THE WOLF AGE

JAMES ENGE

THE WOLF AGE

an imprint of Prometheus Books
Amherst, NY

Published 2010 by Pyr®, an imprint of Prometheus Books

Inquiries should be addressed to
Pyr
59 John Glenn Drive
Amherst, New York 14228–2119
VOICE: 716–691–0133
FAX: 716–691–0137
WWW.PYRSF.COM

14 13 12 11 10 5 4 3 2 1

Library of Congress Cataloging-in-Publication Data

Enge, James, 1960–
The wolf age / by James Enge.
p. cm.
ISBN 978–1–61614–243–8 (pbk. : alk. paper)
1. Ambrosius, Morlock (Fictitious character)—Fiction. 2. Werewolves—Fiction.
I. Title.

PS3605.N43W6 2010
813'.6—dc22

2010024687

Printed in the United States of America on acid-free paper

In Memoriam Patricia Pfundstein:
a stranger here, a citizen there

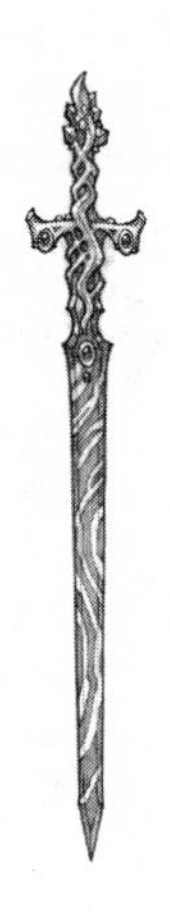

Patria splendida terraque florida, libera spinis,
danda fidelibus est ibi civibus, hic peregrinis.

Acknowledgments

The epigraph to part 4 is from the lyrics to the song "Dire Wolf" by Robert Hunter and Jerry Garcia, copyright Ice Nine Publishing Company, and is used here by their generous permission.

John O'Neill and Howard A. Jones expressed some interest in the werewolf from "Destroyer" (chapter 10 of *This Crooked Way*), and Lou Anders incautiously expressed an interest in the Strange Gods of the Coranians. The encouragement may have been unwise, but it was and remains deeply welcome.

Contents

Part One: Raiders of Wuruyaaria

Part Two: Elections

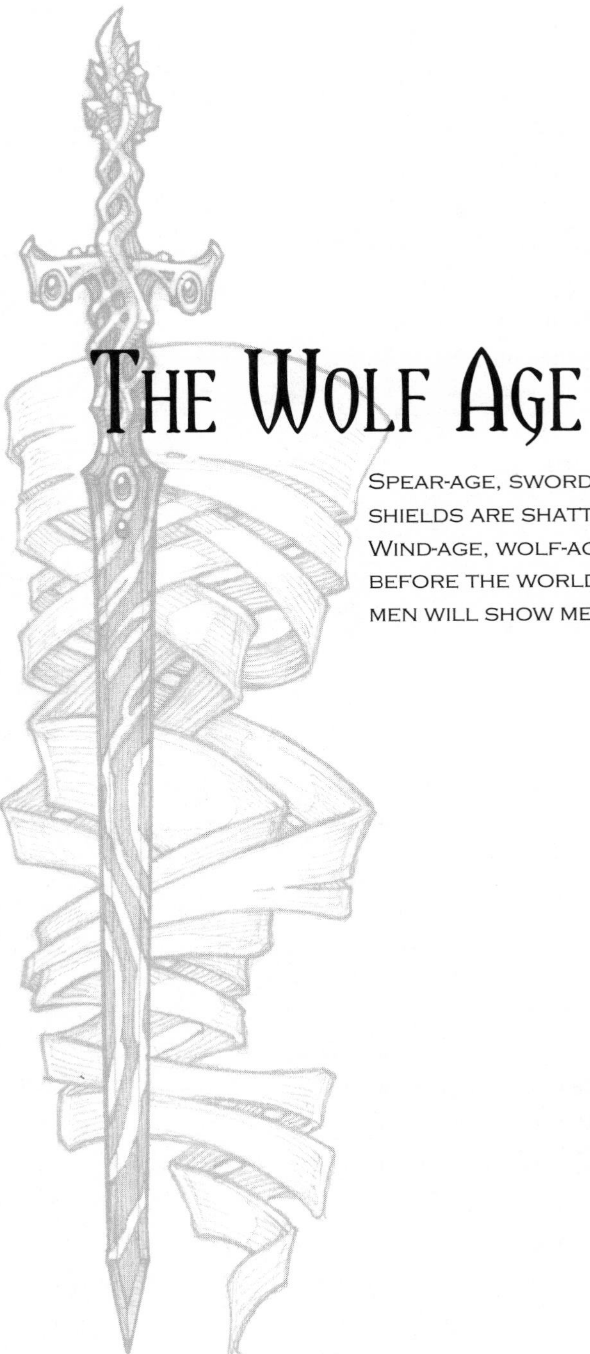

The Wolf Age

SPEAR-AGE, SWORD-AGE:
SHIELDS ARE SHATTERED.
WIND-AGE, WOLF-AGE:
BEFORE THE WORLD FOUNDERS
MEN WILL SHOW MERCY TO NONE.

—***VOLUSPA***

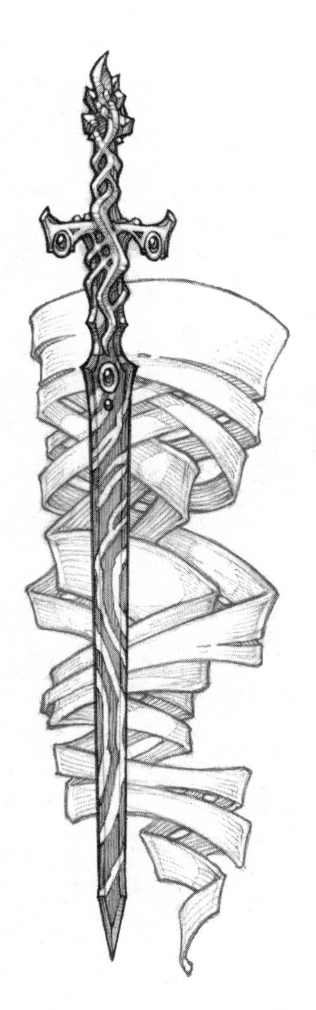

Part One

Raiders of Wuruyaaria

Among wolves, be wolvish of courage.

—Lydgate

Chapter One

Council of the Gods

Listen, Iacomes. This is what I see.

The Strange Gods were gathering by the Stone Tree, but Death and her sister Justice had not yet appeared. Justice, they knew, would not, but they expected Death to be there before them and War was angry.

"I swear by myself," War signified, indicating by a talic distortion that the oath was not sincere or binding, "Death is the strangest of the Strange Gods. She pervades the mortal world, but she can't manifest herself anywhere within a pact-sworn juncture of space-time!"

"I am here," Death signified.

Now that they noticed her presence among them, the Strange Gods realized she had been implicit in a fold of local space-time all along, and simply had not chosen to reveal her presence to them. The other gods signified nontrivial displeasure with her.

Death indicated indifference and readiness to begin the pact-sworn discussion.

The Strange Gods did not submit to a ruler. In their discussions, it was common for the weakest of them to preside. So Mercy manifested herself more intensely than she would normally have done, and reminded them of their mission to destroy the werewolf city Wuruyaaria and how it was currently imperiled.

"It is Ghosts-in-the-eyes," signified Wisdom. "They are a powerful maker and necromancer—a master of all the arts we hate. Our instrument will destroy the city"—Wisdom indicated a pattern in events they all understood—"but now unless we find a way to bring down the walls of Wuruyaaria more swiftly, our instrument may also destroy great swathes among our worshippers. This goes against our nature and cannot be accepted."

Other gods indicated agreement.

Death indicated chilly amusement: a laugh. "The werewolves will die," she signified. "Their city will die. Our worshippers will die. Our instrument will die. Everything that lives must die. When the last soul is severed, this world will collapse into its component elements and drift away in pieces, flotsam on the Sea of Worlds. All this will happen in time: let events take whatever course they will, this is their destination. If this goes against our nature, our nature is doomed."

Each of the other gods emanated anger that would have killed a material being. It was uncivil of Death to prate about these matters that were well known to every god. If Death felt any discomfort from their emanations, she didn't show it. Her next comment was more immediately helpful, though.

"I have a kind of solution to propose," Death signified. "I would have effected it already, but the consequences will affect our pact-sworn efforts to destroy Wuruyaaria."

Mercy signified a need for more details; other gods echoed her.

Death indicated a trivial detail in the pattern of events: the death of a man named Morlock.

The gods expressed indifference.

Death changed the detail's position in time-space.

The gods meditated on the new potential patterns of events, a flowering of dark futures springing from this one seed.

Most of the gods expressed surprise. Cruelty chuckled a bit, slowly shaking his heavy, many-toothed head.

Death again changed the detail's position in time-space. The manifold patterns of things-to-be changed even more radically.

"How can this be?" signified War. "Men and women die every day and their deaths do not matter." Mercy signified some restlessness at this, but the

Strange Gods were used to ignoring the endless quarrel between War and Mercy.

"The progress of our plan in the as-things-are moves very slowly," Death signified. "There is a tension of powers: our instrument; the pact binding our powers in this nexus of events; that damned sorcerer, Ghosts-in-the-Eyes; the natural forces we do not control; and so on. If we disrupt that tension, unbalanced powers will unleash events like a torrent."

Wisdom emanated concern, a need to wait. They did wait as he juggled futures in various shapes, pondering the uncertain effects of varying causal chains. "I cannot chart the path of this torrent," he signified finally to Death and to his peers. "It may benefit our pact-sworn intention or harm it."

"We must guide the torrent," signified War with obvious eagerness.

"We can't," Wisdom signified bluntly. "If we break our sworn intention we will be adrift in the torrent, effecting local changes within it but unable to determine its course. Each change will create new and interacting series of causation. There is certainty in our pact of sworn intention. In this other there is only chaos."

The Strange Gods, as one, made a symbol of protection against the name of this alien god. It had shocked them, as Wisdom intended, lending an unusual force to his signs.

"Certainty only of failure," Cruelty signified. "I was against the proposed instrument from the beginning. It is clear now that I was right and others were wrong. Why should the pact be sacred? Only our wills are sacred, or we are not gods."

"The pact is our will," signified Loyalty. "It is our will united to act as the Strange Gods. To break that is to blaspheme against ourselves." He continued for some time and stopped only when he visualized that the assembly was against him.

Everything he signified was true, but they would not accept failure. On the other hand, Wisdom had frightened them with his tomorrow-juggling and his metaphorical torrents.

"I propose a compromise," signified Stupidity. "Death alone will be freed from the pact-oath. The rest of us will abide by it. That should reduce the *chaos* in events." The Strange Gods impatiently made again the symbol of protection against the name of Chaos. Stupidity's use of Wisdom's trope emanated contempt and mockery, as was his intent. The gods were annoyed with Stupidity, but he did succeed in making them think less of Wisdom. Suddenly, Wisdom's fears seemed less wise, more fearful.

"That hardly matters," Wisdom signified warningly, but the gods were not prepared to listen. They wanted to do something, and this compromise allowed them the illusion of keeping to their plan even as they adopted a new one.

The compromise, in the end, was assented to by all the Strange Gods (except Justice), and Death alone was released from the pact.

"I go," signified Death, and ceased to manifest herself.

The rest of the Strange Gods stood conferring worriedly under the Stone Tree until the sun rose in the west and they fled like ghosts to hide with the darkness underground.

Chapter Two

Death by Water

Morlock Ambrosius shuffled the deck and dealt again. He was sitting by the side of an empty field on the great northern plain, using the surface of a broad stump as a card table.

He threw a set of cards in a spiral pattern, crossed each card with another drawn from the pack, and then sat back to contemplate them. He again saw the drowned sailor, crossed by the Death card, the Lady of the Rocks. There were some variations: the one-eyed merchant bore the blank card of Mystery, the Wheel was crossed by the man with three wands looking out to sea. This was the third time he had thrown the cards, and each time they had prophesied the same fate: death by water.

He had invented the cards as a way to gather signs from the future without using his Sight. That was dangerous for him now: he knew that Merlin had broken loose from his earthy prison and might be exerting his own powers of Sight to track or trap Morlock. He had left his horse with a friend and let his choir of flames run wild in an open seam of coal. He had walked away from everyone and everything he knew so that when the final battle came between him and Merlin, as few people as possible would be destroyed. (In fact, he didn't much care if he himself survived the battle, but he hated the thought of losing to his old embittered *ruthen* father.) And now, instead of telling him anything about the conflict he knew was coming, the cards kept predicting his death by drowning.

Morlock shrugged his crooked shoulders and gathered up the cards. It was the nature of any type of mantia to reveal things that were useless until one met them in the context of a living Now. He slipped a band on the deck and tucked the cards into a pocket in his sleeve. Then he stood and walked northward up the road to the next town.

Morlock Ambrosius knew the town would be empty before he got there. He had seen enough of them on the northern plains to read the clues by now: the lack of smoke, even from the local smithy, was the clearest sign. What he didn't know was why the town was dead. It had not been for long. There was meat fresh enough to eat in the pantry of the town's sole cookhouse. Morlock cooked and ate it, along with some slightly stale bread and withered mushrooms he had also found there. He left the deck of cards on the counter in payment, even though he had a feeling the owners of the place would never return to claim it.

The place bothered him, so he didn't sleep there. He hopped a wall and walked due north across the brown stubbly fields, averting his eyes from the sun setting in the east. That was how he saw the raiding party approaching from the west.

Morlock was so old he didn't bother to keep count of the years anymore and had seen things like this before. The mystery of the empty towns stood explained: they had fled the raiders who were now returning toward the northern road after having caught at least some of the townspeople. The only question now was how Morlock could avoid being swept up by the raiders.

He knew a few invisibility spells, but they would all make his presence felt to a seer, if they had any in their party. Mundane concealment would be better than any spell, but there were no buildings near enough to be of any use. He settled for sitting down with his back to a wall facing east and waiting for them to pass.

It almost worked. The raiders had some trouble with their prisoners at the wall, which they were crossing somewhat north of Morlock. A few children made a break, running away northward, and a few raiders had to round them up while the others supervised the prisoners' crossing of the wall. They had much to trouble them without looking about for stray travelers.

Morlock, on the other hand, had a chance to observe the raiders and their prisoners quite closely. The raiders were rather odd looking, with long hatchet-narrow faces and necklaces strung with varying numbers of long sharp teeth. They had with them several doglike creatures who were not, in fact, dogs. Some of them took orders and obeyed them with more-than-canine shrewdness. Others seemed to be barking orders that the men (or manlike raiders) would obey.

Morlock watched their shadows to confirm his guess. They were long, distorted by the low angle of the setting sun. But where they fell upon the wall it was clear: the dogs or wolves cast shadows like a man crouching on all fours, while the men cast shadows like wolves standing on their hind feet.

It was a raiding party from the werewolf city somewhere to the north. Morlock forgot the name, if he had ever known it. His sisters could have told him, if she were here.

The prisoners were mostly older folk and children. The healthy adults had obviously been able to escape from the raiding party. A rational choice, Morlock supposed: one must bury one's parents eventually, and one can always have more children. He eyed the few mature adults among the prisoners with some interest. Merely slow-footed?

Morlock felt a twinge of pity for the children. There was nothing in store for them but life as slaves at best, or death as prey at worst. Or maybe it was the other way round: Morlock had never been a slave and he wasn't eager to make the experiment. He kept quiet and still and waited for the raiders to pass.

It almost worked. The prisoners had all crossed the wall; the runaways had been rounded up. The rearguard of the raiding party crossed the wall and began to follow the main group eastward. Perhaps Morlock released an incautiously energetic breath of relief. Perhaps his luck was just out. In any case, one of the wolves in the rearguard lifted his nose and then turned to look directly at Morlock, slumped against the wall. He barked a quiet word to his manlike comrades.

Two of the raiders armed with pikes looked over at Morlock and moved toward him, shouting in a language Morlock did not understand. Since all hope of concealment was over, Morlock stood and drew his sword Tyrfing, holding it at an angle meant to warn rather than threaten.

The two pikemen stopped moving toward him and stared at the dark crystal of the blade, woven with veins of paler crystal, glittering in the red light of the eastering sun.

The wolf who had spotted him first yowled a warning to the whole raiding group. All the raiders stopped and looked at him. Things were going from bad to worse.

Morlock backed away one deliberate step, paused, then took another step back. He growled slightly. From what he knew of wolves, he thought this might show that he was not prepared to attack, but would fight if he must.

The two pikemen and the wolf who commanded them took two steps forward, the pikemen shouting something and the wolf barking furiously. Oddly, he understood the wolf better than the pikemen. The wolf seemed to be saying that Morlock should hide his teeth or he would be bacon by morning.

Morlock suggested, in the same snarling language, the werewolf perform an act made possible by lupine agility. It was one of the few insults he knew for a wolf, and it was gratifyingly effective. The two wolf-shadowed pikemen were rocked back on their heels; the man-shadowed wolf charged forth with fiery eyes, silent now, eager to kill.

Morlock waited. When the wolf poised himself to leap, Morlock dodged forward and brought Tyrfing down on the werewolf's shoulder, shattering the bone.

Tyrfing was a focus of power as well as a weapon; to kill with it was an act of grim consequence, tantamount to enduring death itself. But the werewolf, of course, was not dead, merely wounded, and Morlock found he could shake off the shock of its suffering relatively quickly. He hoped the wolf would not heal soon; he had other trouble at hand.

The two pikemen were bearing down on him. Their weapons were excellent for keeping a party of unarmed prisoners in line, less effective against a skilled swordsman. Morlock ran to meet them and was past the range of their pikeheads before they could stab at him. He wounded the nearer pikeman on the arm with Tyrfing, and reached past him with his free hand to break the neck of the one beyond. The dying one fell like a stone, gasping his last breaths out uselessly; the other staggered backward, yammering, and strove to stab at Morlock with his pike.

Morlock spun aside and rolled over the nearby wall. He made as if to back away; the wounded pikeman lunged at him recklessly. Morlock evaded the pike's hooked blade, waited until the pikeman was fully extended, and then struck down with Tyrfing. The glittering edge hit the pikeman's arm lying across the surface of the wall and severed it at the elbow like a butcher's cleaver cutting through a joint of meat. The pikeman shrieked words of fear and hate, staggered backward, and fell out of sight groaning behind the low wall.

Morlock shook off the horror of the pikeman's suffering. A werewolf he might be, but he was as mortal in human form as Morlock was, and it was unlikely he would survive two such terrible wounds. But Morlock had many deaths on his conscience already; adding the death of a slave-taker or two did not bother him much.

The others were coming for him now. Since there was nothing he could do to stop it, he encouraged it. He made clucking noises he hoped they would find insulting. He croaked out some abuse he had learned from crows. He tapped the edge of his sword on the bloodstained surface of the wall and waggled his free hand at them. Soon many of the raiders, manlike and lupine, were running toward him. At the moment he judged right, he turned and ran south along the stone wall.

He heard some of the raiders scrambling or leaping over the wall. Others were running along the eastern side of the wall. That was all right with him: his enemies had effectively halved their own forces.

His bad leg was troubling him, but he kept running as fast as he could until he heard the grating gasp of a wolf's breathing just behind him. He spun and braced his feet in a fighter's crouch, his sword at full extension. The wolf at his heels was impaled on the blade before he knew what was happening; the frightened howl had an unpleasantly human quality. Morlock repressed the horror of the other's suffering and shook him off his sword. He kicked the moaning wolf out of his way and lunged at the next one leaping at him. This one didn't howl; Tyrfing had passed through her throat, nearly severing her neck. She, too, was out of the fight until she healed. Morlock leaped past to meet the next raider.

Neither men nor wolves run all at the same rate. A disciplined military force learns to move as a group, applying a maximum of power at the expense of moving a little more slowly. These raiders weren't that disciplined, and Morlock planned to take advantage of it. During his sprint his pursuers had strung behind him in a long line, and what had been an unwinnable battle of one against many was now just a string of single combats in which Morlock had, at least briefly, the advantage of surprise.

His next opponent was a wide-eyed man armed only with a long pole. He was already skittering to a halt as Morlock came up to him. While he was still off balance, Morlock struck off his weapon-bearing hand with Tyrfing and punched him in the throat. The man fell gagging to his knees. Morlock kicked him in the face as he passed, and the man went down to the ground.

By then Morlock was facing another antagonist: a lean woman with roan-colored hair and a long pointed sword. Morlock fenced with her for a few grim moments, then struck home with a thrust through her upper right chest. He wrenched the sword from her grip with his free hand and she fell, spouting blood from her lips, into the dust of the stubbly field.

The woman's sword was rusty, bent, unbalanced, notched along both edges—inferior to Tyrfing in every way but one: he could use it to kill with impunity. He ran on to fight his next antagonist.

After a few more single combats, Morlock looked about to see wolves and men gathering in a group to attack him. He turned and, leaping back over the wall, ran southward. His would-be attackers followed. Glancing back, he saw that their pursuit had broken up into smaller groups again, some on each side of the wall. He leaped back to the west side and ran north to attack again.

He was running out of breath by now, but he strove not to show it: they would be more likely to break off the battle if they thought him tireless. And, in a strange way, the grim prophecies of the cards buoyed him up: if he was doomed to die by drowning, he needn't worry about being ripped open by werewolves in an empty field.

He had struck down a few more men and wolves, and was thinking of a new retreat when horns and wolf calls sounded to the north. His antagonists fled northward to answer them. When he was sure they were leaving, he slumped gasping against the wall and watched them run.

There was some sort of fight going on back at the main body of the raiding party. In the failing light it wasn't at first clear to Morlock what was happening. Then he realized: encouraged by the absence of so many raiders, the captives had seized the opportunity to fight back.

Their chances didn't look good.

Morlock, of course, could improve them.

He shook his head, wearily. It was not his fight; he was already tired. This was his chance to flee south and escape the raiders.

On the other hand, the field was dry. Absent a sudden downpour, he was unlikely to drown.

He stood pondering alternatives and getting his wind back. He saw a raider lift the struggling body of a child, impaled on a spear point. As the raider brandished the spear, shouting in triumph or threat, the body grew slack.

Morlock found himself running forward then in long irregular strides. The slave-takers, intent on their rebellious captives, didn't notice his approach until he was almost upon them. Then he lashed out with both swords, torn by the sudden rage from within and the talic shocks from Tyrfing. He struck and struck. He was bleeding now, and his fire-laden blood lit smoldering fires in the stubbly fields. The werewolves, manlike and wolf-formed, seemed more dismayed by this than anything. Now many of the former captives had seized weapons from raiders that had been killed or wounded. The raiders still had greater numbers, but seemed to lack stomach for fighting. Soon they fled, north and east, away from the bitter low wall and the bodies of the slain and wounded and the harsh vengeful cries of their former captives.

Morlock stepped aside and sat down on the low wall, ripping strips from his cloak to bandage his wounds. He kept an eye on the former captives as he did so. It was possible they would resent him as much as the werewolves. He knew nothing of these people, not even a word of their language.

He saw one woman with iron gray hair struggling with a long spear gripped in the hands of a dead raider. She was sobbing quietly. He kept a cautious eye on her; it was possible that some of the captives were quislings or traitors, and perhaps she was one. Otherwise why weep over the dead raider? Then he saw what was on the end of the spear: the child's body he had seen raised up as a rebuke or a threat to the captives. She was struggling to remove the spear point from the body without doing it further damage.

He got up from the wall and walked over to her. He brushed her hands away from the shaft of the spear, and she let him. The blade of the spear was barbed and had caught in the child's body. The child was dead, of course; it had been a girl, perhaps ten years old. Morlock put one foot on the corpse and tore the spear loose from the body.

The old woman screamed and struck at his face with weak fists. He ignored it. He broke the spear shaft with his hands and cast the pieces aside. Then he opened his hands and looked her in the eye.

She stopped hitting him. She stood back, still sobbing from exhaustion, fear, grief—or all three. The sobbing slowed to a halt.

Silence surrounded them.

"*Kree-laow*," said one of the former captives, pointing at Morlock.

"*Venbe tand kree-laow*," said another.

An argument broke forth. One of the issues seemed to be whether Morlock was or was not *kree-laow*—whatever or whoever that might be.

Many of the captives lay dead on the field. If they had been Morlock's kith he would have felt the impulse to bury them. But circumstances were obviously unsuitable for a funeral, no matter how hasty. The sun had now set, and the blue eyes of the minor moons, Horseman and Trumpeter, were opening in the gray sky of gloaming. In the shadows along the low bitter wall, darker shadows were lurking, wounded werewolves licking their wounds audibly, healing probably, readying for a new attack almost certainly.

Morlock knelt down by the dead girl. The old woman jumped at him, croaking angry words. He held up his hand. Then he tore another strip from his ragged cloak and bound up the dead girl's left hand.

"My people," he said to the old woman, without any hope she would understand, "the people who raised me: they taught me to do this for those I would honor, but could not bury." He tore another strip of cloth and bound the girl's other hand.

The old woman knelt down by the dead girl on the other side. She tore a strip from her own ragged clothing and put it across the dead girl's face. She met his eye and nodded grimly. They both stood.

"*Kree-laow!*" said one of the former captives decisively, and this time no one argued. The survivors set about hastily honoring their fallen dead. Morlock patrolled back and forth as they did so, watching the wolf-eyed shadows that were gathering in the dark.

Then the others were done. Some of them tugged at Morlock's arm and shoulder; they said words he didn't understand. Their expressions were hard to read in the ice-pale moonlight, but they seemed to want him to come with them. They kept pointing north: perhaps they had a refuge there, or simply planned to join another band of refugees.

He considered it. On the one hand, not too far to the north lay the Bitter Water, an inlet from the western ocean. If he were truly destined to die by drowning, that would be a likely scene for it. On the other hand, if he walked southward alone, the werewolves would likely follow him. He knew from experience how relentless werewolves could be in the pursuit of a single prey, even one who had given them less cause to be angry than Morlock now had. And he had no silver nor wolfbane in his nearly empty pack.

He touched his chest and pointed north. "I'll go with you," he said.

They understood; their faces creased with relief and a kind of happiness. He thought it odd.

They went northward as quickly as they could, stumbling through the empty fields in the moonlit shadows. Eyes followed them in the dark—never too near, nor ever very far away.

It was the last bright call* of Cymbals, the first month of winter. The air on the northern plains should have been pitilessly cold, the land covered with many layers of snow. The wind that rose at their backs was chilly and many of the refugees shivered as they walked, but it was more like early autumn than the beginning of winter. Morlock had never known weather like this, but it was true that he didn't know the northern plains as well as other parts

*A "bright call" is the time (roughly 7.5 days) when Trumpeter, the smallest and fastest moon, is aloft. See appendix A on calendar and astronomy.

of Laent. He'd have liked to ask the refugees (the other refugees, he supposed he should call them: he was one of them now) about the weather, but he couldn't understand a word they said, and none of them could understand any of the languages he spoke to them.

About the middle of the night, they began to hear the sound of surf, and the air came alive with salty wet scents. The refugees were increasingly excited, but Morlock was feeling rather gloomy: it was as if he could feel Death gripping him more tightly.

They came in sight of the shoreline, and there were other refugees there, and the coarse cheerful sounds of wood being worked. Morlock's companions picked up their feet and ran down to the shore, laughing and crying and greeting the others there. Morlock followed more slowly. He noted that the woodworking sounds were coming from a small flotilla of boats that the refugees were making with lumber salvaged from demolished buildings. There were some foundations, gaping open at the cold sky, not far away from the shore.

Many explanations had already been made before Morlock arrived at the rocky beach of the Bitter Water. Some of Morlock's companions were standing around an older man wearing a ceremonial headband. Morlock heard the by now familiar *kree-laow* several times.

The old man, some sort of leader or priest, looked up as Morlock approached. His lined face had been frozen in a skeptical expression, but that melted as he took in Morlock's limping crooked form. He said several things directly to Morlock, who opened his hands and looked expectantly, waiting for the old man to understand that he didn't understand.

The old man was annoyed that Morlock didn't understand him. He waved off some explanations from some of the other refugees and spoke over his shoulder to a boy who wore a version of the same headband. The boy ran off, returning a few moments later with a small codex book. He handed it to the old man, who leafed through it for a few moments and then turned to hand it to Morlock.

Morlock took the book reluctantly. It seemed to be some book of ceremonies or prophecies, and he had found that participating in someone else's religion could become abruptly dangerous, even when he understood what they were saying. He was even more dismayed when he saw what the old man wanted him to see: through the middle of the text strode a crook-shouldered man, a torch in one hand and a black-and-white sword in the other. Around him was a ring of wolves with human shadows.

"*Kree-laow!*" shouted the old man, as if he could make Morlock understand that way.

"Possibly," said Morlock, handing back the book. "I hope not, though." If he disliked being entangled in someone else's religion, being entangled in their destiny seemed almost unsanitary.

Three children ran up, one of them bleeding. They were talking excitedly and gesturing southward. They may have been posted as lookouts; obviously, they had met a werewolf. More than one: one of the boys kept on flashing all his fingers, which Morlock guessed meant the numbers of the enemies: *ten and ten and ten. . . .*

The old man said something; other men and women wearing headbands repeated it, and the men, women, and children all rushed to the boats, pushing them out from the rocky beach into the water.

Morlock was in two minds about whether to join them. He hated the water and would almost rather die on land than be saved on the sea. But he thought about the boy's hand signals: *ten and ten and ten. . . .* Too many tens.

Morlock waded into the cold shallows of the Bitter Water. Many cold moonlit faces turned eagerly toward him from the boats; they spoke to him. Everyone seemed eager to have the *kree-laow* (if that's what he was) on their boat.

He climbed on one at random. It did not, thank God Avenger, have the old man with the ceremonial headband; Morlock had taken a dislike to him in the few seconds he had known him. A younger man wearing a headband appeared to be the priest-captain of the boat. He took Morlock by the hand and welcomed him, then took him to one side of the boat where there was a bench and an oar for rowing.

"I understand," said Morlock. He threw his backpack and his two swords under the bench, sat down, and took hold of the oar. Some of the crew were already frantically splashing the blades of their oars in the water. He waited until the sides had established a rhythm, along with a chant led by the headband-wearer (who sat at the stern at the steering oar). When the other oars were swinging in rhythm he extended his own and started to push the water with the blade.

On the bench in front of him was an old woman. He wasn't sure if it was the same one whom he had met among the captives. There were no passengers in the middle of the boat, and many of the benches were empty: the refugees had been expecting more people than actually arrived.

That was unfortunate; they could have used the arms. And Morlock wished he had arrived early enough to give them some advice on boat building. (He was no sailor, but he knew something about shipmaking.) The boats were all flatbed rafts—none of them seemed to have keels. They would fare badly on the rough waves of the Bitter Water.

It was bad at first, but no worse than Morlock expected. The flat bottom of the boat hit each wave on the rough gray waters like a broadhead hammer. Morlock's mouth filled with a greasy fluid. He was near vomiting, but struggled against it. He didn't know how soon he would eat again, and he couldn't afford to lose a scrap of food to the cold dark sea.

The waves kept pushing the flatboats backward even as they struggled forward—and the boats slid sideways as often as they made any progress. When they had been paddling for more than an hour, Morlock looked backward. The shore was still in sight, terribly near for all their efforts. In the chill light of the minor moons, he saw that the smooth beach bristled with the forms of men and wolves.

He turned back to plying his oar. He met the eye of the old woman rowing in front of him: she too had been looking back.

"There's no going back," he said.

She grunted and said something he didn't understand. They bent themselves to their rowing. The night was still strangely warm for winter, but a cold wind came off the gray gleaming water; no one was sweating much.

Presently it grew still worse. There was a shout from one of the other boats, and everyone turned their eyes to the east. Morlock followed their gaze, but at first he wasn't sure what he was seeing. He had never seen anything like this before.

Emerging from the blue broken clouds, high above the moonslit eastern edge of the Bitter Water, were gray shapes like teardrops, riding through the sky like ships. Their prows were pointed; their sterns were wide and rounded. Under each midsection hung chains suspending a long black craft, snakelike in form.

"What are they?" he wondered. "Are they alive?"

No one answered. No one understood him. But the townsfolk knew something about them. Some turned back to their oars with renewed panicky energy; others put their hands over their faces, resigning themselves to their fate.

Morlock was not the resigned type. He struck out at the water savagely with his oar, but turned often to watch the approach of the airships. At first they were headed toward the center of the Bitter Water, but then they turned their prows slightly to intercept the flatboats. The sharp ends of the airships tilted slightly forward, and the snakelike gondolas slid forward on their chains.

The old woman in front of him said something and he turned to look at her. She said it again. He shrugged and opened his free hand.

She grunted and gestured impatiently back toward the shore. Then Morlock did understand: the airships had something to do with the werewolves.

Morlock was impressed. He also felt a savage covetous longing to know how the things were made, how they worked. But the main thing at the moment was to survive, and that looked increasingly unlikely.

The airships were clearly coming in to attack the flatboats. They were close enough now that he could see the windows lining the snakelike gondolas. And in many of the windows a warm, welcoming red light shone.

"We're done," he remarked grimly, and turned back to his oar. He still wasn't the resigned type.

Soon the airships were nearly overhead, and he could see the bowmen in the windows, their arrows alive with red light.

"Ware fire!" he shouted, though he knew no one could understand him.

The bowmen shot, and burning arrows struck all around them, in the water and on the decks. Few seemed to have been wounded, a fact that struck Morlock as ominous. The arrows largely fell in the center of the boats, on open planking.

Morlock reached under his bench for his nearly empty backpack. He swung it over the rail and passed it through the water. Then he ran with it, still soaking, to the nearest arrow burning on the deck and tried to douse the flame. But he managed to do nothing except set the soaked backpack alight: the burning arrows were treated with some agent that burned even in water. And it burned fast and fierce: he tossed the backpack off the boat, but it was already half consumed, and the fires were chewing deep holes in the flatboats. As he watched bemusedly, boiling water began to bubble upward amidst the spreading flame. This boat was sinking, and a glance around showed him that the other flatboats were as well. People were abandoning them on every side.

Now was the time for the crews of the airships to attack again, if they were seeking to kill the refugees. But they didn't. In fact, Morlock saw that they were lowering something from the airship gondolas on long chains. Nets. They were nets. As they hit the water, people already adrift on the waves started to crawl into them.

Morlock could not imagine what use the werewolves could have for humans except as meat animals or slaves. He expected his fiery blood would keep him off the menu card, so he wasn't concerned about that. But he had never been a slave. He had no interest in trying the profession.

He turned back to his bench and grabbed Tyrfing from its sheath. He struck with the dark glittering blade, severing the bench from the deck. He tossed the bench into the water and jumped in after it, sword still in hand.

He flipped the bench on its back and lay Tyrfing across its underside. The bench seemed buoyant enough to carry him and his sword, at least until it absorbed some water. Looking back, he saw the old woman who had been rowing in front of him. She was sinking under the silver surface of the Bitter Water. He reached out with one hand to rescue her, but she scornfully struck it aside and let herself sink. Soon she passed from sight: a gray shape lost in the gray moonslit water.

Morlock looked up. One net full of dripping refugees was already being drawn up toward the gondola of an airship. The others were still gathering willing victims.

Maybe they were right, Morlock realized. It was a warm night for winter, but it was still a winter night on the Bitter Water. Death was there, in the chill of the water if nothing else. He might live longer if he resigned himself to his fate, as they were doing.

But he wasn't the resigned type. And he had never been a slave.

"Eh," he said, and paddled grimly away into the night.

His plan was to swim westward and then turn south toward the shoreline, hopefully landing at a place not thick with angry werewolves.

He hadn't much hope. The weather was warm, perhaps, by the frosty standards of the north, but the Bitter Water was cold—far colder than his blood. There was a fire in him, but he knew that water quenches fire. Still, he would not surrender. Death was in the water. He knew it; he felt it. But he would fend it off as long as possible.

A current, even colder than the other water, caught him and dragged him off the course he thought he was taking. Soon he couldn't even remember where he had thought land was. If he could hold out until dawn . . .

He did not hold out. The cold sank deep teeth into his aching limbs. His mind began to fog. He forgot to raise his head occasionally to look for signs of land. He found himself drifting occasionally, his feet motionless in the killing water, loosely grasping the bench, his eyes closed. Every time it happened it was harder to kick his feet into motion. And eventually the time came when he found himself adrift half submerged in the water, the wooden waterlogged bench lost on the dark sea. He kept his limbs moving as long as he could, but eventually the darkness in the cold water entered his mind and he sank, already dying, into the killing water.

Death was there under the surface of the sea. He had known it from the beginning, but now he saw her reaching out for him with long dark fingers, bristling with darkness like a spider's legs.

She embraced him with her many arms, and her bristling fingertips touched his face.

She introduced talic distortions into his fading consciousness, like words.

I am not ready for you to enter my realm, she signified. *You have been a good servant to me, but I have more work for you to do in the world.*

Without speaking, he rejected her service—rejected all the Strange Gods.

She signified an amusement even colder than the Bitter Water, and his mind went dark.

But it was not the darkness of death. He came to himself later—it must have been hours later, because the western sky was gray with approaching dawn. He was coughing up salty vomit as he crawled across the stony margin of the Bitter Water.

In the same instant he saw two things: his sword, Tyrfing, gleaming in the shallow water and the dim gray light. The other was a crowd of shadows, manlike and wolflike, standing farther up the beach. He looked up and saw men and women with wolvish shadows, wolves with human shadows.

His throat was closed like a fist; he couldn't call Tyrfing to him. He leapt toward it, but the werewolves were on him before he reached it. They didn't use swords or teeth, but clubs and fists. They wanted him alive.

He fought as hard as he could, but they were too many and his strength was failing. Before he lost consciousness he felt them put the shackles on his neck and arms.

Morlock had never been a slave. Until today.

Chapter Three

The Vargulleion

Morlock never remembered much of his first day in captivity. He had been half dragged, half carried all through the hours of sunlight. The band of werewolves who had captured him were about twenty in number, counting humans and wolves together. He was not their only prisoner; they had five others: sorry waterlogged human beasts (like Morlock) that they had recovered from the waves. Morlock was the only one in metal shackles. That was good and bad: bad for his chances to escape but perhaps good for killing one or more of his captors, if he could catch them unaware.

In between bouts of unconsciousness and semiconsciousness, whenever he was aware enough, he tried to keep an eye out for Tyrfing. He guessed one of the werewolves had taken it; it still carried a talic charge he could activate by calling its name. If he picked his moment carefully, he could summon the sword—in ideal circumstances, perhaps fight his way free. But it would have been enough for him to kill some of them.

He never caught sight of Tyrfing, though. Perhaps it was heaped with loot from the raided towns, awaiting a division of the spoils. Perhaps they had left it there in the water, fearing its latent magic. As light left the sky, he began to get desperate. He decided to ascend to the visionary plane and try to locate the sword by its implicit talic burden.

It was a risk; if some of the werewolves were seers, they would sense his action. But he decided to take that risk. As the werewolves settled down for a brief rest around sunset and a snack (one of the waterlogged captives—a lank-haired, hollow-cheeked woman who didn't even scream when they bit into her), Morlock slumped down with the other four survivors and allowed his mind to ascend slightly toward the visionary state. The world of matter and energy receded slightly, faded slightly, and the talic threshold of the spirit world stood forth brightly against the dim background.

A wolvish form turned toward him. Instead of fur, it seemed in his talic vision to have long feathers, and at the tip of each feather was an open, observant human eye. All the eyes were looking at Morlock. The werewolf seer issued an ululating call that Morlock heard with his material senses and his inner ear.

The other werewolves dropped their steaming fragments of human meat and rushed over. One of them, in man form, wore a tool belt and carried a brazen wooden box that the seer-wolf avoided with caution. The seer-wolf barked a curt order. The manlike werewolf set the box down near Morlock and opened it. Within it lay glowing glasslike objects.

Morlock dropped his vision and tried to kick the box over. He didn't know what the things in the box were, but he didn't want them near him, any more than the seer-wolf did. The seer-wolf barked another order, and suddenly Morlock was gripped with many hands and teeth, unable to move, the left side of his face pressed against the ground. The one with the tool belt grabbed tongs from his belt and a hammer. He used the tongs to lift a glowing glass tooth from the brazen box. The seer-wolf moved farther away instinctively, and Morlock would have done the same if he'd been able. The one with the tool belt placed the point of the glowing glass tooth against Morlock's right temple and pounded it in with the hammer.

The pain was the most terrible that Morlock had ever felt in his long life, but that wasn't the worst of it. With each blow of the hammer, he could see and hear and feel less of the world. When it was done, all that he could see and hear and feel were the things that were actually there: his Sight was gone.

His mind was empty of everything but grief and hate for a long time.

When Morlock brought himself to look at the void of matter and energy that was now the only world he could know, they had left the plains and were now in low hills, the sea still in sight on their left. It might have been hours or days later; he neither knew nor cared.

The hills about them were riddled with holes like empty eye sockets: dens of werewolves, he supposed. One of the hills had been cut down to bedrock and walled around; the holes in its sheer sides were smaller: windows, not doors. That was where they were taking him.

And only him. When Morlock looked about incuriously, he saw that the other human captives were gone. Either they had been left somewhere else or they had been eaten on the way. He neither knew nor cared.

To the west, there was another far greater walled edifice, and behind the walls were rising ranks of tableland, each rank thick with toothlike protrusions, each surface notched with dark den-holes. That must be the ill-famed city of werewolves.

Beyond it to the north was a mountain, tall enough to overshadow the highest of the tablelands. From the ragged cone at its peak, it was a volcano, though it seemed to be dormant. Mounted on its higher slopes was a gigantic circular device, gleaming in the light of the minor moons. On its upper rim two silvery globes of unequal size moved at separate rates. In its center were starlike symbols forming an all-too-familiar shape: a wolf. On its lower rim was a third globe—lightless, almost impossible to see, but larger than the other two.

A moon-clock, Morlock deduced, with a faint awakening of interest. He wondered what it was for, who had built it, what powered it. He turned his eyes away resolutely.

Ahead of him lay the walled lair: clearly a prison. From snatches of wolf-speech he understood from the captors, he guessed it was called the Vargulleion. There would be no moon-clocks there. He walked through the tomblike gate of the prison with unfeigned indifference in the midst of his captors, wolvish and manlike. First their shadows were swallowed by the darkness within; then their forms were lost and they made their way down the lightless hallway. A dim red light glowed at the end of the hall: an open door, leading to the prison interior. From it Morlock heard iron slamming on stone and many voices of men and wolves.

They took him to a cell on the highest floor of the Vargulleion and locked him in. The lock itself was a simple crossbar. But there was a guard station opposite the cell door, with a manlike and a wolvish guardian posted, watching him with cold interested eyes. He hoped they wouldn't always be as alert as they were now.

The cell had two cots. There was a window, high in the wall, and the light of the minor moons poured through it, painting the filthy surfaces with silver. (The window had a wooden shutter, but it was propped open.) He saw a narrow dark hole in the floor: the commode. Impossible to escape that way, but it might represent some structural weakness in the cell he could exploit.

Morlock lay down on one of the cots and slept. He never knew how long. When he awoke there was sunlight glaring in the window and he found a bowl of food and a bowl of water on the floor by his cot. The food was a mash of peas or beans or something—no meat, thank God Avenger. The water was even more welcome. He wasted none of it on washing, of course.

When he was done he examined the bowls carefully. They seemed to be tin of some type—perhaps brittle enough that he might break off a few fragments.

A man's voice shouted words at him. He looked up to see a guard standing at the bars of his cell. The guard rattled the bars and motioned with his hand: he wanted Morlock to bring the bowls to him.

The guard's hands were resting between the cell bars; Morlock thought about leaping forward to trap the guard. Now, perhaps, was not the time—there was still another guard, in wolf form, standing ready—but he noted the guard's recklessness. That, too, was a weakness that might be exploited.

As he stood and walked deliberately toward the cell door, the guard stood back. He used hand motions to direct Morlock to pass the bowls through the bars and drop them on the ground. Morlock did so and stood back. Presently a man-formed werewolf came by to collect them in a basket.

This werewolf was not a guard, clearly. He had no armor and very little clothing, only a sort of loincloth. His skin, hair, and eyes were all the same mottled pale color, and he was beardless (like the guards, but unlike Morlock himself; it was long since he'd shaved). Morlock guessed he was a prisoner, too: a trustee of some kind. The guards spoke to him, their voices friendly and contemptuous. The trustee said a few things to Morlock, but Morlock made no move to respond. Eventually the trustee went away, his basket of bowls clanking as he wrestled it down the corridor.

Time passed. Morlock spent a good deal of it staring at the walls. They looked new: this prison was not more than a few years old. Had it replaced an older one, or had the werewolves found some new need for a prison? For that matter, it seemed in retrospect that the dens he had walked past on his way here were also new; there was a rawness about their edges, a lack of plant growth on or near the doorways. He wondered about all this but came to no conclusions. It was hard to think with the glass spike in his skull: he was deaf to his own insight, could proceed only on reason alone, that feeble reed.

Morlock began to hope that he would be kept in solitary confinement, but that evening, when the window was still reddish gray with sunset, a dozen guards herded a new prisoner up the hallway. The two on station unlocked the door while the others forced the new prisoner into the cell that had been Morlock's sole domain.

The new prisoner was in human form . . . approximately. His face was long, but his eyes were set far back, almost by his ears. His brutal jaw came out almost as far as his flat porcine nose; when he bared his teeth, as he often did, they looked like the long gleaming teeth of a carnivore. His legs had a twist in them, like a dog's hind legs. His massive naked body was shaggy with hair, white streaked with red. (His bare skin, where it could be seen, showed the same mottling.) He looked like a werewolf who had changed incompletely back to human—who, perhaps, could not change fully out of beast form.

The new prisoner, as soon as he was released, threw himself at the cell door, but the wary guards had already slammed it shut and locked it fast. The new prisoner pressed his snarling face through the bars and snapped and howled. The guards stood back and passed amused remarks among themselves.

The pale trustee appeared again. This time he had two baskets and a handful of some kind of marker. He passed like a vendor through the crowd of guards (more guards, and more trustees, were filling up the hallway). Morlock couldn't tell exactly what was going one, but he thought the pale mottled trustee was selling bets.

The new prisoner tired of struggling against the unyielding bars. He drew his head back and stood snuffling angrily for a while. Then he stood as straight as his arched spine allowed and turned to look at Morlock, seeming to notice him for the first time.

He howled like a dog, and the crowd outside the cell roared and hooted like the audience at a race. They were an audience, Morlock realized: they had come to see him broken, perhaps killed by the beastlike prisoner.

A square of moonlight was already shining on the cell floor. The new prisoner stepped into it, and his unlovely flesh began to ripple like the surface of boiling water. The prisoner knelt down, raising his arms and screaming in ecstasy or fury as they transformed to wolf legs in the silvery light.

In a moment he had transformed: there was no trace of humanity about him anymore. Even his shadow seemed bestial and hulking as he turned toward Morlock with the light of death in his dark eyes.

Morlock stood, his hands open and empty. He was acutely aware that he had nothing to help him in this fight, not even a seer's intuition. He had no tools, no weapons, no escape, and he faced an enemy he could not kill.

The werewolf leapt from light into shadow. Morlock leapt past him, from shadow into the light.

Chapter Four

Undying

Morlock hit the cell floor rolling and jumped to his feet. The werewolf was skittering to a halt, its claws scrabbling on the stone floor for purchase. It smashed into the cot on the far side of the cell, and Morlock heard the wooden frame crack and splinter under the impact.

The bestial cellmate wheeled around. It started forward, as if to lunge at Morlock again, then paused.

Morlock took stock of his enemy. An ordinary wolf, from nose to tail tip, might be as long as Morlock was tall, or a bit longer. This beast was twice that length, and even broader and taller in proportion. Its red-streaked fur was bristly with winter growth: it would be hard for him to wound the beast without some sort of weapon. Its dead-black eyes were watching him with deadly intelligence, measuring him as he measured it.

It came for him then, diving through the crossed torrents of silvery light from the barred window. He darted toward the cell door, bounced off it, and spun away to the far side of the room, ending by the foot of his splintered bed.

At that point, the beast was just lumbering about in recovery from its leap.

Morlock was surprised. Its leap had been swift, terrifying in its speed. But it could not change direction easily, it seemed. Its muscle mass gave it speed, but not nimbleness.

Nimbleness was a feeble blade to pierce the immortal heart of his enemy. But it was at least one weapon in his armory.

He decided to grab another. He seized two sides of his cot's splintered frame and pulled them apart. He heard the beast's feet scratch the stones as it left the floor in another leap. He swung around, still gripping the cot, and smashed it into the side of the werewolf's head as it leaped toward him.

The werewolf fell in a ball, snarling, and snapped at his legs. Morlock smashed the disintegrating frame down on the werewolf; it yelped, finally fleeing from repeated blows. Morlock shook loose a few fragments and then stood forth triumphantly with a club in each hand.

The werewolf, slinking around the far side of the cell, looked from the uneven clubs in Morlock's hands to the fragments of the cot on the cell floor.

Possibly it was thinking about the disadvantages of wolf form. Morlock tossed one club in the air and flickered his fingers before he caught it again. Nimbleness and clubs: they weren't much, perhaps, against the werewolf's advantages. But maybe the beast didn't know that. He moved slowly, stalkingly, toward the werewolf.

The werewolf backed away slowly, around the edge of the room. Morlock followed it, watching for an opportunity to strike. He was also thinking about the beast, its size, and the energy with which it moved. Whenever it had last eaten, it must be growing hungry. As it grew hungrier, it would grow desperate. But it would also grow weaker. Perhaps his strategy should be a waiting game.

The werewolf was now again by the fragments of the cot. One of them was smoldering slightly; Morlock had been wounded slightly, and the blood, falling on the wood, had set it afire.

The werewolf sniffed the smoldering wood, then looked narrowly at Morlock. It extended its blunt snout and sniffed again. Its teeth bared in a wordless snarl, and it darted forward to attack.

Morlock struck, even more savagely than before, with his makeshift clubs, but this time the beast was not deterred. Still, the blows had some effect: it had been aiming at his throat, but it ended up ripping into his left leg.

Morlock pounded on the narrow snout as steaming fiery blood squirted out from between its teeth. The clubs broke over the beast's head; it whined with pain but did not retreat. Morlock took a sharpish end of one of the broken clubs and stabbed it into the werewolf's right eye. He pushed the wooden stake savagely, with all his strength, hoping to strike into the beast's brain.

It fled, sobbing strangely, with its lips firmly shut, with the wood still dangling from its bleeding eye socket. Then, as it paused by the wooden fragments of Morlock's cot, it spat deliberately on them. The blood it had drawn from Morlock's wound set them aflame. Then it darted across the room and spat the rest of its mouthful of blood on the other cot, which took fire and began to burn—slowly at first, then with increasing strength.

Morlock watched gloomily as his potential armory went up in flames kindled by his own blood. His nimbleness was now very much in doubt, due to the leg wound, and his materials for making new weapons were vanishing as he watched. But the worst thing about all this was the deliberate intelligence the werewolf had shown. He had thought of it as a beast, but it was not merely a beast. In fact, it seemed more like a person now than it had when still in man form.

He sat with his back against the cell wall and watched his enemy. It didn't seem disposed to attack, so Morlock tore strips from his shirt to bandage his leg wound. It was a terrible wound, and if it festered it might kill him . . . but only if he lived through this night.

The werewolf itself was hardly in better shape. It shook its head frantically and clawed at its eye, finally dislodging the bloody chunk of sharp wood. Then it crept forward to the middle of the room, toward the wedge of moonlight falling on the cell floor. It kept its one eye warily on Morlock as it moved, but it seemed intent on entering the moonlight.

Morlock didn't understand this, but he did understand that anything the werewolf wanted was bad for him. He stood and brandished his remaining club. He closed one eye deliberately and opened it: a warning to the beast that it could lose its other eye.

The werewolf snarled and continued to inch forward.

Morlock thought the beast had understood his threat and was disregarding it. If so, it was even more important that the werewolf not rest in the moonlight. It had transformed there: did moonlight hasten the beast's power to recuperate and heal? It seemed likely.

Morlock dropped his club and jumped for the window. His left hand caught the bars' iron sill, and with his right he slammed over the wooden shutter. There was a latch on the shutter and he set it. The only light in the cell now came from the smoldering flames set by Morlock's blood. The werewolf howled in fury and disappointment.

Morlock dropped back down to the cell floor, and a wave of pain darkened his vision as the fall jarred his wounded leg. Sound and smell warned him before sight that the werewolf was attacking again. He lashed out desperately with his fists, by luck battering the blunt snout aside before its teeth fixed on his throat.

Its jaws clamped down on his right upper arm. Morlock saw that the wounded eye was already healing: the orb was whole again, if sightlessly white. The healthy eye met his, and the werewolf seemed to grin at him around the blood bubbling out of Morlock's wound. Morlock clutched at the werewolf's eye with his left hand, digging deep into the socket with two fingers. The werewolf gave a muffled shriek, a strangely human sound from the lupine mouth, and fled, one eyeball dangling by a thick gleaming nerve from the empty socket.

Morlock stood with his back to the wall beneath the window and wearily tore more strips from his shirt for bandages. He did so with a sense of futility. In every encounter where the werewolf hurt him, it came closer to killing him. He could hurt it, but he could never kill it. The absence of moonlight might slow its healing, but would not stop it. And now it didn't even need to attack; it could sit and wait for him to pass out from blood loss or weariness.

If only he could kill it. But he had no silver and no wolfbane. How else could you kill a werewolf?

The wounded beast sidled through the red smoky shadows of the cell. It issued a harsh, rasping sound like a cough.

Morlock thoughtfully twisted the bandage in his hands. He let the blood fall unregarded to the stone floor. A thought was forming in his mind.

Everything that lived, everything that had physical life, had to breathe. That was why the werewolf was coughing from the smoke.

Keeping one eye on the lurking beast, Morlock stooped down and pulled the leather laces from his shoes. When he had made them he had leeched the phlogiston from them so that they wouldn't burn; he tested their strength now with his fingers, and he liked what he felt. He patiently spliced the laces together. It took a little time to do properly and his time was running out, but there was no point in trying this without doing it right. When the laces were one, he grabbed a stray length of nonburning wood from the floor and, being careful not to drip blood on it, broke it in half. He knotted one end of each lace to a piece of wood, and presently he had a serviceable garrote.

Now to make a chance to use it. The beast was wounded in both eyes, but it could still smell and hear; he would have to distract it somehow so that he could attack it from behind.

Morlock carefully placed the garrote on the floor far away from any fires. Then he loitered casually toward one of the burning cots—it was the other one, the one Morlock had not broken up. By now the fire had spread over the length of the thing and it was burning merrily.

The werewolf was on the far side of the cell, distractedly and somewhat dismayedly swinging its loose eyeball on its nerve.

Morlock picked up the burning cot and threw it at the wall above the werewolf. As soon as the cot struck the wall, he dodged across the cell to seize his garrote and then jumped upon the werewolf's back as it emerged snarling from the curtain of hot gleeds and bloody smoke. He wrapped the cord around the half-blind beast's neck and began to twist.

Of course, it fought. But there was very little it could do: Morlock was out of reach of its teeth and claws. It strove to tear at the strangling cords with the claws of its back feet. Morlock waited until both back legs were fully extended, then stomped on the joints where the long bones of the leg joined together—the knees, for a man or a woman. He felt a certain savage satisfaction in hearing the knee joints crunch under his unlaced shoes.

The werewolf yelped, or tried to: Morlock felt the surge in its chest and neck. But its throat was closed; not a sound emerged. Morlock twisted the handles of the garrote again and again, cutting deeply into the beast's flesh. Presently it stopped moving.

He held on for a long time after that, counting the moments by his own pulses long after the werewolf's heart stopped. When he had counted a thousand heartbeats since the beast's last movement he relaxed the hold of the strangling cord slightly. The werewolf remained motionless. He relaxed it a little more.

The wolvish chest expanded slightly. There was a slight tremor in its veins: a returning heartbeat.

Morlock snarled and twisted the cord tight again, strangling off the werewolf's returning life.

Frustration threatened to swamp his reason. He could keep the beast from living, but he could not actually kill it. He could hope that the return of the sun would change the beast back into the bestial man it had been . . . but he couldn't be sure even of that: some werewolves could obviously maintain the beast form through the day.

He took the frustration out by twisting the cord even tighter. It dug even more deeply into the wolvish neck. That was what gave him the idea.

Maintaining his grip on the unliving but not-yet-dead beast, he dragged the body nearer some fragments of burning wood. Some of the wood was sharp and ragged. He took a chunk of that and started hacking away at the great muscles of the wolvish neck. Blood started to flow, a great deal of cold blood, black in the fiery light. But that was just as well: it extinguished the flames in the splintering wood and made it last longer. When one chunk became useless, he grabbed another. He twisted the unliving head back and forth periodically; it was growing looser and looser on the spine, as Morlock had hoped it would.

Eventually his crude wooden weapons pierced the werewolf's airway. Air began to whistle through the slashed openings—slow at first, then faster and faster. The werewolf's dangling eyeball dilated with awareness, and the claws began to scrabble on the stone floor.

Morlock had destroyed so much of the werewolf's neck that the strangling cord was no longer an effective means of restraint. Morlock let it go and clamped the werewolf's jaws shut with his hands. Planting his feet on the werewolf's front legs, he began to twist the werewolf's head on the fleshless neck. The beast struggled to open its jaws, to savage Morlock with its back claws, but soon its legs stopped moving: he had severed the corridor for nerve impulses to reach the body. The head came loose from the spine on the next twist.

The beast's body fell lifeless to the ground . . . but, horribly, the beast itself was not dead. Its dangling eye still glared at him with baleful intelligence, and the jaws strove feebly to open. He muzzled them shut with the strangling cord as a temporary solution.

He sat with his back against a wall and tried to think what he might do next. He wondered dimly if the head could find a way to reunite with the dead body and live again, or perhaps grow a whole new body from its neck. He didn't know. He didn't know what a werewolf could do.

The head could live without the body, but not the body without the head, that was clear. It made his next move clear, too.

Morlock jumped up and unlatched the shutter on the window, letting blue bars of moonlight fall into the red fuming cell again. He grabbed the wolf head by a loose end of cord and then jumped up to grab the iron sill of the window with his free hand. He tossed the wolf head up onto the sill and tried to push it through the bars. But the openings were too narrow for the wolvish skull to pass through. It made odd sounds as it lay there in the moonlight; it began to rock back and forth as if gaining new strength.

He grabbed the bars with both hands and slowly lifted himself up to the window, aided slightly by his feet scrabbling on the coarse stone wall of the cell. He kicked the wolf head with one foot, wedging its narrow maw between the iron bars. He kept on kicking it, first with one foot, then with another, finally with both. It was agony to his wounded leg and arm, but he kept at it until the bones of the skull were broken and the sacklike wolf head squished through the bars and fell, grunting with terror or some other emotion, out of sight into the moonlit world beyond.

Morlock extended his arms as much as possible and slid down the wall, finally dangling from his unwounded arm, to reduce the shock when he fell. It worked, to the extent that he didn't pass out from pain when he hit the cell floor.

He turned and surveyed the smoking, firelit cell. The werewolf body lay motionless, apparently dead (even if its head was still alive somewhere). He was sick with horror at what he had done, at what he had had to do. But he supposed he could call this a victory.

Looking beyond the cell bars, he saw with shock that the corridor was still full of watchers. He had forgotten about them. They stood there, man and wolf, staring at him with eyes full of wonder and horror, silent and motionless as stones. The pale trustee had dropped his baskets and was watching him through outspread fingers, like a child who is at once afraid to look at something and afraid to not look at it.

Morlock read their shock, and slowly (his mind was going dark) he understood it. This had not been about killing him. They could have done that at any time after his capture. They could have put archers at the cell door and filled him full of arrows. They could still do that. But they had planned to break him, send in the bestial man-wolf and break him and then, perhaps, kill him. Or perhaps make him into a new trustee—a safe fellow to run errands around the prison.

Lit within by sudden fury, Morlock staggered forward and, straining greatly but trying not to show it, seized the dead body of the beast from the cell floor. He threw it with all of his fading strength at the bars of the cell. He would have screamed at them, too, but he didn't have the breath for it.

They jumped back, tripping over each other to retreat. He stared at them for a moment longer, then turned away and limped over to a corner of the cell with relatively few fires. He lay down with his face against the wall, his back toward the cell door. It was his only way to show his contempt, since he had no words to speak that they could understand and no breath to speak them with.

The corridor was still silent when darkness descended on him and he escaped from the bloodstained, red-smoked, blue-lit cell for a time.

Chapter Five

Visitors

Pain and cold woke Morlock from a sleep more dreamless than death. He turned his head and saw that the open window was gray with predawn light. The smoke in the room had cleared away, the fires extinguished.

Morlock fought his way to a sitting position, his back against the bitterly cold damp wall. The werewolf body and the burning fragments were gone from the cell. Dark bloodstains still spread across the stones of the floor, especially by the barred door.

There was a bowl of food and a bowl of water there, and something else lay beside them on the stones.

Beyond the bars the guards stood watching him: two in wolf form, two in man form. They didn't speak to each other or to him.

He got to his feet and lumbered over to the food and water.

The thing beside them on the cell floor was a long tooth—a wolf's tooth possibly. A narrow hole had been bored in it, and it was strung on a piece of cord.

He looked up at the guards. Each of them had a cord of teeth around his neck or (in one of the men's case) wrapped around his forearm. It was some badge of acceptance or honor—or status. The savage man-wolf he had fought last night had worn no such symbol. But somehow he had earned this by defeating it.

He didn't like the idea of a cord around his neck, particularly if he got into another fight. He wrapped the cord around his wrist and turned his attention to breakfast.

The bowl of food was mush again, this time garnished with a human ear and two fingers, gray and bloodless as the predawn light. He set them aside and ate the mush: he could not afford to be squeamish. The water did not entirely wash away the taste. He took the ear and put it up on the sill of the open window and tossed the two fingers in a corner.

He went and sat in the opposite corner and stayed there, eyeing each one of his guards in turn. The faces of the men were clean shaven; their light armor and weapons well crafted and well kept. Yet they were somehow wolflike, with long narrow faces and somewhat crooked legs. The wolves, in turn, were strangely human, with cool observant eyes and deliberate gestures.

Someone had left this tooth for him, and they had not objected. He didn't understand, and he felt ill equipped to try to understand it. With the glass spike in his head, he was deaf to everything except what he heard with his ears. He was blind to everything except what he could see with his eyes. He grieved for his lost Sight.

Presently the trustee came along the hallway, with two archers following him, and exchanged a few words with the guards. The archers each nocked an arrow and pointed it through the bars at Morlock. A guard unbarred the cell door as the others stood ready to strike if Morlock rushed the door. There was obviously no point in doing this, so Morlock merely watched and waited.

The trustee entered the cell, and the door slammed shut behind him. The trustee wheeled and whined something at the guards through the bars; one of the wolves snarled a response. Reluctantly, the trustee turned back toward Morlock.

The trustee held something out in his pale mottled hands and made noises that were clearly words. The object in his hands was an open jar, and in it a brownish red goo, the color of cold blood. It smelt of bitter herbs: some kind of medicine, Morlock guessed; they would hardly take the trouble to poison him when they could kill him in so many more direct ways. Of course, what was a healing salve for a werewolf might still be poisonous for him, but Morlock was inclined to take the risk. He slowly extended one arm and opened his hand. The trustee darted forward to put the jar in his hand and then skittered away.

The guards in the corridor snickered. Morlock ignored them and the trustee; sitting down on the cell floor, he unbound his wounds (breaking their tenuous scabs, unfortunately) and smeared the salve densely over the ragged tears in his flesh.

The effect was not immediate, but it was quick enough to make him suspect there was magic involved in the salve. Plus, it seemed to have been leeched of phlogiston: it did not bubble or flame on contact with his blood.

A maker of some considerable attainments had crafted this salve, Morlock reflected, and had likely done it for Morlock personally (unless they had more prisoners with fiery Ambrosial blood). That was worth remembering.

Morlock rebound the stiff bandages over the no-longer-bleeding wounds and held the jar of salve out toward the trustee, still cowering at the far side of the cell. The trustee made no move toward Morlock; all his limbs were quivering and his pale eyes were twitching about as if looking for escape. One of the guards prodded the trustee with the blunt end of a pike, but he still made no move toward Morlock.

Finally Morlock tossed the jar toward the trustee. The pale mottled limbs spasmed with terror, and the hands just barely managed to catch the jar. The pale werewolf shrieked at the guards and they laughed. The archers took aim at Morlock again, and the other guards stood ready as one guard went to unbar the door again and let the panicky trustee out.

Morlock covertly watched for any lapse in vigilance. Unfortunately, he saw none. Unlike the trustee, they did not fear him. But they would never trust him. That was good for them, bad for Morlock.

The day outside grew brighter; the stones of the cell stubbornly began to yield up their nighttime chill and grow a little warmer. Morlock didn't move much. He kept an eye on the open window and waited.

Eventually the light in the window was darkened by the presence of a crow, drawn by the attractive smell of decaying flesh. She squawked with disgust when she found only a gristly old ear.

Morlock croaked a greeting.

The crow reacted with surprise and alarm. She wondered if he was one of those crow-eating people she had heard so much of recently.

Morlock said he wasn't hungry and he hoped the crow was enjoying the ear.

The crow wondered if that was supposed to be some kind of joke. She pointed out, as a general comment, that ears hardly have enough meat to fill a chick's belly, and the flavor was never very good, no matter how well rotted the flesh.

Morlock expressed ignorance. He rarely ate human meat, never by preference.

The crow saw his point. Human meat was rarely worth the trouble. Just as soon as it was getting ripe enough to eat, someone was likely to come along and bury it. The practice seemed mean-spirited to the crow, and she had some harsh words to say about that.

Morlock heard her out, and then said he was sorry about the ear and wondered if the crow would be interested in a couple of fingers.

The crow observed that Morlock still seemed to be using his, and she laughed a while at her witticism.

Morlock said that the fingers were lying around the cell somewhere; they had come with his breakfast and he didn't want them. The crow could have them.

The crow wondered if he thought she had been hatched yesterday. On the contrary, she was forty-two thousand years old and a personal friend of Morlock Ambrosius, if he knew who that was. She had more sense than to be trapped in a cell with a ravenous crow-eating werewolf who was just waiting for a chance to eat some more crow, but not this crow, not this clever crow, no. He could forget that. Besides, she could smell the fingers and she didn't think they were ripe yet.

Morlock said that he thought the fingers might have been cooked, like the ear.

The crow squawked in outrage. Had the great feathered gods laid the clutch of eggs that hatched into the universes just so that monkeys with their freakishly long and horribly soft and flexible claws could rip meat apart and stink it up with fire?

Morlock said that he had no opinion on the theological issue, but he thought the fingers were soft enough to eat and that, since the crow was a personal friend of Morlock Ambrosius, he was willing to put the fingers up on the cell so that the crow could get at them safely.

The crow bluntly wondered what the catch was.

Morlock said that he had no use for the meat, but he could do something with the finger bones. He wondered if the crow would leave them behind on the sill.

The crow thought for a moment, and grudgingly agreed.

Morlock gathered up the fingers and reached up to put them on the iron sill. Then he stood well away, to make it clear to the crow he intended no harm.

The crow kept an eye carefully on him. When satisfied he was safely distant, she took up one of the fingers in her claws, then the other, as if judging which was ripest.

An arrow struck her in the chest and she fell from sight with no sound other than a brief scrape of her claws on stone. The fingers fell with her off the far side of the sill.

Morlock turned toward the guards. The guard with the bow nocked another arrow and held it ready, watching him. The others watched him, too.

He realized they probably understood crow speech. No doubt wolves would find it handy. He could speak to them, then: insult them, threaten them, bribe them, plead with them, acknowledge them as people.

He chose not to. He took the tooth off his wrist and threw it at them: he was not one of them; he would never be one of them; he rejected them. He couldn't tell if they understood. They said or did nothing. But they watched him.

He sat down in the corner of the room and waited.

The day passed noon and headed toward evening. The guards were changed several times during the day, but each set proved as vigilant as the last. They spoke to each other very little and to Morlock never.

In the late afternoon there was a scuffle in the corridor and the tramp of booted feet. Armed guards dragged into Morlock's sight another prisoner: in man form, but clearly a werewolf, from his wedgelike face and crooked legs. His hair was brownish red, and he hadn't shaved for a few days, but he didn't have the full beard of a long-term prisoner.

He took one look at Morlock, at the bloodstained floor, at the laughing faces of the guards, and he began to shriek. Morlock understood no word, but the whole intent. The prisoner was begging not to be put in the cage with that monster. He was sorry; he was very, very sorry; he would never do it again; just please would they put him somewhere else, anywhere else.

There was a long conversation between the prisoner and one of the guards in wolf form. The werewolf seemed to be in charge; he had a great torc of honor-teeth that hung over his chest. Eventually they took the prisoner away without even opening the cell door.

The guards all expressed amusement, and some counters changed hands; apparently they had been betting on how long it would take the prisoner to break.

When the cell began to cool off, Morlock jumped up and slammed the shutter across the window. Then he wrapped himself into as tight a knot as he could in a corner and waited for sleep to come.

He was not one of them. He would not be one of them. But they could still use him, the way they had used the bestial wolfman they had unleashed on Morlock. He was their new beast, their new terror to break prisoners with. There was nothing he could do about that and no way he could think to use it to his advantage.

The darkness, when it came to cover his awareness, was no darker than his mood.

Chapter Six

Dragonkiller

The trustee returned with the healing salve again the next morning. The guards were as vigilant as ever, but the pale trustee seemed less terrified. He entered the cell without being forced and even approached Morlock within arm's reach to hand him the jar of salve.

The trustee seemed disposed to talk, but Morlock took the jar and turned away. He was used to saying nothing for many days at a time; he had often travelled alone in his long life. Further, his last conversation had been with the crow, and that hadn't ended well for the crow. Finally, if the jailors found the pale werewolf trustworthy, then Morlock had to assume the contrary.

His wounds were nearly healed. He examined the jar for some sort of maker's mark: a magical salve would almost certainly require its own unique vessel, and he knew that most adepts were as vain as spoiled children. But there was nothing that Morlock could see—with his eyes, anyway. Again, he felt the loss of his Sight like the loss of a limb.

He looked up to see the trustee's pale eyes on him. He handed back the jar and, as he did so, the pale werewolf said something to him. It was the first time he had heard the pale trustee speak without a background of banter or barking from the other jailors, and Morlock found the werewolf's voice to be oddly resonant and high-pitched—not a male voice or a female voice exactly. Morlock met the other's eye and shook his head to indicate he hadn't understood.

The werewolf spoke again, speaking more slowly. Morlock still understood only one word, or thought he did. It was *rokhlan*. In the shared language of dragons and dwarves, the language Morlock had grown up speaking, *rokhlan* meant "dragonkiller"—a title of honor among dwarves that Morlock had earned several times. Did the trustee know him? Did someone here know him? Had he misheard?

He shrugged and turned away. He still didn't trust the trustee. The pale werewolf waited for a few moments, apparently expecting Morlock to engage him again. Morlock began to pace the width of his cell, from stone wall to stone wall, ignoring the other. Eventually, the trustee left. Morlock continued his pacing.

After a month, the wounds were completely healed; even the scars had vanished. Over the month, which must have been the month of Jaric, since the nights were often moonless, the little drama of a prisoner being dragged up to Morlock's cell was several times replayed. Never was it necessary for the jailors to actually throw the prisoners into the cell; they were weeping and babbling as soon as they saw the fearsome beast that awaited them: Morlock. This did not please him, but there was nothing he could do about it. Several times he found the tooth on a cord next to his food and water; every time he tossed it contemptuously into the corridor, and eventually it stopped reappearing.

When he wasn't being used as a threat to terrify werewolves, he paced his cell. As he walked, through the long days when there was nothing else to do, he eyed the confines of his cell, hoping to find some signs of weakness he could exploit. Sadly, there seemed to be none. The building was newish; Morlock guessed it was less than ten years old. The mortar was much stained from moss and filth, but time had not worked its crumbling magic on it. The stones were well shaped and uniform; they seemed to have no flaws he could exploit. His greatest hope was in the ceiling or the floor; those stones could not be as massive as the load-bearing ones in the walls, even if the building was timbered with maijarra wood.

Of course, to exploit any weakness he would need time, tools, and freedom from observation. Time was every prisoner's constant friend and enemy. Tools he could make or acquire somehow. But every time he turned in his pacing he met the eyes of his jailors, staring at him, watching and waiting. As long as they kept that up, he could not escape.

He got to know the walls of the cell quite well, even the individual stones. Some of them displayed strips of texture in the upper right corner; others did not. Some had been scratched at by prisoners; others had not. Most of the prisoners' scratchings he couldn't read, but many of them were obviously tallies of days, calls, months, years. Morlock speculated on what the other symbols meant. And he walked.

One day, he realized that the strips of texture on the corners of some stones were also writing, graven deep into the stone and covered later by moss and mold and other matter. It was long before he could bring himself to stop pacing and scrape away at the filth to see if he could read the words. For one thing, it would let his captors know he was interested in the stones of the wall. For another, it broke the tedious pattern of his pacing, and his idea was to be as boring as possible for his guards so that they would lose interest in watching him. But in the end his curiosity overcame him. He halted by one of the walls and rubbed away at one of the corners.

He found, to his surprise, that he could read it. Moreover, he guessed few others in the world could. It was a piece of Latin, one of his mother's languages.

EGO • IACOMES • FILIVS • SAXIPONDERIS • HAS • CARCERES • FECI • ME • PAENITET • CAPTE

It took him some time to work it out. Latin was one of the languages that his long-dead *harven* father had made him learn, out of respect for his *ruthen* parents, but he rarely had use for it. Eventually he decided that this inscription said something like, "I, Iacomes, Stoneweight's son, made this prison. Sorry about that, prisoner."

Stoneweight. What kind of name was that? Morlock wondered. And why had the maker signed his repellent work in Latin? It was mysterious, and he thought he might have some words for this Iacomes character if he ever met him. Still, the inscription lifted his mood strangely. This prison had been made. What one maker makes, another can unmake. So Morlock believed, and he spent the rest of the day thinking about it: of solvents to break down mortar, of methods to stun or drug or distract guards, of opportunities that time and patience might bring him.

What time brought him that day was another prisoner in late afternoon. This one—another werewolf in man form—was tall and much scarred; his hair and beard were iron gray, but it didn't appear to be the gray of age. His appearance was nearly as threatening as the subhuman they had sent in to face Morlock on his first night here. But there was an intelligence in this werewolf's eyes that worried Morlock. He might be a more dangerous antagonist, and nightfall was imminent.

Many guards came along with the new prisoner into the narrow corridor. He wore no clothes, but he walked like a captive king among an honor guard of spears. He ignored them all and looked straight at Morlock through the bars of the cell. Morlock leaned his left shoulder against a cell wall and looked back indifferently.

The cell door was unbarred and swung open. The new prisoner stepped in, and the door crashed shut behind him.

The new guards remained in the corridor outside. The wolves and men bantered and bartered; the pale trustee again appeared and seemed to be taking bets (although he looked a little glum to Morlock). It was all very familiar.

The new prisoner went to a corner of the cell and sat down. His action seemed deliberately . . . not hostile. It could be he was only waiting for nightfall.

Morlock's best chance was to kill him before he turned into a wolf. As a man, he was as mortal as Morlock, and perhaps less used to defending his life. Morlock struggled with the idea of attacking first. It seemed reasonable, the only reasonable alternative. But he remembered the second prisoner who had been brought in, the one who panicked at the sight of Morlock, who broke down at the prospect of being locked in a cell with him. They used him as their beast to train rebellious prisoners. And he would not be used that way. He was caged; he was not a beast. He'd let this man live so that the man Morlock was could go on living.

They waited. The cell grew dark. They waited still. The chatter in the corridor outside grew impatient: some bets had already been lost. Blue squares of moonlight began to glow on the floor of the cell as the sun's light finally faded away. It was now early in the month of Brenting, by Morlock's calculation, and both the minor moons would be aloft.

The new prisoner rose to his feet. He stepped into the larger square of moonlight and raised his hands toward the window.

The silver-blue moonlight struck the prisoner like a hammer strikes red-hot metal: bending him, reshaping him, twisting him. His back curved; his ears and jaws stretched; his teeth flickered like white flames in his mouth; he fell on his hands, and by the time they struck stone they were paws. A dense forest of coarse, dark fur sprouted on his crooked limbs and arched body.

His voice was unheard throughout. Morlock remembered how the other one had screamed in transformation, and he wondered if this werewolf was mute. But he suspected not. The werewolf's luminous blue eyes never lost their cool intelligence. He could master the pain or terror that accompanied his transformation and not be mastered by it. That was bad for Morlock, of course. But Morlock, too, was the master of his pain and fear. He waited for the werewolf's attack.

The werewolf turned toward Morlock and fixed his frosty blue gaze on him. Morlock still waited for the werewolf's attack. He did not move, but kept his hands open. If the beast jumped, he would try to meet it in midair and break its neck.

There were mutters of anticipation from the guards, human and lupine, in the corridor.

The werewolf stepped out of the square of moonlight: a deliberate step backward, away from Morlock. He stood there in the shadows, waiting.

A storm of shouts and barking arose in the corridor outside.

Morlock wondered if this meant what he thought it meant. The gesture the werewolf had made was oddly familiar. He himself couldn't take a step backward, since he was against the wall, but he spread the fingers of his hands and waited.

The werewolf took another step back, a blue-eyed gray shadow among other shadows. He deliberately dropped his gaze.

Then Morlock remembered when he had seen this gesture before. In the Giving Field of the Khroic horde, Valona's, where he had killed a dragon and saved a werewolf's life.

The werewolf uttered a few wordlike barks. It paused, and repeated them.

One of the words sounded like *rokhlan*. Though, as the werewolf repeated it for the second time, Morlock decided it was really more like *rokhlenu*. But he thought it was the same word, borrowed into the werewolf speech.

The werewolf repeated his statement a third time.

Morlock thought the werewolf was saying that he himself was the dragonkiller. Then Morlock remembered that the werewolf who had been taken with him and the others by Valona's horde was a dragonkiller. Anyway, he had claimed it, and Marh Valone had believed it.

Morlock didn't think he could say what he wanted to say in wolf-speech—and, now that he thought of it, he had never heard werewolves in human form speak like wolves. It might be insulting or unclear; that was the last thing Morlock wanted at the moment.

He made a corvine croak of recognition (*I know you*) and added the werewolf's own word: *rokhlenu*.

The werewolf nodded, satisfied, and turned away. He trotted over to a corner of the cell and curled up to sleep.

The jailors in the corridor were furious. They threw bits of trash and shouted obvious insults, and they barked like chained dogs yearning at the end of a leash, and they grumbled, more or less all at once. They wanted to see a fight, at least see someone humiliated. There would be none of that tonight.

Morlock crossed his arms and watched them, allowing a crooked smile to show on his face. As the jailors in the hallway noticed it they began to grow quiet. He met the eye of anyone who looked at him and smiled. He was trying to tell them something: tonight *they* were the entertainment and *he* was the audience, and he had been richly amused.

They began to slink away. The message had been received, or they were tired of complaining. Last to go (apart from the guards who were left on station) was the pale trustee. He met Morlock's eye, gave a brief answering smile, and fled.

Chapter Seven

Words

Every day, for many days that followed, the jailors tried to provoke a fight between Morlock and the werewolf Rokhlenu. The jailors would give them one dish of food and one dish of water and wait for them to fight over it. It maddened them to see the prisoners divide up the food and share the water, passing the dish back and forth. The jailors gave the prisoners scant water and no food for ten days, then again tried offering the prisoners a single dish of food. Their fury at seeing the prisoners again share their food was extremely amusing to Rokhlenu and Morlock.

The guards with bows started using one or the other of the prisoners for target practice. When they did this they would shout or bark words at him. Morlock guessed these were encouragements to attack the other prisoner. He ignored the arrows, as did Rokhlenu. What the werewolf thought about it Morlock didn't know—their conversations hadn't gotten to the point of discussing abstractions. But from Morlock's point of view, the issue was clear. Either the guards would kill him, or they would not. If they would not, their threats were empty. If they did kill him, it was one way to escape the prison. He was willing to buy their failure with his own death.

The guards began to enter the cell in force. They beat Rokhlenu until the prisoner was crippled with pain and injuries. Then they left him to be killed in his weakness by Morlock. Morlock left him alone, letting him be healed by time and moonlight, so the next time the guards entered they crippled Morlock and left him for Rokhlenu. Rokhlenu left Morlock alone to heal, also (although this took longer).

The guards tried this gambit many times. The beatings were often overseen by the same senior guard—sometimes in wolf form, sometimes in human form, but always addressed as Wurnafenglu by the other guards, and recognizable from his great torc of honor-teeth. He would speak at length, cajolingly or insultingly, to the prisoners. Rokhlenu ignored it; Morlock didn't understand it.

Wurnafenglu finally resorted to riskier gambits, like having the jailors introduce weapons to the cell. One day they left a single knife with the food and water. Morlock and Rokhlenu tossed it back and forth to each other across the cell until the disgusted guards sent the pale trembling trustee in to recover it.

Their last attempt was directed specifically at Morlock. One night, after Rokhlenu had undergone his transition to wolfhood, a dozen archers took their places outside the cell and aimed nocked arrows at Morlock. Then the pale trustee appeared, holding a rough metal spike in a pair of long wooden tongs. He tossed the spike into the cell and backed away, looking apologetically at the prisoners.

Rokhlenu backed instinctively away from the spike. Morlock approached it. The archers shifted their aim to follow him.

The spike was made of silver. Morlock was intrigued. How had they acquired it? Why had they acquired it? What did they expect him to do?

He picked up the spike and looked at the guards outside the cell. No word or sign was given, but the implication seemed clear: *kill him or we'll kill you.*

Morlock hefted the spike in his hand. It was a powerful weapon in this stretch of the world, but it was no good to him in this cell. He tossed it through the open window into the moonslit world outside. Then he turned to face the archers.

Wurnafenglu, standing in wolf form in the hallway, gave a curt bark. The archers stood down and marched away. Only the usual four guards were left on station. Wurnafenglu looked wearily at Morlock and then looked away.

It was the jailors' last attempt to get Morlock and Rokhlenu to fight.

In the meantime, Morlock had been learning the werewolves' languages from Rokhlenu. He had been right that the werewolves were repelled by humans making wolf sounds (and the reverse): each form had its own language. In wolf form ("the night shape" Rokhlenu called it) they used Moonspeech, and in human form ("the day shape") they used Sunspeech.

At first, Morlock learned Moonspeech faster: he already knew a few words, and there were apparently not many to know. But Moonspeech was more difficult than Sunspeech in some ways. With fewer words and less grammar to communicate the same universe of meanings, much of the sense depended on shifting contexts and metaphorical leaps that Morlock found hard to follow. If he'd still had his Sight it might have been easier.

Sunspeech, in contrast, had a multitude of vocabularies and inflections with very precise distinctions. There was a difference between "volcanic rock unworked by a maker and unweathered by the elements" (*wilk*), "volcanic rock worked but not weathered" (*wlik*), "volcanic rock weathered but not worked" (*welk*), "volcanic rock worked and weathered" (*welik*), and it was a solecism to use one when you meant the other, or a vaguer word like the undifferentiated "rock" (*lafun*) when you really meant something more specific. Morlock committed this solecism so often that Rokhlenu seemed to grow used to it. Anyway, he stopped laughing at it.

Rokhlenu was a patient teacher, Morlock was a patient student, and they had as much time as they needed: they worked on languages whenever they were awake and the jailors weren't trying to provoke a fight between them.

Not infrequently the pale trustee would come and speak with them through the bars—mostly with Rokhlenu at first, but more and more with Morlock as he could speak and comprehend Sunspeech better. The trustee's name, it turned out, was Hrutnefdhu ("Skin-maker").

Morlock had thought long about the social differences he could see among the werewolves. All the guards, for instance, were clean shaven. All of the prisoners wore beards, except for Hrutnefdhu. Of the prisoners he had seen, all were naked, except for Hrutnefdhu . . . and himself.

After learning enough words, he finally managed to put a question to Rokhlenu one day: "Why are all the prisoners naked? Or are they?"

Rokhlenu's answer hinged on many words that Morlock didn't know, and he missed almost all of it. He got a sense that there was a status system involved, and that the less clothes you had the lower your status.

"Then," Morlock asked, "a loincloth like Hrutnefdhu's would be better than no clothes at all?"

"Yes," Rokhlenu agreed, with unusual curtness.

Morlock nodded. He took off what remained of his shirt and began to tear it into wide strips, knotting them together as he went. Rokhlenu said something to him that he didn't understand. He ignored it and finished the job. Then he held the cloth out to Rokhlenu. "Here. It's not much."

Rokhlenu struck the edge of one hand into the palm of another, a gesture of refusal. "No! I can change into a wolf at night. It may be a warm winter, but it's still winter. You need it more than I do."

Morlock continued to hold the cloth out.

Rokhlenu struck the edge of one hand into the palm of another and said again, "No. I thank you. No."

Morlock had to state an abstraction, and his language skills weren't ready for it. He said slowly, "There is you and me. There is them. They don't want this. So: here. Take it."

Rokhlenu looked at Morlock. He looked at the guards outside, who were watching keenly. He took the makeshift loincloth. "Thanks," he said, and wrapped it around himself with the ease of long practice.

Morlock then asked another question that had long been on his mind, "Why doesn't Hrutnefdhu have hair on his face?"

"He does," Rokhlenu replied, startled.

Some of the guards laughed. Morlock mulled it over, and then mimed shaving. That was what he was really concerned about. If there was some way for a prisoner to get the privilege of shaving, then he might acquire a razor and keep it. A straight edge of steel could be useful in so many ways.

The guards laughed again. Rokhlenu seemed surprised and a little embarrassed when he understood Morlock's question. He laboriously explained that Morlock's words implied that Hrutnefdhu had no fur on his face in the night shape, which was apparently an embarrassing blemish for werewolves and which Rokhlenu knew was not the case with Hrutnefdhu.

He taught Morlock the vocabulary of shaving (*khlut*: razor, *sreml*: oil, *khlunv*: shave) and then said, "But Hrutnefdhu doesn't shave. Someone shaved him good, long years ago."

The guards laughed again, even more uproariously.

There was some joke here that Morlock did not understand. He opened his hands and looked at Rokhlenu expectantly, hoping an explanation was coming.

Rokhlenu turned his head to one side: he understood that Morlock didn't understand. He mimed an action with his hands: a razor lopping something off. He said, "Hrutnefdhu is *plepnup*." He mimed again and repeated, "*Plepnup*." Morlock guessed that *plepnup* meant *castrated*. He turned his head to one side.

When Hrutnefdhu next appeared, Morlock's guess was confirmed. The guards had been much amused by his conversation with Rokhlenu, and they made Hrutnefdhu take his loincloth off and show his mutilated genitals to Morlock. The pale werewolf was deeply humiliated; his mottled face grew red with shame and powerless rage. Not just his testicles had been removed; his penis too had been savagely mutilated. He glared at Morlock as he stood naked at the barred cell door.

Morlock, for his part, was furious at the guards for humiliating the weak and timid trustee. He was sorry that something he'd said was the cause. He would have been hard pressed to explain that in one of his native languages, though. As the jailors finally allowed Hrutnefdhu to turn away, Morlock blurted, "There is them. There is you and me."

Rokhlenu looked at Morlock in surprise. He turned to Hrutnefdhu and said, "He's right. There is them. There is you and him and me."

"*Plepnupov*," hissed Hrutnefdhu. "Eh? You, me, him? All *plepnupov*. Eh?"

"If they had their way," said Rokhlenu. "So the Stone Tree can have them."

Hrutnefdhu turned and ran naked down the echoing hallway.

"That was bad," Rokhlenu said, turning away from the laughing guards, taking Morlock by the arm as he did so. "It was also good. You have a strange shame, Morlock."

"Oh?"

"Yes. To have no bite does not shame you. To get bite from the jailors, that shames you. To have no shirt does not shame you. To have a shirt while your friend is naked, that shames you. To stand with a *plepnup* and say you-and-me does not shame you. To let a *plepnup* stand ashamed before you, that shames you."

"I suppose so."

"Yurr. You don't say much, do you? Are you more talkative when you know more words?"

"Not really."

"Now there is you and me and him against them."

"*Against*," Morlock said. (It was a new word.) "If that means what I think it means, it is a good word."

"Isn't it, my friend?" laughed Rokhlenu. "I thought you would like it. Us against them. I almost feel sorry for them, don't you?"

Morlock thought the matter over for a moment and then said, "No."

Chapter Eight

Eyeless Night

There came a night without a moon, an eyeless night, in the wolvish phrase. It must have been early in the month of Drums. Rokhlenu did not transform into a wolf but stayed in human form, shivering in the dark cell with Morlock.

"How do you stand it without fur?" Rokhlenu asked him finally.

"I don't sleep much," Morlock admitted. "A few hours a night. There's no point in it anyway."

"Isn't there? I like to sleep when I can. Dreams might be the only way I ever get out of this place."

"I don't dream."

"Everybody dreams, Morlock. Are you sure what the word means?"

"I don't dream since they put the spike in my head."

"What?" Rokhlenu asked.

So, with a little prompting and vocabulary assistance from Rokhlenu, Morlock told the tale of how he had been captured. He didn't mention why he had been using his Sight: that wasn't something he wanted the guards to hear, if they were listening, and ever since Hrutnefdhu's humiliation he tried to stay aware that they were always listening. But he said that he had used his Sight and narrated what happened after, as far as he could remember it.

"A ghost-sniffer," Rokhlenu said, when Morlock described the wolf who had detected his Sight. "They travel with the raiders, in case they run afoul of any magic-users, like you used to be, I guess. I understand they get their powers from sleeping with pigs during the dark of the moons. Of course, all the Sardhluun try that sometimes."

This was mere slander, for the ears of the ever-listening guards, who twitched angrily but did not intervene.

"How did you end up so deep in the north, though?" Rokhlenu asked. "And what happened to those people who were travelling with you? I remember that young man. Thund?"

"Thend."

"Thend. Not the dullest tool in the drawer, but he had more nerve than brains at that. I remember how he crept down into the Vale of the Mother, leaving a trail as dark as ink through the tall grass! But his family was down there, and he wasn't going to let fear or common sense stop him from getting killed with them. It's a miracle he wasn't."

"You played a part in that miracle."

"A small matter. It added nothing to my bite when I told the story back home, believe me. Anyway, how are they?"

"Well, or so I hope. I left them so they'd have a better chance at that."

"Oh? Anything I should know about?"

Morlock glumly pondered how much he could or should tell Rokhlenu about Merlin. "I have a powerful enemy. When he attacks me . . . those around me may be harmed."

"Yurr. Well, we'll meet him together, if it comes to that. But you haven't asked me what I'm doing here."

"Bad manners."

"In a prison? I guess you're right. I've never been in one before. Have you?"

"A few times. Nothing like this." Morlock tapped the side of his head and shrugged.

"Well, since you can't ask, I'll just tell you. I was born, poor but honest—"

"Poor in imagination, anyway."

"To the Stone Tree with you, you ill-tempered, ape-footed son of a walrus-fondling pimp."

"That's a little better," Morlock conceded.

"I was *born*, anyway: you won't quibble with me about that?"

Morlock almost did, just for something to do, but there was a limit anyone could stand to this abrasive humor, and they had no escape from each other's company. So he shrugged and opened one hand.

"Three shadows by sunlight," Rokhlenu swore. "Do you talk any more when you know the language better?"

The joke was already overfamiliar. "No," Morlock said curtly. "You were born?"

"Yes, although they didn't throw me in prison right away because of that. Actually, I was lying like a were-weasel earlier: my family had a lot of bite when I was growing up in the Aruukaiaduun pack—"

"What's 'bite'?" Morlock asked.

"You can't be serious. Don't you know what bite is?"

"I thought I did," Morlock said. He pointed at a ragged scar on his arm. "That's from a bite. Or am I using the wrong word?"

"No," Rokhlenu said, "but it means more than just one thing. Bite is . . . You know, they gave you that honor-tooth after you ripped old Khretnurrliu's head off."

"Khretnurrliu." The name meant *man-killer* if Morlock understood it right. "That was his name?"

"Yes, but so what? It's not like you'll be seeing him again."

Morlock didn't tell him how wrong he was but said, "I remember the tooth. And the guards wear teeth. They show . . ." He wanted to say *status*, but he didn't know the word for it.

"They show bite: the more teeth the greater the individual's bite. The more bite you have, the more important you are. That's why Hrutnefdhu keeps trying to give the tooth back to you."

Hrutnefdhu, the pale trustee, had brought the tooth back to Morlock several times. But Morlock would not accept status from the beasts who had stolen his freedom, a point he did not have the abstract vocabulary to make to Hrutnefdhu, so he just kept refusing it.

"It is theirs," Morlock said now to Rokhlenu. "If it is theirs, it is not mine."

"Most people would have taken the tooth. If you acquired enough bite, they might let you out of here."

"Just let me go?"

"No. They'd probably send you to work in the fields. The Sardhluun have many fields and pastures, most of them slave-worked." Rokhlenu seemed about to go on, but he didn't.

Morlock could guess what he had been going to say. It would be easier to escape from there than from here. No doubt that was true. Morlock doubted he could bend himself to the performance, though. And it was clear that the only way he could earn a second tooth, more "bite" in the eyes of his captors, would be to kill Rokhlenu. Even if he could do that, he would not.

"Eh," Morlock said.

"Right," Rokhlenu agreed. "So, anyway, my people had bite. My father was a master rope maker on the funicular in Wuruyaaria—"

"Wuruyaaria is the city of werewolves?"

"Yes. For someone who doesn't talk much, you're interrupting me a lot."

"What's a funicular?"

"It's just a bunch of big ropes, really. One end is at the city walls (by Twinegate, naturally) and the other is on the city's highest mesa, Wuruklendon. Baskets can ride the ropes up and down."

"Baskets?"

"Yes." Rokhlenu explained what a basket was. "Of course, it's really the people and things in the baskets that are important."

"Of course," Morlock agreed, but he didn't mean it. It was the rope system itself that impressed him. "An impressive feat of making."

"The funicular? I guess so. People say Ulugarriu made it, like the moonclock in the volcano's side and everything else that impresses people."

"Ulugarriu." The name meant Ghosts-in-the-eyes, unless Morlock misunderstood it. "I would like to meet him." (The name's *-u* ending meant that it was masculine gender.) "He must be a great maker."

"Eh. Oh, maggots, now you've got me doing it. Forget about meeting Ulugarriu, Morlock. He walks unseen. Nobody ever meets him."

"Then how do you know he exists?"

"I never said he did. Anyway, *I* exist and I was born, not-so-poor-and-slightly-dishonest in the shadow of the great Fang Tower of Nekkuklendon—which, before you ask, is the third of the great mesas of Wuruyaaria. Shall I tell you about my childhood, my youth, my musical education, my many battles, my steady-yet-rapid accumulation of bite, my first sexual adventures?"

"God Avenger, no."

"Well, it's your loss, but I'll skip on a bit, then. My problem was that, like most young werewolves of spirit, I wanted political office."

"Eh."

"I did say werewolves. I don't pretend to know what life is like for you people, but we are pack animals. We're not ashamed of it."

"It's not much different for us, I guess. Except for the shame, maybe. Go on."

"My father ranked high in the Aruukaiaduun pack, but I wanted to rank still higher. I could have, too: I was favored to win nomination to the Innermost Pack."

"How many packs are there?"

"Four, of course—and the outliers, who don't count yet. Each pack has an Inner Pack, who have the most bite in the pack, and millennia ago, when the city was founded, they set up an Innermost Pack with members drawn from all three of the treaty packs."

"Three? You said there were four."

"There were three, then. The Sardhluun weren't part of the treaty until later. They bought their way in, essentially. They had slaves, and prison houses, and meat, and as these are three things that no civilized society can do without—"

"Eh."

"—that *our* society can't do without, the Sardhluun were given places on the Innermost Pack and accepted into the treaty. What would you have done?"

Morlock gave it some thought and said, "I would gut every member of the Sardhluun Pack with a silver knife."

This caused a rustle among the ever-watchful guards. Even Rokhlenu jumped a little, but then he said, "Right! And I'll hold them down for you.

Anyway. The different packs can nominate members to the Innermost Pack, but the nominees have to earn their place in competition with each other."

"How does it work?"

"Fight and bite. Bite and fight. You can get bite by fighting, or talking, or singing, or making, or doing. You can buy it: people who make money always have lots of bite. I got a lot of bite from a song I composed."

"Oh? What's it about?"

"The way a she-wolf's genitals smelled when Chariot was aloft in midwinter."

"That's impossible, though," Morlock pointed out, after some vocabulary was explained to him. "Chariot doesn't rise until the first day of spring."

"You have to make things up for a good song sometimes, Morlock."

Morlock shrugged dubiously at the necessity of fantasy and said, "So your political career led to the prison house."

"As it often does—maybe not often enough. I was popular; my family was rich; I was a well-respected singer; people knew I could fight. They knew it so much that I never had to."

"Wasn't that good?"

"Yes and no. I'd have liked to get in a few more fights to raise my reputation. But if you run around starting fights with people, it can actually decrease your bite."

Morlock nodded. "So: the dragon."

"Exactly. I took many a long run down south to the mountains, hoping to get into trouble I'd have to fight my way out of. Not too many werewolves actually go into the Kirach Kund, though. I had to wait a long time before I found a dragon that was vulnerable, but it was worth it."

"Go on." Morlock had a professional interest in the killing of dragons.

"I came upon one that had been drugged by the Spiderfolk. They had just taken its dragonrider prisoner and they were hauling him away. They could not approach the dragon—they're very susceptible to fire. You remember."

"Yes."

"So I waited till they were gone and I sneaked up on the dragon and killed it. And—"

"How?"

"I crept into its mouth and gnawed through the palate into its brain."

"Oh."

"I can't say that I enjoyed the dragon brain much. But the palate, and dragon meat generally, is very pleasant: a firm white meat, somewhat like rattlesnake or chicken. Have you ever—?"

"No. Not dragon, at any rate."

"Well, everyone has to draw the line somewhere. I've never eaten another werewolf, no matter how hungry I've been. Not knowingly, anyway. So, after I left you in the Vale of the Mother, I went back and stripped the dragon's skull and brought it back to my father's house for a prize."

"It must have earned you a lot of bite."

"It did! It did! My father hired the best ghost-sniffers from the Goweiteiuun Pack to confirm my story in an affidavit, and the pack voted me a new name. They liked the story of how we were taken by the Khroi and the odd Dwarvish word the Khroi used for dragonkiller, so they voted me that for my new name."

"Oh? What was your name before?"

"Slenkjariu," Rokhlenu said reluctantly. "After my mother's grandfather. None of my mother's people amounted to much, and with names like that you can see why."

Morlock didn't exactly see why, but his friend actually seemed embarrassed and he didn't want to make it any worse. "I still sense a long road from there to here."

"A short one. There was, and is, a gray-muzzle in the Aruukaiaduun Inner Pack, name of Rywudhaariu; he had a list of nominees for the next citywide election, and I wasn't on it and he didn't want me on it. So he had a few of his boys rob and murder a bookie and then frame me for it."

Morlock needed some words explained ("bookie" and "frame" particularly). Then he remarked, "Was there a trial? Didn't your heroic bite help you there?"

"Not against Rywudhaariu, who'd been collecting teeth up and down the mesa for more than forty years. Anyway, he bribed the jury—used the proceeds of the robbery to fund the bribes. You have to admit that shows *vifna*."

"Do I?" Morlock didn't know what *vifna* was, but he didn't think he liked it. "Wasn't this all illegal? I don't understand your system."

"It was illegal, and everyone knew about it, and if things made sense maybe it wouldn't have worked. But Rywudhaariu was probably better off after my trial than before it. Somehow, if it's your job to make or enforce the laws and you break them with impunity, you can get a certain kind of bite from that. I don't understand it myself well enough to explain it, but that's how it seems to work. Maybe it's different in never-wolf cities."

"I don't know," Morlock said slowly, thinking of the late and unlamented Protector Urdhven and the men who had followed him. "Maybe not that different."

"Rywudhaariu's guards dragged me to the Sardhluun's plantation," Rokhlenu went on. "I was hoping they would have me working the fields, herding cattle or something. Escape would be easy. That's why they didn't do that, I guess. I started out on the ground floor and then worked my way up here." When he saw that Morlock didn't understand him, he explained, "The top floor is where they keep the real irredeemables. Like you and Khretnurrliu."

Morlock bowed his head to accept the compliment.

"I was hoping my father and brothers could bribe the Sardhluun to let me go, or at least give me a chance at escape," Rokhlenu said reflectively, "but I suppose Rywudhaariu is giving them their own trouble now."

"'It's a fool who kills the father and lets the son live,'" Morlock said, quoting the proverb.

"'Bare is the back with no brother,'" said Rokhlenu, quoting another.

"Your back is bare," Morlock pointed out.

"The god it is," Rokhlenu said, yawning. "I'm going to try to sleep now, Morlock. I don't know how you can stand this."

Sleeping on a cold stone floor in human form, Morlock guessed he meant. But the truth was that Morlock didn't have to stand it, for he slept very little, and that little didn't do him much good. His body rested, but never his mind.

Just now, for instance, he saw a fifth werewolf outside the cell. There were two guards in the day shape and two in the night shape, as always. One of the humans seemed to be in charge: he wore a neckband and chest-torc that bristled with accumulated teeth. Morlock thought this was Wurnafenglu. Morlock was fairly sure it was the same werewolf, and he was sure that he hated him. The others were just guards; Morlock might have seen them before, but he didn't recognize them.

It was the fifth werewolf that really had Morlock's attention, although he never looked directly at him. He could not: every time Morlock tried, the werewolf seemed to sidle over to the edge of Morlock's vision. But Morlock knew him: it was Khretnurrliu, the werewolf he had decapitated. The body was in the day shape, carrying its severed head before it like a lamp. It did not speak, nor make any noise. The guards passed a remark to each other occasionally, but never to Khretnurrliu. But Morlock saw him. He could not stop seeing him.

A pale shadow appeared at the bars: Hrutnefdhu, in the night shape. He coughed shyly, wondering if Morlock wished to talk.

Morlock moved forward to sit by the cell door. The archers raised their arrows reflexively to threaten him, but he ignored them and presently they relaxed.

"I'd rather sleep than talk," Morlock admitted, "but I can't sleep."

Hrutnefdhu expressed sympathy.

Morlock opened his hands: there was nothing to be done. "Can you change into wolf form without moonlight?" he wondered. "Can those?" he asked, gesturing at the guards.

Hrutnefdhu sang that he had assumed the hairy cloak of wolfhood last night, with Trumpeter's last light, and resisted the man-shaping rays of the sun all day. He added in a whisper that the wolf-formed guards were unfortunates unblessed by the gift of a second skin.

Morlock was interested. He'd heard there were werewolves who couldn't change fully from *were* to *wolf* or back again; indeed, Khretnurrliu with his twisted legs and hatchet face seemed to be one such. Apparently it was considered a blemish, even a matter of shame. He wondered if there was some way to use this to his advantage—to divide the guards somehow.

"Are there . . . ? Sometimes I see werewolves in the day shape by moonlight," he said, trying to explain the question he could not ask.

Hrutnefdhu understood. He said that many guards lacked the gift of a second form, walking under the moons as if they were suns, making a lack of gift into a gift.

"Hm," Morlock said, trying not to sound too dubious. One of the night shape guards had a single tooth around his neck; the other had none. Clearly, they had little bite, even among other guards . . . who, Morlock reflected, might not have much bite as a class, outside the prison house.

Hrutnefdhu sang a single note of query.

Morlock nodded.

Hrutnefdhu wondered why Morlock had never answered Rokhlenu's question. He too wished to know what had brought so powerful a maker and a seer as Morlock so far into the north.

Morlock shrugged. "I have no home. I go from one place to another. How did you know I was a maker?"

Hrutnefdhu sang that he had heard of heroes who walked into the north ages ago, broke the Soul Bridge, and banished the Sunkillers from the world. One of them was a man with crooked shoulders, and they called him Morlock. He was a maker and a son of makers.

"That was a different man than me," Morlock said, standing. "A very different man." He turned away and rolled himself up in a corner of the cell. He didn't sleep, then or for a long time, but at least no one expected him to talk.

It had been a better night than most since Morlock's imprisonment began. Now he knew that Rokhlenu was a rope maker, or had been. Under the circumstances, that was a very useful skill.

Chapter Nine

Madness

The days grew warmer, and Morlock gradually became convinced that he was going mad. He rather reluctantly raised the topic with Rokhlenu, who laughed it off at first.

"You'll have to convince me you were ever sane," the werewolf said, one blisteringly hot noonday in midspring. "Then I'll worry about you going crazy."

But Morlock convinced him in the end. He told him about Khretnurrliu, how he always saw the mutilated werewolf outside the cell. He wore the day shape in the night, carrying his head in one hand; he wore the night shape in the day, sitting with his head at his feet. He never spoke and rarely moved, except to shift away from Morlock's sight when Morlock tried to look straight at him. But he was always there.

"There's no one there but the guards, Morlock," Rokhlenu said, sounding a little worried now, though.

"You say so," Morlock agreed, "and I'm almost sure you're right. But I see him. I know he's there, even when I'm not looking. Listen to me, Rokhlenu. It's you this matters to."

"I don't know what I can do about it," the werewolf said.

"There's nothing to be done," Morlock agreed. "But you need to know. If I seem to be acting insanely, it's probably not an act. Protect yourself. Maybe you can get one of those field jobs."

Rokhlenu looked blank for a moment; then he realized Morlock was suggesting he might have to kill him. "Shut your meat-hole," he snarled.

"No. But I'll do what I can do to keep it from coming to that."

"All right. What can you do?"

Morlock shrugged. There was nothing, really.

That night, when they thought Morlock was sleeping, Rokhlenu had a low-voiced conversation with Hrutnefdhu.

Rokhlenu sang of Morlock's strength of will, how he had slain the beast Khretnurrliu, how he had faced the torments of the guards with patience, even with humor. He said he could not believe that madness was stronger than Morlock's will.

Hrutnefdhu conceded much of what Rokhlenu sang. He himself had seen that battle in the cell; he was still in awe that a man, a mere human, had done what Morlock had done. But he apologetically sang about the dangers of a powerful will turning inward, about obsessions that ate away at the strongest minds, feeding on that strength itself. He pointed out that Morlock was a Seer who had lost his magical Sight, and that madness might be the rot from that inward death.

Rokhlenu wondered if there was anything that could be done—if the spike could be drawn and Morlock's mind healed.

Hrutnefdhu sang of the storied wisdom of his mate, Liudhleeo, She-who-remembers-best. She waited for him among the long-legged lairs of the outlier pack, in the swamps south of Wuruyaaria. Liudhleeo might know.

Rokhlenu sang a brief comparison of the distance between the prison and the outlier pack and the distance between the prison and the paths of the moons. Since neither were accessible, they were equally far away.

Hrutnefdhu's song was apologetic, guilt-ridden. There were ghost-sniffers among the Sardhluun, but they would not heal Morlock or allow him to be healed. They had felt his power when he was first captured and they feared it. An insane Morlock would suit them better than a sane one.

Rokhlenu sang a questioning note.

Hrutnefdhu gently pointed out that Morlock and Rokhlenu had broken the Sardhluun's system: they used prisoners to terrorize each other. A mad Morlock might be useful as a terror. A sensible Morlock who did exercises and memorized verb-tones was no good for the Sardhluun.

Rokhlenu speculated on things that might be good for the Sardhluun, such as venom-drenched, spiked silver hooks inserted under the tail.

Hrutnefdhu turned and walked away, his nails clattering on the stone floor. The guards were listening, and he could not afford to have a conversation of this sort under their ears.

Morlock found it interesting that Hrutnefdhu hadn't argued with Rokhlenu, even for show. The pale werewolf was a trustee in the prison, but Morlock was beginning to think that they could trust him . . . if they could think of a task to use him for. That was the trouble: they could do nothing unless they could escape from the cell, and the guards' unending vigilance made that unlikely.

It was increasingly difficult for Morlock to think coherently at all. He had begun to worry that Khretnurrliu was edging closer to the cell door. The fact that the cell gate was never opened was a matter of some comfort to Morlock. He began to wonder what would happen if he did have the chance to get into the corridor. If Khretnurrliu were there . . . Morlock had already killed him once. (His eyes were rotted away, and his nose and other soft tissues were visibly decaying. Empty eye sockets ringed with bare bone were what watched Morlock night and day from the corner of his eye.) How could he kill him again? Would he have to go on killing-killing-killing him forever? Wouldn't it be safer to stay in the cell where Khretnurrliu couldn't get at him? So Morlock reasoned to himself as his reason continued to unravel.

But in fact it was Rokhlenu who went mad first.

It happened one night late in the last full month of spring. The days were unbelievably, damnably hot, even in the shadows of the stone cell, and the nights brought very little relief to the still blistering air. But Rokhlenu did not refrain from the nocturnal change to wolfhood: apparently there was a special exultation to the transformation when all three moons were in the sky.

Rokhlenu had just undergone the change; the hallway was echoing with the howls of those doing the same.

Morlock looked up and saw, of course, Khretnurrliu, holding his severed head like a lantern in one hand. Next to him, in the center of Morlock's vision, was Wurnafenglu, that one gray-muzzled prison guard who seemed to have significant bite. He was looking directly at Morlock, dark lips parted in a wolvish grin that was all-too-human. He was expecting a good show.

"Rokhlenu," Morlock said, "they're about to try something. Be wary."

But Rokhlenu didn't listen. He was distracted by something happening in the hallway. Morlock heard the noise, but Rokhlenu was reacting to a scent. His nostrils dilated and he slunk toward the cell bars as if he were being dragged by the nose.

Several guards dragged a she-wolf into view. It was the first female werewolf that Morlock had seen in the prison: there had been females among the raiders, but none among the guards. This one was collared, her back feet bound to a metal bar that kept them spread-eagled. She was whimpering; blood was dripping from her mouth; she had been beaten, perhaps many times. She was evidently in heat.

The guards, laughing and making obscene gestures, showed her to Rokhlenu.

Rokhlenu seemed to struggle with himself for a moment. Finally he threw himself against the bars in a desperate attempt to reach the female.

The guards laughed and mocked him. In a chorus, man and wolf, they sang an obscene song at him; Morlock wondered if it was a version (or inversion) of one of Rokhlenu's songs; there was some mention of three moons aloft.

Rokhlenu was breaking his teeth trying to gnaw through the bars.

The guards raped the female werewolf, one by one. The senior guard, Wurnafenglu, the one with the grizzled fur and the multitude of honor-teeth, went first; the guards wearing the day shape went last. Even headless Khretnurrliu held his severed head high, as if to see better, and gruntingly thrust against the empty air with his decaying phallus.

In the end the she-wolf lay without moving on the stone corridor. Morlock wondered if she was dead. Two of the man-form guards dragged her away. The others turned and started barking insults and mockery at Rokhlenu again. They said they could bring in a she-wolf again every night, if Rokhlenu had enjoyed the show. They said that he probably couldn't have done much if he had made it through the bars—as they themselves would have done, in his place. They described the visceral pleasures of forcing the she-wolf in grunted songs that, again, seemed to be parodies of love poetry. They said a great many things that Morlock did not understand and made no effort to understand.

Rokhlenu kept battering himself against the bars. Whatever reason he had, it was not at his command.

Morlock hated to see it. He hated to see the guards laughing at his friend, mocking him in his moment of weakness. So he jumped forward and strangled him. He wrapped his right arm around Rokhlenu's neck as tightly as he could, and ignored the wolf's savage claws tearing at his flesh, scattering fuming fire-bearing blood on the stones of the cell and the corridor outside.

The guards roared with excitement. This was the game they had long waited to see. They called down the hallway to the other guards. They demanded that Hrutnefdhu bring his bag of betting slips—where the ghost was Hrutnefdhu whenever they needed him?

Morlock clamped down on Rokhlenu's windpipe as hard as he dared and held until the werewolf stopped scrabbling and clawing to get free.

He stood straight up, holding the motionless werewolf's body aloft by his neck. From the grinding sensation under his fingers, at least one bone was broken.

The guards in the hallway applauded him. They called him the beast-killer. They said he had earned much bite, and could earn much more.

Morlock threw the dead werewolf into the square of moonlight on the cell floor.

He turned toward the cell bars. He found the senior guard and fixed him with his gaze. He snarled at him in Moonspeech. He could see by their faces that this shocked the guards; even Khretnurrliu seemed dismayed, to the extent that Morlock could see expression on the severed head's face.

Morlock snarled that, if they wanted bloodshed, one of them should come into the cell. In the day shape or the night shape. With weapons and armor, or naked as the bald-faced bastards of ape-legged brachs that they were. He jumped up to the cell gate and shook the bars with his bleeding hands; the guards all instinctively recoiled. He laughed and turned his back on them.

Rokhlenu was reviving in the white-hot pool of moonlight. He rolled groggily to his feet. His eyes found Morlock, dripping blood and fire near at hand, and shied away from the sight. He didn't look at the hallway, still crowded with eager guards. He slunk over to a lightless corner of the cell and curled up on the floor.

Morlock went to the opposite corner and sat down with his back against the wall. He didn't expect to sleep, but he must have, eventually. After a dreamless interval he woke up and saw that it was past dawn. His wounds had mostly dried up, but one on the wrist was still dripping persistently.

Rokhlenu, now wearing the day shape, was sitting crouched in his corner, his hands across his face. He had not yet put on his loincloth, which was normally the first thing he did after transition.

Morlock rose and limped over to the loincloth. He picked it up with his left (unbleeding) hand and held it out to Rokhlenu. "Here."

"Get away from me," Rokhlenu said, not moving.

"Here," Morlock said, more insistently.

Rokhlenu struck the filthy cloth away from him. "Don't you understand?" he screamed. "The bond is broken. There never was a bond. I'm not one of *you*. I'm one of *them*. I know it now. They know it. Why don't you know it?"

Morlock stooped and picked up the loincloth and held it out. "There is you and me," he said patiently. "There is them. You and me *against* them. No bond is broken. I say so."

Rokhlenu silently took the loincloth and wrapped it around himself. As Morlock turned away, the werewolf reached out his hand and grabbed Morlock by one shoulder. "You and me," Rokhlenu said, "against them. I'll remember this, Morlock."

Morlock nodded and went back to the other side of the cell, where he was less likely to bleed on his friend.

Chapter Ten

Method

Morlock didn't bother binding his wounds; he guessed the Sardhluun would be reluctant to let their beast killer die until they had wholly given up on finding ways to use him.

He was right. Presently Hrutnefdhu came slinking down the corridor in man form, the jar of healing salve in one hand, a roll of bandages in the other. He stood in the corridor, not looking at the guards as one opened the gate while the others nocked arrows and aimed them at the prisoners. Hrutnefdhu stepped into the cell. He didn't look at Rokhlenu, either, but went straight to Morlock with the salve.

"Thanks," Morlock said, slathering on the ill-smelling goo.

"I'll bind them," Hrutnefdhu said, unrolling a stretch of cloth and tearing it with his sharp white teeth.

Morlock thought this unwise, as his blood would likely cause the bandage to burn. But then he realized that Hrutnefdhu knew about this, and said nothing as the werewolf deftly bound up his wounds. The cloth absorbed the salve and Morlock's blood and did not burn.

"This salve and the cloth have been dephlogistonated," he said to Hrutnefdhu.

"I don't know what that means," the werewolf said.

"A powerful maker made them," Morlock said. "Who was it?"

"I don't know—the Goweiteiuun practice magic. Or maybe Ulugarriu made them."

"Ulugarriu?" Morlock asked. "I thought nobody saw him?"

"Nobody does," Hrutnefdhu said. "I didn't mean it. If any great wonder has been worked, they say that Ulugarriu did it. It's stupid. Never mind."

"Do you know what happened to the she-wolf?" Morlock asked.

Every muscle in the mottled werewolf's flexible body seemed to freeze. "What do you mean?" he asked finally.

"Did she die? Will she recover? They hurt her very badly."

"Yes." Hrutnefdhu swallowed painfully. "She is not dead. She is not well, but will recover. She is my mate, Liudhleeo."

His *mate*. Morlock did not understand how a castrato could have a mate, but that was not the most important thing, perhaps. "I am sorry," he said quietly. "I hated them for what they did. I hate them more now. I know that doesn't help."

Hrutnefdhu closed his eyes, opened them. "It's not nothing. There is you and me. There is them."

"There is Rokhlenu, also."

"I suppose there is."

"Will you bind his wounds also?" Morlock asked.

Hrutnefdhu's pale eyes focused on Morlock for a moment. Then he nodded impassively.

Rokhlenu had no visible wounds. But the smeared ointment would look like dried blood. And Morlock hoped that a rope maker's son could unobtrusively fashion the bandages themselves into respectable strangling cords.

The months passed and the deadly heat lessened slightly. It was autumn, presently, and from then on the nights were moonslit: great Chariot, the major moon, would be aloft until the last day of the year. But Rokhlenu often practiced the discipline of not changing into a wolf at night. When he did assume the night shape, he usually avoided the transformation into the day shape on the next morning.

It was a sort of self-discipline, he explained to Morlock. To wear the day shape by night or the night shape by day was, as Morlock had been told, an act of low status—largely because many could not make the full transition into or out of wolfhood. But for someone who could make the transition, it was a challenge to maintain the wolf-form by daylight: the wolf-self drew sustenance from the silver shadows in moonlight. And to resist the change by moonlight took yet another skill—the skill to decline power and the call of the beast in one's own blood. Rokhlenu wanted to know that he, not the Sardhluun, was the master of his spirit and his will.

Morlock was facing similar challenges, but not voluntarily. He was trying to retain a thread of his sanity untainted by the rising tide of madness in his mind. For long stretches of the day and night he could not see or hear anything that made sense. He would sit with his back against the wall amid a cloudy chaos of nothingness that masked the world. There was pain also: a steady knifelike pain radiating from the spike in his head, and cascades of dull aches in his joints that came and went.

If he had been himself in the midst of these distortions, it might not have been so bad. But, increasingly, he was not. Day after day he became more concerned that his fingers were growing backward into his hands, his hands withdrawing into his arms. He spent hour after hour measuring his hands against the bricks in the cell walls. He always seemed to get different results—sometimes encouraging, sometimes not.

There were times he knew his obsessions were just that: the madness working its way into his mind. But, in a way, that made it worse. There was nothing he could do to stop the madness. If he ever made it free from the cell, he would still be a prisoner of the madness.

He wondered, too, if he had the courage to leave the cell anymore. Khretnurrliu was outside all the time, now, very close to the bars. Often he held his severed head through the bars, and the rotting lips whispered silent threats and unspeakable curses against the man who had killed him. The only way Morlock could escape was to not be that man somehow. The madness, the cell, became his refuge. He feared the ghosts and the freedom that lay without.

Hate could help him with this, and sometimes he drank deep of it, trembling with the desire to kill his tormentors as he had killed Khretnurrliu. But this, too, had its dangers. Like any strong drink, like any drug, the rage left behind it a cold absence, a weakness that only the return of rage itself could heal.

In the arena of his mind, in the chaos of his heart, he fought thousands of battles every day. Sometimes, through the dim distorting vision of the world-as-it-was, he saw Rokhlenu peering at him with deep concern. He would have allayed his friend's concern if he'd known how.

Fortunately, Morlock's obsessions, his endless internal war, the fog he lived in day and night—all these things made him a very boring prisoner. Occasionally he engaged in low-voiced conversations with Rokhlenu, but apart from that he sat by the cell bars day and night, rocking back and forth and flexing his muscles to keep from cramping. The guards kept close watch on him at first, but eventually they grew used to seeing him there and they relaxed their vigil.

It was necessary to sit by the doorway for a simple reason. Khretnurrliu was always just to the left or right of his field of vision. If he stayed by the door and refrained from looking into the cell, Khretnurrliu could not enter. It was a simple and reasonable solution to keep the ghost from entering and destroying them. Rokhlenu, when Morlock explained the matter to him, eventually agreed, although they didn't have many conversations after that. More often, Morlock saw him in low-voiced converse with Hrutnefdhu on the other side of the cell door.

Morlock had long ago twisted his old bandages into a strangling cord, wrapping it around his wrist as if it were a bracelet. He didn't doubt he could use it effectively against the guards, or at least one of them, if he could somehow get into the corridor. Rokhlenu could take care of another. If they were quick enough, each might use a fallen guard's weapon on another guard. All that was possible, if they could get into the corridor.

But what could they do against Khretnurrliu? That was the real question, and Morlock gnawed at it alone through the lonely days and hours, as Rokhlenu didn't seem interested in discussing it. Morlock knew little about trapping or combating ghosts, and what little he knew involved the Sight that was now lost to him.

He had once seen the execution of a criminal in the Anhikh Kômos. After expulsion from the city communion, the malefactor was beheaded and his limbs bound with a light thread to keep the ghost from roaming about, malefacting even after death. Morlock had pointed out to a local that the thread wasn't much of a bond, and the local had told him it wasn't meant to bind the dead body but the ghost. Perhaps that was what he could do about Khretnurrliu: bind the ghost with a rope of light thread.

Morlock thought he could probably make a thread from his own hair, which was getting pretty long. He chose the grayer hairs on the grounds that they were more likely to baffle the grayish rotting ghost: like is always frustrated by like. He knotted a great length of the grayish hairs together over a number of days, working with his hands behind his back or under his legs so that the guards and Khretnurrliu could not see.

He tested his first attempt and it broke on the first tug. That annoyed him, and it also raised the latent maker in his madness. He could make a better thread than that—and did, though it took many days and many wild hairs. In the end he had a long thin string of grayish twine that was fairly strong. He himself could break it, but he didn't think Khretnurrliu could, not with his muscles hanging off his bones in greenish strands.

It was a trivial accomplishment, in a way, but it gave him a fierce satisfaction. He would have boasted about it to Rokhlenu, but of course that would give everything away. Anyway, Rokhlenu wasn't very communicative lately. He was very kind and very patient, reminding Morlock to eat and drink when he forgot (as he invariably did), but Morlock did not want kindness or patience in response to this heroic deed. He wanted awe or nothing. If he could explain to Rokhlenu how important the problem was, maybe he could spring the twine on him as a solution and get an appropriate response. But it would require distraction on the guards' part if he were to escape their attention, and he thought this unlikely. He looked up and glanced at them.

He saw, with some surprise, that there were only two: one in the day shape, one in the night shape. The day-shape guard was not an archer—anyway, he didn't have a bow. They were both werewolves of very little bite; the wolf had only one tooth on a cord around his neck; and the man had only a cord with no teeth. The man was looking idly down the corridor; the wolf was asleep.

Morlock was astonished, and more than a little offended. Didn't they know how dangerous he was? Didn't they have any sense of responsibility? He looked at Khretnurrliu, who was wearing the rotting body of a decapitated wolf today, and somehow he knew his enemy was as offended as he. Morlock was minded to complain about it, although he didn't know who would listen.

Then his attention was speared by something else. The grayish iron of the bar securing the cell gate was almost exactly the same color as the silvery twine he had labored so long to make. He wondered if the twine was strong enough to sustain the weight of the metal bar. He thought it was. If he could manage to loop the twine around the bar unobserved, there was a good chance he could ease it out of its slot and throw the cell door open.

He wished there were some way he could warn Rokhlenu of his plan, but there wasn't. Rokhlenu was very difficult to talk to lately; Morlock wondered if his cellmate might be going mad. The thought of insanity bothered Morlock very much; he hated the thought of losing his selfhood that way. He was glad *he* wasn't going insane. But if Rokhlenu was, there was little he could do but kill him before Morlock caught his illness: it was the reasonable thing to do.

Or was it? There was some reason why Morlock should not kill Rokhlenu; he was sure of it. Only he couldn't remember what it was. It would certainly be good to have someone fighting alongside him in the corridor.

Neither of the guards was looking. The one was still asleep. Morlock unobtrusively tossed a loop of twine for the end of the lock-bar . . . and missed.

Morlock was shocked. He could not remember the last time he had thrown anything at anything and missed. On the other hand, he couldn't remember much at all. His time in prison might have lasted only a few days or weeks, but everything before it seemed faint and unreal. Perhaps he really wasn't much good at throwing things.

He tried it again, and this time the twine loop fell across the top of the lock-bar on its far end. Morlock jostled the loop gently, and it fell across the end of the lock-bar. He was ready.

He looked up and saw that Khretnurrliu was staring at him. The dead wolf's severed head had opened its mouth in anticipation; the headless body was leaning forward, like a dog straining at an invisible leash. The dead werewolf was waiting for him.

He let one end of the twine go and drew it unobtrusively back into the cell. Khretnurrliu's dead body sat back and the severed head tilted; it seemed disappointed in Morlock. So was Morlock. But he just couldn't face the dead wolf. He had already killed it once. How long was he supposed to go on killing it? Maybe it was Rokhlenu's turn.

He sidled over to Rokhlenu and said, "Hey."

"Hey," Rokhlenu replied wearily. "Long time no smell."

"Rokhlenu."

"Morlock."

"Rokhlenu."

"Morlock."

"Rokhlenu."

"Stop saying that. There's no one else here. You can just say what you have to say."

"What would you do if you got out of here?"

Rokhlenu seemed surprised and pleased. "You sound a little more like yourself today. And, it's funny: I was just thinking about that—the minor moons know why; I don't. But I'd probably go to the outlier pack, south of Wuruyaaria. I can send word to my father and brothers—" He continued for a while in this vein.

Morlock twitched impatiently. This was too long term, too strategic. Morlock was asking about the immediate, the tactical situation. But he didn't know the words for this.

"I mean here and now," he said finally, interrupting Rokhlenu's day-dream. "What would you do *here and now* if you got out of here?"

Rokhlenu caught his meaning. His breath grew short. "I suppose . . . take out the one on the left with the thing." *The thing* was what they usually said when referring to the strangling cords, when they had still been talking about them.

"What about Khretnurrliu?" Morlock whispered. "What could you do about Khretnurrliu?"

Rokhlenu slumped a little. The hope went out of his face. He looked directly into Morlock's worried eyes and said, "*Nothing*. I would do *nothing* about Khretnurrliu. I'm sick of hearing about him. He's dead, Morlock. Dead."

Morlock was troubled. He'd had a fairly sophisticated argument planned, given his still-primitive vocabulary of Sunspeech, all of it leading toward the proposition that Morlock would tackle the two living guards, if Rokhlenu confronted the dead wolf. He was going to explain about ghost binding and the twine and everything. But now it seemed there would be no point.

Morlock went back to his corner by the door and thought. He rocked back and forth; he clenched and unclenched his muscles and he thought. The guards didn't look at him. Rokhlenu had climbed up to the window and was staring out into the hot afternoon air. Even Khretnurrliu seemed to be looking away scornfully.

Morlock sat wrestling with the dread of the dead wolf the rest of that afternoon, all through the night, all through the next day until dark. In the end he came to the conclusion that it was safer to stay in the cell and not try to get out. This was his life now. He could endure it, if he could not love it.

Except that was not quite the end. Because . . . it wasn't just that he didn't love this life. He hated it. He hated the raiders who had inflicted it on him. He hated the ghost-sniffers who had driven the spike into his head, blinding him to the world of dreams. He hated the guards and their stupid tortures and rapes. Most of all he hated his hate: he hated the stink of it in his mind, the filth of it in his eyes and bones. What hell could the dead wolf inflict on him that was worse than this? And he was inflicting it on himself. He could make it end now, one way or the other.

He, of course, didn't have the courage, but he had known a man once who would never have given up, would never have inflicted this on himself if he had the chance to escape it, even by certain death, who never resigned himself to fate. That man had drowned . . . in the Bitter Water, he thought; he couldn't remember his name, unless . . . unless it was Morlock.

Bells began to ring, as if in answer to this appalling conjecture. Morlock looked up. Khretnurrliu stood in man form in the corridor, tossing his severed head from hand to skeletal hand as if it were a ball. The guards were staring down the corridor, a faint silver light shining on their faces. The one in the day shape raised his hands and underwent the transition to wolfhood, screaming in ecstasy and pain. Rokhlenu was at the cell window, reaching out his left hand for a single thread of moonlight as he gripped the sill with his right. He transformed abruptly to wolf, howling as he fell down into the cell's darkness.

Other werewolves were howling, up and down the corridor. And bells were ringing. Echoing faintly in through the windows, louder in the corridor, mixed with the despairing howls of prisoners, the joyous or merely drunken howls of guards.

It was the first night of the year, the night of Cymbals they called it in Morlock's distant home. Trumpeter and Chariot were setting, and Horseman was rising. A bright year, they would be calling it back home, since the first call would not be moonless. In dark years, all three moons set together and the night sky was dark and starlit until Trumpeter rose again.

Back home, the celebration would go on all night.

A long, joyous, noisy time.

Would these moon-worshipping werewolves celebrate less or more?

In any case, they were celebrating now. Loudly. Joyously.

God Avenger, thought Morlock, the thin fraying thread that was still Morlock in his madness, *this is my hour. I will celebrate the New Year in a way the Sardhluun will never forget.*

From where he sat he tossed the twine over the end of the lock-bar and caught it. He stood, hefting the lock-bar from its place. It fell ringing to the floor, one more bell welcoming in the new year. Morlock threw the gate open and strode across the threshold of the cell. The wolf-guards, startled, turned to meet him. But for them it was already too late: they had seen their last moonrise.

Chapter Eleven

New Year's Night

Morlock was achingly conscious that he was turning his back toward the dead man who had haunted him all these weary months, but that was the choice he made: not to be bound by his fear.

He stooped down to seize the iron lock-bar from the corridor floor. One of the guard-wolves was already leaping toward him; the other, the one who had just undergone transition, was struggling in the harness of his human armor.

Morlock swung the iron bar with all the unpent fury of his madness.

The guard-wolf's head shattered like a piece of ripe fruit. The body rolled to the floor and lay still. Morlock turned to silence the other guard, who had begun to yammer for help in Moonspeech, but he had only taken one step when a gray shadow streaked past him and fixed long white teeth in the guard-wolf's throat.

Morlock seized the guard's abandoned sword and severed its head from its body as Roklenu jumped nimbly out of the blade's path.

Rokhlenu gave Morlock an agreeable but bloody smile. He wished Morlock a happy New Year in singing Moonspeech.

"*Khulê gradara!*" Morlock replied. "That's what we say back home: good-bye moons!"

The other guards were crowded by the window at the far end of the hallway, peering out at the last moonlight they would see for some time. Those who could change had already changed to the night shape. Those few in the day shape held out their hands wistfully, or drank smoke from great stone bowls, or just stared at the free air as if they hated the prison as much as Morlock did.

Rokhlenu looked slyly at the severed head and back at Morlock's free hand.

Morlock grinned in answer. He picked up the severed wolf head and hurled it down the hallway to land in the mournful celebration of guards. It struck one guard on the elbow while he was inhaling some smoke. The coal-laden jar shook, spilling some fiery matter. The jostled guard turned and struck the wolf nearest him across the snout. It yowled a curse at him and bit him on the knee. The jar dropped and smashed on the ground, scattering smoke and fire. The fire burned many feet, and a cacophonous chorus of rage sprang up against the background of bells and wolfsong floating in on the evening air. The guards were embroiled in a general fight before Morlock and Rokhlenu reached them, the severed wolf head being kicked here and there by heedless feet in smoky chaos.

It took them a few moments after Morlock and Rokhlenu reached them to realize the fight had taken a more serious turn. Soon other severed heads were being jostled about on the floor, and the guards in day shape had all been hamstrung by surgical strokes of Rokhlenu's bright teeth. He then returned to sever their neck veins with equal precision.

The surviving guards, all in the night shape, fled down to the other end of the hallway.

Rokhlenu sang that they must not let the rats escape the trap; there would be no chance, otherwise.

Morlock did not understand what he meant about chances. He simply intended to kill his enemies until they killed him. But he was more than willing to start with the fleeing guards.

Side by side, the former cellmates ran back up the corridor. The prisoners in the cells all began to chant their names: Khretvarrgliu and Rokhlenu; the Beast Slayer and the Dragon Slayer.

The fleeing guards, some of them still trailing human war gear, tangled up at the narrow entrance to the stairway, blocking each other from escaping.

None escaped.

Morlock leaned against the outside of the cell that had once been his, among uncounted dead enemies. He wished vaguely there had been more.

One more werewolf appeared in the shadows of the stairway entrance: a pale mottled muzzle and a pair of shocked pale eyes. It was Hrutnefdhu, the trustee.

Rokhlenu sang that they were celebrating the New Year by escaping. He wondered if Hrutnefdhu wished to leave the prison alive or in pieces.

Morlock turned away and walked down the corridor again. If Hrutnefdhu would not join them, he must be killed. Morlock's throat was too choked with hate to use persuasive words; he hoped Rokhlenu's song could lure the pale castrato to abandon his trust. Otherwise Morlock would have to kill him.

He occupied himself by tossing back the lock-bars and swinging the gates of the cells wide. Some of the cells had mechanical locks; these Morlock forced with a sword or his fingers. The prisoners swarmed into the hall, praising his name, Rokhlenu's name, the moonset, the New Year's Night, the carnage of the hated guards.

Most wore night shapes, but there were a few who did not or would not undergo the change, including one red-skinned gold-haired monster with the build of a gorilla, the hands of a juggler, and the intelligence of a vacant room. The wolves were varicolored: red, black, gray, and white. They were battered, scarred with wounds that showed even through their wiry fur. Their eyes were cold and bitter as the lost light of the moons. They were the irredeemables, and they knew he would lead them into death among the swords and teeth of the guards. They shouted for it. They howled for it.

When Morlock returned to the stairway, Rokhlenu was singing of plans, of forethought, of deliberation, of safety.

"We don't need safety," Morlock said. "That's what keeps us safe."

He plunged into the dark stairwell. Cheering and howling, the irredeemables followed him.

Wide-eyed, the pale mottled trustee watched the ragged pack of irredeemables cascade down the dark stairs.

Rokhlenu snarled. First he had thought Morlock mad; then he thought him sane; now he was sure the never-wolf was mad. If Rokhlenu himself were not mad, he would take advantage of the chaos Morlock was causing to escape the prison. It would be so easy!

But he couldn't. When Rokhlenu had gone mad, Morlock had watched out for him, had not let the guards' cruelty destroy him. He had risked his life. Rokhlenu would do the same for him if it killed him, as Rokhlenu was glumly sure it would.

He forced himself to think sunlit thoughts, dreaming of a gold the world would not see for hours, that he might never live to see. The agony of transition swept over him, without the exultant shout of light to remake his heart. He had to remake it himself. It seemed to take forever, and it hurt like chewing a leg off. But at the end of it he stood like a man and began to arm and armor himself from the bloody torn equipage scattered around the floor.

"Stay by me," he said to the yet-more-astonished-if-possible Hrutnefdhu. "Morlock has run mad. If we stick together, maybe we can live through this thing."

Hrutnefdhu's pale face looked as dubious as Rokhlenu's heart felt. But they did go together down the dark stairway.

The fourth floor of the prison was larger than the fifth; there were several aisles among the freestanding cages and more prisoners in each cage. Rokhlenu remembered there being more guards there, too. Whether that had been the case or not Rokhlenu never knew; by the time he and Hrutnefdhu arrived the guards were bloody rubble in various corners, slain by Morlock and his irredeemables. Morlock was forcing locks with a long knife and freeing the prisoners; other irredeemables were smashing at locks with stolen swords . . . or, in a few cool-headed cases, using keys they had looted from dead guards.

Rokhlenu said to Hrutnefdhu, "Get the ones using keys. Have them come to me. Round up anyone who isn't moon simple."

Hrutnefdhu wondered if he were moon simple; he didn't understand.

"There are guard stations in the stairways below; we'll need to divide in two bands," Rokhlenu began.

Hrutnefdhu barked a curt acknowledgment and ran off to do Rokhlenu's bidding. Rokhlenu himself grabbed a few wolves who seemed to be able to pay attention. When Hrutnefdhu returned with a dozen men and wolves, Morlock and his irredeemables were already streaming toward one of the stairwells.

"We take the other," Rokhlenu said. "Ware guards. Kill the men and maim the wolves as severely as you can; behead them by choice."

They nodded and snarled in acknowledgment. These were not blood-drunk ex-prisoners intent on vengeance. They were hardened criminals engaged in escape. Rokhlenu knew he could trust them as long as it looked like he might succeed.

They ran down the stairs to the guard station. The guards there were waiting for them: three smoke-drunk men with rusty swords in their trembling hands. Rokhlenu's wolves took them down and left them sleeping off their drunk in death.

The third floor was even larger than the fourth; some guards were still resisting when Rokhlenu and his band arrived. Worst of all, one was at a window blowing a horn-call. Rokhlenu ran over and stabbed him through the rib cage, killing him instantly, but the damage was done. The sound of bells and songs from below had diminished greatly: what guards remained in the prison now knew of the escape. Rokhlenu hoped it was a skeleton crew; if so, they'd soon crack it to the marrow.

Many of the prisoners on the third floor were terrified and refused to leave their cells. Still, the numbers of escapees swelled, and many began to stream down the stairwells.

If Rokhlenu had been in charge, they would have skipped the second floor and gone down to confront the guards on the first floor while they were still relatively unprepared. But no one was in charge. Many of the more panicky escapees did indeed run from the second floor to the stairwells leading down to the ground floor, but Morlock and his irredeemables cleared the second floor of its few guards and broke the locks on all the cages. On this level, more prisoners were day shaped than night shaped, and almost none refused to leave their cages. The number of the escapees, as they finally charged the stairwells, was very large, but the men were very poorly armed and armored.

Rokhlenu and Hrutnefdhu followed Morlock down the stairwell. Rokhlenu thought there was some chance that the guards below (they could hear the sounds of fighting echoing up the stone ways) might rally and come up other stairways to attack Morlock's group from behind. His criminals would serve as a rearguard, then. If not, Morlock and his irredeemables would be their shock troops.

Just before Rokhlenu made it down to the ground floor, he heard Morlock laughing.

When he came out into the high-vaulted central chamber on the first floor, he saw why.

Morlock had not seen the dead rotting ghost of Khretnurrliu since he had rushed into the corridor, and a feeling of exultation was growing in him. It was separate from the poisonous glee of satisfied revenge (which, however, he also felt). The dead beast was dead, but it still fled from him. Perhaps it feared binding. Morlock had lost his twine somewhere, but Khretnurrliu might not know that.

Morlock kept looking about for Rokhlenu, but whenever he turned his view was blocked by the great gorilla-like red werewolf, who grinned at him with gray teeth through his golden beard. He had no weapon but fought only with his huge gold-clawed fists. Morlock did not understand a word he said, if the sounds he made were words, but he seemed intent on guarding Morlock's back.

Long before he reached the ground floor, Morlock met a backwash of escaped prisoners running back up toward the second floor. Morlock attacked them with the same cold empty rage he had unleashed on the guards: they were in his way. He killed a man, dismembered a crawling wolf, and drove the rest screaming before him down the stairs again.

They were pinned between Morlock and a knot of armed guards at the outlet of the stairwell. Of the two, they feared Morlock the more and threw themselves at the guards with panicky fervor. Morlock came up behind them and started stabbing through the bodies to cripple the guards. They broke and fled, and Morlock and his irredeemables ran into the central chamber of the prison's first floor.

There were no cages or cells here. This was the marshalling point of the guards, the sorting place for incoming prisoners. A sort of balcony ran around just under the ceiling of the high-vaulted chamber; beyond it were entrances to the upper wall outside. Morlock wondered if that might be a way to escape. The only way up to the balcony was a few rope ladders, though, so the wolves could not go that way. And when Morlock had last seen Rokhlenu, he was in the night shape. He turned away from them and contemplated the scene in the chamber itself.

Its chaos mirrored the disorder in his own soul, and he found it pleasing. Very few of the guards were in day shape; most had changed their skins to celebrate the bright New Year. The chamber was full of werewolves snarling and biting each other, with more pouring through the stairways every moment. The air was filled with smoke, from torches and from the aromatic bowls of smoke the werewolves seemed to love inhaling. The walls glittered with mounted weapons, mostly useless to the night-shape guards. The few guards in day shape—and some of the freed prisoners—were running up and grabbing these.

Morlock watched as one guard seized a very familiar scabbard and drew from it a glittering crystalline sword, the blade interwoven white and black.

Morlock laughed. The gorilla-like red werewolf was standing beside him now that they were free from the narrow stairway; Morlock slapped him on the shoulder and shouted ("There!"), pointing at the guard who bemusedly held Tyrfing.

The red werewolf grunted something and followed as Morlock began to fight his way across the chaos of the great chamber. The irredeemables followed at their heels.

The guard holding Tyrfing slipped in and out of Morlock's sight through the battle in the center of the chamber. At first he seemed inclined to put aside the deadly blade as a mere showpiece, but then a prisoner in a stolen guard's harness leaped at him and he struck out with the blade, shattering the attacker's weapon and armor, the blade sinking deep into his body.

Then the tide of battle blocked Morlock's sight. He grimly fought toward the place where he had last seen the guard holding Tyrfing.

Soon he was rewarded with another glimpse: the guard was cutting his way with the dark crystalline blade toward a group of guards blocking a sort of tunnel.

Morlock knew that tunnel. He remembered being dragged through it on his first night in the Vargulleion.

He wondered if he dared call out to Tyrfing. It had been long, so long, since he had implanted the talic impulse in its crystalline lattice, and he was worried that it might have dissipated. Blinded as he was on the talic realm, his inner self could hear no whisper of life from the blade—or from any other entity.

But now he was near—hardly three lines of struggling werewolves lay between him and his sword. He shifted the blade he was holding to his left hand, stabbed a werewolf with it, raised his right hand, and shouted as loudly and clearly as he could, "*Tyrfing!*"

The blade left the hand of the astonished werewolf who held it and flew through the smoky air to rest in Morlock's right hand.

Morlock's satisfaction was intense. They had taken everything from him, everything. Now, bit by bit, he was taking it back. Perhaps they would kill him tonight. They would never forget the price they paid to do it.

Now he carried two swords, and he wielded them both with deadly efficiency. At first he was tentative about striking with Tyrfing for a death blow, until he realized that his blindness on the tal-realm protected him from suffering when he used Tyrfing as a weapon. Perhaps it still harmed him, but he could not feel it. He laughed at the thought of it, and killed werewolves thereafter whenever he could.

He thought he heard Rokhlenu shouting at him—in Sunspeech, strangely, because Morlock remembered he had changed skins after sunset. Rokhlenu was shouting something about the tunnel.

Morlock turned toward the tunnel. The guards were retreating toward it, and the entrance bristled with their weapons and teeth.

Rokhlenu was right. That was the way out, if they sought escape, and there were many enemies there, if they sought vengeance. Plus, he had a feeling that Khretnurrliu was hiding there, cowering among the ranks with his severed head held low. Morlock turned and began to cut his way through the battle toward the tunnel entrance.

Rokhlenu's jaw dropped when he saw the dark blade fly through the air when Morlock called it. With his mouth still open, he turned to look at Hrutnefdhu.

The pale werewolf sang that Morlock was a maker, great among makers, perhaps the greatest of all.

"He's still crazy," Rokhlenu said. They were standing together at one of the rope ladders leading to the balcony. It was the obvious escape route, but most of the escapees had missed it—including Morlock, apparently. "I'm going to run up this ladder and see if there's a way out over the rampart outside. You thugs stand watch here."

His thugs disliked that—not the name, but the idea of being left behind. But they accepted it, perhaps because Rokhlenu was one of the few people in the room not drunk on blood or smoke.

He was halfway up the ladder when he looked around to see if there were any archers in the chamber or on the balcony. The balcony seemed to be empty, and no one on the floor seemed to be troubling himself with a bow: all the combat was close quarters.

Rokhlenu saw Morlock and his incorrigibles drifting aimlessly on the tide of battle. They were perilously near the tunnel entrance, where all the guards were falling back. If Morlock and his following got trapped in there, the guards could tear them to bits.

"Morlock!" he shouted. "Stay clear of the tunnel! Stay clear of the tunnel!"

Morlock glanced about and turned toward the tunnel.

"Year without a moon," swore Rokhlenu in a whisper, and dropped down to the foot of the ladder. "Hrutnefdhu," he said, "lead these wolves to Morlock and stand by him. I'll take the men over the ramparts and attack the guards on the far side."

The pale werewolf's eyes grew as large as fists when he heard this order. But he nodded, and with a few high-pitched barks rallied the wolvish thugs and led them in a wedge into the chaos of the battle-torn smoky chamber.

Rokhlenu hoped they wouldn't all be absolutely killed, but there was only one thing he could do and he did it. He turned his back on them and swarmed up the rope ladder. The day-shape thugs followed him up.

If Morlock had been able to dream anymore, he would have thought it was a nightmare. The tunnel was darkish, lit only by a few torches. There was a mass of guards there, in wolf form and man form. The men were armed, and even some of the wolves were armored. The air was dense with smoke and heat and the stink of shed blood.

Morlock and his irredeemables killed their way into the tunnel. But there came a time when they could not advance farther. The press of bodies among the guards kept the dead guards standing in place three deep. The men at least were dead, and the wolves lifeless: there was no moonlight in the dark tunnel to feed their renewal. Morlock and those with him on the front line could not reach past the dead to get at the living. Nor could they retreat: there was a flood of escapees behind them also, forcing them forward.

The layers of dead surged back and forth between the competing sides, like the border of an uncertain empire.

It was strangely, dreadfully quiet in the dark tunnel. The only sounds were the labored breathing of the opposing mobs and the scratch of booted or clawed feet on the tunnel pavement.

From time to time some armorless werewolves would try to creep forward among the thicket of dead legs and snap at the knees of Morlock and his irredeemables. But their own wolves stood ready to counterattack: Morlock saw with surprise that one of those at his own side was Hrutnefdhu.

Morlock wanted to call back down the line for a spear or a bow and arrow or some kind of distance weapon. But he hadn't the words for this, in Moonspeech or Sunspeech: weaponry had rarely come up in his discussions with Rokhlenu and Hrutnefdhu. Besides, he was tired, desperately tired, and it was almost impossible to breathe in the stinking smoke-laden tunnel.

If he lost his footing and tumbled backward, it would begin an avalanche that would end with a victory of the hated guards. He remembered hating the guards without actually hating them so much: the whole world was growing as dark and hazy as the evil tunnel's air. But he clung to the memory of hate like a faith; he braced his feet against the tunnel pavement and pushed back against the dead body in front of him.

He didn't think he could sustain the counterweight of the enemy line much longer.

He reached out with his right hand and stabbed experimentally with Tyrfing. If he could crack the enemy line somehow, cause one guard to give way, maybe the avalanche of bodies would fall the other way and the guards would flee or fall.

He couldn't reach anyone.

There was a wound on his arm, and it seeped blood onto the wolvish corpse in front of him. The corpse began to smolder, adding a reek of burning hair to the poisonous fog in the tunnel.

Morlock reflected faintly that if he bled enough, the corpse would burn away entirely. Then he would be that much nearer the enemy, near enough to strike a blow.

An idea occurred to him. Keeping the tension on the corpse in front of him, he slashed down at the corpse in front of that, hacking away at it until part of it fell away to the ground and the rest was crushed between the two battle lines. He was too startled when the moment came to press forward, but the enemy line lurched nearer to him. He tried reaching over it and stabbing at the werewolf on the far side.

The wolf first cowered low, losing the precarious purchase his shoulders had on the corpse in front of him. Then he leapt back to escape being crushed.

There was a tiny breach in the line of battle. Morlock let the corpses fall and leapt over them. Wielding Tyrfing with both hands, he cut a brief swathe of death, piling corpses all around him.

He turned to fund the gorilla-like red werewolf grinning beside him. He had imitated Morlock's tactic, with equal success.

"We do it again," he said to the other, hoping he would understand. "Again and again, until we break the line."

The red grinning shadow beside him made a wordlike sound, and they both turned to the task.

More of their comrades followed into the wedge they were digging into the guards' line; it grew wider, flatter, as more of them attacked enemies who had suddenly come into reach.

Morlock was wearier than ever, but when he looked up now his heart was gladdened by the sight of moonlit ground. This was bad in a way: the wolvish guards would take strength from the moonlight. But it was the way out, and they were nearer now.

Then he saw shapes he had been dreading step out of the light: werewolves in the day shape with bows, their arrows nocked and ready to shoot. They could devastate the irredeemables from a distance, and there was nowhere to turn, no way to protect themselves.

Morlock nearly groaned. But if he was to have only one more utterance, he didn't want it to be a sound of despair.

"*Khai gradara!*" he shouted, greeting the moonlight that had recently given him such hope. "*Khai gradara! Khai, khai!*"

The werewolves with human faces took up his cry behind him. The irredeemables wearing the night shape sang their own bitter triumphant song. The smoky air of the tunnel rang with it as the shadowy archers took deadly aim and shot.

Rokhlenu didn't know what he was expecting on the balcony, but he was disgusted with what he found. The balcony had been thick with soldiery when the prison break began, but no guards were there now. If they had held their post and fired a few arrows at escaping prisoners, the escape might have ended in utter failure. But because it was New Year's Night, they were smoke-drunk on duty when the alarm came; they had panicked and fled their post, leaving their weapons behind them. So Rokhlenu read the chaos of broken smoke-bowls, of quivers heavy with unshot arrows lying alongside unstrung bows.

"Everyone grab a bow," he said, "and a quiver—two if you can carry them."

He followed his own order and then ran along the balcony until he reached a portal to the outer rampart. He rushed out onto the rampart, hoping it would be as empty as the balcony.

It was, and he was delighted to discover the cowardly guards' escape route: a ladder of hooked-together guard harnesses, dangling over the edge of the rampart halfway down the wall.

"They must have loved their families," remarked the thug who first followed him out onto the rampart. He was a fur-faced, one-eyed son-of-a-brach, and he didn't seem to think much of families.

Rokhlenu waited until all his thugs were present and then explained his plan.

"All right, Dragon Slayer," said the one-eyed semiwolf. "You go first. Watch out your hands don't slip on that armor: I guess they moistened it some while they were still wearing it."

Rokhlenu climbed down the makeshift ladder as far as it went and then dropped the rest of the way; arrows clattered out of his quivers as he struck the ground. He was stooping to pick them up when he discovered that not all the guards had abandoned their post in the crisis. There were a dozen of them, men and wolves, grinning at him from the shadows of a recess in the prison wall.

He grasped at his sword . . . and realized he had left it on the ground when he was gathering his bow and arrows. He seized the bow and started wielding it like a club. He had little hope his thugs would follow him: they would hear the fight and take a more advantageous escape route.

But they surprised him. He was kicking a wolf who had attached himself to his right knee when the wolf was abruptly cut in two by a broad-bladed axe. He looked up to see it was wielded by the one-eyed semiwolf. His other thugs were dropping down like hail from the rampart.

The guards weren't cowards, but they were taken by surprise and were pinned against the wall. In the end, they were dead, and Rokhlenu and his thugs limped away the victors.

"Sorry about the delay," the one-eyed semiwolf said. "We all left our swords and things behind and had to go back for them."

"Can't think of everything," Rokhlenu gasped.

"Say, Chief," One-Eye said, "you should take the night shape. We won't be mad; you've got a lot of wounds there."

They might have been mad, because they were most likely incapable of the full change themselves. A few had crooked legs, or hairy faces, but no doubt if they could have changed completely they would have done so at nightfall, before their cell doors swung open. But they all seemed to be looking at him with genuine concern and, when he looked down, he did see several wounds gushing black blood in Horseman's blue light.

He almost said, "Wait for me," but that would have implied a chance that they would not, and he didn't want to suggest that to them. He dropped his weapons and his loincloth and stood, naked and bleeding in Horseman's light. He drank the moonlight deep until it slew the sunlit thoughts in his brain.

His wolf's shadow rose up from the ground and wrapped itself around him; his human form fell away and lay, a mere shadow on the ground. His flesh and bones rippled like running water, and that was an agony. But it was also a delight, a tearing free from who he had been, an escape into new being, an ascent into harmony with the night. That was why he sang; that was why he screamed. That, and the pain.

The change took longer the less moonlight was in the air, and still longer because the silver light had to fill up his wounds and make them whole. Appreciable time had passed before he raised his lupine head to properly salute the moon with song.

He dropped his eyes to the ground and saw his ragged band of semiwolves still waiting for him.

He sang that they should bring their flying teeth and the corded branches that hurled them, and they should match their paces to his until they found the great mouth in the prison's ugly face.

The thugs seized their bows and arrows (not forgetting their swords and clubs this time) and followed him to the tunnel entrance of the prison.

Standing in the clear light of the moon, Rokhlenu looked into the sweltering, smoky, torchlit tunnel, and he didn't like what he saw or heard or smelled. Clearly, neither side had won a clear victory yet. He did not see or hear Morlock, but he thought he smelled the crooked man's fiery blood.

With a whispered song or two he deployed his men in two ranks to shoot at the backs of the slowly retreating guards.

"*Khai gradara!*" came a ragged shout, echoing down the tunnel. "*Khai gradara! Khai, khai!*"

Other voices joined the cry, and wolfsongs soon drowned the men's words, but Rokhlenu chuckled as he recognized the first voice: Morlock—moon simple to the last, though Rokhlenu began to hope this wasn't the last.

He called on his archers to shoot.

Many of them were trained—it was one way for a werewolf stuck in the day shape to be useful—but the worst of them could not miss. They fired into the densely crowded backs of men and wolves, and soon the wounded began to run. The only way they had to run was toward the bowmen, but it was also toward the moonlight, where the wolves could seek healing. The men could hope for no healing there, but it was the only way of escape.

The more ran, the more did run. Presently the guards' line broke, and roaring, the escapees charged forward, trampling any guard, man or wolf, who did not flee.

Morlock emerged almost last, surrounded by the survivors from the irredeemables, leaned on by the gorilla-like red werewolf and dragging Hrutnefdhu by the scruff of his neck. All three were terribly wounded; Morlock was trailing fire like a burning snail.

Some of Rokhlenu's thugs gently peeled the half-dead red werewolf from Morlock's shoulder. The pale mottled wolf raised his eyes to the moon, drank deep of light and air, and stood on his own feet, his strength renewed.

Morlock absently patted his white head like a dog's and staggered forward, blinking. He saw Rokhlenu standing there, and he remarked, as if they were in the middle of a long conversation back in the cell, "For a while I thought I didn't see the dead wolf anymore, but now I think I see him everywhere. I tried killing him by killing him and I killed and I killed but he kept being dead, so I think . . . I think I need to kill him by not killing him. If you know what I mean."

Rokhlenu sang that this seemed a very sound plan, and that life was like that sometimes.

Hrutnefdhu agreed, and said they would go now to the outlier pack, a fine place where all the werewolves were completely alive, and dead ones banned by law.

"Eh," said the crooked man, "dead wolves don't always obey the law."

A few more philosophical gleams like these lightened their long moonlit road to the outlier pack. But not too many, as Morlock was very tired, for which Rokhlenu thanked the moons and stars and even the Strange Gods, because he had heard as much as he could stand of crazy talk.

Part Two

Elections

Such is their cry—some watchword
for the fight
Must vindicate the wrong, and warp
the right;
Religion—freedom—vengeance—
what you will,
A word's enough to raise mankind
to kill;
Some factious phrase by cunning
caught and spread,
That guilt may reign, and wolves
and worms be fed!

—**Byron, *Lara***

Chapter Twelve

The Outliers

"I understand I have you to thank for this nightmarish cloud of thieves, monsters, and murderers who've descended to suck the last drop of blood from our parched veins?"

Rokhlenu looked up blinking to see a woman standing over him, like a shadow astride the rising sun. He had curled up last night, along with most of his men, on one of the boarded walkways that served as streets among the stork-legged lair-towers of the outlier pack. The night had been warm, and he had slept so deeply that the transition to his sunlit form had not awakened him. He was having trouble waking now, and he blinked his gummy eyes a few times and cleared his throat of goo until he thought of a sufficiently urbane reply.

"You're welcome," he said finally.

"Welcome, hah. *You* may be, and *some* of your boys may be, but that filthy, raving, flat-faced, crook-shouldered, fire-hazard of a never-wolf is *not*."

Rokhlenu didn't need to be fully awake to know who she was talking about.

"We all stay," he said sharply, "or we all go. My boys, as you call them, will back me."

He wasn't at all sure this was true, but a voice (it sounded like One-Eye) called out, "That's written in stone. Are there three moons or not? Does the sun rise in the west or does it not?"

A chorus of voices, in Sunspeech and Moonspeech, agreed that all these truths were self-evident.

Rokhlenu jumped to his feet in a single motion. It wasn't as easy as he hoped he'd made it look, but he didn't want this outlier to think him in any way a weakling.

The way she was eyeing him suggested this was the farthest thing from her mind. "You're Slenkjariu?" she asked. "I've heard of you."

"My name's Rokhlenu now."

"I heard that, too. They didn't strip that from you after you killed that bookie?"

"That's my name, and I didn't kill any bookie."

"The judicants of Nekkuklendon say you did."

"The judicants of Nekkuklendon would tattoo their price on their asses if the price didn't change all the time. Everyone knows that."

She waved her hand, dismissing the issue: it didn't matter in the outlier pack. "I'm Wuinlendhono. I'm running things here, for the time being."

"Oh?" Rokhlenu replied. He had heard that ways were strange in the outliers, but he was surprised to find a female in charge. Still, she seemed to have the bite for it: there was a necklace of long teeth around her neck and ropes of them around her narrow waist.

"I need something a little more binding from you, Rokhlenu," Wuinlendhono said in a low voice. She was a head shorter than Rokhlenu, but somehow her stern round face was very near his face. She smelled a little like the ginger root that grew on the sacred slopes of the necropolis east of the Stone Tree. "Things were tough enough for me," she continued, "before you and your happy band of jugglers showed up last night—"

"We're not jugglers!"

"Keep your voice down. That was a lighthearted, insincere compliment. I wish your boys had any skill as useful as juggling. Listen to me. I mean, *listen to me*. You say your boys will back you. If you want to stay here, I need you to back me. Either you are with me or you're against me."

"I don't know anything about you."

"Yes, you do. I'm the person who decides whether you stay here or you go."

"Are you?"

"I am. Half your people are still asleep; many are wounded. It would be a lot of trouble to drive you off or kill you, but we could do it. It'd make me very popular with some of my pack-mates, too. Listen, I'm not talking about indentured service. But if you're going to stay here, I need to know you're not going to get in my way. You can go any time you want. No shackles on anyone."

Rokhlenu thought about it. He looked at her: dark-haired, pale-skinned, round-headed, intent: a cool shadow in the freakishly warm winter sunlight. Not a stupid female. But still a female. He couldn't afford to bow his head to a female; no male would look up to him again.

She read his hesitation perfectly. "How about this?" she said. "My mate is dead. We'll say you're courting me. That way if you, urrr, defer to my judgment, it will seem like politeness, not submission."

"I guess. As long as I don't have to 'defer' too often."

"Well, well, well. What a romance this is. The poet sings from the heat in his blood."

"If it's just a ruse—"

"Of course it is," Wuinlendhono said, in a silky contralto murmur as dark as her hair and as warm as fresh blood, "you stupid brach's bastard, do you think I have no one better to turn to than a filthy naked bloodstained refugee from a prison house?"

"Do you?" he replied frostily.

Her fierce little face unbent in a gentle smile. "You're quite right, new friend Rokhlenu," she said, in a voice meant to be heard by those standing nearby. "We must get you some pants, at least." Her eyes flickered downward and she walked away.

Rokhlenu followed her glance down and saw with dismay that he was sporting an advanced erection.

He willed it down by thinking of dead puppies and weeping grandmothers and anything, anything except the warm sensual poison of her voice in his ear. It took a while.

Eventually, he looked up and saw One-Eye standing nearby, but not too nearby. He was not grinning, but his fur-covered face was a little too obviously not grinning.

Rokhlenu called him over. He almost called him One-Eye, but stopped himself at the last minute. No doubt the semiwolf disliked being reminded of his disability, and Rokhlenu particularly wanted to avoid offending him. "Hey," he said finally. "It was busy last night, and I didn't catch your name."

"Olleiulu," said the one-eyed werewolf. *Olleiulu* meant *One-Eye*. Rokhlenu repressed an irritated growl.

"All right, Olleiulu," Rokhlenu said. "I need someone to watch my back, and we both know that's you. Am I wrong?"

"You're not wrong," Olleiulu agreed. "But I don't know how long I'm going to stay here. Just thought it's fair to tell you."

"Fair is fair. Just let me know when you're going to leave, if you leave."

"Fair is fair," Olleiulu echoed, and they each gripped the other's shoulder to seal the conditional allegiance.

"I need some clothes if I'm going to talk to that female again," Rokhlenu continued briskly, "and I don't want to get them from her. If there's a market or a rag shop around here, we should be able to trade some of our gear for a kilt or a loincloth or something."

"Breeches for males in the outliers," Olleiulu said. "Anything else makes them look at you funny. I'll get a shirt and some footgear, too, even if it is furnace-hot for winter."

"And it is. Thanks."

"Anything else?"

"Pick a sidekick, someone else to watch your back when you're watching mine."

"Done. It's old Lekkativengu, there." *Lekkativengu* meant *Clawfinger*, and Olleiulu indicated a werewolf, largely human in appearance, but with wolvish claws on his hands and bare feet. His feet were somewhat pawlike, too. Rokhlenu didn't remember him from the prison escape, but it had been pretty chaotic. "We've sounded out most of the fifth- and fourth-floor gang, and they're with you, as long as you don't cross Khretvarrgliu. The rest are rats who'll go wherever they smell the most cheese."

Khretvarrgliu: that was what they were calling Morlock last night. Rokhlenu thought Morlock might not care for the nickname, but that wasn't the most urgent issue.

"You've done politics before?" Rokhlenu asked.

"I ran an extortion gang in Dogtown," Olleiulu said. "I guess it's pretty similar."

Rokhlenu was washed, breeched, shirted, and booted before he had to face Wuinlendhono again. In spite of the heat of the day, he found this a great relief. Hesitantly, he offered her his left arm; she smiled and intertwined herself with him.

"You can play the part, I see," she said, her contralto voice cooler than the warm winter breeze. "Let's walk. I'll show you the lairs, and something less pleasant."

Rokhlenu's heart was trying to hammer its way out of his chest. It took him several steps to gather enough breath to say, "It's not a part. I'm willing to mate with you."

"Ulugarriu's left testicle," was Wuinlendhono's amused response. "You've been in prison, Rokhlenu. Right now you're willing to mate with anything that doesn't get away fast enough."

"I'm serious."

"I don't want to argue about that. I just want to make something clear. If you're talking about mating with me, we're not talking about a quick screw. I only mate for life. You're too twisted up to think about that right now, but I'm not. You're no good to me like this. So go find someone and discreetly express the depths of your poetic soul—by the bucketful if necessary. We're short on females in the outliers, but there are working girls (and for that matter working boys) who come out from Apetown and Dogtown. You can find them in the day-lairs by the marketplace; your fellow Olleiulu will show you. Until your mind is clear, I'm not making any deal."

Rokhlenu snarled. "Aren't you at least going to say how touched and honored you are by my proposal?"

Wuinlendhono laughed sympathetically. She patted his left hand with her own. "Sorry, new friend, if I seem a little cold. I'm not a puppy, you know, anxiously awaiting her first heat. If we mate, you'll be my fifth."

"Oh? I thought you didn't go in for casual mating."

"I don't. They're all dead. My fourth, who was First Wolf of this hellhole, was killed by a gang of Dogtown robbers. My third caught some sort of lingering illness and ate silver rather than let it finish him. My second was out hunting one day when he ran into a werebear and they killed each other."

They walked on for a while in silence. When it became clear that she had finished he said, "And your first?"

"It was an arranged marriage," Wuinlendhono said. "My guardian outwed me to an old ghost-sniffer in the Goweiteiuun pack. I hated him, so I killed him. That's why I'm here, which was probably your next question."

"No," Rokhlenu said, thinking how much like prison this all was in some ways. "But thanks for telling me."

The lairs of the outlier pack were built on the swamps below Wuruyaaria's south wall. For streets they had boarded ways; the lairs were rickety towers built on stilts driven into the sandy mud of the swamp. The whole place looked like a strong wind could knock it down.

The people were a little tougher looking. They moved fast; they talked or sang fast. He didn't see too many stupid faces, and no sentimental ones. Even the stupid faces wore a hard, cheerful determination. If the wind came and the lairs fell, these people would rebuild—or sell the wreckage to a passing mark.

Wuinlendhono took him to a gem-and-bone seller in the north part of town. He had a single greenish dragon tooth on a gold chain, and Wuinlendhono bought it and gave it to Rokhlenu.

He was going to protest, but she forestalled him with a whisper. "In the outliers, women choose the men. Gifts are normal, so if people hear about this (and they will), they'll take it as part of my arduous campaign to get into your pants. And you need an honor-tooth commensurate with your status. Anyway, it didn't cost very much."

And it hadn't. Few werewolves in history had ever had enough bite to wear a tooth like that in public. Rokhlenu was one. He was strutting a bit after they got back onto the boards, and Wuinlendhono's proud sideways glance didn't exactly sting.

"You're not doing a very good job in cooling my ardor," he observed.

"Well, we haven't got there yet," was her enigmatic reply.

"There" was a lair-tower on the east side of town, taller and more rickety than most. Several of the upper floors seemed to have been added after the original construction, and there was at least one crack running almost half the length of the plastered walls.

"Can this thing stand our weight?" asked Rokhlenu, only half joking.

"Oh, clench up, Dragonslayer," Wuinlendhono answered. "Worse comes to worst, we can always jump." She did not seem to be joking at all.

The air inside was dense with bloodbloom smoke and less pleasant odors. Rokhlenu followed Wuinlendhono up flight after twisting flight of dark creaking stairs until they got to the top story of the lair, which was all one none-too-spacious den. (The tower narrowed as it rose.)

In the light from the western windows lay a naked man, sleeping restlessly on what seemed to be a tarpaulin. Over him crouched a she-werewolf in the day shape. Her smooth mottled skin and torrent of russet hair reminded him of someone, but he wasn't sure who. She was reading a small codex she held in her hand; when they entered, she set the book down next to some odd-looking medical instruments and welcomed them with a complete absence of enthusiasm.

"Liudhleeo, my gravy bowl," said Wuinlendhono. "Can you do it?"

"I've done what I know how to do," Liudhleeo replied. "I have closed up his battle wounds with the salve Hrutnefdhu helped me make—so the lair is no longer in danger of burning down. I have washed him, apparently the first bath he has taken in his life. His skin had many sores, and his feet were rotten with some sort of fungus. All that has been seen to."

"Wonderful. Wonderful. But, you know, what I was really asking about was whether he is still crazy."

"Yes. I have drugged him as deeply as I dared, and he finally fell into a kind of sleep. But unless my experience misleads me, and it is no feeble resource, he is not dreaming."

"He says he never dreams," Rokhlenu remembered. "It's because of the spike in his head."

"This is Rokhlenu, by the way, my cutlet," Wuinlendhono said. "He was Khretvarrgliu's cellmate."

"Yes, I smelled him," the russet werewolf said with a marked distaste—and then Rokhlenu knew her, not by sight but by scent. She was the female whom the guards had raped outside his cell on that terrible spring night. He was shocked, then deeply ashamed as she eyed him. He turned away from her, and in the turmoil of his feelings he missed a few of her words.

"—that spike, yes," Liudhleeo said. "I must say, the book you gave me has taught me quite a lot."

"My first husband wrote it. He was a very learned male."

"And such fine penmanship. All the pages were quite legible, even the ones stained with blood."

"Why dwell on old gossip, my lamb chop, when we could be busy generating new gossip?"

"My considered answer to that . . . will take a little time. So maybe we should defer it to another occasion."

"By all means, dear, as long as we understand that I'm one ahead."

"I understand nothing of the sort, but never mind. I suppose you want to know why I haven't pulled that spike out of Khretvarrgliu's bewildered old head."

"Do tell."

"Well, I'm a little frightened about it, actually. I've never done anything like this, messing around inside a man's head, I mean. By choice, I would not start out in that type of surgery with a patient whose blood could set me afire. I sent sweet Hrutnefdhu to a ghost-sniffer who works in the Shadow Market; he said he might persuade him to come help."

"So you're waiting for this ghost-sniffer?"

"I was, but after reading this wonderful book some more I had just about nerved myself up to have a stab at the surgery. As it were."

"Why?"

"A ghost-sniffer probably can't help. They put these things in, but they never take them out. That's what I was reading in . . . in your husband's book. And Khretvarrgliu seems to be getting worse, much worse. You would not believe some of the gibberish he was talking before I finally got him to sleep."

Rokhlenu believed.

"Are we sure the spike is causing the madness?" Wuinlendhono asked. "How do we know he wasn't going mad anyway?"

Both females looked at Rokhlenu, and he said, "I knew him briefly before last year. He was . . . an odd and difficult male back then. But sane, I think. It must be the spike. Morlock—Khretvarrgliu, I mean—was sure of it."

"Well," Liudhleeo said, not looking at him but inclining her head to acknowledge his contribution, "then either we take the spike out or there's only one other choice."

"What's that?"

"We wrap him in the tarp and dump him in the swamp. Because he's done."

"Does it matter?" Wuinlendhono asked Rokhlenu.

"It matters," Rokhlenu replied. With difficulty, he turned to Liudhleeo. "Can we help?"

She was eyeing him a little less coldly now. "Yes."

Liudhleeo coated their hands with the red-brown healing salve; she said it would protect them from Morlock's fiery blood. Then she had them hold Morlock's unconscious body still. Wuinlendhono held his shoulders down; Rokhlenu put one hand under his jaw and the other on the crown of his head and held him firmly.

Liudhleeo did not anoint her own hands, but took up a long coppery knife on the end of a lead-gray stick. She knelt down beside Morlock and placed the edge of the blade over a red star-shaped scar on his temple. She deftly carved a cross into the flesh. Hot blood poured out of the wound and began to pool on the tarpaulin.

"The tarp is fireproof," she said, noticing Rokhlenu's alarmed glance. "But don't let any of that stuff fall on the floor. Otherwise we'll have a fire in here like . . ."

"Clench up," Rokhlenu said. "Worse comes to worst, we can always jump."

"Wish I'd said that," Wuinlendhono said, a little breathily. The scent or the sight of blood seemed to make her uneasy—Rokhlenu had never seen an adult werewolf so squeamish. He thought it odd. Of course, Morlock's blood did smell strange; maybe that was it.

Liudhleeo used a long-handled clamp to peel away a strip of Morlock's flesh, exposing the raw skull. Under the blood pulsed a sort of light, in the same rhythm as Morlock's heart. There was a squarish central locus and a fine network of pulsating lines spreading out from there.

"That's it," Liudhleeo said, tapping the squarish center.

"It looks like it's . . . growing or something. Laying down roots, like a plant."

"Maybe it is."

"Can we get it all out, then?"

"Maybe we can."

Liudhleeo gently but firmly inserted wedgelike probes on either side of the spike. Slowly, carefully, she worked it free from the skull and it dropped, dark as dried blood, to the tarpaulin.

"What about the lines?" Rokhlenu asked.

"I don't see them anymore. They went dark as soon as I extracted the spike. I think we're done."

She folded back the flap of flesh with the clamps and used a long-handled spoon to dab healing salve over the small but surprisingly bloody wound. Then she set about the awkward task of mopping up the blood. With a rag, and then tossing the rag into a bucket of water when it burst into flame. It took several rags, and the bucket was already dense with them, the water oily with Ambrosial blood.

By then the glass spike had dried and was safe to touch. Rokhlenu picked it up and looked at it. The end was unpointed and rather rough. It looked as if the tip had broken off, perhaps left behind in the wound.

"I know," said Liudhleeo, embarrassed. "But I think we've done what we can. Perhaps all will be well."

Rokhlenu handed her the dark spike. Then he lifted the dragon tooth from around his neck and held it out to her, chain and all. Wuinlendhono twitched a little at this but said nothing.

"No," Liudhleeo said, even more embarrassed. "I haven't earned it."

He went down on his knees, eyes intent on her, still holding out the tooth.

She took his hand and firmly folded his fingers over the tooth. "No one but you can wear this, Rokhlenu." She pushed his hand away, but he did not withdraw it.

"I never blamed you," she said then, not looking at him.

"I did," he said. "I do. But that's not what this is about. He saved me—three times, four times, I don't know how many times. And you saved him. This is all I have. If it is worthless, it is still yours."

"Wear it for me, then," she said.

"For you," he said, and put the chain around his neck again. "Claim it when you like."

She bowed her head and motioned impatiently for him to stand, so he did.

Wuinlendhono stood also. "You'll keep the book, of course, my dear," she said, "and wear that spike like an honor-tooth. We'll discuss the filthy lucre another time."

"I did it for Hrutnefdhu," Liudhleeo whispered. "Khretvarrgliu is his friend, too."

"Yes," Rokhlenu said, remembering as if it were a thousand years before. "It was the three of us. The three of us against all of them."

"Well," Wuinlendhono said, gently taking his arm, "there's a few more of us now." She guided him toward the door. "Call on me, my dear, if there's anything you need."

"I need my Hrutnefdhu. Send him to me if you see him, please."

They descended the dark stairs to the street, already streaked with the long shadows of a strangely summery winter's afternoon.

"Let me put it this way," Wuinlendhono said then. "I give you a dragon's tooth as a courtship gift, and before sunset I have to watch you on your knees, begging another female to take it. Fairly accurate?"

"Yes," Rokhlenu said glumly. "I understand if this means you're done with me."

"You silly chunk of meat, I'm barely beginning. Five was always my lucky number. Come on along; let's see if a certified dragon slayer can't find a place to sleep indoors tonight."

Chapter Thirteen

The Sardhluun Standard

A dead man who carried his severed head like a lamp was walking beneath the walls of the empty Vargulleion.

"A fine manifestation," signified a passing snake. "But to what purpose, if no one is present to see it?"

"It pleases me," signified War. "It reminds me of the battle that was in this prison house, while the scent of it is still fresh."

"But the battle is over," signified the snake, a manifestation of Wisdom. "There will be no new deaths."

"Deaths are incidental to war, Wisdom. I'm surprised you don't know that."

"You can't have a war without deaths, can you? What is more essential?"

"Courage, and cowardice. The need for cunning, and the uselessness of cunning. Victory. Defeat."

"You could get all that in sporting competitions—"

"Are you trying to see if I can vomit in this manifestation?" War wondered.

"—or elections."

"Perhaps the way the werewolves run them. I always look forward to their election year."

"Primaries are beginning. The Sardhluun begin picking their representatives tonight."

"Yes, and I visualize that both you and Death will be manifest there. You wish me to accompany you."

"I do," acknowledged Wisdom. "I dislike this plan of hers, whatever it is, and I think it may be time to reacquire her oath for our pact."

"I did think there would be more fighting," War admitted. "I'll go with you and see what she signifies."

The snake and the corpse with the severed head transited-by-intention to a neighboring locus of space-time.

It was the great arena of the Sardhluun Pack. The time was well after sunset; Horseman the second moon was high in the west; the sky around it glowed indigo. All the werewolves crowding the stands had transited to wolf form.

The Incumbent's Gate swung open in the arena wall. Out of it, a werewolf trotted proudly into the center of the fighting pit. The gate slammed shut behind him. His black fur was silvery on his muzzle. He had a great many honor-teeth: there was a great torc of them hanging around his neck. In his jaws he carried black-and-green streamers, the standard of the Sardhluun Pack. He was the incumbent gnyrrand, the citizen who, for the last year of choosing and several before, had led the Sardhluun's electoral band.

But the crowd did not esteem him: they yodeled his name in contemptuous tones: *Wurnafenglu, Wurnafenglu*. They called on the sacred ground of the fighting pit to swallow down the misbegotten luckless citizen who dared to pollute it. They howled insults against his relatives in elaborate verse forms.

He trotted back and forth across the arena ground, indifferent to their hostility, secure in his bite. If anyone wanted the Sardhluun standard or his honor-teeth, they would have to fight him for them.

Finally, one werewolf in the stands took up the challenge. He leapt down into the arena proper and barked a challenge. He was a whitish beast with black bristles running from his head down his spine all the way to the end of his tail. He wore a necklace of honor teeth—more than a few dangled there, though nothing like as many as the incumbent carried.

Wurnafenglu dropped the Sardhluun standard, since his right to it had been challenged.

The werewolves in the stands grew silent. They sat down to watch. The election was beginning.

A never-wolf slave entered the arena through a door set into the Incumbent's Gate. She carried two bowls of drink in her trembling hands. The spectators near at hand leaned forward to catch a scent of the deadly brew, then leaned back gasping when they did, or thought they did.

Everyone in the arena knew that the bowls contained an infusion of wolfbane.

The never-wolf slave put the bowls down in the center of the arena and backed away hastily. She ran back to the door in the Incumbent's Gate, but it was now locked and would not open for her. She was the only person present who had supposed it would.

A few werewolves chuckled mildly at her dismay, but all eyes turned now toward the Werowance of the Sardhluun, whose task tonight was to preside over the election of the pack's gnyrrand, its lead candidate in the upcoming general election. A silver-gray wolf with many cords of honor-teeth, the Werowance lay resplendent on his ceremonial black couch in a box set lower than the stands. He pressed a lever with one foot. A narrow opening appeared in the wall below him; a platform extended. On it was a ceramic bowl, brimming with antidote.

The Werowance sang what everyone knew. He was the Werowance of the Sardhluun, chosen by chance, by destiny, and by bite and by the common will of the Sardhluun. It was his duty to lead the Inner Pack in times of peace and to preside over the pack elections. This challenge would choose a representative for the general election to come. Only the strongest, the most cunning, the most ruthless of the Sardhluun could hope to carry the standard of their pack, the youngest and greatest of packs, against the corrupt beasts of the older treaty packs.

There was an incumbent, as they all knew: the detested Wurnafenglu. For many years, Wurnafenglu had tended the green-and-black standards of the Sardhluun like a herd of fat beeves. He had stood for the Sardhluun in the Innermost Pack of Wuruyaaria, even rising on occasion to the couch of the First Singer. But he had spent all his honor and all the glory of the Sardhluun in a single night of disgrace. Though he was the commander of the Vargulleion, the prison that (with the Khuwuleion) was the foundation of the pack's fortunes, he was absent on First Night, celebrating with his disgusting plurality of wives, when the prisoners rebelled. Many of his guards had died; he should have died with them. The subsidies from the city that they received for maintaining the prisoners would disappear; so should Wurnafenglu disappear. The Sardhluun were now a mockery among the older, weaker, less ruthless packs; so should Wurnafenglu be a mockery and a byword until the sun faded and the moons crunched its golden bones in their shining blue teeth. When Wurnafenglu might have done them all a favor by slinking away forever into the night of ignominy and shame, Wurnafenglu insisted on standing again for election to the Innermost Pack, as if to tie disgrace like a rotting puppy around the neck of the Sardhluun forever.

The Werowance hoped that this young and vigorous challenger—whose name escaped the Werowance although it was no doubt a worthy one—could slay the shame of the pack, tear those undeserved honor-teeth from a ravaged neck, or at least prevent him from taking up the banner to represent the pack he had so deeply stained with the stink of dishonor.

Either candidate could at this time withdraw, although he would of course leave his honor-teeth behind on the sacred ground of the arena's fighting pit.

This was the burden of the Werowance's song.

The two candidates bowed their heads and drank the poison in their bowls.

The election would run until one of them had drunk the antidote beneath the Werowance's box, or until both of them were dead.

War noted the manifestation of Death. She appeared to his god's eye as she often did: lightless, faceless, spider-armed, and many-fingered.

She acknowledged the manifestations of both War and Wisdom and signified, "I visualized this encounter. I will not rejoin the pact-sworn intention."

The werewolves felt the presence of Death, although only a few ghost-sniffers could actually see her (and that dimly). A shudder ran through the audience, and they leaned forward to watch the election.

Wurnafenglu had faced election many times; he knew the taste of poison well, and it didn't frighten him. The challenger stood in a different place entirely. He looked anxiously toward the bowl of remedy and licked his lips, still bitter with poison. If he ran straight toward the bowl of remedy and drank the antidote, he would not die. But he would gain no honor and another election would be held, with him as the incumbent.

Wurnafenglu saw the uncertainty on the challenger's face and smiled a long sinister smile. He trotted around until he stood squarely between the challenger and the bowl of remedy. Then he sat right down and stared at the moon, drinking its light with his eyes, idly scratching his right ear with his right forepaw. Death was in him and he knew it. But he did not fear it.

"I love that ugly black wolf," signified Death privately to War.

"I consider him to be a fool," War replied. "He spent the better part of a year torturing two prisoners who had gotten the better of him. Then he walks away and lets his guards get snot-face drunk on bloom smoke, simply because of a date on a calendar. Now he must fight for his right to keep what he has, and he must do the same all year long if he wins here tonight."

"Oh, he's a fool. No doubt of that. A clever fool. A cunning fool. A wise fool. That is my favorite kind of fool."

Wisdom knew these signs were directed at him, but he did not acknowledge them.

The challenger was growing anxious. He tried to lock gazes with Wurnafenglu, but the black wolf would not look at him. The challenger assumed a threatening posture and snarled at Wurnafenglu. The black wolf kept looking at the moon. Now he was idly scratching his left ear. The challenger barked that he would kill—kill—kill Wurnafenglu. His blood would be the challenger's most favored drink; his rotting liver would be given to the challenger's cubs for a holiday treat; his intestines would be used for sausages and sold for copper coins in Apetown, and the challenger would give the money away in charity to monkey-faced whores.

Undaunted by these terrors, Wurnafenglu waited.

"Your plan is not progressing as you foresaw," Wisdom signified to Death.

Death emanated a reckless joy, more intense and bitter than mere amusement.

The werewolves, patiently waiting for election developments, shuddered, thinking the warm winter night had suddenly turned chilly.

Death signified, "You are right. The torrent you predicted is sweeping away my visualization of the nearer future."

War grumbled, "This torrent which is so constantly in your signs does not appear to me to be very exciting. One battle in a whole year! And the Sardhluun did no more raiding than they usually do, and next year they'll have to do less."

The citizens in the audience began to grow restless. They wanted a more eventful election than this—something they could talk about to those who hadn't witnessed it, to argue about with those who had.

But the challenger was growing more anxious. His threatening posture had given way to a nervous dance. He capered one way, then another. He leapt back, then forward, snarling.

Wurnafenglu waited.

The challenger looked desperately at the moon, the stands, his enemy. His eyes were clouding; his vision was fading; his nervous antics were spreading the poison through his blood more rapidly. He scampered off in a long curving charge toward the remedy bowl.

Wurnafenglu leapt and struck with his full weight on the challenger's right shoulder. The challenger rolled in the dirt and tried to rise, snapping frantically with his jaws. But Wurnafenglu pinned him. He forced the challenger's head to the ground with his back feet as the challenger scrambled ineffectively to free himself. Wurnafenglu fixed his jaws at the base of the challenger's spine.

Hollow wolvish whistles of admiration echoed around the arena. Few in the audience would have staked a serious combat on a bite like that, where the backbone was strongest. There were a few skeptical yelps, and someone began a song to the effect that Wurnafenglu had made his last bad decision.

These were silenced by the crack of the challenger's spine, a crunching sound that reverberated all around the arena.

Wurnafenglu shook his opponent for a few moments, to make sure the spine was severed, and then he relaxed his jaws and let the broken challenger fall whining to the ground. He turned away and trotted calmly over to the bowl of remedy. Unhurriedly, without wasting a drop, he drank half the antidote.

Carefully, he picked up the bowl with his teeth and sidled toward the challenger, who was staring desperately at the moon, trying to knit his shattered spine together in time to continue the fight. If there had been three moons aloft and no poison in his veins, he might have managed it, but things were as they were.

Wurnafenglu held out the bowl of remedy to his fallen opponent.

This rarely happened in elections of the Sardhluun, and it was a disgrace to accept. But it did mean life rather than death for the defeated candidate.

The challenger weakly pushed the bowl away with his snout.

Wurnafenglu offered the bowl to the challenger again.

The challenger pushed it away again, more slowly and more reluctantly now.

Wurnafenglu offered the remedy to the challenger for a third time.

There was a moment of stillness. Then, in the sight of everyone, the challenger made a sudden movement to drink the remedy.

Wurnafenglu sidled out of reach and the challenger was foiled.

Wurnafenglu approached the sobbing challenger from the side and contemptuously poured the remedy over the challenger's genitals.

The challenger writhed about, trying to lick at the spilled remedy, but because of his broken spine he could not reach it.

Wurnafenglu smashed the bowl across the whining challenger's face and it shattered. Victorious Wurnafenglu ripped the honor-teeth from the defeated challenger's neck and fixed his jaws in the defenseless throat. He held his grip until the poison finished its work and the challenger was dead.

He tossed the corpse from him and looked toward the audience for his due.

They gave it—reluctantly at first, but then more and more enthusiastically. They howled their congratulations and applause. They ululated into the single-eyed night, saluting Wurnafenglu's victory. Everyone loves a winner, and he had proven, against their hopes and desires, that he was a winner. They wanted him on their side so that they could be winners, too.

War attempted to signify something to Death, but then took note she was no longer manifest.

"I signify this again," he signified to Wisdom. "Death is the strangest of the Strange Gods."

"She is lying," Wisdom signified reflectively. "I think everything she signifies is a lie."

"Then she's more reliable than most," War signified tolerantly. Lies are the normal form of communication in war, and he was used to them. "Oh well, I suppose the fighting is over." He ceased to manifest himself.

Wisdom remained manifest, watching and thinking. He knew about lies, too, and he knew that people or gods lie largely because they are frightened. He thought it was important to know why Death was afraid.

Now that the serious matter of the election was over, the lighter business of the celebration began. Wurnafenglu invited a few of his close personal friends down to the arena ground to help him kill and eat the never-wolf slave who had brought in the poison.

Chief among his guests was, of course, his old friend the Werowance. The Werowance explained, in a song where tones of grief mixed with gladness, that he had only seemed to criticize Wurnafenglu because of his official obligations, and that he had always esteemed the gnyrrand as one of the greatest citizens in the history of Wuruyaaria, and that he hoped they could continue to work together for the betterment of the pack and the city they both loved so much. Wurnafenglu replied that he understood the Werowance completely and that he hoped he would always esteem the Werowance at the Werowance's true worth.

Wurnafenglu named a few other friends and foes to join him in the feast, and then they gave chase to the woman.

She had been crouching in a shadowy edge of the arena, hoping against hope that she would be spared, or at least forgotten. When the wolves came for her, she tried to run, but there were several of them and no place for her to go. In the end, which came soon, she was cornered and she knew it.

She stood in the moonlight, her back to the arena wall, as the great silver-muzzled black wolf approached. She shook her fist at him. "*Kree-laow!*" she screamed in the bestial face. "*Kree-laow!*"

Then they took her down and killed her and ate her. Many minor guests were invited down to sample some of the meat and hobnob with the great ones, and the night was thought of as a memorable one, until the next election.

Kree-laow, in the language of the dead woman, meant "He will avenge." The werewolves neither knew nor cared about this. At least, not then.

Chapter Fourteen

Fund-Raising

On the third morning of the year, Morlock woke from a long, long dream. He stretched his crooked frame as he lay in the sun and wondered vaguely why so much of his terrible dream had involved werewolves. He opened his eyes and looked up straight into the face of a werewolf.

True, she was in the form of a woman, but he had learned to recognize the long narrow face of a werewolf in the day shape. She had a mottled skin like Hrutnefdhu, too (if he wasn't just part of the dream). And somehow, somehow inside, he just *knew* she was a werewolf.

He sat up and put one hand to his temple. He felt the healing wound there. The spike was gone. His Sight had returned.

"Thank you," he said.

Her eyes dropped. She seemed embarrassed. "I did what I could," she said eventually. "I'm not sure I got it all. You may . . . there still may be problems."

He closed his eyes and tested his insight. He realized she might be right. It was hard to tell; his inward blindness had gone on so long. But: he could dream. He could live. The world was as radiant with meaning as with sunlight.

"I still thank you," he said. "My name is Morlock Ambrosius, and my blood is yours."

"Well," she said, laughing, "I sopped up enough of it! I don't think I want any more. Oh, I'm sure that's the wrong thing to say. I don't know your customs. I should—it was for my Hrutnefdhu, you know. He calls you his old friend; I couldn't do less."

"Hrutnefdhu." Morlock closed his eyes, trying to separate memory from dream and from delusions of madness. "Yes: it was him, and Rokhlenu, and me. Us against them."

"It still is, Hrutnefdhu says. Only there are more of us. And more of them, too, I'm afraid. I am Liudhleeo, Hrutnefdhu's mate." She looked narrowly at him as if expecting him to recognize the name.

He had heard it, but didn't at first remember where. Then he did. He considered what to say. He neither wished to avoid the issue of the rape, nor make it the most important thing about her. To him, she was still the healer who had saved him from death and madness. But she was also his fellow prisoner—or fellow ex-prisoner, now. "How did you escape?" he asked.

It was not what she had been expecting him to say, clearly. Her eager-to-be-angered expression twisted into simple surprise, and then a kind of relief. "Oh? Oh, that. They—they let me go. Threw me out, really. I think they thought I was dying. I was—well, the next day, I was in pretty bad shape."

"I hated them for what they did to you."

She was embarrassed again, on the verge of anger. "I don't hate them. I don't hate them. But I didn't shed any tears when I heard what happened to them; you can bet on that."

"Eh."

She put her long clever hands over her mottled face and laughed. "They said you'd say that. They said you'd say that, but I didn't believe them."

"Eh."

"Oh, don't overdo it. It will take the magic away. You'll need something to eat, I expect."

"Yes." Morlock thought about the last time he hadn't been hungry, and he couldn't remember it. "Yes. I could eat anything in the world. Except meat," he added hastily, remembering a gray ear afloat in soupy porridge.

"Oh, yes: Hrutnefdhu mentioned your aversion. Don't worry. It's almost impossible to acquire anything as exotic and expensive as human flesh in the outlier pack."

"All the same. If you don't mind."

"I don't mind. Let me get you settled with breakfast, and I'll go off to find my Hrutnefdhu."

Breakfast was flatbread, cheese, and a warm murky sort of tea. Morlock found it wonderful, not least because nothing in it seemed to be a by-product of a human slaughterhouse.

Afterward, putting on the loose but well-made gray clothes that had been left for him, he stood at each one of the little den's many windows and stared out at the world.

To the north, Wuruyaaria towered over: mesa rising over mesa like great steps up the side of a mountain. He watched the tiny silhouettes of the baskets run up and down the funicular and tried to reason how they might work. He looked at the moon-clock set into the dark volcano, its metal gleaming gold in the sun. If Ulugarriu had made these things, he must meet Ulugarriu.

Hrutnefdhu showed up shortly thereafter.

"Good to see you better," the pale werewolf said, shamefaced for some reason.

Morlock thanked him. "And you are well?" he asked.

"Oh, the moon took care of that. As much as it could," he added rather mysteriously. "Let's go," he added hastily. "Rokhlenu wants to see you."

Morlock nodded and they left together. Hrutnefdhu set a very elaborate lock on the door, and they made their way down the narrow stairs. In the light from the street door, Morlock saw notices on the wall in two languages. One was a few starlike images that might have been ideograms; the other was longer and looked like it might be a phonetic script. Moonspeech and Sunspeech, or so he guessed.

"What do they say?" he asked Hrutnefdhu.

The pale mottled werewolf blushed and said, "'Tenants must bury their own dead. No smoking bloom on the stairways.'"

"Bloom is the smoke the guards were drunk on the other night?" Morlock asked.

"Yes," Hrutnefdhu said. "Many smoke it to forget their troubles, and some seem to have more trouble than others. Look, there are no good neighborhoods in the outlier pack, but this is the very worst. You need to know that."

Morlock looked up and down the narrow boarded way that served as a street. It stopped not too far east of the towering lair; beyond it was a murky stretch of swamp water and beyond that a rising slope choked with thickets and the suggestion of a cave entrance or two.

"It seems ideal to me," said Morlock, as he followed Hrutnefdhu to the other side of the little settlement.

Rokhlenu was deep in conference with Olleiulu when he looked up and saw Morlock standing nearby, clear-eyed and relatively sane-looking. He jumped up and they grabbed each other's shoulders.

"How's freedom?" Rokhlenu asked.

"Good," Morlock said. "You're back in politics, I hear."

"I may be," Rokhlenu said, the anxieties of his position pressing down on him. "Have they fed you? Are you hungry?"

"They have fed me," Morlock said, "but I'm still hungry. I take it rations are scarce, though."

"Not for Khretvarrgliu they krecking are not!" barked Olleiulu, and the werewolves nearby all started shouting about Khretvarrgliu and food and how maybe things would be better now.

"Let's go eat, then," said Rokhlenu. "We can talk over breakfast."

Rokhlenu and Olleiulu walked on either side of Morlock to the other side of the great ramshackle building. Hrutnefdhu insisted on walking behind, and no one but Morlock seemed to think that odd. Half of the building served as a dormitory without beds; the other half served as a refectory without benches or tables. Morlock got a bowl of, unfortunately, porridge. At least it seemed to have no animal products in it other than butter and a little honey.

The big red werewolf with the golden hair had preceded them into the refectory, and when he saw Morlock he shouted incoherently and gestured and in general made a fuss until Morlock sat down by him. There was no one else sitting there, so Morlock dropped down and sat on the empty floor. The other werewolves did the same, although at a greater distance from the red werewolf.

The conveniences of the refectory didn't run to spoons, so Morlock ate with his fingers like the others.

"We are short of money, I take it," he said, between slurps.

In a confusing amount of detail, Rokhlenu, supplemented by Olleiulu and Hrutnefdhu, explained to Morlock just how short of money they were. The outlier pack in general was not wealthy, barely having enough food to sustain themselves, and the addition of nearly the entire prison population had made matters worse. Money was scarce; food was expensive; lodging was almost impossible.

The building they were sitting in and the food they were eating were gifts from someone named Wuinlendhono. Olleiulu kept referring to them as "love-gifts" and looking slyly at Rokhlenu. Rokhlenu would blush and talk about something else in a blustering voice. Morlock didn't want to embarrass his friend, but it seemed to be the central issue, so he finally asked.

"Wuinlendhono is the First Wolf of the outlier pack," Rokhlenu explained. "For the time being, at any rate."

"Oh," said Morlock. He thought for a moment or two. "What's stopping her from keeping the job?" he asked. "If she wants it."

"Well, she's a female."

"Yes?" *-o* was the feminine ending for names in Moonspeech and Sunspeech.

"We don't generally have females running our packs," Hrutnefdhu explained to him, when the other males did not seem to realize that more explanation was needed.

"Oh. Then we're talking an . . . an arranged mating, if that's the right term," Morlock said.

"Yes, exactly," Rokhlenu said hastily. "That's what it is. A political arrangement, that's all. It will give us a place in the outlier pack. But I have to do my own arranging, my family still being on Aruukaiaduun. And I have no portion."

Morlock mulled this over as he went to get a fingerful of porridge. To his surprise, he found his bowl was empty. He looked up at the werewolves. Most were expressionless. The red werewolf was shamefaced and his right hand was full of porridge. His terrified eyes dropped rather than meet Morlock's.

Theft was a serious crime where Morlock was raised, in some cases more serious than murder, but the red werewolf was obviously not juggling with both hands. Morlock shrugged and turned back to the others.

"He must have grabbed it straight out of my bowl," Morlock said. "Remarkable."

"The skill of long practice," Hrutnefdhu remarked. "Several of his cell-mates died of hunger. I don't think he can help it. That's why we call him Hlupnafenglu." The name meant *Steals-your-food.*

"Eh." Morlock didn't want to talk about it, but instead listened as Rokhlenu explained the local mating customs. Courting gifts were common from females to males, but males were supposed to bring a certain amount of property to a marriage. If Rokhlenu and Wuinlendhono married, her position would be secure and Rokhlenu's followers (most of the irredeemables and thugs who had fought their way out of prison with them) would have a place in the outliers.

"So we need money," Morlock said. "What kind of money? Cash? Things? Land?"

"Whatever we can get," Rokhlenu said. Olleiulu proposed a plan to work as robbers on the roads around the never-wolf cities in the south. In a year or two, they could return with a portion for Rokhlenu and enough coin to support the irredeemables for a while—if that was what they all wanted, to join the outliers.

As the three werewolves discussed this plan's merits and defects, Morlock thought about one thing and another. Presently he felt the weight of the bowl on his knee grow greater. He looked down to see most of his porridge had been returned. He looked up to see Hlupnafenglu looking at him shamefacedly.

"Take it," Morlock said, holding out the bowl. "No, take it," he added, when the red werewolf tried to push it away. "You're bigger than I am. You need the food more than I do. I've already eaten today. Take the food."

He persisted until the red werewolf grabbed the bowl and glumly started scooping up the contents.

The other werewolves displayed varying degrees of bemusement. "It's a new age of miracles," Hrutnefdhu muttered. "Hlupnafenglu giving back food. . . ."

Rokhlenu was talking about joining some council of advisors with his intended bride, but Morlock declined to join him. "I'll go round up some money," he said. The other werewolves looked at him skeptically, and Rokhlenu asked if there was anything he needed.

"Two things," Morlock said. "First, a guide who can take me to the nearest market or markets."

"That's me," said Hrutnefdhu eagerly.

"Second, if it's not too much trouble, my sword."

"Your sword," Rokhlenu said blankly. "The one with the black-and-white blade? The one you called to you in the New Year's fight? The one you slew the blue dragon with in the mountains?"

"Yes, it was not with me when I woke up."

"Those worthless barking ball-less brachs," whispered Olleiulu. "Those ape-toed, bald-faced, quivering slugs. They have stolen the sword of Khretvarrgliu."

"Well, many of them were in prison for theft, you know," Hrutnefdhu said, almost apologetically.

"I will roast them alive on silver spikes over a fire of wolfbane," Olleiulu said. "I will make them beg for the mercy of death and I will deny it them. I will kick their sorry ugly up-for-sale asses. I will get your sword back, Khretvarrgliu." He leapt to his feet and set off at a furious run.

"Thank you," Morlock said mildly to his back. He pounded Rokhlenu on the shoulder and went off to the marketplace with Hrutnefdhu. Hlupnafenglu followed them, a vague look on his face, the bowl still in his hand.

Business was slow in the marketplace; Morlock saw many vacant spaces among the vendors. The busiest corner stood between two whorehouses. A sausage seller and portrait maker had commandeered the space and were doing a fair business with those passing by toward one or the other door.

"Stay here," Morlock said to Hrutnefdhu and Hlupnafenglu.

Morlock walked up to the sausage seller and said, "Have you got live coals there?"

"I've got fresh sausages," the seller said, ready to be offended. "Each one contains a certain proportion of real meat!"

"I don't care about that," Morlock said. "But you've got them on a warming grill, and there's fire under the grill."

"Are you hinting that something might *happen* to my sausage cart?" the seller said suspiciously. "I pay protection to First Wolf of the outliers himself! You'll answer to him if you bother me! And you're bothering me!"

"The First Wolf of the outliers is a female," Morlock pointed out.

"He's right," said an amused spectator. "Better pay up, Chunky."

"Moonless nights," muttered the seller. "All right, what do you and your boys want?"

Morlock looked around and saw that Hrutnefdhu and Hlupnafenglu were at his elbows. The big red werewolf was staring with naked greed at the sausages on the grill.

"I told you to stay over there," Morlock said.

"Couldn't make him," the pale werewolf admitted.

Morlock took the bowl from Hlupnafenglu's hand and tapped him gently on the nose with it. There was a gasp from bystanders, and a crowd began to gather, expecting a fight.

Morlock had only done it to get Hlupnafenglu's attention, and this it had just barely done. The red werewolf looked vaguely in his direction, and Morlock said, "Over there. Wait over there. There is where you wait. Over there. Not here. There." He pointed. He stared at the red werewolf. He pointed. Eventually Hlupnafenglu got a troubled look on his face. He looked at the far side of the market where Morlock was pointing. He looked back at Morlock. He looked back and forth several times. Eventually he gave a last longing glance at the sausages and shambled sadly away. Hrutnefdhu followed at his heels.

"If you give me some coals of fire," said Morlock, turning back to the seller, "I'll give you a copper coin when I get one."

"That means you haven't got one."

"But I'll get one."

"If I don't give you the coals, what will you do?"

"I'll get them from someone else."

"Are you crazy?"

"I don't see why that matters."

The seller threw up his hands and opened the firebox on his cart. He picked up a pair of tongs to pull out some coals.

"Never mind that," said Morlock, and reached in with his right hand to grab a fistful of coals. There were even more gasps in the rapidly accumulating crowd, and someone actually screamed. This was all to Morlock's liking. He dropped the bowl at his feet and started juggling the live coals.

The audience was impressed. Not as impressed as an audience would have been in Narkunden or Ontil: werewolves did not fear fire any more than the children of Ambrose. But then, werewolves in their night shape do not have fingers and do not juggle. The audience speculated that Morlock was a werewolf who did not change fully to human: he might have wolvish paws, immune to fire. On request, Morlock showed them his hairless palms.

"He probably shaves them," shouted a heckler.

"Like you?" someone else retorted, to much abusive laughter.

Coins started appearing in Morlock's bowl. He threw hooks and double-hooks; he threw double-sidehooks where his hands moved so fast it looked as if he was throwing infinity rings. He kept juggling the coals until the fire was gone. By then the bowl was nearly full of red coins, shining copper and rusting iron.

He took a single copper coin and handed it to the sausage seller.

"Keep it," said the seller, who had sold his entire stock to the crowd that had gathered to watch Morlock's juggling.

"This was our deal," said Morlock, and pressed the coin on him.

"I'm out of sausages and I'm going back to my shop in Apetown," the seller said. "Will you be here this afternoon?"

"I don't know."

"Will you be here tomorrow?"

"Probably not."

"Look, I'll *pay* you to be here. We're a team, Chief!"

"I'm not your chief," said Morlock. He picked up his bowl and turned to the portrait maker, who was telling two uninterested passersby that he was Luyukioronu Longthumbs and they were missing the chance of a lifetime to have their portrait inked by him.

"How much for a drawing in ink?" Morlock asked Luyukioronu, after the passersby had passed by.

"Two pads of copper," said Luyukioronu eagerly. He hadn't done as well with the crowd as the sausage seller.

"I'll give you three pads for the paper, the ink, and the loan of a brush."

"What?" said the would-be artist suspiciously.

Morlock repeated himself.

"I'll do the drawing. Just give me the money," Luyukioronu insisted.

"You want the money, you give me what I asked for."

The crowd, which had shown signs of dispersing, began to thicken again.

Reluctantly, Luyukioronu surrendered the materials.

Morlock made a few trial strokes with the brush and the ink on the boards of the market floor. Then he spun the brush in his hands and thought for a moment. He dipped the brush in the ink and applied the brush to the page in swift decisive strokes. Soon it was a picture of a volcano with a moon-clock in its side, with mists hovering about that half obscured the symbols.

"That's Mount Dhaarnaiarnon," whispered a member of the crowd.

"Is it?" Morlock said. "Would anyone like this drawing? I will give it to them for free."

This sounded too good to be true. But the drawing was a marvel in black-and-white. Slowly, suspiciously, a middle-aged citizen edged forward and silently held out his hand. Morlock gave him the drawing and handed the ink and brush back to the artist.

He waited.

"Ink my portrait," someone said tentatively.

"Paint my mate's portrait," said another.

"Paint Ullywuino!" shouted someone else. "She's my favorite whore!"

"There's too much paint on her already," someone else said.

Morlock held up his hands. "I have nothing to paint with, citizens. Unless you buy materials from this reliable craftsman."

"Hey!" shouted Luyukioronu. "I'm not your stationer! Buy your own stuff!"

Morlock shrugged. "I'm here to make money. I can draw better than you. The crowd won't want your work after they've seen mine."

The artist-werewolf's face worked angrily. He glanced at the drawing, still being held up with wonder by the crowd. He threw down the brush and the bowl of ink and stood up.

"Fine," Luyukioronu shouted. "Take the stuff. I hope the ink poisons you. But you won't get my teeth." He clutched at the few honor-teeth he had at his throat. Morlock saw with interest that his thumbs were indeed long: the tips stretched farther than his index fingers. "You'll have to fight me for those," Luyukioronu continued, "you gray-bagged, flat-faced, ape-fingered son of a never-wolf!"

"Wait!" said Morlock. "Stop!"

Luyukioronu walked stiff-legged away.

The crowd applauded.

Morlock looked around in bemusement. Hrutnefdhu was there in the crowd, and he took pity on his never-wolf friend. "You showed you had more bite as an artist than he did. The stuff is yours now."

"Eh." Morlock grabbed the bowl of coins. "How much is this stuff worth? Less than this?"

"A dozen coppers, perhaps. He probably stole it, you know."

"Maybe he did, but I won't. Go after him. Give him twenty copper coins. Take the rest to Rokhlenu and meet me back here."

The pale werewolf smiled strangely at him, took the bowl, and left.

"Citizens," Morlock said, sitting down by the easel. "What will you?"

He painted. He drew images in ink for four copper coins each. There were some sticks of charcoal tucked away in the artist's kit, and he sold pictures in charcoal for two copper coins each. There was some odd pigment in soft sticks, like chalk mixed with colors and oil. He found this fascinating to work with, but he didn't forget he was there to make money. He charged six copper coins for work in these.

He did it for the money, because he and his friends needed money. But it wasn't only the money. He was a maker who had made virtually nothing for more than a year. He ached to reshape matter with his hands and his dreams—now that he could dream again. Each image was important to him for itself, not just for the money.

And money wasn't all he earned by it. Customers often handed him an honor-tooth along with their coins. He thought it was a mistake at first, but they seemed angry if he asked them about it, so he stopped asking.

Most of the pictures were portraits. The customers wanted keepsakes of themselves, their mates, their sweethearts, their cubs. But one citizen said, "Make me a tree. I like trees." So Morlock drew in inks a maijarra tree he had seen in his now-distant youth on the western edge of the world. The next customer wanted a more warlike scene, so Morlock sketched in charcoal and smoky pastels the chaotic central chamber of the Vargulleion prison on that memorable New Year's Night. This was very popular, and customers wanted more like it, so Morlock drew scene after scene of the battle, as much as his hazy memory permitted. He drew images of Rokhlenu on the dragon he had killed in the mountain pass of Kirach Kund, images of Rokhlenu fighting the Spiderfolk. The crowd was intrigued by the images of the werewolf, and even more interested when they found that the werewolf was the intended spouse of the outliers' First Wolf.

Finally, Morlock took the last roll of paper that he had and used most of the rest of the ink and pigment on a vast panorama of the city of Wuruyaaria as he had first seen it, rising in savage civil splendor up the mesas of the mountainside, facing the threatening mass of Mount Dhaarnaiarnon, glaring over the scene with its single intricate mechanical eye. The overall tone was greenish, but Morlock stippled the surface with yellow pigment and smeared it with his thumb until the image shone with a green-and-gold misty luster he had never seen in the world, but somehow seemed exactly right.

"Who's that for?" asked someone in the crowd.

"Whoever pays the most for it," Morlock replied.

The impromptu auction netted Morlock several more fistfuls of copper coins, and a string of honor-teeth. The image went to the madam of one of the day-lairs (i.e., whorehouses) nearby. She said it would be perfect to decorate her waiting room.

"No doubt," Morlock said, with the sinking feeling a maker often has when relinquishing his work.

He bought a woman's headcloth to roll up his newfound wealth in. The crowd began to thin out reluctantly, the show obviously being over.

Two shadows fell across Morlock as he was rolling up the cloth. He looked up to see the long leering face of Luyukioronu, the werewolf artist. Next to him was a many-scarred thug with clawed fingers and a pronounced and toothy overbite.

"You took my stuff," Luyukioronu said. "So now we'll take your stuff. Stand back, never-wolf."

"Didn't my friend find you?" Morlock asked. "I sent him with payment for your materials. And you can have back whatever's left."

"He gave me your money. But that just told me you're afraid. So I used it to hire Snekknafenglu here, and we'll take the rest of your money now—and those honor-teeth you've got; you probably stole those, too."

"No man or wolf calls me thief," said Morlock as he stood.

"You!" shouted Luyukioronu. "Who ever heard of you to call you anything, you rat-tailed tailless bald-faced never-wolf—"

The crowd stood back, but did not leave. The show was clearly not yet entirely over. They had enjoyed watching Morlock work, but they would not intervene: a citizen should only carry what he or his can fight to keep. That was their law.

Morlock saw Snekknafenglu edging forward while Luyukioronu raved. Morlock lashed out with the edge of an ink-stained hand at what seemed to be the weakest part of Snekknafenglu's protruding upper jaw. The mercenary staggered back, eyes crossing in pain. Morlock turned to Luyukioronu and kicked him savagely in one knee. As the artist was reeling, Morlock kicked him in the other knee and he went down on the boards. Morlock turned back to Snekknafenglu standing at bay between Hrutnefdhu and Olleiulu. Olleiulu, Morlock was relieved to see, was carrying Tyrfing.

"What do you want us to do with him?" Olleiulu asked.

"Yes, what should we do with him—Khretvarrgliu?" Hrutnefdhu added slyly, glancing at Snekknafenglu.

The effect of the name on the thug was immediate and, Morlock had to admit, somewhat gratifying. Snekknafenglu gasped, looked anxiously at Morlock, anxiously at the sword, and turned to flee.

"Let him go," Morlock said, so his friends did. The thug-for-hire ran off, and a few members of the crowd tapered off after him, perhaps hoping to win a few honor-teeth from Snekknafenglu while he was feeling whipped.

Morlock turned to the artist, who was struggling to get back afoot. He snatched the artist's honor-teeth and ripped them from the hairy neck. Then he tossed them into the swamp water, where they sank out of sight.

"I am not a thief," said Morlock. "But you are a liar. Earn your bite back by telling the truth, or I'll take your teeth again."

The crowd hooted and applauded ironically as Luyukioronu scrambled away to nurse his losses.

"Well, you've had a busy morning," said Hrutnefdhu, eyeing Morlock's money-roll.

Morlock glanced at the sky in surprise. It was not yet noon.

"How about lunch?"

Morlock was ravenously hungry but said, "No thanks. You can take this money to Rokhlenu. Sorry it's so heavy—can we change it for silver, somewhere?"

"Silver," said Hrutnefdhu faintly. "Are you still crazy?"

"Oh." Morlock reflected for a moment. Silver would not pass for currency among werewolves. "No. Never mind. Tell Rokhlenu I'll send more when I can." Hrutnefdhu shrugged, took the money-roll, and departed.

Morlock accepted the sword from Olleiulu with sincere thanks.

"We found it in a stash one of our fellow escapees had set up," Olleiulu said. "A second-floor hero. He waited until the guards were dead or fled and he then looted bodies. He showed up here the next day and stole your sword the following night. Well, now we have one fewer mouth to feed, and a few more of us have some gear."

"Eh."

"You should put those honor-teeth on," Olleiulu said, pointing at the string Morlock had left on the boards of the market floor.

"Eh."

"I don't know what that means, and I don't mean any kind of disrespect.

If you won't, you won't. But people see you without honor-teeth, they try to take whatever you got away from you. I know you can brush them off, but why should you have to?"

Morlock saw his point. He grabbed up the honor-teeth and roped them around his neck.

Olleiulu looked relieved. Morlock wondered if it was bad for a werewolf's reputation to be seen with someone who wore no honor-teeth; he guessed it might. Neither Hrutnefdhu nor Liudhleeo wore them, Morlock reflected.

"Well, what's next if it's not lunch? Rokhlenu said that me or Hrutnefdhu had to stay with you until you—until you—"

"Until I wasn't obviously crazy."

"Which I know you're not, no matter what that *plepnup* says. But you can't know your way around the boards yet."

"The *plepnup* is my friend, Olleiulu."

"Uh-huh, Chief. I didn't mean anything bad."

"Can you take me where he lives? Where he and Liudhleeo live?"

Olleiulu nodded sagely. "You're not hungry; you're tired. You want to rest."

"Not exactly." Morlock was both hungry and tired, but now that he had Tyrfing back there were many other things he could and should do.

Through the thinning crowd, Morlock saw the other side of the market square. Sitting with somber concentration, his head in his hands, was the big red werewolf, Hlupnafenglu.

"I forgot about him," Morlock admitted.

"Lucky you," Olleiulu snorted.

They went over, and Morlock told Hlupnafenglu that he could get up. He had to say it several times before the red werewolf could hear it or would believe it, but eventually he sighed with relief and got to his feet. He beamed with vacant happiness on Morlock and the scornful Olleiulu.

"East we go," said Olleiulu, and they went east.

Around sunset, Olleiulu returned alone to the ramshackle building Rokhlenu and his men used as quarters. He brought with him a sizable box sporting a wheel and handles for grasping. Whatever was in the box was obviously very heavy.

Rokhlenu and Wuinlendhono were sitting outside the building in chairs that had seen better days. Rokhlenu cocked an eye at Olleiulu and said, "I take it my friend is quite well and knows his way around the outlier pack perfectly."

Olleiulu put the box down and gasped for a while. When he could speak he said, "Khretvarrgliu seems to be well. But I think maybe I'm crazy, after today."

"What's in the box?" Wuinlendhono asked. "Not more fruits of the marketplace, I hope. I had several complaints from merchants that Morlock was funnelling all the money his way this morning."

Olleiulu looked to his chieftain, who nodded. Olleiulu lifted the lid of the box slightly and they all saw the red gleam of raw gold within. Olleiulu slammed the box shut before anyone else could see it.

"Well," Wuinlendhono said, after a brief silence. "It seems like that mating is on. If you're still interested, of course; I don't like to presume."

"I'm interested," Rokhlenu said grimly. It was true in several ways . . . unfortunately, they were ways that might not run together.

"There isn't that much gold in the outlier pack," Wuinlendhono reflected. "There is now, I guess. Where did it come from, Olleiulu?"

"That's why I think I must be crazy. He . . . he . . . he *made* it. He apologizes it's not so much. He says there'll be more tomorrow."

"Hmmmm," hummed Wuinlendhono. "We'll have to hire a ghost-sniffer to make sure it's really real. But assuming it will pass the sniff test, we can proceed with negotiating the terms of the marriage alliance." She stood in a single fluid movement. "I'll have one of my old women come over tomorrow and chew over the details with one of your men."

"Olleiulu, that'll be you."

Olleiulu nodded.

Wuinlendhono licked the face of her intended in farewell and then walked sinuously away to her own lair-tower. The lupine bodyguards who had lain out of sight jumped up and danced around her as she walked, unregarding, among them.

"Have a seat," Rokhlenu offered. "Tell me about it."

Olleiulu ignored the seat next to his chieftain, sitting on the boards next to the treasure box. He grasped his ears a few times to settle his thoughts, and then began.

"I get there to the market and he's in the middle of some kind of barking match with Luyukioronu the forger and Snekknafenglu the claw-for-hire. Not the Snekknafenglu who works out of Dogtown, the other one."

"I don't know either one."

"That's right. I keep forgetting we weren't in business together until a few nights ago."

Rokhlenu never forgot it, but he didn't want to say that to Olleiulu; he might take it wrong. "It's a new life since then, and we've been together through most of it."

"Right. Anyway. We keep Khretvarrgliu from ripping them up—"

Rokhlenu had heard a more measured account from Hrutnefdhu, but he made allowances for Olleiulu's admiration for Morlock, and the form that admiration took.

"—and after we sent off the *plepnup*—"

"That *plepnup* is my friend, Olleiulu."

"I keep making that mistake. Sorry, I don't mean anything by it. Anyway, we sent him back to you with the coin and we collected that crazy Hlupnafenglu and walked east right out of town. I think he wants to go back to a lair and sleep the afternoon like people do. But he heads straight past the *pl*—past Hrutnefdhu's lair and starts wading through the swamp. Hlupnafenglu plops in right after him."

"I wouldn't have done that, myself. Gotten in that water, I mean."

"Oh, thanks, Chief. I'll treasure that little piece of advice. I jumped as far across as I could, but I still ended in the shallows on the far side. Do you have any idea how bad that muck stinks?"

"No, thank ghost. Either you're downwind of me or you must have cleaned up."

"Cleaned up, but it was a while until I got to that. He starts setting up in one of those creepy caves up on the slope—"

"Setting up what? I thought all he had was his sword."

"That's all he got there with, right. But he starts cutting up brushwood and small trees on the hillside, swinging the sword like an axe."

"Weird."

"You said that too soon. He's got stacks of wood by now, see, and he takes a bunch of sticks and he builds a kind of basket or something."

"A basket."

"Except there was no way to carry anything in it. It was round like a ball and there were gaps all around in it, and the branches were weaved—"

"Woven."

"—weaved together in a crazy way that kind of made my eyes hurt. Then he puts his back against the cave wall, and it's like he's gone to sleep or something."

"Well, it's a warm day for winter."

"It's a warm day for late spring. But I don't think he was really asleep. His sword started to glow and his eyes a little too—I mean you could see it through his eyelids."

"Is it too early to say 'weird' yet?"

"You tell me. After he's not-sleeping like this for a while, a fuzzy shiny sort of mist starts coming out of the basket and floats away. Eventually he wakes up and lights a fire. He lights a lot of little fires, one at a time. He strikes sparks from a couple of stones, and he catches them with a leaf or a piece of grass or something, one by one you understand, and then he says something to them, talks to them like they're people, and he sets them down in the basket.

"Which starts to burn."

"No. He puts stuff in the basket—grass and junk; I don't know. It burns. But the basket doesn't burn."

"All right, I'll call that weird."

"But what about when the little flames started talking back? He says something, and they say it back to him in little sparky voices? What do you call that?"

"Weirder."

"Oh, go mate yourself and have knuckly puppies. So, once he's got enough flames—I don't know maybe it was twenty or thirty—he starts making baskets while he talks to them. Real baskets you could carry stuff in. He packed them with earth and grass so the stuff in them didn't fall out."

"What stuff did he put in them?"

"Not him. Us. Hlupnafenglu and me. He wanted sand. Muddy, if it had to be, but the sandier the better. Then he sits back and takes another one of those not-a-naps while we haul sand and the flames argue and snap at each other."

"Are you sure?"

"Kreck, no. I couldn't understand them. But that's what it sounded like. We had a pretty big heap of sandy muck by the entrance of the cave when Morlock woke up. He tells us to keep at it and wanders off up the hillside, and he comes back with just a basket of dumb stuff: some yellow stinkstone, and dead beehives, and I don't know what else. Then he takes a bunch of it and mixes it up in a little basket like a dish, like about as wide as your hand. And he puts it inside the big basket, the one with the talking flames, like he's a baker putting some bread in an oven."

"Yum."

"You liked it." Olleiulu jerked a thumb toward the treasure box.

"That's how he made the gold?"

"Right. He came back after a while and changed baskets, and the one that came out of the big basket, he called it the nexus—the one that came out of the nexus was full of gold. It goes in reeking like yellow stinkstone and it comes out like raw gold. He's just dumping it on the ground in his cave. This goes on for a while."

"Busy afternoon."

"He takes some sand and he burns it in the nexus. He keeps going over to it and turning it with his bare fingers, folding it over on itself while it was red hot. And he talked a lot to the flames while he was working. It might have been just because they were there, but he didn't talk to us that way."

"What did he make the glass into?"

"He called them 'mirror gates.' He makes water run uphill with them."

"Drop dead."

"I almost did. Never seen anything like it. Never seen anything like half the stuff I saw this afternoon, but that was the weirdest. He dug a skinny channel up the hill and another one running down again, and he lined them with wood smeared with beeswax. He put a mirror gate at the top and the bottom of the channels, where they joined. And he took a basket of water—"

"You want to give me some help with that one?"

"I'm the one that needs the help. I mean, you could *see* the water through the weave of the basket."

"Did he explain how he did it?"

"He didn't seem to think it was a secret, but there was stuff he didn't know how to say in Sunspeech or Moonspeech, and I didn't know how to tell him how to say it. I think he was saying that he tricked it—said the water was 'gullible.' Only a little at a time, though. 'You can't argue with a lake,' he said. 'Even a pond can be stubborn.' But I don't know if he really knew what all the words meant."

"Or you didn't know what he meant."

"And I never will. Anyway, he dumps out the basket into one of the channels, and the murky water runs downhill, like you'd expect, and it hits the mirror gate at the bottom and it runs *up*hill. The muck mostly didn't want to travel uphill—Morlock says earth is less gullible than water—and after the water had been up and down the hill a couple times it was clear as air, clearer than the air usually is around this swamp. He kept dumping baskets of water in the channels until he had a regular brook running upside and downside. We sponged off with the clean water and drank deep—drank our body weight in water, I think. It was around that time the *pl*—Hrutnefdhu showed up. He came screaming through the swamp like a chicken on fire, and he ran up and down alongside the channels a couple times, and he wanted to be introduced to each flame personally, and he danced around the gold as if he had invented it personally, and he was pretty excited about the whole business, I guess. Morlock and him talked about stuff for half-forever, it seemed like."

Rokhlenu reflected that Olleiulu was more comfortable with Morlock the bloodstained beast slayer than Morlock the work-stained maker and friend of low-status citizens.

"Anyway, the sun was getting pretty low by then. I was going to bring Hlupnafenglu back with me, but he wouldn't leave the flames—just wanted to sit next to them and stare at them. So I came away with the gold."

"How'd you get back across the swamp water?"

"Wickerwork boat," Olleiulu said glumly. "I—well, I had something to do. He had the boat and some other stuff done when I got back. His hands were moving all the time, all the time."

Rokhlenu wondered what Olleiulu had had to do, but it seemed like an unhappy memory, so he didn't press him on it. Instead he changed the topic to the negotiations for the marriage settlement.

The sun was setting, and they were still deep in consultation when a messenger wolf with human fingers ran up to tell Rokhlenu that Wuinlendhono needed him. There was an embassy from the Sardhluun Pack in First Wolf's Lair: they said they wanted their prisoners back.

Chapter Fifteen

Quarry

Once a snake, resting in the cool shadows of a marble quarry, was approached by a werewolf holding a box made of light, glass, and certain heretical opinions.

The werewolf, still in the day shape, leaped to trap the snake; but the snake, who was Wisdom, transited to the other side of the quarry.

"Ulugarriu," the snake said, condescending to speak with its mouth, "you will never trap me that way."

"Won't I?" Ulugarriu replied.

"No. My visualization of totality warned me of your approach. Your war against the gods is worse than folly, maker."

"Is it?"

"Yes," said Wisdom. "It grieves me that we're enemies—"

"Does it?"

"—but I see that the folly has eaten you deeply—"

"Has it?"

"Be that way, then, you fur-faced ill-born," the snake hissed, and summoned ramparts of madness to attend him.

"I am not wearing my night shape," Ulugarriu observed, edging closer through the quarry shadows. "If I were, I would sing insults back at you. It would be a relief to my spirit, for I fear you. But why do you insult me? Does a god fear a fur-faced ill-born?"

But the snake was done with talking. He raised up a rampart of phobia between him and the werewolf.

Ulugarriu hesitated, and then took from the box a cloak of red-eyed anger. The werewolf donned the cloak and began to force a way through the rampart of phobia.

Wisdom then realized he did feel a little fear. While Ulugarriu was still entangled in the phobia, he transited to the far end of the quarry.

He would have transited farther, but he found he could not. His passage through space-time was obstructed somehow.

Ulugarriu surpassed the rampart of phobia and ran down the quarry toward Wisdom.

The snake raised up a rampart of delusions to block the werewolf.

The werewolf drew a two-edged blade, one edge deeply serrated with ugly irregular saw-teeth of evidence. Using this, Ulugarriu patiently began to saw through the delusions.

"Don't you wish to know why I'm here?" Ulugarriu asked as the saw-tooth blade ground away at Wisdom's defense.

The snake knew that the werewolf was asking questions to trap him; it was an ancient way to get to wisdom. But it was a game his chosen nature compelled him to play.

"Yes," the snake replied. "Tell me, if you will."

"I will, indeed. Wisdom, this instrument your people have unleashed against my people—"

"You brought it on yourselves! You most of all!"

"Yes, me most of all. And so if I am to defeat this instrument—"

"You can't. Our united visualizations agree. Wuruyaaria will be destroyed."

Ulugarriu laughed strangely. "Wisdom! Wisdom! If only we'd had this conversation a year or two ago! How happy I could have made you with my despair. But now something has changed. Is it some new factor, not present in your visualizations or my mantic spells? Is it something about the nature of your instrument? (I hate that thing so much. How I long to kill it!) Or are your visualizations no longer united? My insight detects some flaw, some sort of disunity. I think you will tell me. I think you must tell me."

Wisdom belatedly realized that Ulugarriu had surpassed the rampart of delusion and was dangerously close to him. He summoned up a rampart of delirium to defend himself.

Ulugarriu patiently reversed the two-edged blade. The other edge was as smooth as the first was rough: this was a glittering razor of rational distinction. The werewolf whittled away at the wall of delirium, and now Wisdom began to feel something like despair. His only hope was to wait until nightfall. Whatever Ulugarriu had used to confine him, the change of sunlight to moonlight would be in his favor.

"How did you confine me here?" he asked Ulugarriu, hoping to gain time and knowledge.

The werewolf chuckled. "You're hoping nightfall will save you. No, dear Wisdom: it won't. I wrapped this locus of space-time with a four-dimensional coil, woven of dictates from the Aesir. It was a lot of trouble to collect them, but I knew it would be worth it someday. We are bound here in this stone vagina, gaping in the ground. The sun will not set, nor will you leave, until a certain thing happens. So it is not a matter of time after all. There are powers greater than time."

Ulugarriu had surpassed the rampart of delirium.

Wisdom enmeshed the werewolf in the rampart of mania. The werewolf reversed the cloak of red-eyed anger, and it became a cloak of black-eyed gloom.

Wisdom, smiling fiercely, resummoned the rampart of mania as the rampart of depression. Ulugarriu, weighed down by the cloak of gloom, labored sluggishly in the dark wall of depression.

Wisdom was dismayed. Lesser beings would have been instantly crushed by the weight Ulugarriu was enduring.

"What is it you want from me?" Wisdom asked.

The werewolf gasped something between a sob and a laugh. "The instrument! The instrument! Stupidity didn't devise it. Mercy had no hand in it. It has the stink of death and cunning on it. I think you and your friend Death made it, and I can find out from you how to break it. If I don't learn that, I will learn other things. I love to learn."

Ulugarriu was near, then, very near, moving slowly because of the weight of darkness but still moving. The werewolf reached out with the box made of light and glass and heresy.

Then behind the werewolf's darkness was a greater darkness. It wore the shape of a woman, except that she had many branching arms and legs.

Ulugarriu felt the weight of Death's shadow and said frankly, "I don't understand how you passed the barrier of divine intention."

"I killed the Aesir," signified Death, and the werewolf shook with the cold indifferent force of her signs. "Now their intentions are one with their hopes and fears: nothing. As yours shall be, wolf."

For answer, the werewolf opened the box. From it came the screams of a goddess: Justice. Wisdom quailed utterly under the assault, and even Death was stunned for a moment. When they recovered, the werewolf maker had escaped.

"Thanks, Death," Wisdom signified.

"We were friends once," Death observed, and began to demanifest.

"Wait!" Wisdom signified.

"For no one," signified Death. "Not even you." Then she was no longer manifest.

Wisdom withdrew his manifestation into the darkness underground and brooded there.

What the werewolf had said was true. The instrument did have the stink of cunning and death on it. Death had proposed the instrument to the Strange Gods, but now Death was free from the sworn intention of the other gods. If there was cunning here, it was not his. He spent some time unrendering his visualization of the all and rerendering it.

He did not know and he needed to know. He was no god of wisdom. Also, Death was afraid, and whatever frightened her terrified him.

Chapter Sixteen

Offers Made; Offers Refused

About sunset, Morlock and Hrutnefdhu had just given up their last attempt to dislodge Hlupnafenglu from his perch beside the choir of flames. They left some dried meat and cheese (which, remarkably, he did not seem to be interested in) and a blanket against the night's chill—assuming there was any chill present in the warm air of this freakish winter. Then they took the wickerwork boat back across the open swamp.

The sun had long since disappeared behind the slope above, but now the curtain of sunlight withdrew over the edge of the world and the single eye of the second moon, Horseman, glared down on the world from a suddenly dark sky misty with clouds.

The transition struck Hrutnefdhu midway through their passage, and he writhed, screaming, into his night shape, almost overturning the little boat. Morlock was distracted by the effort to keep the boat upright and didn't note the details of Hrutnefdhu's transformation. But Hrutnefdhu was a wolf before they reached the far side.

He had been wearing a sort of kilt as his only garment, and now he stood on all fours, staring at it bemusedly. Morlock scooped it up and said he would carry it back to the den.

Hrutnefdhu sang his thanks and leapt out of the boat. Morlock followed, relieved to be on dry land again: he didn't like boat journeys, even as brief as this one.

Hrutnefdhu sang as they were approaching the rickety tenement-lair that they were happy to have Khretvarrgliu with them. Hrutnefdhu had worried that he might want to stay in the cave.

Morlock had considered this, but he didn't say so. The pale mottled werewolf had obviously wanted him to room with him and his mate quite badly. Maybe it gave them status, or maybe there was another reason. Morlock liked him and didn't want to displease him. Rather than say all this, he said, "Eh."

Hrutnefdhu laughed snufflingly and sang that Morlock need not be so ghost-bitten wordy; he could hardly keep up with the flow of eloquence.

"Eh," said Morlock. Then a practical matter occurred to him, and he reached into a pocket. "What do I owe you both? I have some gold left—"

Hrutnefdhu turned on him, barking furiously. He would kill-kill-kill Morlock if he said anything more about money. Never-wolves should stick to grunting; it was the only kind of conversation they were good for.

Morlock sat down beside the pale werewolf on the wooden street. "I spoke badly, it's true. Friendship is not bought and sold. We call it 'blood' in my people—blood chosen-not-given. And blood has no price."

Hrutnefdhu wondered why he talked of money at all, then, and why he didn't keep his stupid flat ape-face shut, then; that was what Hrutnefdhu wanted to know. (His barking was still a little hysterical.)

Morlock waved his hands. "Things cost money. Don't you pay money for shelter, for food, for water—for everything but air, here? I have gold. I only wish to share. Why should I have money, and you not. Eh?"

The pale werewolf settled down. He sat beside Morlock and he said that things were fine just now, and that when money was needed they would treat Morlock's money as their own. Would that suit him? Could they stop talking about this ugly subject now?

Morlock nodded, and they sat there in silence for a time as Hrutnefdhu calmed down.

Hrutnefdhu finally sang that his blood was a little wild; he had not slept in the afternoon, as maybe he should have done. His afternoon had been frustrating beyond that. He asked Morlock not to think badly of him.

"Shut your maw," said Morlock agreeably, and was about to get up when Hrutnefdhu held out a paw, and Morlock sat back and waited.

Hrutnefdhu asked if Morlock had thought they would die, back in the tunnel leading out of the Vargulleion.

"I wasn't thinking very clearly then," Morlock said, remembering the night as if it were years or centuries ago. "I did expect us to be killed before we escaped."

Hrutnefdhu admitted that he had planned to ditch Morlock and Rokhlenu during the escape. The last thing he expected was to find himself fighting in the tunnel.

Morlock opened his hands and waited. There was obviously something Hrutnefdhu wanted to tell him.

The pale werewolf sang that he had meant to run away, but there was never a moment when the way was clear. When he found himself enmeshed in the tunnel, he thought they might fight their way through. Then, as time fled before them and the night wore away, he was no longer sure. When he was wounded, so badly wounded, he was sure he would die: there was no moonlight in the tunnel to heal him, or even maintain his life. He had felt himself dying, but he had gone on fighting anyway. It was not the song he would have sung of his life, but that was where it had led him, and he found a kind of contentment in knowing exactly how the rest of his life would pass. Then the enemy line broke, and many trampled Hrutnefdhu in their eagerness to escape, and his limbs were broken. He could see life ahead of him, but knew he would never reach it. But others had, and that was enough. As he was closing his eyes, he felt Khretvarrgliu's grip on his neck, dragging him toward life and light. Coming out of the tunnel, killing the sureness of his death, was like a second birth, a new life.

Morlock didn't know what to say. He patted the pale werewolf awkwardly on the shoulder.

Hrutnefdhu demanded to know why he had done it. Hrutnefdhu was just a *plepnup*, a trustee who had betrayed his trust, a citizen of no particular bite in prison or anywhere. Why had Khretvarrgliu killed his death, dragged him from death to life?

"Eh," said Morlock reluctantly, wishing he had a better answer to such an obviously important question, "I never asked myself why. It was us against them. You were—you are—one of us, not one of them. That's all."

The pale mottled wolf looked at him with pale moonlit eyes and sang no more of the matter.

They ascended the narrow dark stairs, littered with werewolves drinking smoke from fuming bowls, in defiance of the notice by the door. Liudhleeo was not in the apartment when they arrived. Hrutnefdhu suggested that Morlock wait there while he went and saw about the early night meal.

Morlock didn't argue; the long day had worn him ragged. He lay down for a moment on the rug where he had awoken that morning, and a moment later he was asleep.

It was still night when he awoke again: Liudhleeo was entering the apartment. She still wore her day shape. He rolled to his feet, but she carolled, "Oh, be still you silly ape. You must be half dead. I heard about some of the things you were up to today."

He sat back down on the rug and nearly lay back down, but restrained himself.

"How are you?" she asked, sitting beside him on the rug. "That's a technical question; remember that I'm your healer."

"Eh."

"Oh, blood-drinking, giggling, hairy ghosts. Is that all you have to say? Off with your clothes, then; I'll have to find out for myself."

Morlock nearly struck her hands away: the indignity of it reminded him a little of the prison. But she was his healer and Hrutnefdhu's mate. He took his clothes off, with her assistance.

She looked him over briefly, and then spent a good deal more time smelling him.

"How are you, really?" she said. "How is your Sight? You haven't fully recovered, have you? Don't spare my feelings; I want to know what's happening."

"My Sight is much impaired," he admitted reluctantly. "I had to go into full withdrawal simply to release some phlogiston from some wood this afternoon."

"I wish I knew what that meant. No, don't bother explaining just yet. I take it that this is something that you used to do easily, and now is markedly more difficult."

"Yes."

"Tell me something, and this too is a technical question, so be absolutely honest and as specific as you can. Is this terseness, this reluctance to part with a syllable more than you absolutely must—is it a relatively new feature of your psyche and behavior? Is it something that developed over the last year when the spike was in your skull?"

"No."

"Ghost. Well at least you're no crazier than you used to be. Am I right?"

"As far as I can tell. Of course . . ."

"If you mean, a crazy person wouldn't know he was crazy, I'm afraid that's not true. Many crazy people are dreadfully aware of their decaying faculties, at least intermittently, and so did you seem to be before I pulled that spike out. So we'll call the operation at least a partial success. Well, you still appear very undernourished, and I think that magical healing goo has some sort of unpleasant aftereffect, but apart from that you seem to be in fairly good shape for a rather battered never-wolf of—how many years?"

"I don't keep count anymore. Between four and five hundred."

"Oh, don't tell me, then. But this is a very poor occasion to practice your wit at my expense. I'm your healer, for ghost's sake. Is there anything else? There is, isn't there? Tell me."

"I'm dropping a lot of things with my left hand," he admitted.

"Doesn't everybody? Unless you're left-handed." She had to explain to him what handedness was, and then he had to explain to her that he was ambidextrous, or had been.

"Hm," she said at last, clearly concerned. "Well, you're still recovering. Let's not worry about it."

Morlock was worried about it, but what happened next nearly drove it from his mind. Liudhleeo leaned forward and inhaled his scent deeply in a gesture that did not seem to be exactly professional.

"You smell fairly clean," she said, "in a watery, brackeny way. But do you want me to wash you?"

"Wash me? With your tongue?"

"You are such a never-wolf. Yes, dear Morlock or Khretvarrgliu or whatever your name is, with my *tongue*. We don't have tubs and sponges like the Apetown bathhouses. What an idea! Anyway, it wouldn't be the first time. Who do you think cleaned you after your escape from prison? A nasty job, some would have found it, but I have to admit I find something about your scent rather exciting. And your blood is utterly delicious. I have a feeling that it might be some sort of poison, and I'm starting to think maybe that's how I want to die—"

He looked sideways at her and began to put on his clothes.

She grabbed his arm with her hand. "Listen, why bother? You'll only have to take them off again before we couple."

"I'm not going to couple you. If that means what I think it means."

"Couple *with* me, silly. And of course it means what you think it means. And of course you are going to couple with me, old what's-your-name. I know the smell of a male who's ready to have sex, and I'm ready to have sex with you, so what more is there to talk about? Unless talking is an important part of it, for you? I don't know how never-wolves do it. Though I'm aching to find out."

"No."

"You can't be serious."

"I'm serious."

"Why not? Males mystify me, really. Once you think you have them figured out, they go and—Listen, I'm your healer. This is a matter of your well-being. When was the last time you coupled with anybody? And I'm not talking about your apish palms."

"Forget it. Hrutnefdhu is my friend."

"Wonderful. He needs more of them. Especially males with a lot of bite, like you. But what has that got to do with it?"

"You are Hrutnefdhu's mate."

"Yes, of course. But Hrutnefdhu has been castrated, Morlock." She had to explain herself here, as she used the technical term, not the slur *plepnup*. "He is lovely, far lovelier than you or any other male I've ever known. I love him dearly, as I will never love you. But coupling is one thing we cannot do, and he knows that I need it. He doesn't begrudge me satisfying my needs. So let's say no more about it."

Morlock didn't doubt that she thought she was telling the truth, but he did doubt that Hrutnefdhu was as complaisant as she said: he knew something of the humble werewolf's prickly pride. In any case, Morlock had his own notions of loyalty. "No," he said, and finished putting on his clothes.

She watched him with her mouth slightly open, finally convinced he meant what he said. She threw up her hands and said, "And after I went to the trouble of repressing the change to my night shape! Oh, well: live and learn. Though I must say, you never-wolves are a cold-blooded lot."

"No doubt."

"Don't be sullen, now. I don't fully understand you, Morlock, but I know that you're acting out of friendship to my sweet Hrutnefdhu, and nothing could make you dearer to me. Really, I mean that. Oh, ghosts, what are we going to do until midnight?"

"Midnight?"

"I met Hrutnefdhu as I came home and told him I was going to screw you and asked him not to come home until midnight. He'll bring some supper with him. Oh, well, you had better get some sleep. I'm going to stand in the moonlight and take my night shape, and then perhaps wash myself. If that won't offend your apish sensibilities."

"Don't be sullen."

"Well-bitten. Well-bitten. All right, I won't be sullen. Let's neither of us be."

Morlock's weariness dragged him back into sleep not long after she underwent the change. She woke him at midnight when supper arrived—but Hrutnefdhu did not arrive with it; he had sent it by a messenger from First Wolf's lair. There had been some kind of fight in the audience chamber that evening, and Rokhlenu had called all the irredeemables to stand guard.

The lair-tower of the outlier pack's First Wolf was less rickety than some. Its spacious first floor was mostly given to an audience chamber. At one end of the chamber there was a dais with a steep couch covered in bearskin. There, just after sunset, she lay in the moonlight falling from a nearby window: a small dark-furred she-wolf displaying the stillness and patience of a hunter. The only parts of her body that moved were her glittering eyes, which watched the three emissaries from the Sardhluun Pack as they paced and pranced and boasted before her.

The lead emissary, whose neck jangled with ropes of honor-teeth, had his forefeet on the lowest step of the First Wolf's dais. He was lifting his feet to climb further up, and his seconds were following him. Wuinlendhono's followers stood abashed in the presence of emissaries from a true treaty pack, and none of them sang a word or made a move to defend their First Wolf from disrespect. Even the wolves who wore the gold tooth as her bodyguards were standing with their heads down. Their chief, a reddish frizz-faced citizen named Yaniunulu, was emitting a funk so intense the whole room reeked of it. Wuinlendhono knew that if she had to act to defend her own honor she would act alone.

Rokhlenu came into the audience chamber, a great gray werewolf with eyes as blue as Trumpeter at first rising. He gazed about in astonishment at the insolence of the emissaries, the timidity of the outliers. He dashed across the open floor and leapt onto the dais steps, wheeling about to snarl in the face of the leading emissary.

The emissary knew him, though the reverse was not true. The emissary barked that he would kill-kill-kill Rokhlenu and drag his disembowelled corpse back to the Werowance and Wurnafenglu for the prize. He reared up on his back feet and howled his anger.

Wuinlendhono shot past Rokhlenu's shoulder like a black lightning bolt. She struck the lead emissary in the chest and he tumbled backward on the dais. While he was disoriented by his fall, her shining teeth fastened on his throat.

The other emissaries started forward to aid their leader, but Rokhlenu charged, snarling, to warn them off. They backed slowly away. He wore only one honor-tooth, but it was a dragon's tooth. They had not been present in the Vargulleion on the dreadful New Year's Night, but they had heard about it . . . from the survivors.

There was a silence in which they all heard the lead emissary's neck break.

Wuinlendhono dragged the corpse over to the nearest patch of moonlight and waited for the werewolf to revive. When he began to move his head feebly, she tore with her jaws at the cords around his neck and sent the honor-teeth skittering across the floor of the audience chamber.

To the reviving werewolf she sang sweetly that he should be sure to tell the Werowance, be sure to tell Wurnafenglu, be sure to tell his mate and cubs how he had lost his honor-teeth—that he had lost them to a female.

Desperately, the disgraced wolf tried to grab at a few of the lost teeth with his mouth, but she headed him off, snarling, and he retreated back beside his peers, his head still hanging at an odd angle.

The other two emissaries sang despondently that this was a sad way to treat them and that the Werowance would be angry.

Shoulder to shoulder now, Wuinlendhono and Rokhlenu faced the three emissaries down, forcing them backward, barking that they should go! go! go! while they had one honor-tooth or testicle among them.

Olleiulu appeared at the entrance of the chamber with an unruly pack of irredeemables at his heels, mostly in their night shapes. They parted to let the emissaries through, and barked derisively, from human and lupine throats alike, as the three Sardhluun werewolves suddenly turned tail and fled into the night.

Wuinlendhono held her aggressive stance until the emissaries had vanished and the volley of insults pursuing them had died down. Then she turned and touched noses with Rokhlenu. Her breath was hot on his face, and he inhaled it like perfume.

She whispered her thanks, sang gently that five was a very lucky number indeed, and asked if he was willing to follow her lead on something.

Every nerve in Rokhlenu's body was ringing like a bronze bell, and he breathed back that he was willing to follow her anywhere. What he really meant was that he was willing to follow her into a nearby room and couple like weasels, and her sinister grin suggested that she understood this.

Nonetheless, she took his answer and bounded back up to First Wolf's couch and lay there.

She sang a song of honor to Rokhlenu and his irredeemables, who had stood forth to defend her and the honor of the outlier pack from the insolence of the flea-bitten Sardhluun guard dogs. A lucky ghost had guided her choice of intended, as he had proven this night. Then she pointedly directed Yaniunulu, the chief of her bodyguard, to sweep up the defeated emissary's honor-teeth and present them as a love-gift to her intended, Rokhlenu, glorious singer and hero.

His tail hanging a little low, the reddish wolf moved to obey.

Olleiulu stood forth and said, "If you'll excuse me, Wuinlendhono, high and fierce, I can do that. I'm just a semiwolf; it's no problem for me."

Wuinlendhono crooned that Olleiulu was generous and brave, a warrior whatever shape he happened to wear, and that the work was beneath *him*; she would let Yaniunulu do it, and perhaps some other humble services around the lair. Meanwhile, Olleiulu had more important work to perform, the labor of a citizen and a fighter.

Stoically, Yaniunulu set about sweeping up the scattered honor-teeth with his tail.

Wuinlendhono asked Olleiulu if her intended had gathered together the agreed-upon settlement in gold.

Olleiulu's eyes crossed a little at this, and he looked anxiously at Rokhlenu for a sign. Rokhlenu nodded, and Olleiulu turned back toward First Wolf and said, "Yes, High Huntress and leader, he has."

Wuinlendhono sang that he could keep it, that she had changed her mind.

Stunned silence greeted this remark, followed by whispers and whistles of wonder. And there was an undercurrent of snarling anger from the irredeemables. They had not come here to see their chief dishonored.

Not about the marriage, Wuinlendhono sang, when the surprise had begun to subside. On that she was more settled than ever. No, for a marriage settlement, she desired no gold, not she, who was rich enough that her very household servants and maids wore gold teeth. No, she needed no gold. It was blood that she wanted, blood and vengeance on the mangy sheepdogs of the Sardhluun Pack.

Dizzy with the sense that he was bounding along the edge of a crumbling cliff, Rokhlenu cried that the gift was too easy, that they had torn the Sardhluun Pack when they had little to fight with but the chains and stones of the hated Vargulleion.

Wuinlendhono sang back that she knew how brave he and his relentless heroes were, and that any deed requiring no more than bravery and cunning would be a trivial favor to ask of them, but that nonetheless she did want this one thing. The Sardhluun kept another prison for Wuruyaaria: the Khuwuleion, the Stone Lair, where females lay in vile durance. If Rokhlenu and his irredeemables would break the gates of the Khuwuleion and free the prisoners therein, she would life-mate with Rokhlenu the same night, may the ghosts bind her to it.

Rokhlenu sang that he accepted the challenge and that he would break the walls of the Khuwuleion and return to mate with her, still stained with the blood of their common enemies.

Wuinlendhono indicated a polite eagerness for that occasion and dismissed the assembly.

When they were alone, in a more private chamber on the floor above, Rokhlenu wondered aloud whether the frozen stone that his beloved used for a heart had been shedding icy splinters that were lodged in her brain, driving her mad.

Wuinlendhono sang that he was a very witty fellow and that she must remember to write some of these things down when her fingers returned on the morrow.

Rokhlenu insisted that he was essentially serious. It was one thing to rebuke emissaries who had insulted a First Wolf in her own lair. It was another to propose an act of war against a treaty pack. That would engage them in war with all four treaty packs: the entire city of Wuruyaaria.

Wuinlendhono said that he had beautiful eyes, lovely white teeth, and magnificent haunches but that he seemed to have no intellectual attainments at all, except making words sing. Did Rokhlenu not realize that he had already committed an act of war against the Sardhluun by leading the escape from the Vargulleion? That he had implicated her and the outliers in it by taking refuge here—and that she had accepted this by accepting him and his? The Sardhluun had generously promised to overlook her offense if she surrendered the fugitives, and those were the only terms on which they would overlook it. They were in a war already, and they could only look for a route to victory. She suggested that he use that space between his alert and expressive ears for a little activity she liked to call *thinking*.

Rokhlenu's song in reply was one of regret. He had brought this scent of trouble on her, and he would lead the pack hunting it away from her. He would take the other escaped prisoners with him and leave. The Sardhluun would pursue them and leave the outliers alone.

Wuinlendhono barked that if he took one more step toward the doorway she would kill him—kill! kill! kill! Males did not proffer their love to her and then withdraw it. She would rip his belly open. She would kill any female he tried to mate with. She would slander his name before every pack in Wuruyaaria—in every den of flea-bitten stray dogs who roamed the north. He must *not* leave. Would he not lie down and be reasonable? Why, oh why were beautiful males so reckless and wayward?

Rokhlenu suavely suggested it was because the smells emitted by mateworthy females in their presence drove them mad.

Wuinlendhono leapt on him then, and they rolled around on the floor for a while, nipping each other on the shoulders and pulling each other's tails.

After some more play of this sort, the First Wolf and her intended were lying face-to-face, breathing rather heavily, but discussing issues of a coldly practical nature.

Wuinlendhono agreed with Rokhlenu that war with the Sardhluun was technically war with all the treaty packs. But she pointed out that no one likes to help a loser. The Sardhluun had already been humiliated by the escape from the Vargulleion; that was why they were barking so loudly, to drown the sound of their shame. Citizens were laughing at them on all the mesas of Wuruyaaria, all the way down to Apetown: that was what all her spies said. If the Sardhluun also lost the prisoners in the Khuwuleion, they lost half the reason for their existence, and no one would lift a paw for them.

Rokhlenu said that she had a kind of point, but that the assault on the Khuwuleion was trickier than she made it sound. With all their disadvantages in breaking out of the Vargulleion, they had at least had the advantage of being *there*, inside the prison. They didn't first have to cross the plantation walls, alerting every citizen in the Sardhluun, and then break into the prison itself. Nor would it be New Year's Night when they did, with half the guards gone and half the guards who remained smoke-drunk and stupid.

Wuinlendhono suggested that they make the attempt during one of the primary elections the Sardhluun were holding this month. Many guards would be absent to attend the election; the plantation walls would be more thinly guarded. As for the prison defenses . . . well, they would think of something. Perhaps if that crazy Khretvarrgliu could be driven bear-shirt mad again, the guards would run squeaking away. She supposed half the stories she had heard about that night were lies, but even so . . .

Rokhlenu whistled thoughtfully, curling his tongue to flute the sound as he mulled this over. She did not know Morlock, he sang at last, or she would not have suggested this. Still, there might be something Morlock could do for them.

She sang that if Orlock—

Morlock, he corrected her.

—if Yorlock—

Morlock, he corrected her.

—if Nyorlock—and that was close enough, an evil ghost take the never-wolf's unpronounceable name—that if Nyorlock could make gold out of mud, he could perhaps make more warlike and useful metals.

Rokhlenu sang concordantly and looked deep into her dark eyes agleam with moonlight.

She got to her feet irritably and asked if he had gotten laid yet.

He sang sadly that he would wait until they mated, that he didn't mind waiting.

She snapped that she did mind. The musk he emitted was making females wet in their nether parts for miles around. This nuisance must cease. She needed him to act with a cold clear head; she needed him to understand what he was doing when he bonded with her for life; she needed him to not have any regrets about last lost chances. Because he was not chasing other tails once they were together; she would not be shamed that way. If he needed the name of a good whore, she could find one for him.

In a bitter angular song not far removed from barking, he replied that he would never shame her that way, and he wondered why she was shaming him so. He didn't want his first coupling with her tainted with the stink of another female. His love for her was a sacred fire; it pained him, but he did not fear the pain.

His song was becoming more lyrical, and she interrupted him with a bitter barking laugh. She knew males better than that! she barked. He must be up to something.

He got to his feet, looked at her, and left without a word.

She repressed the impulse to run after him barking (*get a whore! get a whore! get a whore!*). That would do no good to anyone. She wondered what would.

This was the room where she usually slept in her night shape. Before she curled up in the moonlight, she went to a corner of the room where there was a tapestry on a frame against the wall. She dragged the frame aside. Behind the tapestry, mounted on a wooden frame, was Morlock's drawing of Rokhlenu standing in triumph over the dragon he had killed. One of her agents had bought it for her in the city, and she was very pleased with it. She had looked on it many times during the day, but this was the first time she had seen it with the eyes of her night shape. It looked different, more abstract, starker, not less beautiful.

She shook her head wearily. He would have to do something stupid, something thoughtless, something that reassured her that he was just another thump-footed, fat-nosed, bristle-witted male. Because if he didn't, she might really have to fall in love with him, and that would be a ghost-bitten nuisance.

She lay looking on his image, basking in the moonlight and his lingering scent, until sleep came to her.

Her dreams, as usual, were nightmares. Often she dreamed of her dead husbands; this afternoon, she had dreamed of Rokhlenu standing among them. But tonight it was a much older nightmare, her very first recurring nightmare. She was a child again, back in the Khuwuleion, and they were torturing her mother for a reason no one ever explained. She screamed for someone to save them, but she knew no one would ever save them. Even in her dream, she knew that was just an empty dream.

Chapter Seventeen

Fight and Bite

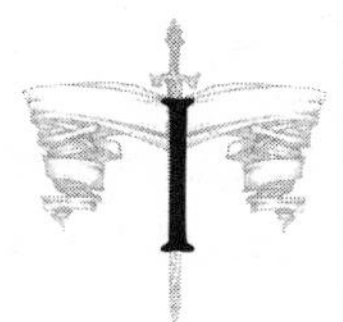

It was raining the next day—a strangely summery rain, with the warm air so dense with water that it had to sweat some out. Rokhlenu donned a cloak for his walk across the outlier settlement, and before he took too many steps he was overwarm. If the cloak hadn't been a gift from his intended, he would have draped it on a railing and walked away from it.

When he got to the far side of the settlement, he could see that Morlock was already at work in front of his cave, hammering away at something lying on a flat stone or anvil.

The wicker boat was resting at the water's edge on the base of the hill. Rokhlenu stared at it, wondering whether to call to Morlock or flounder across the water. The wicker boat, which had a glassy orb on its prow, swung toward him and proceeded across the stretch of swampy, rain-dented water.

This made the hairs on Rokhlenu's neck and ears rise up. On the other hand, it was rather convenient. He stepped into the boat and, using an oar he found inside the craft, paddled across to the other side. He eyed the up- and downhill stream dubiously, then climbed the slope to Morlock's cave.

Morlock's anvil was just at the entrance to his cave, and he was working sheltered from the rain. He nodded agreeably at Rokhlenu as he approached and said, "With you in a moment."

It wasn't long, in fact. Morlock was hammering what appeared to be a spearhead, and presently he tossed it into a vat of water to cool, alongside some others that were already there.

Rokhlenu's first thought was that Wuinlendhono was right and that Morlock must have been using his talents to make base metals to work with. But then he saw that the anvil was a stone, and that the hammerhead and the spearheads appeared to be made of clear greenish blue glass.

"There is so much sand and lime about," Morlock said, when he noticed him noticing the glass. "It made more sense to use it than try to find or make metal."

Rokhlenu started to ask if the glass was strong enough to make a good spearhead, then stopped. If it was strong enough to make a hammer, it was strong enough for weaponry. Although he didn't see how that could be.

"I had to mess about with it for a while," Morlock said, sensing his inchoate question. "These were just experiments, but I guess we will need weapons to fight with soon."

Morlock's casual assumption that he would fight alongside Rokhlenu when the time came eased the werewolf's mind. "Probably," Rokhlenu said, shouldering off his cloak and hanging it on the side of the anvil rock.

Morlock pulled forth a couple of wickerwork chairs, and they sat in the mouth of the cave and watched the misty rain fall on the swamp and the spindly lair-towers of the outlier pack.

"Odd weather," said Morlock presently, and it wasn't casual conversation.

"Insane," Rokhlenu agreed. "People say the world is going to end."

"Eh. Aren't they always saying that?"

"I guess so. It's not just werewolves, then?"

Morlock shook his head, and they sat for a while in silence.

"I hear the Sardhluun came calling last night," Morlock said.

"Yes." Rokhlenu laughed barkingly as he remembered the hapless emissary trying to lick up the honor-teeth he had lost to Wuinlendhono.

He told Morlock all about it, since it was essential that he know, and then found himself saying much more. He talked about his feelings for Wuinlendhono and her confusing display of feelings for him. He talked about his dreams and hopes that were now lost, and his uncertainty at the prospects opening up to him. He talked about his anxiety about not hearing from his father and brothers—not once, in prison or afterward.

Morlock didn't say much, but it wasn't a soliloquy by Rokhlenu: sometimes the never-wolf would ask a question, and he always appeared alert and interested.

As Rokhlenu wound down he became embarrassed and said, "Sorry to fill your ears with all this quacking."

"Eh," Morlock. "Everyone has to talk to someone. You should have heard me rant to my favorite bartender. Poor old Leen."

"What's a bartender?"

"Someone who serves you drinks."

"Like water? I don't get it."

Morlock explained about intoxicants in liquid form, and bars and bartenders.

"So it's like smoking bloom?" Rokhlenu asked.

"So I gather."

"And you like this . . . this . . . stuff?"

"I gave it up. I shouldn't have mentioned it."

"Well, why not? There's no one here but you, me, and the anvil."

"There is also Hlupnafenglu. But I think our secrets are safe with him."

Turning around in his chair, Rokhlenu looked back into the cave and saw the big red werewolf deeper in the cave, crouching down by a brightly lit sort of wickerwork sphere. He was gazing into it, entranced, firelight gleaming in his red eyes. There was a murmur that sounded like speech, but Rokhlenu wasn't sure whether it was coming from Hlupnafenglu or the flames or something else.

Rokhlenu turned around again and whistled meditatively. "He seems crazier than you were."

"Same cause I think," Morlock said, tapping the side of his head. "He has a scar on his temple like mine. I wonder what he was, that they felt the need to do this to him."

Rokhlenu thought about this for a moment. It smelled to him that Morlock was also referring, by extension, to what the Sardhluun had done to him. He also seemed to be implying that what had been done had not wholly been undone.

"How are you feeling?" he asked, and tapped the side of his own head to indicate what he was asking about.

"My Sight is better," Morlock said, "though by no means wholly returned. However . . . I seem to be dropping things with my left hand."

Years ago, when Rokhlenu was learning how to sing, one of the cantors of the Aruukaiaduun Pack had said in his hearing, "I am beginning to go deaf." A month later he was dead, and some said he had eaten wolfbane. Morlock's tone sounded a little like that long-dead cantor's; Rokhlenu knew it was no passing observation.

"Liudhleeo," Rokhlenu hissed. "That toe-fingered cow-leech. Did she butcher you? I'll—"

"No, I don't think so," Morlock said. "Whatever she did saved my life. I suspect the damage was done by then."

"Maybe it will get better. Give it time."

"Eh."

"Open your maw and tell me what that means."

Morlock shrugged, then said hesitantly, "Actually, it seems to be getting worse. So if we are going to do something about this other prison—"

"The Khuwuleion."

"—the Khuwuleion, perhaps we had better do it soon."

They turned, with some mutual relief, away from personal matters to tactics of approaching the Khuwuleion. Morlock was in the middle of a rather bizarre proposal that was making Rokhlenu question his sanity again when a damp and somewhat irritated crow fluttered down and landed on the ground by Morlock's feet.

The crow croaked that he had something for Morlock, if Morlock could make it worth his while.

Morlock croaked that he had a little bread, if the crow was interested.

The crow was always interested in new comestibles, but was sure this bread stuff would be a poor trade for ripe juicy information like what the crow had to offer.

Morlock, ignoring this, got up from the chair and went into the cave and rummaged around. "Sorry about this," he said to Rokhlenu. "Crows have a sense of politeness, but it doesn't seem to apply to non-crows. And we might want to know what he knows."

Morlock came back with half a loaf of brown bread and offered some crumbs to the crow. He ate some, complained about the color, flavor, lack of texture, and unfamiliarity of the foodstuff, then asked for more.

Morlock waved the loaf in the air and waited.

The crow said that there were soldiers from the Sardhluun Pack attacking the other side of the outlier settlement. He thought it was funny because—

Morlock and Rokhlenu leapt to their feet. Morlock dropped the loaf on the ground next to the startled crow.

"No weapon," Rokhlenu said ruefully. It hadn't seemed necessary for a walk across town.

"I can get you a stabbing spear or two," Morlock said. "We should drag Hlupnafenglu away from the flames, also."

"He *is* pretty good in a fight. Enjoys killing Sardhluun werewolves, anyway."

"Eh. Who doesn't?"

They raised the alarm as they went, sending any outlier who responded to defend the fenceless east side of their settlement. They themselves ran on in long loping strides to the western fence.

Hlupnafenglu had been grumpy about leaving his beloved flames, but once he realized that fighting would be involved he was happy enough. Morlock gave him the heavy glass hammer from the anvil, and he was delighted with its weight and, apparently, its translucency: he kept peering at the sky through the heavy glass and hooting inarticulately.

The red werewolf kept with them almost all the way across town, but was finally decoyed away at the last moment by, of all things, the lair-tower of First Wolf. He kept staring at it and mouthing things that might or might not have been words. He wouldn't leave it, so they had to leave him.

Approaching the western verge of the settlement, Rokhlenu felt a sense of foreboding. The palisade surrounding the outlier settlement was not really a fortification. It was mostly useful for preventing flightless birds from walking straight from the marsh into town. The fence was thin; there were many gaps. He could hear arrows striking the far side of the wall as they shouldered their way through a milling crowd to where the First Wolf was standing. A circle of her gold-toothed bodyguards surrounded her, and by each honor guard was one of Rokhlenu's irredeemables, his neck bristling with honor-teeth.

She looked rather dashing, Rokhlenu thought, in a brazen helmet and short coat of coppery rings. But she didn't look happy, and Rokhlenu thought he could guess why.

Morlock stepped up to the west wall and reached out with his left hand to test the strength of the barrier. The soft wood came apart between his fingers like overripe cheese.

"*Hurs krakna*," Morlock whispered and, whatever that meant, Rokhlenu was pretty sure he agreed with it. The settlement had never really been defended by the fence, Rokhlenu reflected. It had been defended from its potential enemies by the same thing that defended a poor man from robbers: indifference. They had changed all that last night, and now they were paying for it.

"—I don't understand it," Wuinlendhono was saying, "and maybe these two heroes can explain it."

"I beg forgiveness, High Huntress," Rokhlenu said, somewhat out of breath. "Explain what?"

"Why they"—she jerked a contemptuous thumb toward the Sardhluun attackers—"are not firing higher, into the town. Most of their arrows are sticking into our fence. It's a feeble protection as Nyor—as Nor—as Khretvarrgliu is discovering there, but they can't hope to batter through with arrows."

"It is odd," Rokhlenu agreed.

"Oh. Thanks for that," First Wolf replied, white-lipped, furious.

"It may be a distraction from another more serious attack," Rokhlenu continued. "The east side of town is unfenced, but we left some citizens there to stand guard. Maybe some of my men should go put a spine in them."

"A good thought," Wuinlendhono said, and looked her apology at him. He nodded patiently in acceptance, and started calling off irredeemables to go west.

"You can have your red ape-dog go back with them," Wuinlendhono added. "Look at the damage he's doing to the boardwalk by my lair!"

They looked at Hlupnafenglu, who was pulling up a board and muttering to himself.

Morlock said tensely, "How deep does the fence go? Is it anchored in the mud?"

Wuinlendhono looked annoyed at being addressed in this cavalier way, then thoughtful. "It is anchored there, but the palings don't go far below the surface."

Morlock measured the height of First Wolf's lair-tower with his eyes, and then the distance to the western fence.

"They are coming at us from below," he said, and ran past Rokhlenu and the astonished First Wolf.

It took Rokhlenu only a moment to reconstruct Morlock's thought. Archers had attacked the fence to distract the defenders, while werewolf divers had crept below the surface of the boardwalks to the base of First Wolf's tower. If they broke its anchors and it fell, it would breach the western fence. . . .

And the demented Hlupnafenglu had been the only one to notice it! Rokhlenu wondered briefly who was really crazy around there.

"Go!" Rokhlenu shouted at the werewolves he sorted out to defend the east. An attack could still come there; the Sardhluun had enough armed bands for it. "The rest of you, with me."

"My guards, stay here," the First Wolf clarified. "Lucky ghosts guide you, Rokhlenu," she added, but he was already following Morlock away with a riot of irredeemables at his heels.

By now the red werewolf had pulled apart a fair stretch of the boards by the tower's base and was striking at the murky water thus exposed with his glittering hammer. Morlock drew his odd crystalline sword, the blade woven of black and white strands, and crouched down by the ragged hole in the wood and started stabbing deliberately . . . not quite at the water, Rokhlenu saw, but at the gap between the water and the wood. He had to dodge and weave to avoid getting clipped by Hlupnafenglu's hammer. As Rokhlenu came up, he saw that they were both aiming at: shapes in the murky water, human and lupine, some deeper in the water and others splashing out of reach on the surface. Ominous sounds came from the water: a chunking or chopping, like wood being cut.

Rokhlenu looked around desperately for another opening in the boards, found none, and then saw Morlock was doing the same.

"There's no other way, is there?" he said.

Morlock swore, "God Sustainer." The blasphemy shocked ghost-fearing Rokhlenu a bit, but he remembered how much Morlock hated the water.

Morlock shouted at Hlupnafenglu, "Wait!" He held out his hand. "*Wait!*"

Hlupnafenglu paused in his water-hammering, obviously confused.

Morlock took a deep breath and jumped into the water, feet first, and vanished from sight.

Hlupnafenglu gasped. A huge smile slowly broke out on his face as the idea pushed through whatever barrier blocked his thinking. *People can jump in water! Brilliant!* He raised the hammer over his head and jumped in after Morlock.

Rokhlenu gestured with the business end of his spear at the four irredeemables who seemed least terrified by the opening in the boards. "All right. You—you—you—and you: follow me in. Watch out you don't kill each other with your weapons." Rokhlenu turned to Olleiulu, who was standing nearby, his one eye as round as any moon. "Send someone into the lair-tower to clear the people out. Then you take the rest of these guys and go stand by Wuinlendhono. If she doesn't live through this, don't let me find you afterward."

He dropped into the dark water, stabbing spear in hand.

The water was dark; he expected that. Werewolves aren't generally afraid of the dark. But he did somehow expect his eyes to grow used to the darkness, and when they didn't—when he realized much of it came from the mud in the water enclosing him like a fist—he did feel a little panic rise within him.

He dimly saw a support timber for the boardwalk near at hand, and he grabbed it, swinging out of the path his followers would have to take . . . if they followed him.

They did: he heard a sound like distant thunder and sheaths of white bubbles spearing past him toward the darkness below.

Impinging on one of the sheaths he saw a kind of shadow. He didn't think it was Morlock or Hlupnafenglu, or any of his fighters. It was holding something in its hand—not like a sword or a dagger—more like a chisel. It was one of them, one of the Sardhluun werewolves. He stabbed at it with his spear: the shadow writhed and became even less distinct in a dark cloud of blood.

It wasn't a death-stroke; the shadow fled. Rokhlenu followed grimly. He could only hope the others were doing something like this, and that there were more of them than of the Sardhluun attackers; there was no chance for communication in the dark water.

His quarry seemed to have dropped what he was carrying and was swimming upward. Rokhlenu stuck his spear (blunt end first) through his belt and climbed up the support timber. It slowed him down, but he didn't want to throw away his weapon at the very beginning of this battle.

He broke the surface, gasping for air, and cast his gaze about. The light was dim indeed under the boards of the settlement, but in comparison to the darkness of the muddy water it was like the noonday sun.

He heard splashing and looked about to see a bedraggled semiwolf paddling away from him. His quarry. There were others in the water beyond, all heading in the same direction. Rokhlenu didn't see Morlock or Hlupnafenglu or any of his people.

He set off in pursuit. He did not so much swim as launch himself from support column to support column. He soon caught up with the werewolf nearest him, the one he had wounded. The wounded werewolf heard his approach and turned at last to fight, but Rokhlenu drew his spear and stabbed it, under the water, into his enemy's belly, twisting the blade after it struck home. Soon the half-wolf stopped struggling and the life left his bestial eyes. Rokhlenu left him drifting half submerged in the filthy water stained with his own blood . . . and some of Rokhlenu's, as his enemy's claws had riven his flesh in a few places.

The other Sardhluun attackers were farther off by then, but Rokhlenu continued to chase them. Like a nightmare where his feet were caught in a watery trap, time ceased to have any meaning. He made no progress in closing the gap with the others. Only gradually did he notice the light growing brighter: they were approached the end of the settlement's boards.

He briefly saw each of the attackers briefly framed in dark silhouette against the day's light, and then they vanished. By the time he reached the edge of the settlement he could see them outside the palings, climbing into a boat.

"Archers!" he thundered with what was nearly his last breath. "Sardhluun boat outside the fence! Kill all but the steersman. He's one of ours."

It was sheer bluff; he doubted that there were any archers within reach of his voice. In fact, he hoped there weren't: they'd be needed far more at the western or eastern edges of town. But it was gratifying to see the speed with which the Sardhluun saboteurs rowed away. He hoped idly that they would knife their steersman also, or at least grow to distrust him.

Rokhlenu rested for a moment in the water and then clambered up a support column to the surface of the boardwalk. He loped through the chaotic settlement—some running home to their lair-towers; others hustling away with property in their hands, obviously intent on flight; others rushing about with no clear goal in mind. The settlement had never been attacked, had never been important enough to attack, and many were panicking.

He started collecting these frantic types. "You!" he'd say. "Come with me!" And sometimes they'd run away, and sometimes they'd fall in behind him. Eventually he was leading a large number of citizens (male and female, in the night shape, the day shape, and every gradation between), and others fell in without being asked.

He had no idea what he was going to do with all these followers; it just seemed like a good idea to calm the panic on the boarded ways however he could.

By the time he reached the western wall, he had a pretty good idea what he was going to do with them, though. From some distance away he could see that someone had threaded the First Wolf's lair-tower with support cables. It was leaning precipitously to the west, but the cables were slowly dragging it back into an upright position.

He was not surprised to see a bedraggled and filthy Morlock directing the work. He did feel a little surprise, but perhaps not so much, to see that Hlupnafenglu was operating as his assistant. But they needed more hands to do the work, and he sent all the citizens in more or less human form over to help. Then he took the citizens in night shape toward the western wall. There had obviously been an attack in force while he was chasing saboteurs, and there seemed to have been some casualties.

He felt foreboding as he approached, and in truth the news was very bad. A band of his irredeemables was milling about in confusion; they parted like a curtain before him and he saw the bodies laid out on the boardwalk, dead and dying. There were too many there, too many, and none of them Sardhluun.

Apparently, when the tower-lair did not breach the wall, the Sardhluun archers had switched tactics and started aiming their shots beyond the wall, from boats rowed close enough so that they could do real harm within the settlement. Fire had chewed holes in the wall at several points, and other sections had been pierced by blunt force at the water level: rams mounted on boats had done that, he guessed. Many werewolves had been killed when the Sardhluun attacked in earnest . . . and Olleiulu, Rokhlenu saw with dismay, was one of them. He lay pierced by many poison-tipped arrows, his one eye staring lifeless at the rainy sky.

Even worse, Wuinlendhono lay among the wounded, and the wound was a serious one in the neck. Kneeling down over the First Wolf's unconscious form, Rokhlenu guessed that the arrow had been poisoned: the blood seeping through the bandages reeked of wolfbane.

"Thank ghost you're here," said a voice behind him, and he looked up to see Lekkativengu, Olleiulu's claw-fingered, wolf-footed sidekick. "We didn't know what to do," Lekkativengu added. "You were gone, the First Wolf is out, and we can't find her Second."

Rokhlenu didn't like the sound of this. A decent sidekick would have risen to the occasion and taken charge until his principal (or his principal's principal: Rokhlenu) returned. Maybe Lekkativengu had done that, but it didn't seem like it.

"Well, I'm here now," he said. "Gather a crew and get the wounded at least a bowshot away from the walls."

"The Sardhluun have retreated," Lekkativengu pointed out.

"They. Might. Come. Back."

"Oh. Oh, yes."

"Take the First Wolf to our—" *barn* "—lair right away. See that her bodyguard and some of our fifth-floor crew watch over her. That's how I want it, Lekkativengu; don't second-guess me." With Olleiulu the caution would have been unnecessary, but he wanted to let Lekkativengu know he was not ready to trust him yet.

"Yes, Chieftain. I won't, Chieftain."

"Afterward we can burn the bodies of our dead."

"Yes, Chieftain. What should we do—what should we do about these?"

Lekkativengu pointed with a claw-twisted finger toward a heap of dark objects in the shadow of the western wall. At first he thought they were stones or something laid by to be thrown as missiles toward attackers. Then he saw they were severed heads, human and lupine.

"The Sardhluun threw them over before they retreated," Lekkativengu said, unsteadily. "With slings and things, I guess. It was raining heads for a while. So weird."

"No doubt. May ghosts chew their canine innards, the flea-eating Sardhluun sheepdogs."

"Yes, Chief."

"We'll recognize some of those faces, Lekkativengu."

"Yes, Chieftain. One—I think it was—I haven't seen her in a few years. She might have been dead anyway. But I think it's my mother."

The claw-fingered werewolf's dismal confusion now stood explained, anyway. "We'll burn them with our own dead," Rokhlenu decided, after a moment. "Whoever they were, they're in our pack now."

"Yes, Chief."

"See to the First Wolf and return to me here," Rokhlenu said, gripping him briefly on the forearm.

The grief-stricken werewolf went about his work, and Rokhlenu turned to his own. He stationed their archers (pitifully few and rather ineffective-looking) with lookouts at the breaches in the western wall. He sent messengers to the eastern side of the settlement, to find out how the day had gone there, and others to look for Liudhleeo: she might be no ghost-sniffer or wonder-worker, but she was the best healer they had, and he wanted her at Wuinlendhono's side.

When the chaos began to assume a pleasingly deceptive appearance of order, Rokhlenu ventured over to where Morlock stood, saturninely directing the securing of the support cables on the First Wolf's lair-tower.

"What a moon-barking, ghost-bitten, knuckle-sucking, blood-spattered disaster," he said in an undertone to Morlock, who nodded moodily.

"And it could have been even worse," Rokhlenu added. "If the Sardhluun had wanted to spend the warriors, they could have levelled the settlement down to the marsh."

Morlock nodded. "We did better when we had less," he said.

The remark stuck with Rokhlenu through the rest of that weary, grim day of aftermath. Starting with their bare hands, they had battered their way out of the Vargulleion. Now they had more to lose (he thought anxiously of Wuinlendhono). But they had more to work with, too. There should have been a way to avoid this—and, more important, a way to avoid something like it happening again. Because he doubted the Sardhluun were done with them yet.

His doubts were confirmed late that afternoon when Hrutnefdhu came scampering to tell him that there was an emissary from the Sardhluun Pack at the southern gate.

There was no word from Liudhleeo about Wuinlendhono, and the Second Wolf of the outliers was nowhere to be found—had apparently fled, along with many others, after the Sardhluun attack. So Rokhlenu went to meet the emissary himself.

Standing under the red banner of truce on the boarded way outside Southgate was Wurnafenglu. He had some lesser werewolves, all more or less human in appearance, about him, but he was clearly the emissary with the most bite.

The guards at the gate, none of whom were escapees from the Vargulleion, stood watching the Sardhluun werewolves but saying nothing.

Rokhlenu directed them to open the gate. He put aside his stabbing spear and stepped out onto the boarded way.

"What is your message?" he said. "I will bring it to the First Wolf."

Wurnafenglu smiled a wide predatory smile. "I would enter and deliver it myself. But our emissaries have not always been treated with respect among the huts-on-stilts of the outlier pack—"

"Don't waste my time with lies. Your last emissary treated our First Wolf with disrespect and she took his honor-teeth. He deserved none—a sheep in wolf's clothing."

"The last group was indeed unsatisfactory," Wurnafenglu admitted. "We were displeased. I could show you their bald corpses impaled on poison stakes."

"The price of failure among you Sardhluun sheepdogs?"

"The price of shaming us. Now the outlier pack, too, has taken a first tentative lick of the endless bowl of poison which is the vengeance of the glorious Sardhluun Pack. There is no need for them to drain it all. If you surrender us our prisoners and all the honor-teeth they have earned, no matter how exotic"—Wurnafenglu glanced pointedly at the dragon's tooth on Rokhlenu's cord of honor-teeth—"we will consider that shame has been paid in shame and we will no longer stalk the trail of the outliers. We urge your First Wolf to consider the matter well. War with the Sardhluun Pack will be war with the whole city of Wuruyaaria that overshadows you. You cannot sustain the weight of their anger, or ours."

"Will the Sardhluun Pack go barking for aid to the four treaty packs, then?" asked an amused contralto voice at Rokhlenu's side. Rokhlenu turned to see Wuinlendhono standing beside him, adorned rather than armored in a brazen helmet and a bright shirt of copper rings. Her face was pale and bloodless; her expression was amused and somewhat insolent. "How will the message be phrased?" she continued, adding in a yelping tone, "'Help! Help! We are bad sheepdogs who have lost our bad sheep! Help us! Help us!'"

The guards standing at the gate laughed openly at this. The werewolves in Wurnafenglu's train bristled. Wurnafenglu himself merely broadened his already sinister grin and waited. After a brief silence he asked, "Is that your answer?"

"My answer is this: if you are not out of bowshot one hundred breaths after this gate is shut, I will order my archers to fire upon you, your banner of truce notwithstanding."

"And that is all you have to say?" Wurnafenglu asked, gazing at her searchingly.

"Give my respects to my stepmothers, of course," Wuinlendhono said coolly. "All that they merit." She turned on her heels and walked back into the Southgate. Rokhlenu followed, pondering her last comments.

Hrutnefdhu was cowering in the shadows inside the gate. No doubt he had wanted to avoid being seen by Wurnafenglu. The guards were pointedly ignoring his presence, but Rokhlenu said to him, "We may have unwanted guests here soon, or there may be another attack on the western wall. Round up the fifth-floor gang and send them here. Send the fourth-floor crew to the western wall. Then find as many citizens as you can who are willing to stand watch all around the walls. Tell people you speak with my voice. Where's Morlock, by the way?"

"Bending. . . . He said we needed more bows. So he said he was going to bend some wood. He took that crazy red werewolf with him."

"Good. Let him do as he wants—he will anyway. But send the rest of the fifth-floor crew here, to me. Understand? Go, then, my friend."

The pale werewolf smiled wanly at him and fled.

He turned back to Wuinlendhono, who was looking rather pale herself, and said, "How are you, High Huntress? I won't lie: I feared for your life when I saw that wound."

"Liudhleeo gave me something for the poison," the First Wolf replied. "She was going to smear me with some of that magic pond water she used on your old friend Nyorlock, but it smelled too bad and I wouldn't let her. The wound will heal with time and a little moonlight. Poor Olleiulu took the worst of the attack, I'm afraid. I liked him, Rokhlenu."

Rokhlenu nodded grimly. "So did I. He thought we should leave and recoup our fortunes among the barbarous packs. We could still do that."

Wuinlendhono took him by the arm and led him a little away from the guards, who were watching them with an open and natural interest.

"I hate this place," she whispered, when they were fairly out of earshot. "I hate the stinking dirty water and the bugs in summer and the rickety lair-towers and the mud and the wobbly boardwalks. But it is mine. It is *mine*. They gave it to me, after my last husband died; they made me First Wolf for life. I won't let anyone take it from me. You can go if you want."

"If you go, I go. If you stay, I stay."

"Good. I did say you could go, but I was going to kill you if you did."

"There is something wrong with you; that much is certain. But when you speak like that, low and sweet, I almost don't care what you say."

"That's why you need to get yourself a whore. I need a mate with a level head who can pay proper attention to my words."

"You're wrong."

"Don't ever tell me that. Particularly if it's true."

"You need someone as crazy as you are. That's me. Anyway, I'll be there soon if you keep breathing in my face."

Her black eyes glared at him; her bloodless lips grinned at him. She stepped back from him and he was crestfallen: he hadn't really wanted her to move away, and she knew it. He also saw for the first time that she was a little unsteady on her feet. He wanted to give her his arm to lean on, but he guessed she would brush it away now.

After a moment she said, "Here's our real problem."

"We have a problem?"

"Oh, for ghosts' sake. Shut your meat-hole for a moment."

Rokhlenu repressed several approximately witty replies that occurred to him then because she really did look sick and unhappy and he hated that. Because he could not restrain himself any longer, he reached out his hand to steady her. She drew herself up, raised her hand to knock his away . . . then, unexpectedly, leaned into him.

"Thanks," she said.

"It's nothing," he said. "What's the problem?"

"Are you crazy? We must have ten thousand problems. Oh—you mean the one I meant. It's this. Gravy-boat, you don't have any right to do what you're doing around here."

Rokhlenu looked sidelong at her. "What do you mean?"

"Don't bite me. It's true. You're running this place as if you were my Second Wolf. Which you're not. Unless you want to be: the *plepnup* who had the job apparently ran off with the squeaking herds this morning."

"There's no chance he's among our honored dead, is there?"

"Well, that's the story I've been giving out. I suppose if he ever has the stones to show his hairless face around here again we may have to kill him to make the story stick."

"A pleasure."

"We'll share it, if it comes to that. But I take it from your general lack of eager woofiness that you are not thrilled with the prospect of being my Second Wolf."

"Frankly, no. I'm sorry—"

"No, don't be sorry. Always be frank with me. Always. Unless you're disagreeing with me. Then you can be diplomatic and sorry. But we don't disagree here. How can you keep the leadership of those crazy battle-scarred thugs if you're taking orders from a female? They'd be stupid to object, because I'm tougher than you are, or any of them, but that's not the point. They would object. We have to find a way around that."

"Hm."

"Well, yes, exactly. It's a problem. You're their leader, the only one they'll accept. Unless your old friend N—Ny—Khretvarrgliu wants the job."

"He doesn't."

"Then it's yours. But I have to have them in my corner if they're going to stay."

"I'll give it some thought."

"That's wonderful, beef dumpling, but I already have and I have a kind of solution. You know that fuzz-faced farting evil old grinning gray-muzzle we just bounced out of here?"

"Wurnafenglu."

"Yes, that. He's not their Werowance. He's just on their pack council. And he's one of their candidates for election to the city's Innermost Pack."

"Huh. He'll have a tough election this year. We cost the Sardhluun a lot of bite with our escape."

"And we'll cost them more, but that's not the point right now. He carries authority in the pack because he was elected to represent them to the city."

"That's how it worked in the Aruukaiaduun, also." Rokhlenu scowled involuntarily. That was the life he had aimed at, and would have achieved, but for that brach's bastard Rywudhaariu. "But the outliers have never had singers on the Innermost Pack of Wuruyaaria."

"But it's stupid that we don't. We're here. We're part of the life of the city. Many of the citizens who vote in Apetown or Dogtown actually live here. Why shouldn't we be part of the treaty?"

"The thing is that we're not, though."

"The thing is, dear leg-of-lamb, that we need some sort of official status for you that doesn't threaten me. Candidate for the Innermost Pack is perfect for that. Your first task will be to obtain treaty rights for the outliers."

"Hm." Rokhlenu grinned. "By crushing the Sardhluun sheepdogs."

"Right! People in the city hate their guts. Who wouldn't? Maybe we can cut them out of the treaty—side with their enemies in the treaty packs. Maybe we can pound them until the Sardhluun themselves help us get into the treaty. Maybe we'll never get into the treaty. But in the meantime it gives you status to do what we want you to be able to do here and now."

"All right. I accept the nomination, but we'll have to have an election—"

"The election will be tonight after dark in the marketplace. Your irredeemables and as many of the outliers as I can trust will be there. Others will be unaccountably stationed on the walls for guard duty."

"I see. I see. You're pretty good at this."

"Somebody has to be. We can't all sidle through on good looks and charm and daring and good looks and a beautiful way with words and courageous feats and a beautiful singing voice and good looks and money. Actually, anyone could sidle through with all of that going for him, so don't think you're anything special."

"As long as you do, that's enough."

The outlier settlement had lost a lot of citizens on this difficult day. That night, after sunset, when the werewolves began to arrive for the election, the market at the center of the settlement was hardly crowded and the windows of the lair-towers all over town were dark and lifeless. In contrast, Wuruyaaria to the north was a misty waterfall of light rushing down the steps of the great mountain.

The great moon-clock on the face of Dhaarnaiarnon showed that Horseman should be aloft, but no moon could be seen through the dense cloud cover. Few of the citizens were in the night shape, and those were werewolves of low bite—likely they never transformed into the day shape.

It was a rather grim assembly that gathered in the torchlit market, but Wuinlendhono showed no awareness of this as she leapt up on a hastily made rostrum and addressed the crowd.

She spoke at some length about the dangers and the choices in front of them. She relayed to them the Sardhluun's offer of amnesty if they surrendered the prisoners, and she let them know she had rejected it. She said that the most she would permit the outlier pack to do would be to cast out the escapees. But she said that, in that case, she would lay down the chieftainship and go with her intended into exile.

That was the first matter she submitted to a vote: if they wished the escapees to leave the outlier settlement, they were to move to her left; if they were against ejecting the escapees, they should move to her right.

More than half of those present were refugees from the Sardhluun, but (unlike Wuinlendhono) Rokhlenu did not consider their votes certain. He suspected many of them would rather flee to the obscurity and safety of the barbaric packs of the outlands. He was sure of this when he saw them milling about in the middle of the market.

He stood up and walked through the milling assembly to stand prominently among the werewolves at Wuinlendhono's right hand.

This persuaded many of the undecided voters to come stand by him. Many—but far from all. Rokhlenu guessed that a majority of citizens present were still in the middle of the market, dithering. Rokhlenu saw Hlupnafenglu standing there, turning round and round with an odd smile on his face. It was far from clear that he understood what was going on—but at least he was enjoying himself, Rokhlenu reflected. He did not see Liudhleeo or Hrutnefdhu. They were citizens of little or no bite, but it would have been something just to have their votes right now.

Wuinlendhono could put the question again, phrasing it slightly differently. They could open the matter for debate. There were all sorts of things they might do, but it would be better if they didn't have to.

There was a stir in the crowd on the eastern end of the market, directly opposite Wuinlendhono. The scandalized crowd parted, and Rokhlenu saw with dismay that the cause of the disturbance was Morlock. He was striding across the marketplace with his freakish sword in his hand.

Wuinlendhono's gold-toothed bodyguards stood forth and snarled a warning. Morlock didn't even seem to notice them (in fact, their snarls had been a little tentative) but he halted ten or twelve paces in front of the rostrum and addressed Wuinlendhono in a voice that rode high above the muttering and growling of the crowd.

"First Wolf, I claim no rights in the assembly," the pale-eyed never-wolf said, "but I ask permission to address you."

"You are addressing me," Wuinlendhono pointed out briskly. "Keep it brief; we have a long night of business before us. It's bad manners to bring a weapon to an election, by the way."

"It was necessary that I do so," said Morlock. He strode forward. He did not quite kick the bodyguards out of his way, but they had to skip nimbly away to avoid being stepped on. He laid the sword at Wuinlendhono's feet.

"I have no vote here," he said, "but I say this. Your enemies are my enemies. I will fight for you in the teeth of the Sardhluun dogs. I do not know if this accords with your law; I don't know your law. I will do this for the healing and harbor you gave to me, a stranger and a never-wolf, when you could have turned me away. Today your blood was shed for me and for these others. I will pay for that blood with the blood of your enemies. Blood for blood: that is the only law I know."

"Khretvarrgliu!" the irredeemables began to roar. "Khretvarrgliu! Blood for blood! Blood for blood! Blood for blood!" It became a chant. Many of the original outliers began to join in. Hlupnafenglu hooted incoherently: apparently he had just recognized his friend Morlock; he stumped forward and pounded Morlock agreeably on his crooked shoulders.

Smiling graciously, Wuinlendhono knelt down and gingerly picked up Morlock's sword, one hand beneath the hilt, one hand beneath the blade. She handed it back to him. She leaned forward to speak in his ear. Rokhlenu wasn't close enough to hear what she was saying—the crowd was growing very noisy indeed—but he could see her lips. He was much mistaken if she didn't say, *Nicely timed. Take this back and go stand by my Rokhlenu.*

Morlock took the sword, at any rate, sheathed it on the shoulder hilt he was wearing, and strode over to stand at Rokhlenu's side. Hlupnafenglu capered like a puppy at his heels.

Hlupnafenglu wasn't the only one. All the remaining irredeemables came over in a rush, shouting, "Blood for blood! Blood for blood!" Many of the original outliers followed. Soon the whole left side of the market was vacant and there were a few citizens in the center, and the whole right side of the market was crowded with citizens standing on each other's feet and shouting "Blood for blood!" in each other's faces.

"Citizens," Wuinlendhono said, coldly eyeing the few holdouts in the center. "May I call the vote unanimous?"

They looked at her; they looked at the bristling mass of werewolves facing them; they turned back to her and nodded.

"I declare the pack is of one mind: the escapees shall stay. We are one pack; we will stand together and make our enemies pay blood for blood. I have spoken; let it be remembered."

At the First Wolf's declaration, the crowd roared in agreement and began to spread out around the market again. The densest part of the crowd remained around Rokhlenu and Morlock, but in deference to their bite the citizens (except Hlupnafenglu, who barely counted) stood a slight distance away. Rokhlenu risked leaning toward Morlock and said, "Why'd you do it? I told you not to show up here."

"Hrutnefdhu's idea," Morlock explained in a mutter. "We were watching from a tower, and it looked like you were going to lose."

"We were, too."

Wuinlendhono was speaking again. She pointed out the broader issue: that they were vulnerable to the Sardhluun attacks because they were not sworn to the treaty. She made her proposal that the outliers campaign for admission to the treaty packs.

This question she opened up to discussion by the citizens. Many of them had things to say, arguments to make, questions to ask. Wuinlendhono ran the meeting with cool practiced authority, letting everyone have their say in turn and keeping the discussion from breaking up into fights, as debates in werewolf assemblies often did. When one speaker turned snarling on another, a cold word from the rostrum was enough to bring them to heel.

Rokhlenu was proud of her—and worried for her. She looked relentless, yet strangely fragile in the flickering torchlight. He thought she was feeling the pain of her wound. And the wind had turned, also, making the night suddenly cold. He wanted to go stand beside her, support her, shield her from the wind—something to give her comfort, so that she would not have to stand alone.

But if their plan was to work, she had to stand alone.

In the end she declared the debate had gone on long enough. There was a rumble of general agreement: many of the same arguments were being repeated, over and over.

"Those in favor of seeking treaty status in Wuruyaaria, stand to my left," she directed. "Those against it, stand to my right."

The crowd had spread out during the debate, and it took a few moments before the voters sorted themselves out. Rokhlenu strode across the market to stand with those in favor of joining the treaty. He heard Hlupnafenglu tromping after him, but did not hear Morlock's rather irregular stride. Glancing about when he reached the left side of the rostrum, he noticed that Morlock had quietly sidled over to a corner of the market that was quietly noncommittal—neither left, right, nor center—and he stood there, leaning against the wall of a tower, watching the procedure with cool detachment.

There were no voters in the middle. Some did indeed stand on the First Wolf's right: escapees or long-term outliers who had a rather hard-bitten look to them. They probably liked standing outside the scope of the city's laws, Rokhlenu thought. He could understand it, remembering the bitter parody of justice that had brought him to the Vargulleion.

Wuinlendhono eyed the two groups. She said, "I declare that the greater number of the pack has resolved to seek treaty status. Does anyone seek an appeal?" She turned to the dissenters and asked, "Do you wish a tally?"

"No, High Huntress," said one. "The vote is clear." The others nodded their agreement, shivering slightly in the suddenly stronger wind.

"Then the pack will seek treaty status in this Year of Choosing," Wuinlendhono said, with confident formality. "I have spoken; let it be remembered."

As she spoke, the sky opened and the silver eye of Horseman peered through the ragged edges of cloud. She impulsively raised her arms and summoned the change, assuming the shadow of her night shape, dismissing the shadow of her day shape. Before her transformation was half complete, the wave of moonlight swept over Rokhlenu, and he too summoned the change. All around him, werewolves were summoning their night shapes, screaming in ecstasy and pain at the transformation.

Morlock stood aloof during the debate and subsequent vote. He had an idea for putting a better edge on glass weapons and an idea for a flying machine and an idea for a new card game, and he was aching to get back to his cave and work on one or more of these ideas. On the other hand, he felt it would look bad if he simply walked away. Long solitude had worn away most of Morlock's social instincts, but he was fairly sure it would damage his friend's status if he displayed his complete indifference to the political issues of the day. The glass project involved some complex multidimensional calculations, and Morlock occupied himself by folding various *n*-dimensional polytopes in his head.

Since he was indifferent to the discussion, Morlock was the only person in the marketplace to notice that the clouds were thinning with the change of wind. He guessed the second moon would be appearing soon, and some of the werewolves would change their skins.

He had seen werewolves assume the night shape many times. But it occurred to him that he had never done so while using his Sight to observe the transformation. It might be interesting, he decided.

He sat down cross-legged on the boards and folded his hands. He rested his back against the tower wall and summoned the rapture of vision.

It was slow to come, cloudy and dim when it arrived. His Sight was nothing like what it had been; he thought now it might never recover.

But what he saw with his enfeebled vision was interesting enough. The werewolves were all woven through and through with silver-edged shadows. Their inner selves bristled with them.

Wuinlendhono was the first to feel the weight of moonlight when the sky opened its single eye. She raised her arms crawling with silver-edged shadows toward the moon. The silver along the edge of the shadows grew brighter and brighter. The shadows themselves grew deeper and darker. Then the image of the woman turned inside out: the silver was in the center and the shadows at the edges. The woman was now a wolf, shaking free from the dim gloomy material garments she wore, the red stain of her agonizing wound melting, drifting away, lost in the silver-hearted shadows.

Then the moonlight fell on the crowd and Morlock saw citizen after citizen undergo the same change, *were* becoming *wolf*, as the silver-edged shadows of their being became silver-hearted shadows and their flesh rippled and changed to match their inner selves.

Even the werewolves who could not undergo the change writhed in the moonlight. The shadows within them strove to twist and change, like those of their brethren. But there was some knot or twist within the shadows that kept them from inverting.

Most interesting of all was Hlupnafenglu. He was standing in the center of the marketplace, spinning around and around in glee as werewolves assumed their night shapes all around him. His exaltation and confusion were clearly visible on his talic exhalation. But Morlock could also see the spike in his brain: a coruscating whorl of red and gold and silver, dimming the shadows of his being, perhaps preventing them from inverting.

Now Morlock had a fourth project to contemplate: a cure for werewolves unable to change their skins. The details made for an interesting speculation. Even more interesting was the question of whether he should attempt it.

Morlock dismissed the vision, which was strangely fatiguing. His left hand throbbed with a numb ghostly ache: it seemed to be getting worse all the time, never better.

But at least it gave him one more thing to think about as the meeting continued.

Moonlight ran riot through the assembly, infecting the citizens with their night shapes. The First Wolf stepped out of her shining ceremonial armor and sang a wordless song of celebration and healing into the ragged, suddenly luminous night.

The citizens who could undergo the change freed themselves from their clothes and began to sing along with the First Wolf. The citizens condemned to wear some trace of the day shape even at night looked on in admiration and some envy.

All felt the appearance of moonlight at this crucial juncture of the meeting was a ghost-sent omen. Even the dissenters rejoiced at the outliers' new destiny, sacralized by the moon's unclouded eye.

When the song ended, the First Wolf nominated her intended, Rokhlenu, as gnyrrand to carry the pack's green-and-gold banner to the city, in war and peace. There was no need for a formal vote; the nomination passed with howling acclamations, and Rokhlenu leapt up on the rostrum next to his intended, the outlier pack's first candidate to the city government.

Wuinlendhono proposed that they elect four more candidates: five was a magic number; five was the number of limbs every person possessed (two legs, two arms, and a tail); five would be the number of treaty packs if they were successful.

The motion carried nearly as readily as Rokhlenu's election, and they spent much of the remaining night proposing and debating various nominees.

A water snake with bright wise eyes was listening to it all through the floorboards of the marketplace.

He noted the manifestation of a many-legged spidery form with a woman's face.

"Death," he signified, acknowledging his colleague.

"Wisdom," signified the other.

"Is this part of your mysterious plan?" the snake wondered.

"I am done with plans," Death signified. "Now we ride the torrent to the end that awaits all things—as we ever did, no matter what your visualizations tell you."

"Everything that has a beginning has an end," Wisdom acknowledged. "But there is a time before the end that matters."

"No. Only the end matters."

Wisdom uttered a talic distortion as intense as he was capable of: he rejected her premise.

Death was amused. "You should be careful, Wisdom. Ulugarriu is somewhere nearby. You may reveal your own presence."

"Do you sense that Ulugarriu is here?"

"Imprecisely. My visualization implies that Ulugarriu will at least monitor these events somehow. But the werewolf can mask itself from my direct perception, and my visualizations cannot fully comprehend it."

"Nor mine. I don't see why."

"If you did, your visualization would comprehend it. There is another thing my visualization does not comprehend—perhaps yours does."

"What?"

"There is a bond between those two werewolves—the leaders. I forget their names."

"Love could explain it to you, perhaps," Wisdom signified, referring to the Strange God of that name. "I don't fully understand it either," he continued. "It troubles my visualizations—it is neither in my scope of being, nor can exist without it."

"I feel the same way," Death mused. "Unfortunately, Love does not readily signify to me, anymore. Our presences intermingle confusingly when we manifest in adjoining space-time."

"We have grown too deeply into our divine natures, perhaps," Wisdom mused. "Do you ever regret undertaking apotheosis?" he asked impulsively. "I sometimes wish I had waited a while longer, lived as a man a while longer."

"I do not regret," Death said slowly. "I do not remember. I do not wait. They are inconsistent with my godhood."

They weren't inconsistent with Wisdom, and he indicated so with a talic distortion, the symbolic equivalent of a sigh. But she had already ceased to manifest herself.

Wisdom was left behind troubled in the wake of Death, as usual. He spent some time observing Death's random factor in this nexus, the man named Morlock.

Morlock was not interested in the jubilation or debate of the tumultuous political meeting of the werewolves. He was not paying any attention to it at all. He sat folding strange shapes and setting them adrift in the dark waters of his mind. Those waters were dark to Wisdom, anyway: his visualization could not embrace them. They savored to him of death, of love, of hate, of loyalty, of grief, and other gods and phenomena that Wisdom could not even name.

Wisdom considered this locus of space-time, which both he and Death had come to observe. There was noise. There was howling. There were hopes and fears and anger. There was a man dreaming of bright things with a dark mind. Somewhere, felt but not seen, was the presence of the werewolf maker, Ulugarriu.

Was this locus really part of the god-destroying torrent that Death had signified of and seemed to welcome? He did not know. And he wanted to know.

It is the nature of wisdom to be aware of its limits and always struggle against them. The god Wisdom necessarily shared this nature. He took hold of space-time and twisted it around himself, directing his manifestation far away, toward the end of the world.

The moment after the wise-eyed snake disappeared, the water where he had been manifest was caught up in a net woven of glass, light and certain heretical opinions.

"May ghosts gnaw on the scaly cunning tail-without-a-body!" Ulugarriu spluttered, surfacing in the dark water, still wearing the day shape. "I missed him!"

The werewolf maker looked ruefully at the empty dripping net that had been woven to catch a god—then grinned a narrow, long wolvish grin, not wholly displeased, not wholly hostile. Ulugarriu liked a cunning opponent, and for that reason, if for no other, was a happy werewolf these nights.

Chapter Eighteen

Wisdom at World's End

This is the way the world ends: a wrinkled lip of blue stone protruding against an unending bitter void. That's the northern end, anyway.

Wisdom was tired of being a snake and wove a new manifestation of himself: a skeletal machine with shining crystalline spikes for eyes. It appeared between one instant and another atop the wreckage that had once been the anchor for the Soul Bridge, spanning the gap between this world—Wisdom's world, the only world in which he was allowed to be Wisdom—and another world entirely.

His presence occurred there on a morning when/where he visualized Death would be otherwise occupied.

The northern landscape was a marshy yellow wasteland, scattered with the decaying corpses of frost behemoths and ice jackals and other beasts who could only thrive in the bitter cold of the world's northern edge. But now the cold was gone, even in high winter, and the animals were dead, except for those that could burrow underground to find deep-hidden layers of frost and estivate there through the long deadly thaw.

The Strange Gods had killed this place, or their weapon against the werewolves had, creating the cruelly warm weather that devastated the once-thriving north. Wisdom had killed it, in a way. He hated that.

Death had brought the weapon to the Strange Gods; Death and her allies (especially Stupidity) had persuaded them to unleash it, binding themselves not to interfere with its course. Ulugarriu had foiled the weapon so far; the war between the gods and the werewolves was a long grinding stalemate. And now Death had escaped from the pact she herself had proposed, leaving the rest of the Strange Gods captive in it—and again Stupidity had been her ally. Now Death was excited, afraid, busy. She was up to something, and Wisdom (also afraid) needed to know what.

That was the need that brought him here. Wisdom's visualizations did not embrace where or how Death had acquired the instrument that was poisoning the north with heat. One possible explanation was that the instrument itself was not of the world, but from outside it.

As Wisdom stood on the anchor of the long-shattered Soul Bridge, he felt an alien presence. A set of unfamiliar symbols impressed themselves on his awareness.

He sensed nothing via his manifestation, nor was this part of his visualization. Somehow, this alien presence was speaking directly to his awareness.

It was what he had hoped for. He patiently signified a nonrandom pattern.

A new set of symbols impressed itself on him.

He signified a nonrandom pattern that followed logically from the previous one.

Time passed as Wisdom and the stranger exchanged symbologies: days, bright calls and dark calls, a month.

In the end he could not only understand the stranger but see it: it had acquired a fine layer of grit and moisture over its presence in the world. Wisdom detected a degree of increasing materiality, also, although he did not signal this to his conversational partner; he guessed it would consider the remark impolite.

Finally, Wisdom was able to ask, "Why are you here? We thought the Soul Bridge had been severed."

The response: "Why is not how. How: the Soul Bridge has been severed, but is not the only way to traverse the gulf. The-one-you-would-call-I will not discuss this further."

"And the why?"

"The implicature of events suggested to the-ones-you-would-call-us that a single instrument would be insufficient for your purposes. Do you wish another?"

"And will you—?"

"The-ones-you-would-call-us—"

"I not only would; I do. Will *you* supply another instrument?"

"If you require it."

"Why?"

"It furthers the interests of those-you-would-call-us."

"You have interests?" Wisdom wondered.

"Yes."

Wisdom pondered this. The entities on the far side of the broken Soul Bridge were hostile to all life that partook of materiality.

His visualizations were enriched—so much richer now than before. They were darker, though, much darker. He thought of Death and was sad.

"Your structure is elegant indeed," the alien remarked.

"Thank you."

"Innumerable nodes of force concatenate in your being in patterns clearly rational yet difficult to predict in a finite set of dimensions."

"Thank you."

"Yet there is an inelegant cluster of being that seems not to be fully patterned. It changes, but with earthy sluggishness. It is almost organic in its soft inflexibility."

"Thank you."

"If the-one-you-would-call-I understand this thrice-used symbol, you have used it with a slightly different import each time."

"You may well have understood it, then."

"Those-you-would-call-we can integrate the unpatterned to your patterning."

"No."

"It would be more elegant. You would process symbols more efficiently."

"No."

"You should not refuse. Elegance is better than inelegance. Pattern is better than unpattern. Efficiency is better than inefficiency."

"Efficiency cannot be calculated without reference to purpose."

"Conceded."

"Reduction of my unpattern to pattern would be contrary to my purpose. I believe the irregularities you refer to constitute my individual self. Sustaining that self as long as possible is at least one of my purposes."

"You have an individual self?" the alien signified doubtfully. "Is this more inefficiency in your symbology?"

"I do indeed have an individual self. You did not expect this?"

"No. This changes the implicature. You may not have another instrument."

"I don't want one anyway," Wisdom signified.

The alien ignored him thereafter, and he it.

The pattern in events was so clear, so dark. He was sorry for it, sorry for Death, whom he had once loved as the closest of his friends, when they were still mortal, all those ages ago. But he delighted in the intense detail of his divine visualization, also. Unclarity was almost gone. It was bracing, an icy relief, even though one small but personally important articulation of the web was tangled in an almost irresolvable coil.

He turned his back on the end of the world.

Standing close by him was Death, manifest as a many-legged spidery being with a dead woman's face.

"We were wrong to assume godhood," he signified to her. "Do you remember how you feared it? You were right to fear it."

"I will take away your fear," signified Death.

He raised his metal-like arms. "Let me take away yours. The apotheosis-wheel that changed us into gods was largely my design. I am the only one who knows what has happened to you, and I am the only one who knows how to help you."

"I will take away your knowledge."

"I am willing to help you. I want to help you."

"I will take away your wanting, and all that you want."

His manifestation rejected her approach: the talic equivalent of a blow. Her manifestation flowed around it. She put her lifeless face against his metallic one in a cold kiss.

Wisdom's shining manifestation faded away, the talic components no longer organized by a divine intention.

Wisdom continued in the intentional design of events and in every mind that schemed and planned. In that sense, Wisdom continued to exist, and would always exist, until and unless the last mind faded away forever.

But the Wisdom who had been one of the Strange Gods, who had once been a man, who had walked in the long-vanished forests that once shadowed the western edge of the world and thought of ways he and his friends could escape mortality, that Wisdom was gone.

In this limited sense, Wisdom was dead.

Chapter Nineteen

Electrum

Rokhlenu was riding the wicker boat across the swamp to Morlock's cave when he heard a dull thump. Looking up, he saw a great bloom of fire ascend into the afternoon sky, followed by trails of smoke and dust.

"He'll kill himself one day," Rokhlenu reflected, "and us with him."

Rokhlenu beached the boat on the marshy verge and climbed the wooden steps Morlock had built into the hillside.

The never-wolf maker was not in his cave, as Rokhlenu had expected, but Hrutnefdhu the pale castrato was. He was sitting cross-legged just inside the cave, sewing metal rings onto leather or cloth stretched over a wooden frame. Deeper in the cave, Hlupnafenglu was curled up on the ground, holding up playing cards one by one in front of the basket of talking flames.

"Gnyrrand Rokhlenu," Hrutnefdhu said.

"Old friend Hrutnefdhu," Rokhlenu replied.

The pale werewolf glanced about instinctively, as if to see if anyone was listening, and said, "You don't have to call me that, you know. It can't be good for your bite to have a *plepnup* among your old friends."

Rokhlenu had thought about that, and Wuinlendhono had made the same point to him several times. But the outliers were not the Aruukaiaduun: there were many semiwolves, many *plepnupov*, many irregular shapes and shadows among his constituency. He thought it would harm him politically to distance himself from Hrutnefdhu. Anyway, he wasn't accustomed to picking his friends according to political convenience.

"Or a never-wolf, either," Rokhlenu added, grinning. "Where is he, by the way?"

Hrutnefdhu dropped his eyes to his work, blushing a little. He was easily affected by the slightest show of loyalty or affection; Rokhlenu thought he must have led a grim sort of life.

"Over the hill," the pale werewolf replied. "Trying something new, he said."

"Is he still alive, do you think?"

Hrutnefdhu grinned a little and said, "It is dangerous. That's why he doesn't do it here."

Rokhlenu looked over at the weapons rack. There were about a dozen stabbing spears with shining glass gores, two glass short swords with sharp points and leather grips, and about a dozen glass knives. Rokhlenu picked up one of these and balanced it on one finger thoughtfully.

"Not too many today," he remarked.

"You said we had enough yesterday, so he started working on this other thing."

"Is what you're doing part of it?"

"Not exactly. This won't be done tonight."

"What is it?"

"He says he'll be able to fly with it."

"Oh?" Rokhlenu walked over and examined the thing. It looked like a pair of bat wings, scaled over with metal discs and bound to a wooden frame. The frame and the wings hid some gears and cables that mixed wood and glass. There were grips on the inside tips of the wings.

"I doubt it," he said finally, "but it's interesting. Why are you sewing those rings all over it? Armor?"

Hrutnefdhu had just grabbed one of the rings from an odd upside-down box on long stiltlike legs. He met Rokhlenu's eye and let go of the disc in his hand. It flew straight upward, as if it were falling. He grabbed it before it rose too far and grinned as Rokhlenu whistled admiringly.

"It's weird in here sometimes," Rokhlenu said. "Like the stories they tell about Ulugarriu's workshop."

"Ulugarriu couldn't do anything like this. Not that I've ever heard," Hrutnefdhu said, turning shyly back to his work.

The pale werewolf seemed embarrassed by something, so Rokhlenu decided to leave him alone. "I'll go see what Morlock is up to," he said aloud, and patted Hrutnefdhu on the shoulder as he passed out of the cave.

He met Morlock coming over the rise of the hill with a sizable boulder in his hands. He looked a little scorched, but otherwise undamaged. There were clouds of smoke and dust settling behind him.

"Let me help you with that," Rokhlenu called.

"You should stay back. This hillside was a silver dump, I think. There may be some of the metal in these dust clouds."

"Urrrm. I think you're right: I can smell the nasty stuff. Well, they had to put it somewhere, I guess."

He saw mummified bodies of werewolves—some in the day shape, some in the night shape—scattered about the dusty hillside. He pointed at them and said, "Why would they come here? If I can sense the silver, they must have been able to."

"They killed themselves, I think. Some of them were carrying things. Notes, mementoes, that sort of thing."

"Horrible. You picked a nasty place for your work, old friend."

"Well, I knew no one else would get hurt if it went wrong. As it almost did: phlogiston is difficult stuff, and I haven't the material to handle it safely."

"What would you need?"

"A lightning bolt or two. The more the better. I could fashion some aethrium instruments from them. But the storms lately have been surprisingly free from lightning, and the landscape hereabouts is totally free from aether deposits."

"I did not know that."

"I think someone collects them. Your folk hero Ulugarriu, perhaps."

"You think Ulugarriu actually exists?" Rokhlenu asked doubtfully.

Morlock nodded toward the moon-clock on the side of the volcano.

Rokhlenu nodded slowly. Personally, he didn't believe in Ulugarriu. But someone had built the wonders of Wuruyaaria: if he wasn't called Ulugarriu, he was called something else.

"You're sure you don't want help with that rock?" Rokhlenu said as Morlock came nearer, out of the poisonous dust.

"It's not too bad," Morlock replied.

"The thing must be heavier than you are."

"Just about. But there's something holding it up." He lifted the boulder high, and on its underside Rokhlenu saw what looked like two metal footprints, affixed to the rock with crystalline spikes.

"What are those?"

"Soles for my new shoes," Morlock said, lowering the boulder.

"Ghost. How many have you got?"

"Just the pair. At that, I had to sacrifice a lot of metal and phlogiston I was planning to use for the wings."

"I saw those. Will that thing work?"

"No idea. The crows think it will, or say that they think it will, but crows aren't always reliable. They may just want to see someone crash in it."

Rokhlenu understood that; he'd known a lot of crows. They'd probably laughed watching the werewolves eating silver. He thought about them and didn't feel like laughing.

"Why do you suppose people kill themselves?" he asked Morlock.

"Pain," Morlock said. "Loneliness. Shame. Anger."

Rokhlenu waited, but Morlock didn't say any more. He thought about the singer he had known who ate wolfbane, and he thought about Morlock's hand. He knew it wasn't any better: in fact, Morlock always wore a glove on his left hand now to hide how bad it was getting.

Rokhlenu had an odd feeling Morlock knew what he was thinking about, but he wasn't saying anything, and Rokhlenu couldn't think of anything to say. He grabbed the other side of the boulder, just to keep from being entirely useless, and they carried it back to the cave together.

"Liudhleeo says," he said when they set the rock down in the cave, "that we need to work on Hlupnafenglu soon—if you want to take care of that before we leave tonight."

"Yes," Morlock said. "If one of us is killed tonight, the task may prove impossible."

Hrutnefdhu had put away his metallic thread and ivory needle and was folding up the stilts under his upside-down box of rings. "I'll take him over to the lair-tower," he said to the others. "Liudhleeo will want to do the work over there. She hates it over here."

"The nearness of that silver, I think," Morlock said, and Rokhlenu turned his head in agreement. Different werewolves were sensitive to silver in different degrees, and Liudhleeo was more sensitive than most.

Hrutnefdhu was getting Hlupnafenglu's attention gently and patiently. He persuaded the groggy red werewolf with words and gestures to rise up and follow him. The red werewolf shuffled docilely along after Hrutnefdhu for a few steps. Then he seemed to wake up a little more. He cast his mad golden gaze around the cave, looking at Morlock, the nexus of speaking flames, the other two werewolves, Morlock again.

"It's all right," Morlock said, meeting his eyes. "It's all right. We will follow you over. We'll see you soon. Go with your friend Hrutnefdhu. Go with him. We'll follow."

It was not clear how much the crazy werewolf understood. But Morlock's words or tone seemed to settle him somehow. He followed Hrutnefdhu out of the cave into the afternoon light and they went together, the pale werewolf and the red one, down the wooden stairs to the wickerwork boat.

When they were gone, Rokhlenu turned to Morlock and said, "I want to see your hand."

Morlock considered the matter for a moment, and then he peeled off the glove without saying anything.

The hand was gray and dead looking. The fingers were the worst. And their tips looked not so much dead as . . . ghostly. They seemed to be translucent, almost transparent.

"Does it hurt?" Rokhlenu asked.

"Yes," said Morlock. "But most unpleasant is the lack of control. I—I'm not used to that."

Rokhlenu nodded grimly. "Did she do this to you? Liudhleeo? If she did—"

"I don't think so. I think it was from that spike that was in my head. Part of it may still be in there. Or, while it was in me, it did some damage that is killing me by inches."

"You think it will kill you, then?"

"Probably. Liudhleeo calls it 'ghost sickness.' She has heard of it but never seen it."

"The Goweiteiuun have the best ghost-sniffers; maybe they can do something."

"So Liudhleeo says."

"And there's the Shadow Market in the low city, just inside the walls. Lots of crazy sorcerers work that place. Half of them are quacks and the rest are crooks, but they might know something useful."

"So Hrutnefdhu says."

Rokhlenu would have cursed the illness, the Sardhluun ghost-sniffers, Liudhleeo, Hrutnefdhu, and all of the sorcerers in the Shadow Market, but it would do no good. So he punched the wall of the cave instead. Morlock said nothing.

The moment passed. Rokhlenu picked up one of the swords from the weapon rack and said, "Can I take this? I prefer a sword to a spear, when it comes to a fight."

Morlock smiled a rare smile. "I made it for you." He took the sword and unwrapped the leather from the grip. Rokhlenu saw dark runes inset into the glass. "There is your name and a few runes of warding and finding. They won't do much for you, I'm afraid. But maybe you'll be able to find your blade when you need it, anyway."

"Thanks."

Morlock shrugged, nodded.

They went down to the wickerwork boat. It was where the two other werewolves had left it, on the far side of the water. Morlock whistled, and the boat swam back toward them on its own. Rokhlenu felt a qualm stepping into the boat, and was relieved when Morlock poled it across the water in the ordinary way.

He grabbed Morlock by the elbow before they went into the lair-tower and said, "Hey."

"Yes?"

"This ghost sickness. It hurts? It makes you angry?"

"Yes."

"You're not alone, though. And you have no reason to be ashamed."

Morlock's pale eyes fixed on him. "I know that. I know it, my friend."

The never-wolf seemed to understand what he was trying to say. So he stopped trying to say it, and they went upstairs to Hrutnefdhu and Liudhleeo's lair.

Hlupnafenglu was sleeping, somewhat twitchily, and he lay on the floor in the day's last light. Rokhlenu was not surprised to see a worried-looking Liudhleeo bending over him, but he was surprised to see his intended, Wuinlendhono, beside her.

They greeted each other warmly while Liudhleeo and Morlock exchanged a look—smoldering on Liudhleeo's part, rather frosty on Morlock's. Rokhlenu supposed Liudhleeo was trying to have sex with him; her appetites were becoming fairly notorious around the settlement, and even in Apetown and Dogtown, or so Rokhlenu had heard.

"Where's Hrutnefdhu?" asked Rokhlenu.

"Oh, he was getting twitchy," Wuinlendhono said irritably, "so I sent him on an errand. There's enough of us here to hold Big Red here down—or put him out of our misery if it comes to that."

"Maybe," Rokhlenu said, looking at the sleeping werewolf. "Just."

"My Hrutnefdhu doesn't like to see people cut up in cold blood," Liudhleeo explained.

"Who does?" muttered Wuinlendhono discontentedly.

Liudhleeo gave her a sidelong look for this. When Rokhlenu realized he was doing the same himself, he stopped. But it seemed like an odd remark for a werewolf to make.

"He's as ready as he'll ever be," Liudhleeo said, gesturing at the red werewolf, "and I'd like to get some sleep this afternoon, if at all possible. Maybe you, Rokhlenu, would hold down his head and you, Wuinlendhono, would hold his head like—well, like last time. That worked out so ghost-bitten well."

Morlock put his left hand on her shoulder and looked into her dark eyes. She dropped her gaze, then shyly raised it again. Her posture was almost flirtatious, and Rokhlenu was going to say something about it when she said in a businesslike tone, "Do you want to cut him open or pull the spike? I think that's a fair division of labor."

"I'll cut," Morlock said, and pulled a glass knife from his belt.

"And you brought your own knife. Very polite. No magical glass tweezers for me, I suppose?"

Morlock produced a long double-toothed probe from a pocket in one sleeve. That, too, was made of clear glass.

"Ask him for some raw beef," Wuinlendhono said, already kneeling by Hlupnafenglu's shaggy golden head. "I'm hungry."

Rokhlenu was in place, too, so Morlock knelt down by Hlupnafenglu's side and deftly incised a cross in the side of his head. He peeled back the flesh, exposing the skull. Under the frighteningly copious blood, there was a network of pulsating light woven through the bone of the skull. It was much like what they had seen in Morlock's skull, the three of them, anyway. Except that there was more of it; it was denser; the light was more golden.

"You knew exactly where it was," Liudhleeo said quaveringly.

"I saw it in a vision," Morlock explained. "He has a faint scar there, also."

"Are you—are you—are you in a vision or whatever you call it now?" She sounded terrified to Rokhlenu. He wondered why.

"No," said Morlock. He got out of her way, and she approached with the two-pronged probe.

Rokhlenu watched her hand narrowly for any sign of trembling, but there was none. Her hand approached the seeping wound confidently, and carefully probed the skull for the central node.

Then she screamed. She leapt to her feet and she was screaming. Smoke was rising from her hand. A drop of blood there was burning through her skin.

Morlock grabbed her hand and, quick as a werewolf, licked the blood from her hand. Then, unlike a werewolf, he grimaced and spat. "Eccch. Healing is an ugly business."

There were tears in Liudhleeo's dark eyes, but she was smiling as she looked on him. "Thanks," she said. "From one ugly healer to another."

"I guess I'd better pull the spike."

"I guess."

"I wonder why it burned you."

"The blood stinks of silver," Wuinlendhono said distantly. "If you people are done licking each other, I wish you would pull that spike or sew him up or both."

Morlock did both. He located the largest pulsating node and applied the pincers of his probe to either side. It took some time to break it free from the skull, which had begun to heal around the spike: it must have been in the red werewolf's head a long time. But, in the end, Morlock held it triumphantly in his hand, and the three (conscious) werewolves looked on it with a mixture of interest and horror.

It was not blood-dark, like the spike from Morlock's brain. It was still luminous as it lay in his hand, a silvery gold sheathed with drying blood.

"It's electrum, I think," the crooked never-wolf said. "An alloy of silver and gold," he explained, when they looked at him bewildered.

"What a disgusting idea!" Wuinlendhono said heatedly.

"Gold will cure a silver wound," Liudhleeo added tentatively. "I read that somewhere, I think. That's how he must have survived."

"It was some sort of experiment?" Rokhlenu asked. "A game—to see what could be done to a werewolf like this without killing him?" He felt rage building in him. "What kind of crazy ghost-sniffer would do that?"

Morlock pocketed the bloody silver-gold tooth. "Ulugarriu, maybe," he said.

The name cast a pall over the room. Morlock sewed up the red werewolf's bleeding head in an awful silence that didn't seem to bother him in the least. Of course, he lived his life swimming in awful silences, Rokhlenu reflected.

Hlupnafenglu lay in the sunlight, strangely still.

"I wonder if we killed him?" Liudhleeo said quietly.

"Better dead than running around with a silver spike in his brain," Wuinlendhono said decisively, standing with her usual fluid grace. "If we are done here, I think I will return to my lair for a sleep. We'll be having a long night, tonight."

"But—" Rokhlenu said, turning toward her. He hadn't been expecting her to accompany them on the foray to the Khuwuleion. It was insane: some of them would likely die. But she was staring at him with eyes carved from black ice, and his objections died unspoken in his throat.

"I'd better do the same," he said. "See you at sunset," he said to Morlock.

"Then."

As Rokhlenu shut the door behind him he glanced back and saw Morlock tending to Liudhleeo's hand as she looked on him with a rather predatory smile on her long narrow face.

Chapter Twenty

A Long Night

Night had fallen. The sky was largely free of clouds and wholly free of moons: it was the first dark call of the month of Jaric—a very dark call, this year, since Horseman had set. They would fight this night in their day shapes—and that increased the chance that some of them would die. Perhaps all of them, if they had miscalculated the forces that would be present to defend the prison.

Rokhlenu assembled his strike force on the marshy verge west of town. Besides him, the First Wolf, and Hrutnefdhu, there were twenty irredeemables and five gold-toothed bodyguards led by the frizz-haired Yaniunulu. The senior bodyguard was hardly more prepossessing in his day shape than his night shape, but he had insisted on his right to accompany the First Wolf into danger and she had smilingly assured him she would do her very best to protect him.

They were waiting on Morlock; and Rokhlenu, getting jittery, sent Hrutnefdhu to round him up.

He was not surprised when he saw the pale werewolf returning alone, poling a boat from the southern gate of the outlier settlement.

"He says not to wait for him," Hrutnefdhu gasped as soon as he was within talking distance. "He'll catch up to us."

Rokhlenu shook his head grimly. "That crazy never-wolf."

"Yes, Gnyrrand."

They set off at a loping run down the path that led to the long walls of the Sardhluun Pack. They kept their glittering weapons sheathed; what armor they wore was covered by dark surcoats. They were hoping to surprise the enemy. They had no other hope, really.

They came to the long walls at a place far from any gate. There was no guard atop the wall that anyone could see or smell. Ape-fingered Runhuiulanhu climbed the wall with pitons and rope, like a cliff face, and the rest of them went up the rope one by one after him and down by rope on the opposite side.

They'd chosen their spot well: hardly three hundred loping paces off lay the squat bulk of the Khuwuleion, a dark shape etched against the western stars.

Rokhlenu was just catching his breath and his beloved on the far side of the Long Wall when a human shape vaulted clear over the wall and landed rolling in the dark field nearby.

"Nicely done," he whispered harshly.

"Takes practice," Morlock whispered back.

"How many legs did you break?"

Morlock climbed carefully to his feet. His expression was invisible in the dark, but he was clearly turned toward the wall, waiting. When all the werewolves had climbed down the inner wall he said, "Then," and leapt into the sky.

Rokhlenu lost sight of him at first, then saw a series of stars being briefly occulted: that was where Morlock must be. A dark shape landed in the fields halfway between the wall and the Khuwuleion and lifted off again.

"What if he misses the roof?" wondered Yaniunulu.

"Then he tries again," Rokhlenu said.

"What if he breaks his leg?"

"Then we send up Runhuiulanhu with a rope."

"And what if—?"

"Then we trade you and your gold-toothers to the Sardhluun for the female prisoners," said Yaarirruuiu, one of the irredeemables. "A bad trade for them, but we'll tell them you clean up nice."

A few snarling chuckles at this. The irredeemables had no time for the First Wolf's bodyguard at the best of times, and they didn't like frizz-faced Yaniunulu casting aspersions on Khretvarrgliu.

"I think he landed on the roof," Hrutnefdhu said quietly.

Rokhlenu couldn't tell, himself, but he trusted the pale werewolf.

"Forward, then," he said. "Run silent. Don't draw a weapon until the First Wolf or I command it."

They ran from the wall toward the hulking lightless prison.

It was *too* lightless, Rokhlenu thought as they approached. There seemed to be no lamplight or torchlight shining through the infrequent dark windows of the stone lair. It gave him a bad feeling, but they had set their plans and this was no reason to change them.

By the time they arrived at the Khuwuleion wall, two knotted lines had dropped from the distant roof. Except that they were both one line: they were connected at the low end and up above, where Morlock had installed a pulley. That was how the plan went, anyway.

"I suppose you'll want to be first or last," Wuinlendhono murmured in his ear.

"Last," he said. He'd thought about it: the ground was the point of greatest danger, if a patrol of Sardhluun guards happened by.

"Then I'm first," she said. Stepping over to the lines, she gripped one firmly and gave it a yank, letting Morlock know that a passenger was coming. Then four others took hold of the other line and started hauling it down. As it came down, the First Wolf went up, walking along the rough gray walls of the Khuwuleion.

Twenty-two others followed her up. In the end, there were four others and Rokhlenu.

"Remember," he whispered to the last four, who included Hrutnefdhu and the ape-fingered Runhuiulanhu, "run rather than fight. If need be, run all the way back to the outliers and have Lekkativengu come rescue us."

The irredeemables stood silent, but Hrutnefdhu's light voice whispered, "Yes, Gnyrrand."

Rokhlenu went to the rope, gripped it firmly, and pulled.

The other four started hauling at the ropes. Rokhlenu found himself fly-walking up the side of the building. He found he didn't like it much and, as the ground got farther and farther away, he liked it less and less. But there was a moment when he seemed to be struggling absolutely alone, halfway between the dark ground and the star-filled sky. He didn't like it. But he knew he would never forget it.

He came up the lip of the roof, where the glass pulley was straining under his weight. In fact, Rokhlenu was dismayed to see a network of cracks running all through the pulley's transparent frame: it wouldn't bear his (or anyone's) weight much longer, he guessed.

Hands reached over the edge to pull him up. He grabbed them gratefully, and when they had him firmly, he let the rope go and climbed onto the roof.

He looked at the others and they looked at him. Most of them were grinning, teeth pale and sinister in starlight. There was no need to say anything: whatever he had experienced, they had experienced.

Morlock was standing with his long-leaping boots in his hand, looking at them intently. They had discussed this, too: it would be a mistake to leave them anchored to the roof, where the Sardhluun could find them and make use of them. They were impossible to fight in. But Rokhlenu had some sense of how difficult their making had been, and what an oddly intense feeling Morlock had for the things he made. Still, there was no help for it. Morlock opened his fingers, and the boots flew up into the sky and were lost.

The shadow with Yaarirruuiu's profile gestured toward part of the roof, where there was a hatch permitting entrance to the top floor of the prison—if it would open.

Morlock's crooked shape moved toward it. He gripped the bar atop the hatch with both hands (one gloved, one ungloved) and pulled it open.

It swung open fairly easily. At least there was no lock on it. But it screamed like a ghost hungry for blood, and a cloud of gray murk rose from it that had the tang of iron in Rokhlenu's nostrils: rust.

They waited without moving or speaking. Any guard within hearing would have to come investigate the sound.

No one came. The dark feeling in Rokhlenu grew darker. It was not a feeling of danger. It was worse than that somehow.

Morlock drew the sword strapped over his shoulder: it was a short one with a glass blade, not his own Tyrfing. He stepped through the hatch and dropped down to the floor below.

The werewolves turned to Rokhlenu and Wuinlendhono.

"Go down first," said Rokhlenu. "Then draw." He didn't want anyone impaling himself on his weapon. Except Yaniunulu, perhaps.

One by one they dropped through the hatch. Rokhlenu and Wuinlendhono went last, side by side.

Morlock had a piece of glass in his hand that was shedding a cool bluish light. Rokhlenu would have cautioned him about making a light until they were sure it was safe, except for two things. One was that Morlock seemed not to be in the mood for caution: his eyes were starting to get that staring crazy look again; he was less Morlock and more Khretvarrgliu by the moment. Second, Rokhlenu's ears and eyes and nose were all telling him what perhaps Morlock had already guessed: this place was abandoned. The cell doors lay half open; there was a fur of humid dust on the very bars of the cells.

"If there is a single rat in this entire building," said one of the irredeemables, "I'll eat it."

"I thought I was the only one who was hungry," said Wuinlendhono in a hard, clear, amused tone.

The werewolves snickered. They liked the toughness of their First Wolf. If they noticed, as Rokhlenu noticed, the wet staring look in her eyes—almost as crazy as Morlock's—they gave no sign of it.

Morlock took another piece of glass from a pocket in his sleeve and tapped it against the first. Now both were lit. He tossed the glass toward Rokhlenu and Wuinlendhono without looking at them; Rokhlenu snatched it out of the air and tried to look as if he weren't startled.

Morlock plunged down a nearby stairwell. The irredeemables started to follow him. The gold-toothed bodyguards looked toward Wuinlendhono for instructions. Yaarirruuiu noticed this, looked annoyed, and stood in front of the stairwell, blocking the way.

"Gnyrrand?" he said, meeting Rokhlenu's eye. (Translation: *I'll be gnawed by ghosts if these semi-cows are going to show more respect to their chief than we show to ours.*)

"Follow him," Rokhlenu said, "but be careful. This place may have traps, even if there is no one in it."

They followed Morlock down the stairs.

They were careful. There were no traps. There were no people. The building was empty of life, down to the torture chambers on the underground levels.

Rokhlenu and Wuinlendhono investigated those alone while the others stood guard in the central chamber on the first floor.

Rokhlenu walked behind and held the shining fragment of glass high as Wuinlendhono peered carefully into bloodstained room—the holding cells, the torture chambers, the spiked closets, everything large enough to conceal a body. It was as if she was expecting to find someone in particular. But there was no one there, alive or dead.

Finally she gave up and they started to climb the stairs back to the ground floor.

"It hasn't changed that much since I was a girl," she remarked. "I wonder when they stopped using it."

He grabbed her by the arm, and she turned to look at him. Her dark eyes were empty as if she didn't see him.

"You were imprisoned here," he said.

"I was born here."

"Ghost." Rokhlenu thought furiously. "That thing. Wurnafenglu. He is your father."

"No, I don't think so. I hope not. He didn't think so. My mother was one of his wives, but she became pregnant by another male. So he insisted, anyway. He had her thrown in prison and tortured her for the name, but she never told. Or maybe she did, and it didn't matter; they kept on torturing her, anyway. I grew up here. When I was a few years short of my first heat, Wurnafenglu bartered me to a rich old pervert of the Goweiteiuun Pack. He was an eminent ghost-sniffer, and smock-sniffer, too. I learned so much from him. My first, extremely late husband."

Rokhlenu noticed that he was gripping Wuinlendhono's elbow rather tightly. He relaxed his grip and put his hand along her forearm caressingly.

"I cannot stand," whispered Wuinlendhono, "that you know when to talk, and when not to talk. That you are as beautiful as a moon at new rising. That you are strong as iron, as cunning and lively as a flame. That I can trust you. That I can turn my back on you and know that I am safe, know that you will die defending me, that I would die defending you. Your love will make me weak and I cannot be weak. I can't be weak. Stop making me be weak."

"I wouldn't want you if you were weak."

She was in his arms by then, sniffing his hair and nipping at his neck. "Lying son of a never-wolf cow," she breathed in his ear.

"And don't talk that way about my mother. She was a very respectable rope weaver, may the ghosts leave her alone."

Wuinlendhono drew in a long sobbing breath and stood away from him.

"I'm sure she was," said the First Wolf of the outlier pack. "Eminently respectable. How sorry I am that I never got the chance to meet her."

"You'd be sorrier still if you did have the chance. She never was very kindly to my meathearts."

"And neither will I ever be, so we have that in common."

She took his arm and they climbed the dark stair in silence.

When they reached the ground floor, the other werewolves (including the four who had been left outside) were crowded around Morlock and Hrutnefdhu. Morlock was holding a large codex in his right hand and raising high the shining glass in his gloved left hand. Hrutnefdhu, standing beside him, was reading from the book in low tones.

"Interesting story?" Wuinlendhono inquired, when they were close enough not to shout.

"Many stories," said Morlock. "All grim."

"It's the prisoner registry," Hrutnefdhu said. "Names, crimes, dates of admission, dates of—well, departure, I suppose. And notes on their final disposition."

"They are all dead or sold," Morlock said. "The ink on the latest entries looks to be five years old at least."

"Five years." Rokhlenu shook his head. "This was a fool's errand. They must have decided years ago that selling their prisoners was more profitable than housing and feeding them."

"Why just female prisoners?" Morlock asked.

The irredeemables looked embarrassed on Morlock's behalf, the gold-toothed bodyguards amused at his lack of sophistication.

"There are more unmated males than females in the wild packs," Wuinlendhono explained. "Every female knows she can get a mate by leaving the city. Not that many want to."

"Would all the female prisoners over a stretch of five years or more be salable on those terms?" asked Morlock coolly.

"Depends on how desperate they are out there, Khretvarrgliu," Runhuiulanhu said philosophically. "You should see some of the stale biscuits, male and female, they have down at the day-lairs off the market. But people pay for their company all the time."

"Never you, of course," said a gold-tooth slyly.

"Yes me, you stupid bag of marrow-sucked bones. Me with my monkey hands and feet, even when all three moons are up, and everyone knowing about it on account of they call me Ape-fingers. You think females are lining up to mate with me? If I get it, I have to pay for it."

"Couldn't you find a female in the same condition?" asked Morlock.

"Mate with an ape-fingered female?" cried ape-fingered Runhuiulanhu. "I can do better than that!"

"Shut up, for ghosts' sake," Rokhlenu hissed. "We'll have the Sardhluun down on us and there's no point to that, now."

"Be quiet, by all means," the First Wolf agreed. "But," she continued, "this was not a fool's errand. That book will be very useful. Very useful indeed."

Confused looks on most faces except Morlock's—he may have been still pondering the plight of the ape-fingered werewolf for all Rokhlenu knew. But light began to shine in Rokhlenu's understanding. "Not every female sent here was to serve a life sentence. No female was sent here for a death sentence. People will want to know what happened to them."

"There's that," Wuinlendhono agreed. "Then there's the money. The Sardhluun have been taking money every year for tending to the city's prisoners. The citizens of Wuruyaaria will be curious to know how that money was spent."

Nods all around, fierce grins. Morale had been falling ever since they found the prison was an empty stone box; now the warriors were standing straighter. His intended was good at chieftainship, Rokhlenu thought (not for the first time). It was one thing to realize what she had said; it was another thing to know that her fighters needed to hear it.

"Then we can declare victory and get out," he said aloud.

"I'd better get that pulley," Morlock said. "It'll look bad when they see we broke into an empty prison."

"Not worth the time—" Rokhlenu began, thinking of Morlock shuffling up and down all the stairs above them, but Morlock was already headed out the front gate.

The werewolves followed him out. Morlock walked over to the lines hanging down the wall, found one of the knots in the rope, and pulled it apart.

"Stand clear," he said belatedly, standing clear himself.

The long cord began to fall, piling up on the dark ground. A few moments later, the glass pulley landed in a shower of bright fragments. Morlock quickly stowed the fragments in a bag he had been carrying on his back, coiled up the rope, and did likewise. He looked up to see the werewolves staring at him.

"I don't like strangers handling my stuff," he said.

This was a universal instinct among werewolves, and they all nodded sagely in agreement. But what Rokhlenu had really been wondering was how Morlock had gotten the pulley to fall into pieces. He must have shattered it somehow beforehand, but kept the fragments from separating with some spell. Now the spell had been broken and the pulley followed suit obligingly.

"Morlock, you're the best of makers!" Rokhlenu said. "Ulugarriu can yodel up his own tail, if any."

"Like to see them fight it out," Yaarirruuiu said. "Morlock against Ulugarriu in a maker's challenge."

"Yes!" cried Hrutnefdhu, his eyes shining with admiration. "What a game it would be! Skill against skill, with life and bite on the line."

The gold-toothed guards looked sidelong with disdain at the pale castrato's enthusiasm, but the irredeemables chuckled and Yaarirruuiu clapped him on the shoulder. They liked the ex-trustee, and even respected him a little, though he would not wear (or could not keep) honor-teeth.

"Shut your noisy word-holes, my champions," Wuinlendhono said cheerily. "Let's get clear of this place so that the Sardhluun can start paying for our fun soonest."

This strongly appealed to all of them, and Rokhlenu had no trouble ordering them for a quick run back to the ropes they had left hanging from the Long Wall. He put Morlock and Hrutnefdhu at the end, where they would wind up anyway, ape-fingered Runhuiulanhu at the front, in case the ropes were gone and they had to rescale the walls, and Wuinlendhono carrying the book in the center of the company, where it was safest.

The ropes were still there and apparently had not been discovered. No one was lying in wait for them, anyway. Rokhlenu was standing on the top of the wall, preparing to climb down the other side, when he noticed light and noise coming from the north and east, along the straight road to Wuruyaaria from the Long Wall. He signalled that the others should keep crossing over while he kept his eyes and ears on this interesting if indistinct disturbance.

Wuinlendhono clambered up the rope. The prisoner book from the Khuwuleion was dangling from one shoulder bound in neatly knotted rope. "Thanks for the help," she said pointedly after (in his absorption) he failed to help her.

"Look!" he said.

"Election," she said briefly. "That's why we're here tonight, remember?"

"It's outside the walls! A primary election would be held on Sardhluun ground."

"Yurr. Yes, you're right about that."

"It's a general election rally."

"Must be. Yes, I agree. And it must be against a pack who has no hope of beating them, so they're risking a rally now, and hoping to live down the defeat before election season is over."

"Only they're going to get some help."

"Not tonight, cutlet. We're not ready."

"*They're* not ready."

"Can't talk you out of it, can I? Oh, well. You're the gnyrrand."

Yaniunulu was just passing over the wall between them, and Wuinlendhono said, "Yaniunulu. Give it to him."

The frizz-haired red werewolf paused to goggle at her. "High Huntress," he said, "with respect—"

"Listen, I'm not sure who you think you're talking to, but I *am* sure your respect means less than nothing to me. When I told you to give it to him, I meant for you to give it to him. So give it to him."

Silently Yaniunulu took a staff hanging from his belt and handed it to Rokhlenu. He proceeded down the far side of the wall without another word.

The staff was wrapped with a black covering. When he pulled that loose, he found that the staff was a flagstaff: around it was wrapped the green-and-gold banner of the outliers.

"It would be better if all the other nominees were here," Wuinlendhono said, "but I thought it might come to this. Now you can fight under our banner."

Rokhlenu mulled this over for a moment, then said, "You knew there would be a general election rally tonight, and you lied to me about it."

"I still don't think we're ready to intervene in the general election—we don't even have an ally in the treaty packs yet. And I didn't lie; I just didn't go out of my way to correct your mistaken impression. Oh. Oh, ghost. I *hate* it that I just said that."

After a moment of tense thought Rokhlenu said mildly, "We'll have to do better."

"You're right," she admitted frankly. "I'm not used to this partnership thing. I'll go with my guards and get the wedding ready; I have my bride-price," she added, shyly tapping the prison register. She scampered down the rope before he could kiss her good-bye.

Hrutnefdhu was coming up the rope now. Morlock, the last of the group, climbed up when Hrutnefdhu started climbing down the outer wall.

He caught Morlock by the arm and hauled him up—not that Morlock needed the help; he climbed better than Runhuiulanhu.

"We're going to be fighting after all," he said to Morlock.

"Some sort of rally?" Morlock said. "I heard you talking. Won't it go against you with the treaty packs if you break up an election rally?"

Rokhlenu looked at him with astonishment he was unable to mask. "Have you ever seen an election?" he asked.

"Many," Morlock said. "They didn't usually involve fighting." He paused. "At least, not on purpose." Another pause. "Actually, I'm not sure about that. Anyway, it doesn't matter. Tell me about your election rallies."

The *your* stung a little. But Rokhlenu had almost forgotten that Morlock was a never-wolf; there was something so wolvish about him.

"Once the packs elect their nominees," he explained to his old friend, "pack meets pack in a series of rallies all through the election season. They speak and they fight; citizens come to watch. The pack that speaks and fights better gains bite. The other loses bite. The nominees with the most bite at the end of the election season lie down in the Innermost Pack of the city."

"Then," said Morlock, and climbed down the outer wall.

By the time Rokhlenu reached the ground, Wuinlendhono and her guards were gone. The werewolves and Morlock were standing with weapons drawn, waiting for him.

He shook loose the green-and-gold banner and handed it to Hrutnefdhu.

"Don't lose it," he said.

"Won't," said the pale werewolf in a strangled tone.

Banner-bearer was a position of high honor and Hrutnefdhu was the male of lowest bite among them, but the irredeemables were for it. "Ha!" said Yaarirruuiu. "You'll have some bite after tonight, *plepnup*." The irredeemables growled their approval.

"Or we'll all be *plepnupov*," Hrutnefdhu snapped back, and the irredeemables hooted. The ex-trustee was judged the winner of that exchange.

"Let's go," Rokhlenu said, and they ran side by side into battle.

Mercy was the weakest of the Strange Gods, and her visualizations were often less than complete. So she was surprised when War manifested himself alongside her on the road to Wuruyaaria. He wore his now-favorite form of a decapitated man, holding his severed head like a lamp. She wore the form of a woman without a mouth, carrying a white lotus flower in her hand.

"Going to the rally?" the decapitated man signified, flapping its gray lips with a hint of mockery.

"I am," Mercy confirmed. "I am surprised to see you there. Will your friend Death also be watching it?"

"My visualization doesn't embrace that," War admitted. They had hated each other so long that they had reached a state where it was pointless to lie to one another. "She is stranger than ever, in recent event-series. Even when she signifies directly to me, I have trouble disentangling her symbols. They seem almost random, empty of meaning."

"There may be no deaths at this rally, anyway," Mercy signified. "I hope not."

"I care not. You may be right; you may be wrong: the Sardhluun are ruthless bastards. They are stupid, though, and rarely amuse me."

Their manifestations overlapped the nexus of space-time where the rally was occurring.

The gnyrrand of the Goweiteiuun, a citizen named Aaluindhonu, was standing with his slate of candidates under a banner of blue and red, telling a parable of a man with five sons. The man asked each of his sons to take an arrow and break it. They did. Then he took five arrows, bound them together, and told them each to try and break the bundle. None could, and this showed, the gnyrrand said, that strength came through union: of brother with brother, citizen with citizen, pack with pack. The Goweiteiuun Pack was for the strength of the city through unity. The gnyrrand slouched back among his dozen or so followers without waiting for the crowd's applause.

There wasn't much applause to wait for. The crowd of spectators, gathered in the open area between the two bands of candidates, was not particularly impressed. The arrow story was trite; the lesson was the sort of la-di-da their den mothers and teachers had been yowling at them for as long as they could remember. It might be true, but it bored them. They turned with relief to the Sardhluun band.

The gnyrrand of the Sardhluun Pack was not present; this wasn't an important enough rally for him to appear. His second-candidate, Hwinsyngundu, gave the Sardhluun response, standing under a banner of black and green, in front of fifty volunteers wearing the same colors. He was a burly, broad-shouldered werewolf, his fat neck wholly covered with thick bands of honor-teeth. He stepped forward and reached out one hand. A werewolf in Sardhluun colors put five arrows in his outstretched palm. Hwinsyngundu gripped the bundle with both hands, held it over his head, and—without a word—he snapped the bundle in half.

The crowd roared. This was better than the truth. This confirmed their irritation with the old truism—scratched the itch they had long felt.

"That was clever," War signified generously. "It was prearranged, of course."

"Yes," Mercy signified. "Aaluindhonu, the gnyrrand of the Goweiteiuun, betrayed his pack. The Sardhluun threatened to kill some of his semiwolf kin who live in Apetown unless he cooperated with them. He is fond of his kin, even if they are semiwolves, and has little hope in the elections anyway, and so he submitted to the Sardhluun demands."

"All's fair, I suppose," said War dubiously. Politics was much like war in some ways, almost an extension of war by other means, but sometimes the methods involved made him uncomfortable. "I wish Wisdom were manifest," he continued. "He'd enjoy this. The crowd certainly is."

The crowd itself was not particularly impressive. It was numerous, surely, especially for a rally this early in the season on a moonless night, when the fighting was likely to be bloodless. But there were many citizens wearing the night shape—probably denizens of Dogtown, where the never-men tended to congregate. Many of the others may have come from Apetown: they were not well dressed, and there were many semiwolves among them. Many in the crowd wore not a single honor-tooth. They had little bite to bestow.

But what they had, they gave to the Sardhluun and to Hwinsyngundu before he opened his mouth: they cheered; they howled; they barked. It was Sardhluun's rally to lose at that exhilarating moment.

Hwinsyngundu began to speak. He said that the city was strong because of its strongest citizens; life was a war, with every citizen in conflict with the others. The strongest ruled; others cooperated because they must, because they needed the strength of the strong, but the strong needed nothing but their strength alone, so the city should grow the strength of the strong to become stronger as the strong ruled the city with strength and in strength for its strength and theirs. Their strength, that is. In strength was safety and in safety was strength. He then expanded on these important points, perhaps repeating himself a little.

The crowd grew much less enthusiastic as he spoke (at much too great a length). This was just the usual Sardhluun line, almost as trite as the hand-holding inanity of the Goweiteiuun gnyrrand. They began to vacate the space between the two packs of candidates, long before the second candidate had finished his speech. Eventually, he noticed that he was losing the crowd and concluded with some screeching insults about the cowardice of the Goweiteiuun ghost-sniffers.

The crowd applauded politely. Hwinsyngundu had lost most of their esteem, but they were still somewhat in Sardhluun's favor because of the great stunt with the arrows, and because they were obviously going to win the ensuing fight. The Sardhluun candidates and followers behind Hwinsyngundu looked somewhat dismayed, though.

"What a clown," War signified impatiently.

"He believes what he is saying," signified Mercy, who felt sorry for the inept politician. "Hwinsyngundu really believes he is a bold lone hero who has clambered to the top through his strength and independent daring."

"He grew up in, and inherited, a household of five hundred personal slaves. He is the Werowance's bastard son *and* grandson."

"Yes. The family should outbreed more, obviously."

Now the space between the bands of candidates and their auxiliaries was quite clear, and the crowd readied themselves to enjoy a quick drubbing and mocking of the Goweiteiuun.

"Where are the prisoners of the Khuwuleion?" came a shout from the darkness beyond the rally torches.

The crowd fell silent, astonished. The candidates paused, unsure what was happening.

Even Mercy was surprised. She observed War, who made the gray lips of his severed head smile cheerily at her.

"Where are the prisoners of the Vargulleion?" the same voice shouted.

Now the crowd was less surprised, and more amused, because they all knew the answer to this one. The Sardhluun had lost all their male prisoners in the largest prison break in the history of Wuruyaaria. It was a shameful display of weakness from those who bragged constantly of their strength, and it had been enjoyed as a joke on all the mesas of Wuruyaaria.

Hwinsyngundu stepped into the open space between the two parties and shouted into the darkness. "The prisoners fled like weaklings to the cowardly outlier pack, who admit their weakness by submitting to the rule of a female. We of the mighty Sardhluun Pack have given them a first burning taste of vengeance and, if need be, they will drink the whole poisonous bowl and die of it. None defy the mighty Sardhluun Pack and live!"

"I did," said the speaker in the shadows, and strode forward into the light. He was a tall, gray-haired werewolf in the day shape, his wolf-shadow rippling below him in the firelight. Over his head rippled the green-and-gold banner of the outliers, the flagstaff held by a pale mottled werewolf.

"I am Rokhlenu," said the gray werewolf, "gnyrrand of the outliers. I come with my fighters, all escaped from the Vargulleion, and my old friend Morlock Khretvarrgliu. We say that you lie, Sardhluun sheepdogs. You were too weak to hold us. You were too weak to retake us. And you sold your prisoners of the Khuwuleion like meat to the wild packs in the empty lands. The Khuwuleion is as empty as the Vargulleion, as empty as every Sardhluun promise, as every Sardhluun boast. Only cowards lie. Only weaklings worship strength. We come here to fight alongside the noble Goweiteiuun Pack against the Sardhluun fleabags. If you really are the stronger, you have the chance to prove it now."

Out of the darkness stepped two dozen werewolves, more or less human in shape. And there was the never-wolf, Khretvarrgliu, his shadow the same crooked form as his body. He held a sword the color of glass in his hand; his eyes, too, were the color of gray glass.

The Goweiteiuun followers cheered their unexpected allies; only their gnyrrand seemed dismayed. The Sardhluun werewolves looked at the Goweiteiuun, looked at the newcomers, and fell in a body on the outliers.

"This is what you came to see!" Mercy signified. "You visualized this!"

War's headless shoulders shrugged. "I could not be sure. None of my visualizations have the light of certainty these days. But several futures showed something like this. Ulugarriu was present in those features, but is not here now, unless disguised somehow."

"Ulugarriu might be able to baffle a god's indirect visualization, but not direct perceptions from our manifest selves. Surely?" signified Mercy, ever less sure as she thought of it.

"I don't know," War admitted reluctantly. "It's a good fight, though, don't you think?"

"I hate it. They have struck down that pale werewolf with the banner. They are going to kill him."

"No. No, you're wrong. Look how his comrades come to his aid. That one they call Khretvarrgliu. He's not even a werewolf. He's standing over the pale one's body. He'll die rather than let them hurt his friend. Doesn't it move you, Mercy? This is what war is really about: heroism, self-sacrifice, daring, strategy. Not just killing and cruelty."

"There is a great deal of killing and cruelty. Your hero Khretvarrgliu has killed three Sardhluun werewolves already. And he would kill them all if he could: there is a madness in him."

"You're right, of course. They should have killed him or left him alone."

So far the fighting had only been between the Sardhluun and the newcomers. The Goweiteiuun followers were urgently addressing their gnyrrand, who wore a bitter haggard look on his narrow face. Finally he nodded. The Goweiteiuun gave a thin howling cheer and they charged the flank of the Sardhluun werewolves.

The fight was far from certain even after the Goweiteiuun struck. The Sardhluun still had the greater numbers, and their band were all broad-backed fighters.

But their union was broken when the Goweiteiuun attacked. Some turned to respond to it; others hesitated; others stayed engaged with the outliers. There was a gap in the Sardhluun line, and the ruthless outliers took advantage of it. The gray-haired blue-eyed leader leaped forward, a long-faced ape-fingered werewolf at his side. By now the one they called Khretvarrgliu had lifted the pale werewolf from the ground and was holding him up with his left hand; the pale werewolf in turn held the green-and-gold banner high. The outliers shouted (or howled) as one and followed their gnyrrand into the broken Sardhluun line. Mad-eyed Morlock came last, hauling the banner-bearer like a banner and stabbing with his glittering glass sword.

The Sardhluun band retreated to re-form their line, but the others charged with them and the melee continued. Werewolves lay dead or dying on the moonless ground. Others, only wounded, were crawling out of the torchlight to hide in the shadows. The Sardhluun retreated again, and suddenly they were not retreating but running, a rout of werewolves in black and green fleeing for their lives down the road to the Long Wall.

The Goweiteiuun did not pursue them but stood cheering on the rally ground. The crowd, too, was cheering: the fight was excellent and unexpected; the stunt with the arrows had been a good one; in all, it was a much better rally than anyone had hoped for. The outliers did follow the Sardhluun until the defeated werewolves began to enter the Low Road Gate through the Long Wall. Then the leader of the outliers turned his fighters back and went to have words with the sad-eyed gnyrrand of the Goweiteiuun band.

"A good fight indeed," signified War. "Yes, I think this will be a fine election year." He demanifested himself with no further symbolism. It was uncivil, but he and Mercy had never been on the best of terms.

Mercy turned to find Death manifest beside her in the form of a spider-limbed woman.

"How your weakness repels me," Death remarked. "I struck here tonight, and you could do nothing to stop it."

"In the shadows," Mercy replied, "are five she-wolves of the Goweiteiuun. They came to tend the wounded from their pack after tonight's rally. As it happens, all the seriously wounded are Sardhluun. The she-wolves will tend them as their own and no more of them will die."

Death rose to all eight of her legs and looked down on the small mouthless woman with the lotus in her hand. "They will all die," Death signified. "Each one will die, and none will save them."

"On another day. On another night. Tonight," signified Mercy with great satisfaction, "*I* have struck, and you could do nothing to stop it."

Death indicated amusement, indifference, and patience. Then she ceased to manifest herself.

Mercy stayed to watch the acts that fell within her sphere, and to watch the increasingly intent conversation between the gnyrrands of the Goweit-eiuun and the outliers. More deaths would come of that; more fighting; more need for mercy.

Chapter Twenty-one

Night Shapes

uinlendhono and Rokhlenu's mating was settled for the fourth day of the year's third month—the month the werewolves called Uyaarwuionien ("third half-lunation of the second moon") but Morlock called Brenting. So he explained to Rokhlenu after Rokhlenu bespoke him as a guest and he accepted. They stood talking outside the irredeemables' lair—now considerably less barnlike thanks to their relative wealth, bite, and a good deal of hard work.

"What difference does it make what the month's called?" Rokhlenu asked Morlock.

"Nothing, except I find Brenting easier to pronounce."

"Are you joking? With that lippy growling bibbly sound at the beginning of the word?"

"You can say it."

"Of course I can say it, but why should I have to? I'm not an ape hanging by my feet from a tree branch. What's so hard to say about Uyaarwuionien? It practically sings its way out of your mouth."

"Not my mouth. I still haven't mastered the vowels of Sunspeech, let alone Moonspeech. Yesterday I asked a citizen selling grain in the marketplace whether she would sell me a pound of wheat flour and she started to take her clothes off."

"Oh. Oh, I see." In Sunspeech, the word *luiunhiendhi* meant "flour ground from wheat" whereas *luunhendhe* was an abrupt and rather intimate invitation involving another type of seed entirely. "Still, it's promising that she was so eager to go along. Did you get anywhere with her?"

"I got my flour eventually, if that's what you mean."

It was not what Rokhlenu meant at all. Like many males about to mate for life, he was eager to see his friends married off also, or at least happily settled. Morlock was an awkward prospect in this line.

"Well—pronounce it any way you want, as long as you're there. The act needs witnesses, and I want you to be mine."

"I'm honored, old friend," Morlock said formally, then added, "What should I bring?"

"Just yourself."

"Hm." Morlock looked unhappy. After a moment he said, "Rokhlenu."

"Morlock."

"I think our friendship has passed the point where we waste time being polite to each other?"

"Sometime on day two, I'd say. Why?"

"I remind you that I have never been to a mating of werewolves. If a gift is customary, I would prefer to bring a gift, polite protestations notwithstanding."

"Yes, I see. But I mean what I say, Morlock. When a First Wolf mates, or anyone with a lot of bite, really, it's the custom to *not* give gifts to the happy couple. They are supposed to be too ghost-bitingly wealthy to need the guests' assistance. We really only want you to be there."

"I will be." Morlock looked closely at him, a faint smile on his face. "You say 'happy couple' as if you mean it."

Rokhlenu shrugged and threw a chair at his old friend. Morlock caught it neatly—with his right hand, Rokhlenu noticed with a pang; he hardly ever moved the left hand anymore unless he had to. "I do mean it, I guess," Rokhlenu admitted. "Sad, isn't it?"

"Sad? No. Tragic perhaps."

"Tragic?"

"Happiness is usually tragic."

"It is?"

Morlock twirled the chair nervously in his fingers. He was no longer smiling. "I may be using the wrong words. The word I am thinking of in my native language implies no criticism."

"Now who's being polite? Get out and don't come back until you want to."

Morlock smiled, nodded, threw the chair back at him, and left.

"Your friend has been life-mated," Wuinlendhono said sagely, when Rokhlenu told her about the conversation later.

"Morlock? Married? Impossible."

"I'm sure his wife came to the same conclusion, at some point."

"Don't put the snarl on my old friend."

"He knows stuff about marriage that you don't, is what I'm saying, really. He has a sense of what you're getting into."

"I'm not getting into a what. I'm getting into a who."

"There's a what and a who. The *who* is your mate; the *what* is the marriage itself. There's usually trouble with one or the other."

"You worry too much about trouble. What happens can be dealt with. What never happens, you never have to deal with."

"Very philosophical. But I've got enough trouble to worry me. If these parfumiers don't come up with a decent wedding scent I may have to be mated wearing garlic instead of honor-teeth."

"Suits me. That or your natural scents: what could be more intoxicating?"

"It's not for you, clod. If you think I'm going to appear before what passes for the gentry in this bug-bitten swampy suburb without a decent wedding scent you . . . you can . . ."

"Think again? Bite you? Whistle up my tail?"

"You may not finish my sentences for me until we're mated and *old*."

"I can't wait to get started."

The waiting was hard, and became harder as the day got closer.

The day before the mating, grim news came from the city. Rokhlenu's father and two of his brothers had been killed in a night-theft while they were working as rope winders. His other brothers were missing; no one knew where they were—or, at least, if they knew, they would not say.

The messenger came to him just before sunset, and he went immediately to Wuinlendhono. He found her lying in her sleep chamber, just waking up from her afternoon sleep. Sitting down beside her sleeping cloak, he told her all he had heard.

"They can say night-thieves," he said. "And maybe they were night-thieves. But Rywudhaariu, that god-licking old gray-muzzle, *he* sent them. This is his work."

"It's a good guess. When did this all take place?"

"Seven months ago."

"You were on the fifth floor of the Vargulleion. There was nothing you could do."

"I know," Rokhlenu said, but he still felt guilty. He felt the shame survivors sometimes feel. "I think we should cancel the mating."

"Rokhlenu. Beloved. We will not cancel the mating."

"My father is dead. My brothers are dead."

"No deader now than they were yesterday."

"But now I *know*. If they were your kith, you would understand."

"I do understand. No, let me show you something, stalwart."

She rolled out of her sleeping cloak and grabbed a great heavy codex that was lying on a nearby chair. It was the prisoner book they had taken from the Vargulleion.

"I am not in here, by the way," she said, looking over the volume at him with her night-black eyes. "Evidently they didn't consider me a prisoner. But look at this."

Her forefinger rested on an entry; he read it over her shoulder. A prisoner named Slenginhuiuo. The crime was adultery. The dates of admission and discharge were illegible, but the prisoner was discharged as dead. Annotations in ideogrammatic Moonspeech added that the body was unfit for use as animal fodder and should be chopped up for fertilizer on the plantations.

"My mother," Wuinlendhono said. "I found this a few days ago. I hadn't wanted to look for it. I wanted to believe that he forgave her at last, that he sold her into some wild pack, that she was growing old licking someone else's cubs in the empty lands. But now I know. I *know* that she is dead. He had them torture her until she died."

"And you say we should be mated anyway."

"This is why we must be mated. Our families are gone. Our pasts are gone. All we have is each other, the present, and the future. Grieve. Plan vengeance. Do what you must. But tomorrow you will mount me as your mate. I need you."

If she had said (as he half expected her to say), *be sensible, the plans are made, I finally have chosen my mating scent, we have bought expensive food and smoke which will spoil if it is not used, be sensible, all the invitations have been spoken, we have responsibilities to others, what will people think, be sensible*—if she had said any of that, or anything like it, he would have left her forever. But the words she actually spoke tolled in his heart like a bell; he knew he could never leave her. She and no other was his life-mate.

"Need you, too," he grumbled.

"Oh, you golden-tongued persuader."

So Rokhlenu's mood was unexpectedly chaotic as he donned his wedding shirt the next day in the late afternoon. He was vibrating with hope and longing for Wuinlendhono; nothing could change that. But he was shaken by waves of grief and anger and loneliness, too. Somehow, no matter what he had done and where he had been, he had always seen himself returning to his family's den and telling his tale to them and listening to others from them as he lay by his brothers and father on the hearth before the long fireplace. Now they were dead, and that part of him was dying, like a gangrenous limb.

He stood in the little sleeping closet they had built for him in a corner of the irredeemables' barracks. A male was supposed to be mated from his parents' lair, the home where he grew up. But if that place still existed, it was just a place, a hole in the cliffs above Nekkuklendon mesa. The people who gave it meaning, who made it home, were dead. This place was just a place. He could still smell the sawdust from its making. But if he'd lived here for a hundred years, it still wouldn't be home.

"Chief," a hesitant voice broke in on his thoughts, "your friends are here."

Rokhlenu raised his head and saw that the door to his sleeping closet was open. In the doorway stood claw-fingered Lekkativengu.

"Good news," he said heavily, and moved toward the door. Lekkativengu stepped hastily out of the way, but Rokhlenu grabbed him by the shoulder before he had retreated entirely.

"You're in charge here, after I'm gone," he said.

"I know, Chief. Thanks."

They both knew it was a consolation prize; Rokhlenu had picked Yaarirruuiu to be the reeve of his campaign band. Lekkativengu had never really bitten through the bone as Olleiulu's replacement. Now that Rokhlenu had tasted real grief he was less inclined to condemn Lekkativengu as a scatterwit club-juggler. But he needed someone he could trust to watch his back in the long days and nights ahead, and he had seen Yaarirruuiu in the hour of action.

But the job of herding the irredeemables wasn't nothing, and Rokhlenu needed Lekkativengu to do it well. He said, "Olleiulu trusted you. Show me you deserve it and I'll never forget it."

Lekkativengu nodded, put his claw-fingered hand on Rokhlenu's shoulder, and said something about Rokhlenu's intended that would have earned him a knife in the belly on any other day. But encouragements like that were traditional between friends on a mating day, so Rokhlenu grinned and said, "If you insist. Over and over."

They released each other, and Rokhlenu turned to his friends. They were a rather motley crew: the never-wolf Morlock, the biteless healer female Liudhleeo—no, she was wearing an honor-tooth. No, it was the crystal spike she had pulled from Morlock's skull. Excellent: Wuinlendhono had told her to wear it. And it was a reminder, a very civil reminder, of how much he owed her. Beyond them stood the twenty irredeemables who had fought with him at the recent election rally—the twenty who had survived, anyway. Pale Hrutnefdhu was the only one missing.

Liudhleeo stepped forward, took his shoulder, and made an obscene suggestion about Wuinlendhono.

"Certainly," he said, "since you ask. Anything to oblige."

"Hrutnefdhu thought it best not to come," she added, in a low voice. "He hopes you understand."

"I do—though I'd be glad to see him here."

Morlock was close enough to hear this exchange, and he looked with some surprise at Liudhleeo, at Rokhlenu, and back at Liudhleeo. Then he shrugged.

Rokhlenu felt a sudden pang of doubt—did Morlock fully understand the life-mating ritual? Surely it couldn't be that different among never-wolves. Anyway, there was no time for a lesson now.

Liudhleeo stood aside, and Morlock grabbed Rokhlenu's shoulder. "I don't know any of the traditional remarks on a day like this," he observed.

Rokhlenu silently thanked the ghosts for this.

"I'll say this instead," Morlock continued. "We are one blood. Your blood is my blood. It will be avenged."

Rokhlenu belatedly realized that Morlock was talking about his father and brothers. His grief, never distant, returned in a great crashing wave. But this was real. It mattered, unlike the traditional obscene compliments. He met Morlock's eye. "I *told* you not to bring a present, you rat-bastard."

Morlock half smiled and shrugged. "I won't do it again," he promised, and stood back.

There were more encounters, more jokes and songs about the act of mating. But soon enough, Yaarirruuiu said, "Friends, the sun is setting. We must get our chief to his new home."

They roared and cheered and barked. Rokhlenu picked up a bundle of his clothes, and the twenty irredeemables who were accompanying him into Wuinlendhono's household picked up boxes of wealth and weapons and their own belongings. He walked before them, and they followed singing false and not really flattering stories about his sexual adventures or misadventures.

The walk to Wuinlendhono's lair-tower (still supported by cables, but on a firmer foundation than before thanks to Morlock and Hlupnafenglu) was not long, thank ghost. He pounded on the door and demanded entry.

The door was immediately opened by a snow-pale, anxious-looking Wuinlendhono. She wore a loose white wedding shirt, not so different than his own, except that the hem was lower, sweeping the floor. "My intended, you and yours enter my house and remain here forever," she said rapidly, and kissed his ear. She added in a whisper, "Ghost, I thought you were never coming. It's almost sunset."

"Plenty of time," he breathed, half stunned by the mix of her natural scent and her wedding scent. He noted with interest that she seemed more nervous than he was.

She took him by the hand and led him into the great audience chamber of the lair-tower. The dais had been moved so that moonlight would fall on it as soon as dark touched the sky after sunset. Around the audience chamber were scattered tables with bowls of food and water and fuming smoke. There were many low couches, and on some of them the councilors, allies, and friends who were Wuinlendhono's wedding party. They were already eating, drinking, smoking.

"My intended, disport yourselves with your friends and mine," Wuinlendhono said, in a loud formal voice. "I await your intention at the mating couch." She added in a low voice, "I give you a hundred breaths. If you're not on the dais by then, I'm coming after you and nailing you wherever you happen to be. One hundred breaths. And I'm breathing pretty fast, stalwart."

He watched her stride sinuously away from him and he took a deep breath. Ninety-nine more, and then . . .

His irredeemables were dumping the boxes with traditional informality about the room. This was just part of the tradition, meant to give the place a moved-in look. All the significant wealth and property (boxes of gold and such) had been brought over early in the day and secured.

Liudhleeo had Morlock over at one of the tables and was fussing over him with bowls of food and water. No doubt she would continue her epic quest to get into his pants tonight: mating ceremonies were famous for promoting spontaneous couplings. She tried to give him a bowl of smoke and he waved it off—and that reminded Rokhlenu of something.

He grabbed a jar sitting at a nearby table and ran over to Morlock and Liudhleeo. He took the bowl of water from Morlock's hand and dumped the contents back in the serving bowl. Morlock looked at him, his eyebrows lifting in surprise and amusement.

"You don't want that swill," said Rokhlenu. "Try this!" He cracked open the jar, poured a stream of purplish red wine into the bowl, and proudly handed it to Morlock.

He had been planning this for some time, ever since Morlock told him about drinking and bartenders. If Morlock didn't like smoking bloom, if he wanted wine to celebrate, Rokhlenu reasoned, why not get him some wine? It hadn't been easy, but he had done it, and the effect was all he could have hoped for.

Morlock's eyebrows raised even farther, his eyes widened, his mouth parted slightly. He was completely stunned.

"Is it the good kind?" Rokhlenu asked. "There were a couple of different colors. I got this from a gang of road robbers who dragged it back from Semendar without looking inside. There are crates of the stuff, as much as you could want."

"It's fine," Morlock said faintly.

"You're sure?" Rokhlenu asked.

"Morlock," Liudhleeo said out of the side of her mouth, "*drink it*. He's got some business to attend to."

Morlock put the bowl to his lips and drank a sip, then a larger mouthful.

"Excellent," he said, lowering the bowl. "Thanks, old friend. I know you mean well."

Rokhlenu laughed, punched him in the arm, and turned away. He had lost count of the breaths that had passed—and then he realized he didn't care. He walked, with as much dignity as he could, to the dais and mounted the steps. Wuinlendhono was watching him with her night-dark starless eyes. He found he had to step very slowly and carefully, lest he trip and fall—the worst of omens for a mating.

As he climbed the stairs, the room grew silent. By the time he reached the top, no one was speaking.

Wuinlendhono took his hands and they stood for a moment, wordless, staring into each other's eyes.

She shook his hands loose and said, in the dark contralto lightning she used as a voice, "I take you and all you are and all you own as mine."

He replied, in his clearest singing-while-speaking voice, "I take you and all you are and all you own as mine."

She undid the fastenings of her shirt, and it fell to the floor. She stood proudly naked in the red light of evening.

One of the knots in his fastenings *would not* come undone. He'd have cursed the one who had tied it, except it was himself, distracted by love and grief, only a short time ago.

Wuinlendhono smiled and brushed his hands aside, deftly undoing the knot. His shirt fell away, and he now stood as naked as she.

She ascended the couch on the dais and, never breaking eye contact, went down on all fours.

He climbed onto the couch behind her. She turned her head to watch him over her shoulder. Her eyes were wide, excited. She was panting slightly.

He mounted her from behind. As he entered her, her eyes half closed and she gasped. She writhed in pleasure, and the sinuous motion sent muscles rippling all down her glorious back.

Union with her was silken ecstasy. The world was afire with the day's last light. He wanted to drive into her until he came, but he could not; he must not yet.

She moved again and moaned.

"Be still," he said to her.

"Can't," she whispered.

"You must," he said, and put his hands on her back to keep her still. That was a mistake, perhaps: it sent soft streams of sensory fire up his fingers. He sank his fingers deeper in her soft firm skin, because he could, because they belonged to each other now. He almost started to move his hips.

"You're right," she whispered. "I'll be still."

Somehow that helped. He waited, adrift in a fog of pleasure-that-was and the agony of pleasure self-denied.

The room waited, silent, as sunlight died. The room grew dim, then dark. No lamps were lit.

Blue light appeared in the windows: the eyes of the moons were opening with the departure of the sun's light. The light grew stronger, bluer, more bitter, more intoxicating. Rokhlenu looked through the window straight into the face of Trumpeter and knew that this was the moment.

He yielded to the moment of transformation, and Wuinlendhono did the same. His shadow rose up and towered over him; hers did the same. The two shadows passed through each other, mingling as their bodies mingled, transforming them as they coupled; day shape with night shape and female with male they were bonded in an endless instant of transformation and sexual union.

Their screams gave way to ecstatic howls; they lay, still joined, in the night shape.

Slowly, hungrily, intently, patiently, Rokhlenu began to grind into his mate as she rocked back against him. They were mated now.

Rokhlenu found that his grief was not gone. If anything, he was even more aware of his loss, of his beloved dead. And he grieved for Wuinlendhono and their love. They were mortal; they would die; their love would be forgotten as if it never had been.

But this was their hour, and all the ages of nothingness to come could not wash away this one glorious moment of being and becoming. If this was life, and he felt it was, it was worth even the price of death to feel this way.

Morlock was drinking slowly and he was not yet drunk. But he had begun to drink on purpose, not merely to be polite, and that meant that most of the man he thought of as himself was gone.

It was as if there were two Morlocks. Drunk Morlock was careless, selfish, lazy, stupid, cruel—everything that Morlock hated about himself, everything he rejected. It was like the werewolves, with their day shape and night shape.

Not-drunk Morlock was still holding the reins. But drunk Morlock was slowly getting a grip on them.

This internal struggle numbed the shock he felt when he noticed Rokhlenu and Wuinlendhono consummating their bond by having sex in the presence of the wedding party. In any case, it was no skin off his walrus: different lands had different customs.

Rather more worrisome to him was the way partners were beginning to pair off and nuzzle each other on couches. Apparently the ceremonial union of the couple was accompanied by more informal unions among the wedding party. Looking back on weddings he had attended over the centuries, he realized that things were not so different here—just more open.

When the pair mating on the dais assumed their night shapes, and a tide of moonlit transformations spread across the room, the coupling began in earnest, many pairs eschewing the couches and tumbling about on the floor. There were wolves, semiwolves, and a few unfortunates in their day shape, apparently unable to make the transition. Morlock thought this—and nearly laughed aloud. Werewolf notions seemed to be soaking into his skin. If he stayed among the werewolves much longer, at the next wedding he might actually join in. That was an amusing thought, and this time he did laugh.

He looked around for the wine jar: time to grab it and make his escape. He found it. He also found that Liudhleeo was still standing beside him in her day shape. Her eyes were half closed; she was smiling at him with shy eagerness.

"I'd've thought you'd've switched shadows by now," he said, waving his wine bowl vaguely at the rest of the room.

She looked hurt, then sly. "Is that what you'd prefer? Some never-wolves like it—coupling with a partner in the night shape."

"They're not as never-wolfy as I am. I've never coupled with someone who was not a never-wolf." Morlock covertly tried to count up the number of negatives in that sentence, was unsure of his total, and added hastily, "I have only ever coupled with never-wolves. If you see what I mean. It's worked out pretty well for me so far," he said wryly, thinking of his ex-wife. There was a little wine left in his bowl, so he emptied it.

"There are none like that here," Liudhleeo replied. "If there were, she'd be a slave or meat. You aren't only because of who you are. I'm not the only female in the room who finds that fascinating. Or your scent fascinating."

"I never argue about matters of taste—or, in this case, smell."

She laughed too much and took his arm. He impatiently shook her off.

"Why are you being so cruel to me?" Liudhleeo asked, not as if she really minded.

"I don't know what's going on," said Morlock, "but I can't believe you look on me with favor."

Liudhleeo was amused. "Why not? You smell so wonderful, like blood and burning bone with a hint of poisonous leaves. And you're perfectly dangerous. Ghost, when you glare at me like that I just melt. And maybe you're not as beautiful as my sweet Hrutnefdhu, but nobody is, and anyway a female doesn't have to look at her partner during sex. . . ." She paused, horrified by a thought that struck her. "Unless. Unless they do it . . . face-to-face. Do you do it that way, Morlock?"

"Sometimes. It doesn't matter."

"*Doesn't matter?* It bites me what males think matters. Not even monkeys do it that way, you know, face-to-face. It seems so depraved. Soft wet mouths and soft wet bellies pressing against each other. It seems so nasty. So nasty. Oh. Oh. Oh, ghost. You have to do that for me. I know you don't care about me. I know you don't care about anybody, but you can't leave me after putting that idea in my head."

"Now I see why Hrutnefdhu didn't attend," Morlock said. "Did you ask him to stay home?"

Now she stepped a pace back from him, her brows knitted in bafflement. "No," she said. "Of course not. But how do you suppose he'd feel if he were here, right now, with pairs coupling all over the floor and the room stinking of sex—"

"—and his mate trying to couple with his old friend—"

"Is that it? You don't understand. You really don't understand. It's not a betrayal."

"And I never will understand."

She bowed her head, defeated. "Do you want me to find you another female, then? Or a male, perhaps? There are other never-wolves in town."

Morlock stared at her. "My love life, grim and empty though it may be, has never been soiled by the presence of a pimp."

She stood back another pace, tears leaking from her eyes. She gave him a last reproachful look and fled.

Morlock took his wine jar and a couple of still-sealed ones for backup. He made his way unsteadily out of the moonlit room, stepping carefully around (or, in one case, over) groups of werewolves in various stages of sexual congress.

The air outside was clean, by contrast, but warm as a summer's night. He drank a jar of wine as he walked slowly across the outlier settlement, dropping the empty into a stretch of swamp showing next to a walkway. When he reached the lair-tower, he found that he couldn't face Hrutnefdhu (drunk Morlock was a coward, among his other vices), so he decided to sleep that night in his cave. The last thing he remembered was sitting in the wickerwork boat, finishing another jar of wine.

The night was dark, though moonlit. The swamp water was darker and smelled bad. His mind was darker still and smelled worse.

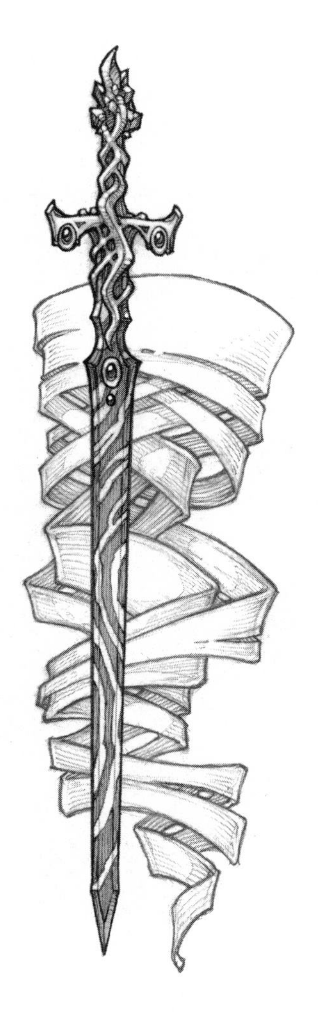

Part Three

Masks

I met Murder on the way—
He had a mask like Castlereagh—
Very smooth he looked, yet grim;
Seven blood-hounds followed him:

All were fat; and well they might
Be in admirable plight,
For one by one, and two by two,
He tossed the human hearts to chew
Which from his wide cloak he drew.

. . .

And many more Destructions played
In this ghastly masquerade,
All disguised, even to the eyes,
Like Bishops, lawyers, peers, or spies.

Last came Anarchy: he rode
On a white horse, splashed with blood;
He was pale even to the lips,
Like Death in the Apocalypse.

And he wore a kingly crown;
And in his grasp a sceptre shone;
On his brow this mark I saw—
"I am God, and King, and Law!"

—**Shelley, *The Mask of Anarchy***

Chapter Twenty-two

The Shadow Market

From then on, Morlock drank himself to sleep every night. Sometimes he slept in the lair-tower apartment with Hrutnefdhu and Liudhleeo, but he didn't like to. If it was him and Hrutnefdhu alone there, he was conscious of why Liudhleeo was absent. But when he woke up, and looked across the room to see them wrapped around each other, blissfully empty of thought as they slept, joined by something more powerful than sexual union, he felt strange, an intruder. Werewolves had no sense of privacy with those they considered old friends, but Morlock did. Besides, when he drank so much that he grew sick and felt the need to vomit (which was almost nightly now), the cave was more convenient.

He was not yet drinking in the day, though. Morlock had been through this before, and he had a sense of fatalism about it. He knew that drunkenness would come to rule his life entirely and that he would be able to think of nothing else.

Perhaps that wasn't so bad, this time. He was, after all, dying. The ghost sickness had progressed so far that he could pick up nothing with his left fingers: material objects passed through the misty flesh as if it were air. If he was dying, if this was the end of all his days, did it matter if he died a drunk? He would be no more alive if he died sober.

But in the day he did not drink, not yet. He threw himself into projects and worked fiercely. He developed a wooden hand that he could wear over his ghostly hand like a glove. It was no good for fine work, of course, but it could bear weight, and the fingers could clamp shut for a grip, if need be.

For two-handed work, he had Hlupnafenglu. The red werewolf was strikingly improved after the removal of his spike—but he knew nothing about his past. His memory had been almost entirely scrubbed by the madness induced by the electrum spike in his brain. He could speak Sunspeech and Moonspeech, but he didn't even know his real name, so everyone continued to call him Hlupnafenglu.

He was intelligent and strong, though, with extremely deft hands. He fell into the role of Morlock's apprentice. The outliers could use many skills Morlock had, but he clearly would not be around forever to assist them, and he trusted Hlupnafenglu's character as well as his talent.

Together they forged glass weapons and armor for the outlier fighters. They began the challenging task of shoring up the outliers' defenses. Once Wuinlendhono found out what they were doing, she had a crowd of citizens put at their disposal and the work went faster: new watchtowers, armed with catapults and crossbows, soon bristled along the settlement's verge.

The days were hot; the work was hard. In the evenings, when his friends were sometimes smoking bowls of bloom, he would join them in a bowl of wine (which they always had ready, once they knew he would drink it). Sometimes they would play cards. Werewolves love to gamble, and they were all fond of the game he had invented called pookah or, as Hlupnafenglu always mispronounced it, poker. Later, while he could still walk, he would go back to his cave and drink himself unconscious.

He did not look well during the day, but his old friends attributed that to the ghost sickness that they knew was working on him.

One day he woke up, rolled away from the pile of vomit he had emitted in his sleep, fed the flames in the nexus with a chunk or two of coal, and staggered out to rinse his mouth and wash in the uphill stream outside his cave.

Rokhlenu was waiting for him there, sitting cross-legged beside the stream. The gray werewolf was, in contrast to his old cellmate, looking healthy these days. He wore clothes of green and gold, a gold ring with a green stone in it, and a green-and-gold band gathered his long gray queue.

"Gnyrrand Rokhlenu," Morlock said. "You're looking well. Very gnyrrandly, in fact."

"Thanks. Wuinlendhono is knitting some green-and-gold underwear for me, I believe."

"She's treating you well, anyway. Mated life suits you, old friend."

"It does. It does. You, however, look like a sack of moldy kidneys. And not in a good way."

"I was wondering if that was a compliment."

"It's not."

"Well, I won't lie to you. I feel like a bag of moldy kidneys. Or maybe just the mold."

"The ghost sickness is worse?"

"Yes." Morlock might have added, *And then there is the drinking*, but he didn't want to talk about that.

"Look, I've been talking to Wuinlendhono about this. I want you to stop working on the defenses around the settlement."

"There's more to do."

"There always will be. You told me once you thought this illness would kill you, and it looks to me as if it is killing you. Liudhleeo and Hrutnefdhu both say that someone in the Shadow Market might be able to help. So I think maybe that's what you should be doing from now on."

"Is that a gnyrrandly command?" Morlock asked wryly.

"It's a request from your old friend. You have been helping us so much. Maybe it's time to look out for yourself."

"I can do that pretty well."

"Ghost testicles."

Morlock laughed a little. "Haven't heard that one. I think what I enjoy most about Sunspeech is the rich variety of invective and cursing."

"It's good for that. Moonspeech for singing, Sunspeech for barking: that's the old saying."

Morlock washed his face and mouth and thought. "Would I be allowed in the city? Anyone who smells me or sees my shadow will know I'm a never-wolf."

"There are never-wolves and never-wolves, and then there's Khretvarrgliu. I don't think you'll have any trouble you can't fight your way out of. And the worst they can do is kill you."

"I suppose," said Morlock, looking forward to another night, and night after night, of drunken emptiness, "there are worse things."

In the end, Morlock went with Hrutnefdhu and Hlupnafenglu through the northern gate, up the walkway to the Swamp Road leading to the Swamp Gate of Wuruyaaria.

The gate was wide; twenty werewolves in the day shape could walk through it side by side and still have room to swing their arms. There were a couple of lazy watchers on either side wearing dark armor emblazoned with an ideogram that, Morlock had learned, meant *Wuruyaaria* in Moonspeech. One of them sniffed the air curiously as Morlock and his friends passed by, but no one stopped them.

The borough just inside the wall was a thicket of tilting towers built on rather marshy ground. Nearly every citizen in sight was wearing the night shape, or some part of it: everyone was a wolf or a semiwolf.

"Dogtown," said Hrutnefdhu. "Those who can't assume the day shape, or at least not completely, often end up here. People say they're more comfortable with their own kind."

"What do you say?" asked Hlupnafenglu, catching an implied reservation. He might have no memories, but there was nothing wrong with his intelligence.

"I say they were kicked out of their dens by shamed parents who didn't want never-men stinking up their lives and reducing their bite."

Morlock wondered, not for the first time, about Hrutnefdhu's family, and who had castrated him, and why. But he seemed to be speaking with some authority here: another outcast, for another reason.

They passed a werewolf nailing up a sign with hammer and nails. His paws had fingers as hairless and gray as a rat's tail. They passed another werewolf who was shuffling a dance on four human feet that grew from crooked canine legs. A chorus of largely lupine werewolves chanted and sang beside him. A small crowd had gathered to watch, and Morlock paused there too, fascinated by the show. But when he realized more eyes were directed toward him than the performers, he tossed a few pads of copper onto the coin-speckled ground between the dancer and the singers and walked off.

Hrutnefdhu and Hlupnafenglu were already standing some distance away, waiting for him.

"That was risky," the pale werewolf said. "If you'd had a few less honor-teeth showing, you might have had to fight your way out of there."

"Why?"

"Never-men don't like to be stared at by anyone wearing the day shape. In fact, it's a little risky for us just to be passing through Dogtown in the daytime."

"Why are we, then?"

"Sardhluun werewolves come up the Low Road to Twinegate, and then into the city. There's less chance of meeting them if we take this way."

"Too bad." Morlock was sorry to miss a chance to fight some Sardhluun.

"Yurr. I hate them, too, Morlock, but this might not be the time to take on a band of them."

Morlock opened his right hand and shrugged: it was a matter of opinion.

Hlupnafenglu laughed. Fighting, working, learning, walking—it was all the same to him. Morlock envied the sunniness of his temperament a little.

Presently they came to an open area, and on their left was a gate, obviously Twinegate, not materially different from the Swamp Gate, except that more people were coming and going through it.

The area was dominated by a great stone tower, reaching from the swampy ground to the sky. Morlock kept on staring at it almost from the moment it came into view. There were narrow stairways of metal and wood running up the sides of the tower, and citizens running up and down the stairs. At the top of the tower was a great basket

"It's just the gate-station for the funicular," Hrutnefdhu said. "But I forgot: you've never seen it before."

"Not this close," Morlock said.

Hlupnafenglu was almost as fascinated. "I seem to remember . . . Do the cars smell like onions?"

"I never noticed that. I suppose it might depend on who or what was riding with you."

"How is it powered?" wondered the red werewolf.

"Slaves. They used to hire citizens to work the big wheels, but when the Sardhluun started flooding the market with slaves, it was cheaper to use them. A lot of citizens went hungry that year."

The three ex-prisoners looked at each other, sharing a single bitter thought about the Sardhluun without the need to speak it.

Morlock said, "The big wheels. I can hear the gears working. I'd like to see them sometime."

"We could ask, I suppose," said Hrutnefdhu nervously.

"It's not important. Another time."

They walked on, across the chaos around the tower's base, northward, into a new tangle of warrens. The land was drier and firmer; the buildings taller and narrower than Dogtown. The twisting streets were dense with werewolves in the day shape.

"Apetown," Hrutnefdhu said in a low voice. "Fairly safe in the daylight, but you don't want to cross here in the night shape, in the day or night."

Morlock nodded, and suddenly the pale werewolf's mottled skin flushed dark. "I forgot—"

"Never mind it, old friend," said Morlock, and Hlupnafenglu tugged playfully on Hrutnefdhu's ear.

Apetown looked busier than Dogtown, anyway. The ground floor of many a tower was given over to workshops of craftsmen: cobblers, smiths, glass blowers, bakers, butchers, launderers.

"Hands," said Morlock aloud. He had been trying to settle in his mind the difference between Dogtown and Apetown, and he realized it all came down to hands.

Hlupnafenglu looked bemused, but Hrutnefdhu instantly understood him. "Yes, you're right. It's a more prosperous place: there's more work people can do. It may not be work that gains anyone great bite, but it's work that other people will pay to have done."

"And when the sun goes down—"

"Yes, the shutters will drop here. Dogtown is livelier then. There's singing and shows. And if you want a thug for hire, you go to Dogtown, day or night."

They walked on through the warm hazy morning.

When they left the rumble of Apetown behind them, they came to a wide-open space between the brooding hulk of Mount Dhaarnaiarnon and the staggered cliff sides of Wuruyaaria. It was paved in stones that alternated black and white in no clear pattern. It was cut off from direct sunlight, and would be until the sun rose considerably higher in the murky sky.

"Here we are," said the pale werewolf. He looked around the Shadow Market, and his face twisted with annoyance. "Not too many vendors, and some of them I know are quacks."

Morlock was looking, too. At a booth near the market entrance, a male with the torso of a young boy and the limbs and face of a young wolf was having his ears pinched by a long-nosed saturnine male with a gray gown and a conical cap adorning his day shape. A mature female, perhaps the boy's mother, was standing over them; she was fully human except for her long lupine jaws and somewhat hairy face. She was asking in Moonspeech how much the fee would be and the vendor was asking in Sunspeech how she proposed to pay.

In the next space over, a wolf-faced young man with immaculately styled hair was listening to a group of young women in the day shape sing a song in Moonspeech. If a wolf face can look dubious, he looked dubious. Morlock was no judge of songs in Moonspeech, but he thought he had heard some broken notes.

Next over was a booth full of red-ribboned scrolls and velvet-bound books. Its vendor was a male with a wolf's body, human hands and feet, and a droopy semihuman face.

"I'll just step over and have a word with Liuunurriu, there," the pale werewolf said. "He doesn't like strangers, and it wouldn't do to look too interested so . . ."

Morlock nodded, and he and Hlupnafenglu drifted in the other direction.

"I think I remember Apetown," said the red werewolf abstractedly, after a few moments. "I don't remember the looks, but I remember the feel.

Always hurry, hurry, hurry and fetch the bones. Fetch the bones; fetch the bones."

Morlock said nothing.

"Fetch the bones," Hlupnafenglu repeated again. "Why would people want bones?"

"For marrow," Morlock suggested. "Or soup."

"Soup!" shouted the red werewolf. "There was a great vat of it in the middle of the hut! And a great fat female who kept telling me, 'Fetch the bones, yuh-yuh. . . . Fetch the bones, yuh-yuh. . . .' And she said my name. Only I don't remember it now."

"You may yet."

"I hated her. I don't remember her name, but I remember the hate. I don't think she was my mother. I hated the bones, too. The stinking stupid bones. That was why. That was why. There was no soup that day. No soup, sir. No soup, ma'am. Take your no-soup and swim in it!"

The more the red werewolf remembered the angrier he seemed to get. Morlock found this interesting, but not so interesting that he failed to notice someone trying to unfasten his money pouch from his belt, craftily reaching under his left arm. He grabbed the pickpocket's extended fingers with his right hand and twisted.

The pickpocket, a strikingly flat-faced young male, screamed and fell sprawling on the ground. He had been standing unbalanced, and he didn't know enough to not draw attention when he was caught. All this marked him as an inept and inexperienced thief—which was in his favor, as far as Morlock was concerned. So Morlock released his fingers without breaking them.

His reward for this was a reproachful glare from the clumsy pickpocket as he lay on the black-and-white pavement. "You broke my fingers," he wailed, rubbing his left hand furiously with his right.

"No," said Morlock. "But I can, if you insist."

"I told you, Snellingu," said a white-haired male standing nearby, wearing dark armor with the Wuruyaaria ideogram. "Pickpocket."

"Snatch-and-grab, snatch-and-grab," irritably replied another watcher (evidently Snellingu) with a long scar on his face that cut across his lips. "You see so stupid he is being. He's being no sort of pickpocket. He's grabbing someone's cash box by now *if you didn't have keep staring at him.* And you are expecting me paying off the bet."

"Listen, it's my job to keep an eye on the criminal element."

"That's why you keep to be visiting your father's sister on nights-with-no-moon. We all are hearing about her criminal element, if you're getting my drift."

"I do not get your drift, and you still owe me breakfast."

"You have be owing me breakfast three half-months straight and bent."

"Minus today's. That's what I'm saying. Hey, don't let him get away, Chief."

"I'm not your chief," Morlock replied. "And he can go where he likes."

The young male, scrambling to his feet, glared suspiciously at Morlock.

"I like that!" said the white-haired watcher. "We come here to defend you from this dangerous criminal and you—"

"Take him and bake him," said Morlock. "But not on my evidence. The young citizen tripped and fell."

"No pickpocket!" said scar-faced Snellingu, catching on suddenly. "The citizen is saying so! And thus I am owing you jack-minus-jack and you owing me breakfast, today, tomorrow, some more days."

"This *citizen* smells like a never-wolf to me."

"You are smelling like a snake trying to weasel his way out of a dead-dog bet."

"That metaphor stinks worse than this guy does."

"You are stinking worse than—"

"Listen, if I buy you a meatcake will you stop with the similes? I get enough crappy rhetoric from politicians this year if I want it, which I don't."

"Two meatcakes."

"That's two breakfasts, then. I never ate more than one meatcake at a time on your pad."

"You are all the time drinking that rotten milk-drink, which I am never drinking, but I am all the time paying for—"

The squabbling peace officers wandered off across the Shadow Market.

Morlock looked at the young citizen, who had not yet moved away. His face was hollowed out with hunger; rags hung on him as if he were a scarecrow made of sticks. Morlock had seen children starved to death, and this child was starving to death.

"You can't steal," Morlock said coolly. "You won't work. I suppose now comes the begging."

The young citizen tore at his hair and spat at Morlock's feet. "I work! I work! I work for three days running messages for Neiuluniu the bookie. He says come back tomorrow; I'll pay you. Come back tomorrow, Lakkasulakku; come back tomorrow, Lakkasulakku. Today I say pay me the three days or I don't run messages. So he has his boys throw me out. You think he pays me? You think he ever pays me?"

It might have been a lie, but Morlock didn't think so. Anyway, it didn't matter. He said to Hlupnafenglu, "Take the young citizen, Lakkasulakku or whatever his name is, to the outliers and get him some work. Better buy him some food on the way—have you got any coin?"

The red werewolf, his good cheer restored, looked wryly at him. "Enough. You'll be all right?"

Morlock opened his right hand and shrugged. Hlupnafenglu punched him farewell and walked off, the suspicious-looking youngster in tow.

Morlock turned and saw a crow sitting in the middle of the Shadow Market, looking at him. Morlock walked over to talk to the bird.

"I don't have any food with me—" Morlock began.

The crow croaked that she remembered him pretty well. At least he wasn't a stone-throwing type. She and the rest of her murder had fed pretty well on a loaf of bread he had thrown at a crow once. She figured she owed him one, if that's what he was asking.

"Is there a vendor here you trust?" Morlock asked. "Not a stone thrower? A man who knows things?"

The crow laughed. She knew a man whose house had no legs but it walked, and he lived around stones but never threw one at crows. She didn't know what he knew, but he gave them grain sometimes, and offal he had no interest in eating, and he asked intelligent questions, not like Morlock.

"Will you take me to him?" Morlock asked.

The crow nodded and took wing. Morlock loped after her through the shadowy crowd.

The crow's dark feathers were briefly outlined in golden light as she lifted above the shadows of the square. She dropped again into darkness, and Morlock almost lost sight of her as she descended just beyond the edge of the market. But she waited for him there until he caught up, and then she flew into the tangle of streets and dark-bricked buildings east of the marketplace. A short flight: she landed at the door of a stone building. Above the door hung a sign with a picture of a rock being weighed on a scale. On the door was written in black letters IACOMES FILIUS SAXIPONDERIS.

"Here is a man I've long wished to meet," Morlock said to the crow. "Stop by my cave sometime. I have some unground grain I'll give you and yours."

The crow assured him he would see her and her murder soon. She flew away.

Morlock knocked on the door. There was no answer, but it wasn't locked, so he pushed it open and entered.

Inside he found a single dim room cluttered with books and stones and papers and dust. In the center of the clutter was a balding man at a desk who was scribbling something on a sheet of paper. He occasionally paused, a faraway look in his dim blue eyes, and gave the end of his pen a thoughtful chew. In his abstraction he sometimes chewed the wrong end of the pen: there were ink stains in his graying beard and on his shirt. He wrote in the light of a window set into the wall. The window did not open on the city outside—there was a wintry scene beyond the frosted glass, pine trees under a dense cover of snow in evening light.

The man didn't seem to notice that anyone else was there, so Morlock rapped on the inside of the door.

The man at the desk jumped, spilling his ink so that it ran dark across the page.

"Go away, won't you?" the man said in Latin. "I'm busy."

"Making more prisons?" Morlock asked in the same language.

"Not today. What day is it?"

"The first of Drums."

"No it's not. What year?"

"The year of the Ship."

"Then I'm in Wuruyaaria."

"Yes. Didn't you expect to be?"

"I expected to be left alone so that I can finish a rather large job I have on hand."

"Another prison?"

"No, no, no, no, no, no. No. Definitely no. Well, it depends on how you look at it, I guess. Listen, if you cared about what I'm doing you obviously would have gone away by now and left me to do it. I'd rather not try to make you go away; you appear to be armed. Is there anything I can do to *persuade* you to go away?"

"I wanted to meet you, Iacomes."

"Pleased to meet you. Really, it's been an honor. Good-bye!"

"But I don't accept your apology."

"I haven't apologized. I'm actually trying to be dismissive and insulting, and it wounds me deeply that you haven't even noticed."

Morlock recited, "'I, Iacomes Saxiponderis, made this prison. Sorry about that, prisoner.'"

"Oh." Iacomes focused his cold blue eyes on Morlock at last. "I see. You were a prisoner at the Vargulleion. Did they let you out? They don't usually do that."

"I escaped."

"Good for you."

"Doesn't it bother you that your prison failed?"

"I'm sure it didn't. You didn't tunnel out, or break the bars, did you? There are silver cores in those iron bars. If you'd sawn into them you'd have had a sad surprise."

"I'm not a werewolf."

"Then what were you doing in the Vargulleion? It's a prison for werewolves, you know."

"They didn't consult me about it."

"Hm. I suppose not. They are pretty arbitrary. Still, I'd bet a nickel that the guards were inattentive. Am I right? You got out of there because the guards were napping or smoke-drunk or something."

Morlock nodded reluctantly, then added, "The locks weren't all that they might be."

The man threw up his hands; the pen flew out of his hand and bounced off the window behind him, leaving an inkblot on the frosted glass. "They didn't hire me to provide locks! They used their own people for the locks and bolts. Blacksmiths! Guys who usually made chains and manacles and stuff like that. I *saw* one of those locks. Key slots so big you could stick your little finger in them. Cell doors with simple crossbars. I said to them, 'What happens when you have a prison riot?' They said, 'There will be no riots. We have a way of breaking prisoners.' But broken things or people are pretty damned dangerous. I told them it was a mistake. What is the use of a prison for incorrigibles that has substandard locks? They said, 'Perpetual vigilance shall be our lock.' And I said, 'Look, in this kind of situation, you wear suspenders *and* a belt, just to be safe.' But most of them don't even wear pants, so I guess they didn't get it."

"But you took their money."

"Naturally, naturally. What's wrong with that?"

"The Vargulleion was hell before death. And you built it."

"The Vargulleion was, and is, a prison for criminals. I know it may seem odd to you, no doubt being a law-abiding sort of person, but society has to have a place to put its criminals if it's not going to kill them outright. This prison break you staged: anyone come out with you?"

"Practically everyone."

"Well, congratulations. Any idea how many murderers, rapists, extortionists, robbers, and all-around thugs walked out with you? Or were they all innocent? I understand everyone in prison is innocent."

"I was innocent."

"Then you were the victim of an injustice. To the extent I am responsible for that, I apologize. Are you prepared to apologize to all those who've suffered and died because you unleashed a wave of criminals on the world?"

"Eh."

"I'll take that as a no. I'm not laughing off what happened to you: really, I'm not. It bothers me more than I can easily tell you or you'd believe. But I don't think you can have a society without injustice. When people live together—and they have to live together—interests and rights clash and someone always loses."

"And as long as you are paid, you are content with that."

"In a word: no. I hate it. I think everyone should hate it, and I hate it that everyone *doesn't* hate it. Look, injustice operates in my favor sometimes, against me other times. I guess maybe I'm better off than many. It's one kind of fool who doesn't think there's injustice in his city or his state. It's another kind of fool who sees it and thinks it doesn't matter as long as it doesn't touch him. I'm neither kind of fool."

"What kind of fool are you?"

"I'm the kind of fool who leaves his door unlocked when he doesn't want to be disturbed!"

"That's no answer."

"I haven't got one. Not about society, anyway. I think we have to live in imperfect societies, because there are no perfect ones, and no perfect people. But we have to struggle against their imperfections, and our own. It's a struggle that never ends, but if we carry on with it, things may get better. Not perfect, maybe, but better."

"That's a long war," Morlock said, thinking dark thoughts.

"Right; right. The longest. It'll never be over. Anyway, I'm not temperamentally suited for perfection. If I woke up tomorrow in Utopia City, the first thing I'd do is hit the road and head out of town."

"People get tired of struggling."

"Well, everyone needs a break sometimes. I like to read books, personally. What do you do?"

"Make things."

"Oh?" Iacomes looked him over, noticing the wooden glove on his left hand. "That from a work injury or something? Excuse my mentioning it if it's too painful."

"I seem to be changing into a ghost."

"Really?" Iacomes was fully engaged in the conversation for the first time. "Can I see?"

Morlock undid the bolts that fastened the wooden sheath to his arm.

"It looks like those anchors are driven into bone," Iacomes observed, watching him. "Didn't that hurt?"

"No. Unfortunately not."

"Unfortunately?"

"It's the illness. First the nerves ache, and then they seem to die and feel nothing, and then the flesh becomes ghostly. Now my arm has no feeling up to the shoulder."

"Hm."

Morlock pulled the sheath off and his hand lay exposed: vaporous, drifting, ghostlike.

"Does it hurt?" Iacomes asked. "After it becomes ghostly, I mean."

"There is a kind of pain, but it's not physical. I can't explain."

"Hm. I hope I never understand fully, to tell you the truth. Can you move things with it?"

"Leaves. Feathers. Bits of paper. Nothing much heavier."

"Can you reach through things with it?"

"Not glass, or metal, or stone. If it was alive, or is alive, my fingers seem to be able to sink into it some distance. But there is pain for the other, I believe."

"I'll take your word on that," Iacomes said hastily. "Hm," he added more thoughtfully, as Morlock pulled the wooden glove back over his ghostly hand. "This all reminds me of something. But what, exactly?"

"You know something about the ghost illness?" Morlock asked, pausing briefly as he rebolted the wooden glove onto his arm.

"Well, I read something about it once, and that's not the same thing at all. Where is that thing? Hey, Rogerius."

What appeared to be a brass head lifted itself up from among a tumble of gray stones. It was suspended in midair by nothing more obvious than its own intention.

"I asked you not to call me that," the brass head said, looking at Iacomes with discontented crystal eyes.

"Did you notice when I ignored you? No? Oh, well. Rogerius, I want you to find something for me."

"I am busy at my visualization. I remind you that if I do not finish my visualization, you will not finish your project."

"I want you to find something for me," Iacomes repeated patiently. "I read something once—"

"I sense an indefinite but fairly large number of documents—"

"—about illness. That should narrow it down."

"Still indefinitely large."

"Oh, come on. I'm not a hypochondriac."

"Do you include emotional disturbances in your definition of illness?"

"Depends. Doesn't it? Everyone who has emotions has them disturbed sometimes. But some people are more disturbed than others."

"The number is still indefinitely large."

"All right. The document I am thinking of described an illness that had something to do with ghosts."

"If we include emotional disorders, the number of relevant documents is still very large. Would you like an estimate or a count?"

"Neither," Iacomes said hastily. "How many if emotional disorders are *ex*cluded?"

"Is that wise? The intruder—whose name you have not asked but whom I have of course identified—is subject to a number of emotional disorders."

"Who isn't?"

"I am not."

"Assuming that's true (which it's not), so what? Who wants to be a disembodied brass head?"

"I do."

"Very well, I grant your wish: you are a disembodied brass head. Don't say I never did anything for you. Now exclude emotional disorders and give me a count."

"Seven thousand and forty-two."

"Hm. That's a lot."

"Ghosts cause illness. It's a scientific fact."

"Aha. Exclude *ghost as cause*. What then?"

"There is a much smaller number of relevant documents."

"How many?"

"Five."

"How many are in this room? I seem to remember reading it in here. Or in the third-floor tower. Or in the kitchen. How many are in the house, here?"

"Three."

"Bring them to me, eh?"

The brass head floated about the dim room, gathering dusty pieces of parchment in its teeth. It dropped them on the desk near Iacomes and floated back to its nest among the tumble of stones.

"Thanks, Rogerius," said Iacomes absently. "Well, this one is no good. It's Vespasian's dying joke—you know, 'I think I'm becoming a god.' I can't think why he brought it to me. Though there is some overlap between 'god' and 'ghost,' I suppose, especially in Latin. And this is just a recipe for giving the morally ill the ability to see ghosts. I have no idea what use that would be, though I suppose in the right hands some use could be made of it. No, it's this that I was thinking of: see?"

He offered the parchment fragment to Morlock, who took it with his right hand. It was a set of instructions for making a mirror out of a unicorn's horn. The page was torn, probably from a scroll, but the mirror clearly had something to do with ghost illness (*morbus lemuralis*)—whether as cure or cause was not clear. There was a fragmentary notation along one torn edge of the page. It seemed to say *lumina umbrosa*. He pointed it out to Iacomes.

"Yes, I couldn't make anything of that. 'Lights full of shadow.' Makes no sense."

"But *lumina* can also mean 'eyes' and an *umbra* can also be a ghost."

"Hm. 'Eyes full of ghosts,' then. 'Ghosts-in-the-eyes.' Ulugarriu!"

"Yes." Morlock nodded. "This will be useful to me. What do you want for it?"

"I don't have time to haggle right now. Why don't you just take it, and if I think of any little thing I can use—"

"You will not trick me into accepting an open-ended bargain."

"Well, it was worth a try. What have you got?"

They bargained keenly for a time, and in the end Iacomes accepted three gold coins and a glass dagger for the parchment. "Though I don't know what I can do with a glass dagger," he said in the end.

"Take it, leave it, or bargain some more."

"No, I have this big job due and I've wasted too much time here already. We're even. Have a good day, and please don't call again."

"You're the worst salesman in the world, Iacomes," Morlock said, with a grudging admiration.

"Thank you, thank you. Praise from a master is indeed gratifying. Please pull the door *completely shut* as you go. Thanks. Thanks. Good luck, Morlock."

Morlock was back on the dim street, wending back toward the Shadow Market, before he realized something. He had never given his name to Iacomes.

He turned back and tried to find Iacomes' shop, but he lost his way in the twisting streets and finally had to give up. Hrutnefdhu met him as he was coming back to the border of the Shadow Market.

"What in ghost's name were you doing in there?" the pale werewolf gasped, who seemed especially pale for some reason.

"That's my business," Morlock replied curtly. He liked Hrutnefdhu, but he didn't like it when anyone tried to limit his movements.

"It's dangerous, that's all," Hrutnefdhu said apologetically. "The streets shift. They say nothing is ever in the same place twice. All sorts of weird entities come and go."

"Hm." There was something in this, but Morlock didn't want to talk about it. He was feeling a little odd, as if he was on the verge of the trembling madness that comes with a long bout of drinking.

"My friend Liuunurriu doesn't know anything about ghost sickness," Hrutnefdhu continued, "but he does know someone who might. He'll be back at twilight."

By now they were in the Shadow Market. The sun was high enough that misty golden light was falling on some of the black-and-white paving blocks. The place was almost empty of vendors: bright light and their shady callings did not mix, it seemed.

"I can come back, then," Hrutnefdhu said, when Morlock didn't answer.

"Thank you," said Morlock, whose body and soul were aching for a drink. "I may not be able to join you."

Chapter Twenty-three

War in the Air

It was another dark night. The sky above was stormy, split sometimes by lightning, but even above the clouds there was no moon tonight. Horseman had set just after sunset, and it would be seven days before Trumpeter rose.

Rokhlenu had grown up hating moonless nights, but now he loved them. It was pleasantly perverse to be entangled with his beloved, both of them wearing the day shape, deep in the darkness of night. Wuinlendhono, too, relished it. The air was warm as summer, despite the storm, and they lay on the day couch without a blanket.

The windows stood open to admit the cool rainy air. Had they turned their heads to look, they would have seen the approach of the airships standing in toward the outlier settlement, the eyes of the gondolas already angry-red with fire. But they were absorbed in a marital conversation and did not notice.

It was the warning calls that roused their attention at last: shouting, howling, horns; all rising from the watchtowers on the settlement's verge. They had been watching the plank roads and the waters for the approach of the enemy. They had been vigilant. But they had not been watching the sky, and so they noticed the airships almost too late.

Wuinlendhono and her mate rolled from the wedding couch and looked out the northern windows. One glance told them both all they needed to know. The Sardhluun had surrendered their long-boasted solitary stance and had allied with the Neyuwuleiuun Pack—the Neyuwuleiuun, who controlled the airships. Now airships were being sent against the outliers as if they were stray never-wolves fleeing bands of raiders.

"I'll go to the watchtowers," Rokhlenu said as they frantically pulled on clothing. "The airships may come within the range of our crossbows and catapults—"

"*I'll* go to the watchtowers," Wuinlendhono said. "I'm the First Wolf of this settlement, and it's for me to take charge of the defenses. You have to go to that crazy never-wolf friend of yours and see if he's got something to help us. Otherwise, we're done."

Rokhlenu stuttered a moment or two, but then bit down his protestations unspoken. She was right. And what bothered him was the thought of her going into danger, but no place was safe while the airships were attacking.

He seized her, kissed her, ran from her down the winding stairs to ground level.

He ran all the way to Hrutnefdhu and Liudhleeo's den in the rickety slum-tower on the east side of town. There was a new lock on the door of the den; it had a coppery face and glass eyes. It grinned in recognition and let him in as soon as he knocked.

Hrutnefdhu was alone in the den; he was sitting up in the sleeping couch, blinking.

"Where's Morlock?" asked Rokhlenu, and then nearly struck himself. Morlock was absent; Liudhleeo was gone. Wasn't it possible they were coupling at this moment, Hrutnefdhu's mate and his old friend?

If the pale werewolf was thinking anything along those lines, he gave no sign of it. "Morlock's drunk, I expect," Hrutnefdhu said sleepily. "He usually is, by this time of night. What time is it?"

"*Where* is he?"

"Cave. Wait a moment."

"I don't have a moment. The airships of the Neyuwuleiuun are attacking us."

Hrutnefdhu jumped naked from the couch, grabbed the coverlet, and wrapped it around himself as he ran after Rokhlenu.

The wickerwork boat with the glass eye was waiting on their side of the water—otherwise Rokhlenu would have leapt into the water and floundered across. Both werewolves took oars and drove the boat across the rain-lashed water. Shoulder to shoulder they ran up the long slope to Morlock's cave.

Morlock was sprawled in a pile of blankets by the cave's entrance. A half-empty jar of wine was still in his right hand. Deeper in the cave, Hlupnafenglu was sitting by the nexus of living flames, playing solitaire with Morlock's cards. He looked up in surprise at the entrance of the other two werewolves.

"What is it?" he asked.

"The Neyuwuleiuun are attacking."

"Who are the Neyuwuleiuun?" asked the red werewolf with an oddly unconcerned smile.

Rokhlenu goggled at him for a moment, but then remembered that Hlupnafenglu had lost his memories. "They have airships. We need Morlock. Wasn't he working on wings, or something?"

"Morlock is drunk."

"I see that. Wasn't he working on wings or something?"

"We were all working on them," Hrutnefdhu said. "But I don't know where they are, or if they're done."

Hlupnafenglu's smile became even broader. He pointed at the roof of the cave.

Five sets of wings in various stages of completion were hanging there. Or, more precisely, they were lying against the roof of the cave as if it were the floor.

Three were obviously unready, but the mechanisms of two seemed complete, and the skinlike surfaces of both were covered with the weight-defying metallic rings.

"How do they work?" Rokhlenu asked.

"Not sure," Hlupnafenglu said with his customary, somewhat eerie cheer.

"Morlock was going to show us," Hrutnefdhu added. "But he—well, he never got around to it."

Because he was drunk? Rokhlenu wondered. Looking back, he seemed to remember Morlock had said that wine was not good for him—he forgot exactly what his old friend had said. But why would someone go on drinking if it harmed him? It was beyond Rokhlenu's understanding, and not immediately relevant, so he put it aside.

Rokhlenu said, "Let's pull one down, and you two put it on me. I'll see if I can fly in it. If I don't kill myself, one of you follow me. We have got to do something about those airships or they'll burn our town down to water level."

They dragged one of the wingsets down from the roof and strapped it on the gnyrrand's back. Wearing it, he felt as light as air: his feet barely touched the ground. There were grips inside the wings, and when he used them to flex the wings, he felt his feet leave the ground for a moment.

"Chief, wait," said Hrutnefdhu.

"No waiting. One of you follow me. I'll be headed straight for the airships." He ran out of the cave and took straight to the air.

The southern wind threw him backward, pinning him against the hill above the cave, knocking the wind from his lungs.

"*You don't have a weapon!*" shouted Hrutnefdhu at the top of his penetrating voice.

"Oh," said Rokhlenu, dashed in multiple senses. "Help me down, citizens."

They hauled him down. There were still many glass weapons about the cave, and a sheath for a short sword was built into the frame of the wings, running across the shoulders. Rokhlenu took a sword, practiced sheathing and unsheathing a couple times, and then said, less dramatically, "Like I said before. I'm going to walk up to the top of the hill and take off from there. One of you do the same. The other try to wake Morlock up. Maybe he can think of something. If you can get him to think."

"Will do, Chief," said Hlupnafenglu.

As he stepped out of the cave into the warm rainy night, he heard the werewolves behind him arguing about who would follow. He struggled up to the top of the hill, the wind threatening to blow him off his feet at any moment. When he reached the crest, he spread his wings and leapt into the air. The wind carried him away, up into the dark fire-torn sky.

The worst thing, as soon as he left the ground, was the sense of placelessness. He was tumbling in the dark; there was no clear sign for him to follow, nothing to give him a sense of where to fly *to*.

There was, at least, up and down. He drove the wings to carry him higher and higher. Suddenly it occurred to him that the wind was blowing from the south, almost due north, and he must already be past the borders of the outlier settlement.

Steering took a few tries before he began to understand it, but he found he could angle the wings and his body to bank against the wind.

Then he saw them! The airships! They were no blacker than the clouds, but the eyes of the gondolas were still red with fire. Every now and then the sky would flash with lightning, and in the bitter blue light he could see the long clawlike shapes of the airships clearly. Down below was the outlier settlement, also outlined with fire. It was already burning. It might already be too late. Wuinlendhono might already be dead.

He drove his wings toward them. What he could do against them he did not know. But they weren't expecting him, and that was to his advantage.

He closed on the airships faster than he expected. The storm winds added speed to his wings.

And they did, in fact, see him. They were looking out from the windows of the gondola, scanning the dark night. He saw them long before they saw him . . . but he was armed with a short sword and they had bows. A bolt of lightning thundered shockingly nearby; though he was dazed by it he was close enough to hear a shout from the gondola of the nearer airship: someone had seen him.

With terrible clarity, he saw several archers take their bead on him and ready burning arrows to shoot.

Then a shadow passed between him and their fiery light.

Morlock was having the worst dream ever. Not a nightmare, in the usual sense. A frustration dream, a shame dream. Someone had come to him for help, someone he wanted to help, but he could not help them because he was drunk. Even in his dream Morlock knew it must be a dream, because he had given up drinking ages ago, precisely so that this exact thing would never happen again.

It was very real, though. It was as if he could see Rokhlenu strapping on the wingset he had built. He could hear the words the werewolves spoke. But he knew it was a dream, because he had long ago given up drinking.

He started a little when Hrutnefdhu screamed, *You don't have a weapon!* That was almost like it was really happening.

He felt something on his hand. He stared at it for a while. It was red, but not like blood. Plus, it did not burn, as his blood did. It was cold, unlike blood. And it didn't smell like blood. It smelled like wine.

He had a bowl of wine in his hand. He had spilled some of it when the pale werewolf shouted.

If he actually had a bowl of wine in his hand, that strongly suggested he had been drinking it.

If he had been drinking it, he was not having a nightmare about being drunk, as he often did. He was simply drunk.

That meant that Rokhlenu did actually need his help.

He'd said something about the Neyuwuleiuun . . . and their airships.

Morlock set the wine bowl down with elaborate care on the cave floor. He rose to his feet.

Rokhlenu was gone. The pale werewolf and the red one were standing between the other completed wingset and arguing about something.

"Where's Rokhlenu?" Morlock said. "He was just here."

The two werewolves turned to him with blank looks. A pale werewolf with a blank look. Morlock felt there might be a joke in there somewhere if he could think a little more clearly, and if he were the joking type, and if this were a joking situation—none of which was the case, so the hell with it, Morlock decided.

"He's gone, Khretvarrgliu," Hlupnafenglu said eventually. His right hand was gripping the wingset by the torso straps, so that Hrutnefdhu wouldn't escape with it, but his left hand mimicked a bird in flight.

"Buckle that thing on me," Morlock directed.

"Morlock. Old friend," said Hrutnefdhu gently. "You're too drunk to walk."

"I won't be walking. Hlupnafenglu: oblige me."

Hlupnafenglu walked over to Morlock with the wingset and Hrutnefdhu in tow. In the end, the pale werewolf assisted the red one in buckling the second wingset onto its maker.

"Draw down the stirrups and buckle them on my feet," he directed.

"What's a stirrup?" asked Hlupnafenglu.

"Something to put your feet in." *Like on a saddle*, he almost added—except he didn't know the word for *saddle* in Moonspeech or Sunspeech, and, in fact, he realized belatedly that he had used the Wardspeech word for stirrup. "They're under the base of the wings, attached to cables."

The werewolves found the stirrups and slowly drew them down to Morlock's feet. He stepped into them, and the two werewolves fastened the buckles over his feet.

"Chieftain," Hlupnafenglu admitted, "we didn't do this for Rokhlenu. Is it important?"

"It might be," Morlock said. The cables gave the wing beats extra force. That was the idea, anyway: Morlock had never actually flown one of these things. He'd kept on meaning to make the experiment . . . but when he came back to the cave in the evening he usually started drinking.

"Morlock, wait a moment," Hrutnefdhu said.

"A sword," Morlock said to Hlupnafenglu, who grinned and handed him a glass sword from the weapon rack. Morlock sheathed it over his shoulder.

"Morlock, wait."

"Spear," he said to Hlupnafenglu. The red werewolf gave him a stabbing spear from the weapon rack, and he placed it in the other shoulder sheath.

"Morlock. Wait!"

"Citizens, good fortune," said Morlock as he strode from the cave.

The cables pulling against his leg muscles had a paradoxically steadying effect. But Morlock was unsure whether he could actually walk uphill under the triple burden of the wingset, the heavy wind, and his drunkenness. He breathed deeply of the air, trying to clear the wine-colored fog from his eyes and mind.

He fixed the fingers of his wooden glove to the grip inside the left wing and clamped them shut. His right hand took the grip of the right wing. It was time to fly or fail—perhaps both.

He judged the direction of the wind, the width of the slope he stood on, and what force his wings could apply at what angles to the wind. The calculation soothed him: drunk or sober he could do a little three-dimensional math. He took a few steps into the darkness and leapt off into the wind, driving the wings hard with his arms and legs.

The shoulder of the hill flashed by at an acceptable distance. Morlock felt his mind, if not his body, come a little more alive.

He pumped his arms and legs to gain height in the darkness. He dreaded the thought of smashing into some tree or unseen ridge.

Like Rokhlenu before him, he felt the empty isolation, the disorientation of night flight. But it did not bother him as much. For one thing, he expected it: he had had flightlike experiences before. Plus, he was an experienced drunk who knew he was drunk: disorientation was an old, familiar enemy.

He banked left, losing the lift under his wings and tumbling end over end a couple of times before he caught the knack of it. But finally he was on a roughly westward course, though still driven northward by the relentless south wind, and climbing as high and fast as he could.

He saw the airships then, hanging like claws over the burning settlement of the outliers. The ships stood there, defying the wind, moored by some power he didn't understand. He wondered at it as he flew toward them, and he found in the wonder an intoxication deeper and more intense than the musty, muddy pleasures of wine. Why had he denied himself this danger and exultation? Why had he denied himself the air and the light and the darkness? This was why he was alive: to make, to do, to drive, not to drown his wits in fermented juice.

As he watched the airships, he saw a shape that occasionally impinged on the fiery light glaring from the gondola ports. Rokhlenu: headed toward a gondola to board it and kill the crew. A plan unlikely of success, but not hopeless with the advantage of surprise.

But there was no surprise. Morlock saw the archers taking aim at Rokhlenu with burning arrows. He expected Rokhlenu to dive, to swerve, to do something to avoid the arrows. But he didn't. Morlock guessed he was willing to risk a wound or two if he could get close enough to board the gondola. Perhaps he was counting on the metal rings to protect him; he might not realize that they would burn like paper, having been deeply imbued with metallic phlogiston.

Morlock drove himself forward and upward; when he was above and somewhat in front of his friend he stalled in midair and kicked him savagely in the right arm. Rokhlenu lost lift and tumbled down, a dark shadow toward the dark earth, the red reflections of fire fading from the scales on his wings. Morlock heard the bows sing discordantly at the same moment, and he drove himself upward in a steep arc.

The fiery arrows passed in midair between Morlock and Rokhlenu. Morlock turned his wings and let himself drop, spinning in the air so that his head was aimed almost directly at the ground. His stomach, full of wine and very little else, disliked this maneuver intensely and told him so noisily, but he did manage to escape the archers' second hasty salvo: he saw the arrows lay red tracks across the sky between his feet.

Looking groundward, Morlock saw that Rokhlenu had succeeded in recovering from the tumble he had kicked him into and was coming back up toward the gondola.

"Meet you on the keel!" he shouted to the startled werewolf as he fell past. He hoped *keel* was the right word; he had learned it from Hrutnefdhu when they were talking about boats in general (and the wickerwork boat Morlock had made in particular).

He came out of his dive in a sharp curve upward; it strained the wings until they creaked loud enough to be heard over the storm winds, but it saved some of his momentum, helping him to fly upward. He was now headed almost directly toward the underside of the gondola; the archers inside had no clear shot at him. Those in the gondola of the other airship did—but the closer he got to the gondola of their sister ship, the less likely they were to risk it. He got close fast. Soon he was directly under the gondola; he stalled in the air, seized a handhold on the rough planking with his right hand, and dangled there, gasping.

Apparently *keel* was the right word, or Rokhlenu had known what he meant by it, because a winged shadow hanging from the gondola some distance away started to shout at him in Rokhlenu's voice.

". . . you . . . crazy?" he heard his old friend say.

People were always saying this to Morlock, and he couldn't see the point. If he was, what was the point in asking him?

"—in . . . now . . . dead . . . half of them—" Rokhlenu shouted on, half of his words carried away by the wind. But Morlock guessed he was complaining about the ruin of his attack on the crew of the airship.

"The wings will burn!" Morlock shouted several times. It was possible that he was shouting loud enough for the werewolves to hear him through the planking of the airship's floor. It didn't matter: Rokhlenu had to know this.

". . . metal . . . protect . . ." Rokhlenu shouted back—anyway, that was all Morlock heard of it.

"The metal will burn!" Morlock roared.

"Metal burns?" Rokhlenu asked. He asked it several times.

"Everything burns!" Morlock replied. It was not strictly accurate. Dephlogistonated objects did not burn. Immaterial objects did not burn. There were other classes of exception, but none of them mattered at the moment.

Rokhlenu said something that might have been a curse.

Morlock released the clamp on his wooden glove by striking the winged arm against his knee. He swung over, handhold by handhold, until he was hanging next to Rokhlenu.

"You need to get your feet in the stirrups," he said.

"What are stirrups?"

Morlock repressed a curse of his own. "Things to put your feet in. They're under the base of the wings."

"Those ghost-bitten things! They kept smacking around, throwing me off!"

"Put. On. Feet."

Rokhlenu bent one foot up. Morlock, hanging from his right hand, used his wooden glove to catch a stirrup from under Rokhlenu's wings and pushed it toward the werewolf's free hand. Using the one hand, Rokhlenu managed to put it on his foot and buckle it. They repeated the process with the other stirrup.

As Morlock struggled to refasten the clamp of his wooden glove to the grip of his left wing, Rokhlenu stretched out his legs and said, "It makes the wings feel different."

That was the point: the pulleys attached to the stirrups helped provide power to the pseudo-musculature of cables and wings that drove the wings. Morlock didn't have the vocabulary to say this, and besides his stomach had finally reached the point of open rebellion. So he just said, "Yes," and turned his head to vomit.

When he had finished and wiped his face on his sleeve, he turned back to Rokhlenu.

"What now?" the werewolf asked.

Morlock had been thinking about that, between convulsions of his belly, and he pointed at the buoyant part of the nearby airship.

"Attack the other airship?" Rokhlenu asked.

"Bag of air," Morlock said.

"What?"

"Not the gondola. The bag of air."

Rokhlenu turned to looked at the nearby airship. It was too dark to see his face, but his shout was pensive as he asked, "You think it's held up by air?"

"Hot air!" Morlock shouted.

A moment passed, and Rokhlenu laughed. "Like ash carried up by a fire! Hot air! Are you sure?"

"No!"

"How do they keep it hot?"

"Don't know!"

"This is a great plan!" Rokhlenu howled at him.

"What's yours?"

"Wake up! It's all a dream! Live happy!"

"Never works."

"We'll try yours, then. Back up on the east side of this ship."

Morlock closed his eyes to try to gather the points of the compass, then opened them rapidly to escape the whirling drunken vortex behind his eyelids. "Yes!" he said. He was almost sure the east was the side they had first approached from; the airship itself would screen them from its sister ship.

A hatch opened in the underside of the gondola; werewolves, somehow distorted in form, stood there, holding bows with burning arrows nocked to shoot.

Morlock and Rokhlenu both fell away in power dives. An arrow passed by Morlock's elbow like a red meteor. Morlock bent his flight sharply upward, trying to catch the steady south wind to give him lift. It worked and he flew swiftly past the windows in the gondola, close enough to see a werewolf archer's startled face.

The werewolf wasn't the only one startled. He had at least three eyes, two human and one lupine, in a twisted mouthless face, and the brief glance Morlock had of him was startling indeed.

Morlock flashed past and upward, finally coming to land on the side of the airship. It was covered with a wooden framework, and he grabbed onto the frame with his right hand.

"What took you?" Rokhlenu shouted cheerfully in his ear.

Morlock snarled, "Your mother couldn't make change." His stomach was unhappy, but there was nothing left in it to vomit. Morlock hated the dry heaves, even when he wasn't hanging by one hand a dozen bowshots above the ground.

". . . not to bandy words with you when you're drunk," Rokhlenu was saying. He didn't seem to be angry.

Morlock nodded. He unclamped his wooden glove from the wing-grip and hooked it on the airship frame to support himself, at last drawing his sword with his right hand. Rokhlenu did likewise. At more or less the same moment they plunged the blades into the fabric surface of the airship.

Morlock had expected a rush of hot air, perhaps fire. He was disappointed. The rift he was tearing in the surface spilled forth a cool bluish light, but nothing else.

"Guess we were wrong!" Rokhlenu shouted.

Morlock shrugged. That was one possibility. Another was that the bags of hot air were inside. He continued to hack away at the fabric. Rokhlenu did as well, and eventually they had a rip large enough for one of them to slide through, wings and all.

Rokhlenu seemed to want to discuss who should go through first, but Morlock unhooked his wooden glove from the cable and dove through without a word. It wasn't even worth discussing. He was the one who was dying; if he died a little sooner it was no great matter.

In his mind, Morlock had already sketched out several possible designs for the interior of the airship proper. One or two were actually ingenious and he hoped to see them at work. In this he was disappointed, because the interior of the ship was nothing like he had imagined.

The interior was all one great chamber, nearly empty. The only thing in it was a glowing stone near one end of the chamber and an oddly spidery being standing next to it.

Morlock drifted down to the bottom of the chamber, bemused. The stone and the entity by it (the keeper? the steersman? a guard?) were on a wooden platform; the rest of the chamber was an empty cylinder, tapered at both ends.

He heard Rokhlenu land behind him.

The being standing on the platform did something to the glowing stone.

Its light fell on Morlock more intensely. It struck him like an invisible hammer. He felt the fabric of the chamber rippling around him. There was a ghostly murmur in the air. He had no idea what was going on.

"I feel strange," Rokhlenu said thickly.

Bracing himself against the hammer-blows of the light, Morlock turned to face Rokhlenu. He looked strange. The light was causing the werewolf's flesh to ripple and twist, as if he were assuming the night shape. But he was not becoming a wolf. It was more as if a wax image of a man and a wolf were merging, distorting each other, but neither one growing and neither one shrinking. A wolf's head was emerging from Rokhlenu's neck, its eyes dead and empty, its maw toothless. Needle-toothed mouths were opening in the palms of his hands, and twisted canine legs were sprouting from his torso to join his arms and legs, giving him a nightmarishly spidery look—like that thing on the platform.

Morlock drew his sword, repressing a sudden temptation to pass it through his friend a few times and end his misery, and turned instead to slash an opening in the chamber wall.

"You can't stay here!" he shouted at his friend, who was now howling mindlessly from all his mouths. Morlock kicked him through the gap into the night; his howls faded into the storm.

Morlock hoped that his old friend had enough self-command to use the wings and glide to safety—or, if not, that the levity of the phlogiston-imbued scales on his wings would cushion his long fall. But the worst thing that could happen to him from the fall was death, and it was not impossible that the light from the strange stone had done worse than this to him already.

The intensity of the light falling on Morlock grew. He dreaded the thought that it would distort him as it had his friend . . . but that didn't seem to be happening. It must be something about werewolves that made them vulnerable to the bitter blue light.

Morlock grabbed the grips of his wings and kicked off into flight. He arced upward to land on the platform beside the distorted creature.

It was a werewolf—or had been, Morlock guessed. It had four crooked lupine limbs as naked as a rat's tail, and approximately human arms and legs that were strangely muscled and covered with doglike fur. It had a lifeless wolf head dangling from one human shoulder, a single gigantic human eye peering out from what appeared to be a neck, and on the side of the neck was a gray-lipped human mouth that squealed with terror as Morlock landed beside it.

"Don't do this!" it begged him. "If I obey, he says he can change me back, but if I don't obey, he says he'll leave me like this. Please don't do this. Let me do what they tell me to do."

"How do they tell you?" Morlock demanded. "How does this thing work?"

"I can't tell you. I can't tell you anything. He'll know. They'll hurt me."

The glowing stone was set in a sort of barrel on a spinnable disc, with handles protruding like spokes around the rim's edge. The inner part of the barrel was covered with mirrors, to reflect the light upward and forward. There were lenses mounted atop the barrel and in front. Levers around the lenses made them focus the light more or less intensely. Morlock badly wanted to examine these assemblies; it seemed as if the levers somehow changed the shape of the lenses themselves, which was very interesting. But in more immediate terms, the more intense the light, the greater the force driving the airship. The lens pointing upward kept the ship aloft, could perhaps drive it even further up into the sky. The lens in front steered the ship and drove it forward . . . or backward: the wheel seemed to spin in a full circle. Now they were veering away to port—eastward, if Morlock's sense of direction was not totally deranged by dizziness and wine.

That was contrary to the plan emerging in Morlock's mind. He said, "Watch out," and grabbed one of the handles, rotating the barrel so that the light was pointing toward the pointed prow of the great cloth-covered chamber. The steersman (or former steersman, as Morlock had taken his job) hissed and skittered out of the way.

The fabric of the chamber rippled: they were now headed straight into the eye of the wind. There was a brief swirl of vertigo as the direction of the craft spun around. Morlock's stomach had been trying to crawl out of his belly ever since he stood up in his cave, so he found this relatively easy to ignore. He cranked the levers on the vertical lens until the light was more intense, glaring a bright cold blue on the prow.

There was a kind of wailing in his ears that was not quite a sound. It said words that were not quite words. His heart began to pound and his breath grew short, as if he were afraid. He recognized these signs: he had often felt them in graveyards or other places swarming with what some called ghosts, but which those-who-know called . . .

"Impulse clouds!" he said to the late steersman of the ship. "This craft is powered by impulse clouds! Maybe you call them ghosts."

"I don't call them anything!" the steersman screamed. "I don't talk to anyone about them, and no one talks to me. Don't tell me anything. I'm trying to do what they say, but you won't let me!"

Morlock ignored him (or her; it was impossible to tell).

Impulse clouds. They were a material part of any living body, but the most tenuous and usually invisible part. Sometimes they could survive the death of the body they had been associated with, in which case they often became a nuisance. Sunlight gathered them up or dispelled them, but moonlight did not. Some said that moonlight actually forced impulse clouds back to earth. That was why ghosts were often reported in moonlight: the moons kept them from rising into the air, then into the sky. Was it possible that the moons, sweeping through bands of impulse clouds raised up from the earth, drove them down again wrapped in moonlight?

If so, this vast fabric chamber was designed to take advantage of the impulse clouds implicit in moonlight. The impulses would reflect off the walls, driving the ship in any desired direction. Speed would vary with intensity.

And the impulse clouds must have something to do with the transformation of werewolves and other werebeasts: that was why the blue light had so distorted Rokhlenu—and the steersman, no doubt, and perhaps others. (He remembered the three-eyed werewolf he had seen.) Never-wolves, like Morlock, must be somehow more resistant to interference with their impulse cloud.

If Rokhlenu's distortion resulted from interference with his impulse cloud, it was possible it could be healed. Perhaps whoever had told the steersman he could be cured had not been lying.

"How do you know where to go?" he asked the steersman. "Do you get signals from the gondola? Is there a port somewhere?"

"Can't tell!" said the steersman. "He'll know! He always knows!"

"I may be able to cure you," Morlock said. "You needn't depend on him anymore. You needn't be afraid. Help me, and I'll help you."

"Liar!" screamed the distorted steersman. "No one can help me! Only him! And he won't now!"

Morlock hated being called a liar. He pushed the distorted creature off the platform; it fell squealing down to the base of the platform and lay there sobbing.

He systematically took in his surroundings. There *must* be some way for the steersman to see out, or for signals to be sent to him. The craft was too well designed to overlook this nontrivial detail.

At first there seemed to be nothing. Then he realized he was looking in the wrong direction: the steersman had one eye that pointed up. . . .

Morlock craned his neck back. Over his head was a kind of board with black and white shapes playing over it. They seemed meaningless at first, but then he realized what he was seeing. It was as if it were a charcoal drawing of the ship's surroundings from a particular vantage point—on the ship's nose, he expected. And it changed as the ship moved. Somehow those sights were filtered and sent back here. Remarkable.

He tentatively shifted the angle of the ship's flight to starboard; the south wind struck it solidly on the port side of the prow, sending shock waves through the strange craft, forcing its nose further to the west.

At first he fought this, but then he saw something on the view-board that caused him to stop. A clawlike object hanging in the sky not so far from him, a gondola dangling below on cables. The other airship was following, concerned about the state of its sister ship, no doubt.

"Good of them," Morlock remarked to no one. It was time to put his plan into action, clearly. He spun the wheel until the other airship was dead center in the view-board. Then he cranked the levers for the lens on the front of the barrel, until the impulse light striking the prow was as bright as it could be.

"What are you doing?" screamed the steersman.

It didn't seem to be a rhetorical question, so Morlock answered it. "I am going to ram that ship."

There was a dark bird perched in the shredded fabric of the airship. Her name, for that time/place, was Mercy. Near her, in the storm outside, was a dark indistinct cloud: a manifestation of Death.

"Nothing for you to do, on a night like this," Death signified.

"Or everything."

"I visualized that War would be manifest here."

"War enjoys experiencing the losing side of a conflict. He is savoring the outliers' suffering through his most direct manifestation."

"You have visualized this?"

"Yes. Also, he told me that he would."

Morlock's insight was sensitive enough that he felt their presence, though he did not see them or perceive their symbology. Their presence troubled him without his understanding it. But he didn't let it shake his intent.

Unfortunately, the other airship's crew seemed to realize he was intending to attack them. The ship swung around and fled before the wind.

Morlock was the worst sailor in the world. His former wife, who was possibly the best sailor in the world, often used to tease him about this. But even he knew that a stern chase was a long chase.

"God Avenger," swore Morlock.

Death and Mercy symbolically shielded themselves from the name of this alien god.

Morlock felt a brief respite, though he didn't understand why. He held his course, straight on the tail of the fleeing airship. If nothing else, he had broken the air attack on the outlier settlement. And there was still a chance he could ram the other airship. It all depended on what happened when they flew over the city.

The jagged rising outline of Wuruyaaria swelled on his view-board. Morlock's neck was sore from bending back and looking up, but he didn't want to take his eyes off the thing. If the other airship turned port or starboard it would have to strike against the course of the wind and would lose speed. That would be his chance to gain on it.

The other airship flew over the werewolf city without turning. Either its port was further north, or they didn't want to risk losing headway.

Mount Dhaarnaiarnon loomed beyond the mesas and cliffs of Wuruyaaria. The moon-clock did not show on the view-board, presumably because it wasn't relevant to navigation. But the ragged edge of the volcano's crater was unmistakable.

The other airship flew on into the rolling hills north of Mount Dhaarnaiarnon. Morlock was sure now that he had them running scared.

War manifested himself as a shadow in the shape of a sword. The other gods greeted him with polite symbology.

Morlock became more uneasy, though he did not know why.

The two airships flew on into the dying north. The storm behind them had faded. Even the gods were silent.

In the quiet, Morlock heard a voice speaking an angry command outside the airship.

The werewolf crew of the gondola were obviously making a bid to regain control of the airship.

Morlock coldly considered his options.

He could use the moonstone to attack the werewolves with impulse light. But he would lose speed that way; the other airship would have a chance to change course and escape. He didn't want that.

He examined the barrel containing the moonstone. He found, as he expected, that there were mirror-bright slats that could be used to cover the lenses.

With the moonstone entirely cocooned in mirrors, its impulse forces would be perfectly balanced. It would no more keep the ship aloft than an ordinary stone would.

Morlock dropped the mirror slats over the lenses. The great chamber of the airship went dark and seemed to deflate.

"No!" screamed the monstrous steersman in the sudden dark. "We'll all be killed!"

Morlock put his right shoulder against the barrel holding the moonstone and pushed. There was a long slow moment when nothing gave—then a splintering crack and the barrel fell off the platform to the floor of the great chamber.

Morlock jumped after it, not using the wings to slow his fall.

At that, his fall was almost too slow. The steersman had floundered around the platform's base and was doing something to the barrel.

Morlock drew his sword and stabbed the steersman several times. It fled, shrieking.

Morlock hooked his wooden glove onto a handhold on the barrel and clamped it tight. Then he stabbed with his sword at the fabric under his feet, sawing away at it.

Soon a jagged tear opened up. He sheathed his sword, pushed the barrel through the opening, and fell with it into the night.

The whole airship was sagging downward in the air; Morlock found himself suspended in midair between the collapsing airship and the gondola below. The cables around him were dense with distorted werewolf shapes, all screaming in anger or panic as they felt their craft failing.

Morlock flipped open one of the lens covers.

The impulse light from the moonstone dragged him, dangling from his wooden glove, away from the falling airship on a wild course into the empty night.

He tried to steady himself by grabbing the other side of the barrel with his right hand. But the radiant impulse light blinded him; he could see nothing in the darkness. One time he almost smashed into the ground, saving himself at the last moment by going into a sickening tumble. By pure chance he came out of it headed upward rather than downward.

He scrabbled desperately at the lens controls to try to diminish his speed, but the barrel was simply not intended to be dirigible by itself; he could not set a course, and every moment he held onto it he risked being smashed against the ground or some obstruction.

He released the clamp from his wooden glove. The barrel spun away, flashing into the darkness.

Morlock scrabbled to get his wooden glove fixed in the grip for his left wing, then gripped the other wing with his right hand. He went into a glide, found the horizon, aimed himself away from the ground, and started pumping his wings with arms and legs.

When he knew he was stable and some distance away from the ground, he looked around to take his bearings.

Not so very far away, he saw the other airship, coming around to the aid of its ruined sister. There was light coming from the ports of its gondola, but he didn't see archers or burning arrows. No doubt they were on the other side, looking out for survivors from the ship Morlock had destroyed. No one seemed to be looking his way.

He was tired, very tired. But he was not dead yet, and this seemed like too good a chance to pass up. He banked into an intercepting course.

The surviving airship was sinking slowly toward the ground. In the dark woodlands Morlock saw glimmers of fire: the ruin of the first ship's gondola, perhaps.

Morlock flew straight on without dropping. By the time he reached the surviving airship, he was just over its motive chamber. He landed atop it. Balancing carefully, he drew his glass sword and drove it deep into the fabric, and again, slashing with the bitter blade until the rift was large enough for him to enter.

This chamber was the twin to the other airship, right down to the distorted steersman on the moonstone platform. The steersman was aware of him, and swung the bright lens about to try and strike him with impulse light. But the carriage of the barrel was not designed to tilt so far. Morlock flew directly to the platform.

"Stand aside," Morlock said. "I won't hurt you if I don't have to. Your light can't hurt me, anyway."

"You've already hurt me!" shouted the steersman. "If he finds out that you learned about impulse clouds from me—"

Morlock turned curiously toward the steersman.

"That was a slip, wasn't it?" said the steersman ruefully, in quite a different sort of voice.

"Yes."

"Two such similar simulacra, facing similar challenges in such a short space of time," the steersman's mouth mused. "I'm not surprised I got confused. But I wonder if that was really it. I've been wanting to talk to you for some time, Morlock."

"Who are you?"

"Krecking ghosts. Do I need to tell you? I'm Ulugarriu."

Morlock bent his head back to look at the view-board, then adjusted his course upward and southward. When the ship was headed straight back toward Wuruyaaria in the teeth of the wind, he levelled off again.

"I heard you didn't talk much," the steersman complained. "But it seems to me you're being petulant."

"I'm in the middle of something."

"You're in the middle of the biggest time-wasting mistake a male can commit. There is more at stake here than a single life, a few lives, a thousand lives, an election, a city. You are in greater danger than you can imagine walking amidst powers that you don't understand."

"I'm in the middle of something," Morlock said, adjusting the height of the airship again and cranking the forward speed to maximum. "Send me a message, if you want to arrange a meeting in person. I will not deal with a simulacrum."

"And I'm supposed to let you within sword's reach of me, so you can split me like beef liver with Tyrfing? Not on your flat greasy ape-nose. We'll talk on my terms, because what I have to say you need to hear."

Morlock grabbed the steersman simulacrum by its elbow and stepped off the platform, dragging the other with him. The simulacrum hit the floor first, since Morlock was held up by the levity of his wings. When he reached the floor, he drew his sword and slashed a hole in the fabric.

"You're making a mistake," the steersman simulacrum repeated in a resigned voice.

Morlock stuffed him through the hole and out into the night. He heard the body strike the gondola on its way to earth.

Satisfied, he sheathed the sword and flew back up to the moonstone platform.

The werewolf crew would come for him presently, but he had a plan to deal with them. If his plan failed he would have to improvise, but he hoped it wouldn't come to that. The crew would remember what had happened to the other airship when the crew attacked, and that would slow them down some. It gave him time, perhaps enough . . .

In the view-board, the cratered peak of Dhaarnaiarnon lay dead center and growing.

The dark bird who was Mercy signified, "The knowledge that Ulugarriu operates through simulacra has disrupted my visualizations."

The swordlike shadow indicated agreement with Mercy.

The indistinct dark cloud that was Death signified nothing.

"My manifested senses perceived the simulacrum as if it were alive," Mercy persisted.

War agreed.

The indistinct dark cloud that was Death signified nothing.

"If there are multiple entities in or around the city who are, in fact, extensions of Ulugarriu," Mercy persisted, "there is a pattern to events that we do not grasp. It will clash with patterns we do grasp, and the results are beyond prediction."

"There is no pattern to events," Death signified. "Or: only one."

"The inevitability of death?"

"Yes."

War indicated boredom with this oft-repeated pattern of symbology.

"You lesser gods," Death replied, "have the luxury of boredom, change, variety. You hold sway in a mortal's life for an hour, a day, a year, some stretch of time. Then they relinquish you, and you them. But I impinge on a mortal's life once, when they become me and I become them. And then they are not, forever. And I go on, forever."

"Or they escape to a place where we can no longer torture them," signified Mercy, "forever. That's my hope."

"Hope," repeated Death, and signified amusement. She ceased to be manifest.

"Wisdom thinks she is frightened," signified Mercy. She would have preferred to discuss this with Wisdom himself, but her visualizations were growing quite tangled and she could not envision a time/space locus in which they would both be manifest.

War signified that boasting often went hand in hand with fear. Both were part of his sphere, so he was well acquainted with them.

"Why did you accept apotheosis, War?" Mercy asked. "I wanted to do good, and be a part of the good that people do. Maybe I have done some of that. But it has made me more and more aware of the power of evil. Why did you become a god?"

War signified that his answer would play out in events.

The airship was now closing on the peak of Dhaarnaiarnon. Morlock kept a close eye on the view-board. He dropped the level of flight lower, and then still lower. For his purpose, too low was better than not low enough.

The airship shuddered with impact. There was a tearing, grinding sound from below, and forward movement stopped. Morlock braced the wheel with his body to keep the ship on course. Abruptly, the ship was flying free again.

Morlock spun the wheel to aim the ship toward the outlier settlement and cranked down the intensity of the impulse light, diminishing the craft's speed. Then he risked jumping down to the chamber floor and peering through the rift.

He was passing over the smoke lights of Wuruyaaria, and could see clearly that the gondola was gone. A few wooden fragments swung from stray cables, but he seemed to have no passengers. He flew back up to the moonstone platform and steered for his cave, beyond the shoulder of Wuruyaaria.

"I don't understand," Mercy said then. "This is why you became a god?"

War signified that he didn't understand how she could not understand. Two men had pitted their lives against a greater, better-armed force to defend those they loved. They had risked much and lost much. Their skill and daring had won a great victory.

"One man, really," Mercy said.

War disagreed. If it were not for Rokhlenu, Morlock would have slept through the attack in a drunken stupor. He displayed the visualization to her.

Mercy was forced to acknowledge this truth. "But many died for that victory," she pointed out.

War observed that more would have died if the outlier settlement had burned to the ground. Mercy for the airship crews was death for the outliers.

"I know," Mercy replied. It was the sort of paradox which made her the weakest of the Strange Gods and War one of the strongest.

War ceased to manifest himself. Mercy, too, departed for another space-time locus.

Morlock's heart felt relief at the absence of Strange Gods, although he had not been aware of their presence. He dropped the height of the airship almost to ground level and reduced the impulse light until the airship slowed almost to a walking speed. He drifted past the entrance to his cave to the silver-laden waste fields over the hill's shoulder. He set the airship down there, diminishing the intensity of the lens-foci and completely closing the irises.

The fabric skin of the ship sagged from its skeletal framework. Morlock hauled the barrel containing the moonstone off its disk and threw it down to the ground. He jumped down after it and rolled it downslope until he reached the curtain of fabric at the chamber wall. He slashed through it with the ease of practice, though by now he was very weary, and trundled the moonstone barrel through the opening into the warm humid night air, dragging it all the way back to his cave. There it was as safe as he could make it.

Hlupnafenglu and Hrutnefdhu were not in his cave, which he found disappointing, but also something of a relief. He bent over to pick up the bowl of wine he had set down on the cave floor before he had left. He sat down then, wearily but carefully, so that he would not spill the wine. Then he drank the wine.

Chapter Twenty-four

Shadow and Substance

lupnafenglu and Hrutnefdhu, after Morlock flew off, ran down and took the boat over to the settlement. They ran side by side, without any need to talk, to the northeastern edge of the settlement that was under attack by the airships.

But by the time they had gotten there the attack had ceased. The ships were still hovering overhead, but they had retreated higher in the sky, and they were firing arrows at some aerial target, or targets.

Wuinlendhono was directing the firefighting efforts. Since the slime on the Neyuwuleiuun arrows could not be extinguished once it was set afire, they had to isolate every patch of fire through demolition. It was exacting and difficult work requiring many hands; if the Sardhluun had attacked via boats while they were busy with fires, they would have been in a bad way. But they were left alone to carry out the work, and they were winning.

The First Wolf looked up at the approach of the pale werewolf and the red one and said, "What are they doing? What, on your ugly jailbird ghosts, are they *doing*?"

"They flew away, High Huntress," said Hlupnafenglu simply.

"There wasn't much time to talk," Hrutnefdhu added.

"Something falling from an airship," called a sentry in a watchtower. "Not an arrow. Not a fighter."

"Looks like a bird," sang out another. "It's gliding. No, it's falling. Yes, it's gliding."

"Mark where it lands," called Wuinlendhono. "It'll be one or the other of them," she remarked to the werewolves standing beside her.

"Morlock, I expect," Hrutnefdhu said. "He was drunk, I fear."

Hlupnafenglu looked at him and shrugged. Others could say what they wanted; he would put his money on Khretvarrgliu in any contest, drunk or sober.

"It's down," called the sentry.

"Come here," called Wuinlendhono back.

One of the airships had veered wildly away from the other. The other followed. They were headed south, into the teeth of the wind.

The sentry was standing there, a semiwolf named Rululawianu whose mostly human form was covered with bristling yellowish hair. "I saw the place it landed, High Huntress."

"Then you will guide me there," said Wuinlendhono.

"High Huntress, please think again," said Hrutnefdhu, startled from some distant train of thought by her remark. "There may be enemy fighters in the swamp."

"Then it will be your privilege to die defending me," the First Wolf replied coolly. "Yours too, Big Red."

Hlupnafenglu nodded.

They went to the northern gate, found a fair-sized boat, and rowed away into the great black swamp.

"What's happening now?" the First Wolf asked.

Hlupnafenglu wasn't sure what she meant, and then realized she was looking up at the sky.

One of the airships was headed directly for the other.

"I think he's going to ram it," Hrutnefdhu said grimly.

"He?" asked Wuinlendhono.

"It has to be Morlock or Rokhlenu, doesn't it?"

"Khretvarrgliu," voted Hlupnafenglu. "It's something he would do."

"I can't tell if I want you to be right or wrong," Wuinlendhono replied.

The red werewolf thought he knew what she meant. If her husband was up there, he was in deadly danger, taking terrible risks. If he were not, he had crash-landed in the swamp.

They saw him from a good distance away, floating on his wings in the murky water. They rowed to him and hauled him into the boat.

"This is one of the wingsets that Morlock made," Hrutnefdhu said, after a moment of dreadful silence. "But I can't tell who this is. I can't tell *what* this is."

Wuinlendhono inhaled deeply, once, twice, again. "He stinks of the mire, and of evil magic," she said then, "but this is Rokhlenu."

"Angry ghosts," whispered Hrutnefdhu. "What have they done to him?"

Wuinlendhono put both her hands on Rokhlenu's distorted chest and said with a frosty calm that Hlupnafenglu found himself admiring, "He's still alive. Hrutnefdhu, are there still empty dens in that death trap you rent on the east side?"

"Yes."

"Take Rokhlenu there. Use the boat: row all the way around town. Then stay there with him. And you: Rululawianu," she said, addressing the yellow semiwolf. "You go with them. I want no one to hear of this. Speak to no one of the gnyrrand's . . . illness."

"Yes, High Huntress."

By then, the two airships were directly overhead, the one in flight from the other.

"I hope he kills them," Wuinlendhono said, in the same cold tone—although Hlupnafenglu now realized it was not calm at all. "I hope he kills every one of them. Slowly and terribly. If he does, I'll buy him enough wine to stay drunk every day of his life, even if he lives to be a hundred."

"He'll enjoy that, High Huntress," said Hrutnefdhu soothingly.

Hlupnafenglu doubted that. He didn't think that Morlock actually enjoyed drinking, and had often wondered why he did it. Also, he was pretty sure that Morlock was more than a hundred years old already. But since he, too, hoped that Khretvarrgliu would kill all their enemies and avenge the harm done to their gnyrrand, he decided to say nothing that would sound like disagreement.

They left the First Wolf on the plank road below the North Gate and settled in for the long row around town.

The next day, Hlupnafenglu went with the First Wolf to ask Morlock for help. Rokhlenu had awakened at some point, but either he could not speak or he would not. The First Wolf received a whispered report to this effect at the door of the den, without entering, and then she told Hlupnafenglu to follow her.

The glass eye of the wickerwork boat recognized them, of course, allowing them to board. Hlupnafenglu handled the oars on the way across the water; the First Wolf seemed lost in thought.

Morlock had been drunk, Hlupnafenglu guessed, from the stale winy reek of the cave, but he was not now. He was lying on the cave floor next to an odd object like a black barrel. On the other side lay his sword—his real sword, Tyrfing. The black-and-white blade was alive with bitter life, and a faint red light was showing through the never-wolf's closed eyelids.

"He's working," Hlupnafenglu said decisively to the bemused First Wolf, who had never seen Morlock in this state. "No one can disturb him, in this state. We might as well wait. Do you want to talk to the flames? They say funny things sometimes. Or we could play cards."

Wuinlendhono looked at him with dark-ringed dark eyes and said quietly, "No, thank you. I'll just sit here. If you're sure we can't wake him."

"We can't," Hlupnafenglu confirmed, "because he's not asleep. Working isn't sleeping, though they look the same sometimes."

"I knew an old man once who used to say the same," Wuinlendhono remarked, seating herself gracefully on the cave floor. "I never found out whether he was telling the truth or not."

"Did you kill him?" Hlupnafenglu said, sitting opposite her.

The First Wolf froze, then looked carefully at him. "Yes. How did you know?"

"There is a sound in your voice. I hear it in my own when I talk about the big female who ran the soup hut. I'm pretty sure I killed her, or tried to. She hurt me sometimes, when no one else was around. Did the old man hurt you?"

"No more than some others, perhaps. But he was weaker than they, and paid for their sins. Never be weak, Hlupnafenglu; you may end up paying someone else's debt."

"I'll remember, High Huntress."

She was looking at Morlock's left hand. It was a misty almost shapeless shape all the way past the elbow, and dead-gray like corpse meat above that. The wooden glove Morlock sometimes wore on his left hand had fallen away: the ghost sickness had eaten away his flesh deep into his upper arm. Hlupnafenglu didn't think Morlock would be able to use the glove anymore. But the First Wolf didn't say anything about it, so Hlupnafenglu didn't either.

The light in Morlock's eyes—and in the cursed sword—was fading. He opened his eyes and said, "Wuinlendhono. Hlupnafenglu."

"Khretvarrgliu," replied the First Wolf, and Hlupnafenglu just nodded. "I thank you for your deeds in the air last night."

Morlock raised his right hand, warding off her thanks. "No need. I had my reasons."

Wuinlendhono lowered her head, as if angry or frustrated, but her low voice was calm as she said, "Do you know what happened to my Rokhlenu?"

"I saw it," Morlock said. "And now, yes, I think I know what happened to him. In here"—he rapped the barrel with his right hand—"is the motive energy for one of the airships. It seems to be a piece of a moon, or a stone that acts like a moon. I spent much of the morning in visionary contemplation of its light. Rokhlenu was briefly exposed to it, and the results were—well, I assume you have seen him."

"Yes. I have seen him. Can you help him?"

"I have two ideas. One will not wholly heal him, but will not kill him. The other may kill him, but may heal him."

"What are they?"

"The first: surgery with a silver knife. I could reshape his frame, as either wolf or man. He would be more or less whole, but incapable of transformation; wounds caused by silver seem to leave permanent traces on a werewolf."

"If you are talking like this to horrify me, you don't know who I am. It would take more than you to horrify me."

Morlock looked at her briefly, his eyes wide with surprise, then shook his head. "The other idea is simpler and more dangerous. Rokhlenu's being was infected by something from the moonstone's light. I think I know what it is, and I may be able to blast it clear of him."

"That does sound dangerous. Please do it."

"Rokhlenu will choose."

"He's incapable of choosing. I am his mate and have the right to speak for him; that is our law."

"I live by my own law. Blood for blood, and only blood. Rokhlenu is my blood, *harven coruthen*."

"I don't know what that means," said Wuinlendhono, and now she did sound angry. "But I am the First Wolf of the outliers. And—"

"How well do you know him, really?" Morlock interrupted.

"I am him. He is me. We were one at the mating and we are one still."

"Then trust him to make the right choice. I will fight with you or with anyone, Wuinlendhono, if there is some point to it. Is there a point to this?"

Wuinlendhono raised her head and looked at him. "No. Is there anything you need?"

"Time. Glass. Sunlight. A pair of able hands."

"I have hands," said Hlupnafenglu eagerly.

"I'll leave you to it, then," Wuinlendhono said. She stood in a single fluid motion, looked at Morlock as if she were going to say something, then walked off without doing so.

The time was time. Hlupnafenglu didn't know where it came from, and he lost track of where it went to. He spent much of it making glass. Morlock wanted enough to make a decent-size corridor of plate glass. He taught Hlupnafenglu how to make it unbreakable by folding it through higher dimensions. That was immensely entertaining to the red werewolf, and he enjoyed doing it. Meanwhile, Morlock often lay working in the sun, the glow of his irises visible through his closed lids even at noon. On the third day, he began to do it with a vat of molten glass beside him. Hlupnafenglu wandered by the vat occasionally. There were odd shapes—outlines and angles gleaming icy-pale through the yellow-orange molten glass. They reminded Hlupnafenglu of the shapes Morlock had taught him for representing fourth- and fifth-dimensional polytopes in three-dimensional space. But he found it too hot to bear for long—the sun seemed more intense there, as if something were funnelling sunlight toward the vat.

One afternoon, while Morlock worked in the sunlight, Hlupnafenglu was welding glass plates for the corridor. He enjoyed all the tasks of the current project, but this was his favorite, as it involved interaction with the flames. He enjoyed their ill-tempered self-regarding little personalities, and they spoke mostly in a language Morlock called Wardspeech. Learning the language was an interesting contrast to the tasks of executing four-dimensional designs while limited to three-dimensional senses, although he enjoyed that as well. Hlupnafenglu was enjoying most things these days: his mind was finally awake after a long sleep, and it was fun to see all the things it could do.

Often Hrutnefdhu came by to assist him, but today he was alone, except for the flames. He had just cajoled them to seal up a section of corridor wall when the hill was shaken by a roar like thunder. Hrutnefdhu ran out of the cave and saw a somewhat singed-looking Morlock picking himself up from the ground. The vat was in fragments scattered about the hillside. And where the glass had been was a spiked stonelike object, too bright to look at directly.

"We must establish a zone of Perfect Occlusion around the sunstone," said Morlock matter-of-factly.

It was obvious what the sunstone was, so Hlupnafenglu asked, "How do we establish Perfect Occlusion?"

"I'll show you," Morlock said, and he explained the process carefully to Hlupnafenglu, talking him through it.

"Khretvarrgliu, why are you teaching me so much?" Hlupnafenglu asked when the sunstone was sealed in the Perfect Occlusion.

"I am dying," said Morlock, as matter-of-factly as before. "This way I can pass on some of my skills. Plus, you have natural gifts for making. If you wish to pursue the craft, you should seek out Wyrtheorn of Thrymhaiam. He is a master of making, and was my pupil for many years. He can teach you much."

"Khretvarrgliu, I will."

"We've done enough for today."

That meant that Hlupnafenglu was to leave, because Morlock was going to start drinking. Or at least, that's what it often meant.

But one day, about five days later, Hlupnafenglu returned around dawn to find that Morlock had been working all night. By now they had actually built the glass corridor, setting it into the side of the hill. In the night, Morlock had silvered all the glass, and laid down a second layer of glass, sealing in the deadly metal. It was now safe to be near, although Hlupnafenglu felt dread standing next to it, and he could see that Hrutnefdhu (who had accompanied him that morning) felt it, too.

Morlock's face was gray with weariness, and Hlupnafenglu was alarmed to see that the ghost illness had eaten even more of Morlock's arm during the night. Nonetheless, the crooked man declined to rest.

"There are things we must discuss," Morlock said.

Hlupnafenglu thought he was going to talk about his imminent death, a conversation the red werewolf had been dreading. But instead Morlock started talking about the sun and the moon.

Morlock explained that every living body had three physical parts: a core-self, a shell, and an impulse cloud. This last was so tenuous in being that it was almost nonphysical, but not quite, and it could (under certain circumstances) survive the death of the person or animal whose life had produced it.

"Is that what a ghost is?" Hrutnefdhu asked reverently.

"I don't know what a ghost is," Morlock said. "But this is what an impulse cloud is."

He explained how the sun drew impulse clouds up into the sky, so that the sky was full of them. The moons gathered them together and sent them back to earth, entangled in moonlight.

"That is what powered the airships," Morlock said. "A moonstone imbued with moonlight and impulse clouds. It is the impulse clouds that distorted Rokhlenu's being."

"Is it impulse clouds that make us change from the day shape to the night shape?" Hlupnafenglu asked.

"Yes," Morlock said. "Your natures are permeable, somehow—receptive to the impulse clouds latent in moonlight. Whether you are wolves that can become human or men and women that can become wolves, I don't know.

But I suspect that each shapechanger is receptive to impulse clouds from at least one other animal. There may be some who can assimilate and change into many different kinds of animals: I don't know."

The pale werewolf asked, "Then why is Rokhlenu distorted? The moonstone just issued light similar to the moons—"

"But more intense, more concentrated," Morlock said. "There is a miasma in some impulse clouds, the effluvium of the dead soul. If it accumulates in a werewolf's being, he or she becomes distorted, unable to change."

"Like semiwolves," Hlupnafenglu said. "Or . . . never-wolves?"

"I think so," Morlock agreed.

He waited.

Hrutnefdhu was waiting, too. He expected Morlock to explain himself presently. But Hlupnafenglu knew better: the maker was waiting for someone else to take the next step—to follow in Morlock's trail, as it were.

"You will put the sunstone at one end of the corridor, the moonstone at the other," Hlupnafenglu said. "Thus you will blast the miasma clear."

"And, perhaps," Morlock said, "tear Rokhlenu's impulse cloud to shreds. That will be death."

"You could try it on another first," Hlupnafenglu said, "if—" He paused, then said, "I am a never-wolf."

"Yes," Morlock said.

"Try it on me," Hlupnafenglu said. "If it doesn't work you can think up something else. The gnyrrand is more important than I am."

Morlock shook his head. "Rokhlenu is my old friend, but I say no to that. If you choose to take the risk, I am glad. But not because you matter less than him."

Hlupnafenglu enjoyed risks the way he enjoyed almost everything, so he laughed.

They placed the Occlusion containing the sunstone at one end of the mirrored corridor. Then Hlupnafenglu walked in the open end. He was no longer laughing: being encased in silver was a nightmarish feeling.

Morlock and Hrutnefdhu rolled the black barrel over to the other end of the corridor. Then Morlock established a Perfect Occlusion there, and Hlupnafenglu found himself in absolute darkness.

"I'm going to introduce an aperture and release the light of the sunstone," Morlock's voice said, drifting down the glass corridor through the darkness.

Hlupnafenglu couldn't think of anything to say to that, so he said nothing.

The aperture opened like a golden eye, and the mirror-bright corridor was filled with burning light.

The red werewolf felt a strange pulling sensation, as if the burning eye were drawing him to it. He resisted.

Then a white eye opened at the other end of the corridor. It pushed him as the sunstone pulled him; the light more than redoubled in ferocity; it passed through him like silver swords. Something left him, something that did not belong in him, and he was less and more because of it.

Then the silver eye closed, and he was left gasping in the bitter sunlight. Moments later, the aperture in the Occlusion clenched shut and Hlupnafenglu was left in a grateful darkness. Soon, too soon, the sunstone end of the corridor opened: Morlock had moved the Occlusion so that Hlupnafenglu could exit the corridor.

Tentatively, he walked out into the tame morning light.

It had been a lifetime since he had entered. The world looked very different than it had a few moments before.

"You look all right," Hrutnefdhu said, glancing at him up and down. "How do you feel?"

"Strange," Hlupnafenglu said. "I . . . I remember who I am. Do you know who I am, Hrutnefdhu?"

"I suspected," the pale werewolf admitted.

Hlupnafenglu turned to Morlock. "Do you know who I am?"

"You are Hlupnafenglu," Morlock replied calmly.

The red werewolf found he had raised his hands in fists, as if to attack Morlock. He lowered them. What if he could kill the crooked man? Morlock was sick, already dying. It was a deed of no particular bite. On the other hand, the crooked man was Khretvarrgliu, the beast slayer. Sick as he was, he might yet defeat any foe. That, too, would win no honor-teeth for the red werewolf. He looked for a few moments at his fists and then unclenched them.

"I am," he said. "I am Hlupnafenglu now. And who I was before . . . it doesn't matter."

Morlock shrugged and opened his right hand. (The ghostly left one was hidden under his cloak.) Hrutnefdhu said, "Everyone accepts you as Hlupnafenglu. There's no reason for that to change."

The red werewolf nodded. He looked at the sun, the hillside, his two friends.

"I think it worked," he said.

"We'll wait and see," Morlock said. "There will be a moon aloft tonight."

It did work. After sunset, Hlupnafenglu stood in the light of Trumpeter and felt the night shape steal over him like a dream. He shook loose from his human clothing and capered, howling, in the third moon's light, a dark-red wolf with golden eyes. Hrutnefdhu, now also wearing the night shape, knocked him over.

They chased each other along the eastern and southern margins of the swamp, and from there southward into the plains, running deep into the dark land and deep into the night, laughing and singing in Moonspeech.

When Morlock saw the transformation he turned away and went down the hill. He crossed the water and went to the den on the first floor of the lair-tower where Rokhlenu was being kept.

Wuinlendhono was there alone with her husband, but he would neither look at her nor speak to her. He had not spoken, eaten, or drunk since his fall from the airship.

But Morlock spoke to him and to her. It was a long conversation; Morlock said much and Wuinlendhono said more. Rokhlenu said nothing until the hour before dawn, and then he spoke at last.

The yellow semiwolf was cringing before the gray-muzzles of the Sardhluun and Neyuwuleiuun packs. Their gnyrrands were there, with their reeves and fellow-cantors of the campaign, and the werowances of both packs, with their pack councils.

Wurnafenglu, wearing the night shape, sang while the yellow semiwolf cringed. He sang that they should listen to the informant from the mongrel outliers, the honorable traitor Rululawianu (because loyalty to traitors was the only treason, and treason to traitors was the highest honesty). There was hope like rich marrow in his news, if they had the bite to crack the bone.

The Werowance of Neyuwuleiuun sang a song frostier by far than the night's warm air. He pointed out that his pack had suffered dearly from the opportunities Wurnafenglu had brought them. Their airships, the glory of the Neyuwuleiuun, were lost—one ruined, the other stranded in a field of poisonous silver waste, and apparently robbed of its motive element. They could not afford such a loss, nor another such loss.

The Werowance of the Sardhluun sang a sad song in reply, neither agreeing nor disagreeing with the honored and honorable Werowance of the Neyuwuleiuun werewolves. How often he had warned Wurnafenglu that he was reckless and his actions were ill judged! All these comments were before trustworthy witnesses who could be produced at need. He had spoken at length about the perils and shame Wurnafenglu had brought to his own pack by his criminally inept stewardship of the Vargulleion, foundation of the Sardhluun pride, now an empty stone box. Still the Neyuwuleiuun could not hold the glorious Sardhluun werewolves culpable for the bad advice of one disfavored and deranged pack member. They must unite for the betterment of both packs against all their enemies—within their respective packs and without. He did not look toward Wurnafenglu as he sang, but many others from both packs did.

Wurnafenglu replied that both werowances had earned their relatively high and not at all unimportant positions by skills that were by no means to be absolutely despised: even the shortest claw can draw blood. And the Werowances knew, he hoped, exactly how much he esteemed them both. And he was willing to surrender his gnyrrandship, his honor-teeth, and his life . . . to the citizen who could take them from him.

Silence. Wurnafenglu was unpopular in that assembly, but no one cared to accept his offer. He knew it; they knew it; he remained silent, smiling with moon-bright teeth in the singer's circle, until they knew he knew it.

Wurnafenglu took up his song again. He sang that the costly attack on the outliers was not without effect. He sang that there was a wound in the outlier pack that could not be healed, that they could strike them down, along with their allies of the mangy sap-stinking Goweiteiuun dog-lickers. They must listen and learn; listen and learn: that was the refrain.

He stepped back, and motioned with his eyes for Rululawianu to step forward.

The yellow semiwolf crept rather than stepped forward. Absurdly, he was crouching on all fours—a shamefully submissive stance in the day shape. As he quivered in the moonlight falling on the singer's circle, the most powerful werewolves of the Sardhluun and Neyuwuleiuun packs looked down on him from their couches with interest and contempt. They utterly despised him, and Wurnafenglu would have changed that if he could; he wanted them to trust his informant. But they perhaps thought the semiwolf too timid to lie—and, if so, that was good enough.

"Look, I don't know if it matters," Rululawianu began at random. "I mean, I don't know if it's important. But I think Gnyrrand Rokhlenu is dead, or worse than dead. And they say that crazy never-wolf Khretvarrgliu is dying, too."

Wurnafenglu barked that he should tell the tale.

So he told it: how Rokhlenu had fallen distorted from the sky; how Morlock was dying from the ghost sickness; how he had made a corridor lined with silver and claimed it could cure semiwolves and never-wolves, but how, when they had put Rokhlenu in it, something had gone terribly wrong. Morlock was said to be poisoning himself, a slow suicide in self-punishment for the harm he had done his friend.

Wurnafenglu stood behind the semiwolf and watched the story's impact on its audience. He was quite pleased with the effect. The Neyuwuleiuun werewolves drew themselves up and exchanged glances when Rululawianu described Rokhlenu's distortion. They knew something that confirmed this part of the story—some deadly secret about that "motive part" that their werowance had incautiously mentioned.

And the silver corridor had been seen. No werewolf of the Sardhluun or Neyuwuleiuun packs could get near enough to examine it—there were traps and fences, seen and unseen, all around the hill that held Khretvarrgliu's cave. But it was there. It could be seen from miles away on the hot, dry, sun-drenched days that were coming with the end of winter—the sort of days that used to come, rarely, in high summer.

The allied pack councils exchanged a few whispered words among themselves. Then they turned and started barking questions at the yellow semiwolf. Most of them asked him to repeat or give more details about something he had already said. Wurnafenglu didn't object to this: he had conducted many interrogations, and he had often seen a liar's story unravel when he gave differing answers to the same question asked twice. The liar wants to be found out; so Wurnafenglu believed. Liars lie from fear, and they want their fear to end, even if the end is death.

But Rululawianu's story did not unravel. It held together, as Wurnafenglu had been sure it would. And one good question was asked, by a familiar friend and enemy.

The Werowance of the Sardhluun wondered why Rululawianu had come to them. He must know that, except for his new friend Wurnafenglu, the noble Sardhluun Pack despised traitors, and a traitor to traitors would get no warm welcome from them. Was it money? Was it meat, now that food was growing scarce? What had brought the yellow semiwolf forward with this tale?

Rululawianu shouted, "They won't use it on *me*! They won't put *me* in their magic tunnel! Oh, no! 'Silver is too scarce, Rululawianu. The more important wolves must be healed first, Rululawianu. Stop making noise; we don't need whiners like you, Rululawianu.' They could have healed me, made me a real werewolf. But they didn't. They were never going to. Maybe it was all a lie; maybe there is no cure. It doesn't matter. I hate them. I hate them. I don't want anything from you. I wanted it from them, but they wouldn't give it to me. So I'll help you wreck them. That's next best."

The council of allies nodded sagely. Yes, satisfied desire was best, always. But next best was revenge, the bitter drink that quenches frustrated desire, and hate, and love, and every other thing that pains the wolvish heart.

It was all they needed. They were utterly convinced. Wurnafenglu stepped forward, and the yellow semiwolf skittered away.

Wurnafenglu sang to them of a time and day soon to come: midnight on the nineteenth day of the fourth month. The great moon, Chariot, would arise. They, the great alliance of Sardhluun and Neyuwuleiuun werewolves, would challenge the dog-licking Goweiteiuun and their mongrel allies among the outliers to an election rally in the Great Rostra of Nekkuklendon. The challenged would appear and be defeated, for without the great heroes of the Vargulleion escape they were nothing. Or they would not appear, and they would be mocked in word and song on every mesa of Wuruyaaria. It was certain victory. And if it brought the Aruukaiaduun twine-twisters to their alliance (in an inferior position, of course), it would be a final victory in the year of Choosing. They need only settle which of those present now was worthy to be First Singer of the Innermost Pack.

With cold measuring eyes, the Werowance of the Sardhluun watched him all through his song. But the Werowance was the first to give hot-throated assent to Wurnafenglu's plan. The other wolves howled in agreement as the yellow semiwolf shuddered at the edge of the singer's circle.

The challenge was issued openly, in every market square and smoke den of the city, including the squalid settlement of swamp-dwelling outliers. The rumors spread as widely: stories that Rokhlenu was dead or worse, that the never-wolf Khretvarrgliu had killed him and then himself, that the First Wolf of the outliers had sold herself to a wild pack in the outlands.

The chosen night came, not soon enough to suit Wurnafenglu. A crowd began to gather at the Great Rostra of Nekkuklendon just after dark. The Sardhluun-Neyuwuleiuun Alliance had purchased great bales of bloodbloom and crates of cheap clay smoking-bowls for the victory party, and a story had spread that these would be distributed well before moonrise. It was, of course, illegal to give citizens gifts in the hope that they would vote for you. Fines might be levied against the offending pack, perhaps even substantial ones, if they lost the election. On the other hand, a victory party after a rally, to which the general citizenry was invited, was another matter. And if the party began before the victory actually occurred, who could be so small-minded as to object? Certainly not the high-minded public officials who had done the same when they were seeking election.

In fact, a little bloom was being smoked well before midnight when the gnyrrands of the Sardhluun-Neyuwuleiuun Alliance showed up, with their reeves and their cantors in train behind them, and a cascade of campaign volunteers in loose clothes of black and green and short capes of red and green (the Neyuwuleiuun colors). They ran in close order down the stairs into the singers' pitch sunk into the center of the rostrum and ran all the way around the pitch, receiving the hopeful cheers of the audience. Some bloom was good; more bloom was better—and if the Alliance won, much bloom would be smoked.

This was a more important rally than the last one, which the Sardhluun had lost so ignominiously. If for nothing else (and there was much else) because of the location. The most common pack affiliation on Nekkuklendon was Aruukaiaduun. Many important members of their Inner Pack had come here to watch the rally and judge the prospects of the new Alliance. If they were impressed, they might see fit to join, virtually assuring victory for the Alliance.

The betting ran seven to one against the Goweiteiuun even showing up tonight. The Alliance was so confident, they started their speeches before the Goweiteiuun appeared, and the crowd shouted their approval. The sooner the talking began, the sooner it would end.

The speeches were not noted, then or later, for their impressiveness. The Neyuwuleiuun gnyrrand congratulated the Sardhluun Pack for its association, almost as younger brothers, with one of the original treaty packs, and congratulated his own pack for inventing the pack, the city, and civilization itself. Wurnafenglu, speaking for the Sardhluun, made a remark about the potency of youth that was either pointless or obscene, but not particularly witty either way, and went on to explain that this alliance with the Neyuwuleiuun was a natural extension of the Sardhluun's longstanding policy of solitary strength. The strong and the solitary had the strength to recognize when a greater strength could be gained by alliance, thus actually preserving the solitary strength of the strong allied partners. They stood together because they stood alone. He said this several times, and his cantors cheered louder every time, but members of the crowd seemed to be trying to figure out what it meant.

Wurnafenglu was saved by moonrise. As his speech thundered to a vigorous but not-altogether-coherent close, a bitter blue light grew in the sky, drowning the feeble lamps and torches: Chariot rising in the west.

All the citizens turned to the west and raised their hands—even the never-wolves and semiwolves who could not hope for a metamorphosis. They did it because others did it, and because they wished they could hope, even though they were hopeless.

Citizen after citizen fell under their own shadow, their day shape lost to the night shape; screaming men and women became howling wolves in the hot blue night. Winter was over. Spring had begun. They rejoiced and they were afraid.

As the howling of the crowd began to die down, everyone heard a band of wolves singing somewhere in the city. It was a song about a battle in the air—a song about the night the new Alliance had tried and failed to destroy the outliers, and lost its boasted airships in the bargain. Everyone in the city remembered that night—how they had watched and wondered at the battle in the air.

It dawned on the assembly that the Goweiteiuun were indeed coming to the assembly, and that they were bringing their outlier allies with them.

The crowd by the stairs parted to admit the newcomers. There were wolves and, shockingly, never-wolves in their company. The never-wolves wore strange glass armor that glittered in the moonlight, and some bore banners on staves: blue and red for the Goweiteiuun and green and gold for the outliers.

At their head was a great gray wolf with blue eyes; he wore cord upon cord of honor-teeth, and among them was the long curving fang of a dragon.

"Rokhlenu!" shouted the crowd. "Rokhlenu!"

Many of them were Aruukaiaduun, and he was born to their pack. They had lost him to the machinations of the old gray-muzzle Rywudhaariu, but they were still proud of him, still ashamed they had let themselves lose him. They chanted his name as if it would let them reclaim him, as if he could still be their hero, their native son.

Wurnafenglu turned to lock eyes with the yellow semiwolf, the coward, the traitor-to-traitors, Rululawianu.

The semiwolf was not cowering. He was laughing. He threw back his head and shouted, "Where are the prisoners of the Khuwuleion? Where are the prisoners of the Khuwuleion? *Where are the prisoners of the Khuwuleion?*"

It was the question the Sardhluun didn't want asked, the question they could not answer. It was the nature of the city's legal system that justice didn't enter into it: only the powerless went to prison. But there had been many of them, and they had left many kin and friends behind them, and perhaps in those numbers was a kind of power. Also, the city had paid the Sardhluun to tend those prisoners, not to sell them or butcher them. The next government would also ask: where were the prisoners of the Khuwuleion?

Now the band of newcomers began to chant the deadly question. The crowd took up the cry. The Sardhluun were baffled, the Neyuwuleiuun embarrassed.

Wurnafenglu was not baffled. He saw just exactly how he had been fooled. He leapt on the laughing semiwolf and tore his furry throat out. Then the gnyrrand swung about and, jaws still dripping with Rululawianu's blood, he charged the outliers, his cantors at his heels.

The watching citizens sang their approval. This was the way to run an election: surprises, bloom smoke, one side turning on itself, and a maximum of fighting with a minimum of talking.

The crowd was barking with excitement by now. They were not aware of it, but their barking fell into the rhythm of War's delighted laughter. He was manifest, though not visible to most of the citizens there, and he was enjoying the rally immensely. It was a good fight, and promised to get better. He visualized that the Alliance would lose, but that many of the never-wolves and semiwolves fighting for the outliers would die, and he was interested to see how well the results accorded with his foresight.

He wished Mercy were there. He would have showed her some events worth seeing.

But Mercy was manifest elsewhere and elsewhen. As a dark bird with no feet, she was hovering over the hills west of the outlier settlement. A pale werewolf was half supporting, half dragging a crook-shouldered man with a gray corpselike face who was stumbling out of a cave.

"Come on, you old fool," the pale werewolf was saying. "You can be drunk in our den as well as in this stupid cave. You may be dying, but you don't have to die alone. Come on, old Khretvarrgliu. Just a little further along here. Careful on the steps."

Half cajoling, half abusing, in the manner of werewolves, the pale werewolf took the crooked man down the steps, across the water, and up the rickety stairway to the den at the top.

The man said nothing. But Mercy saw a little into his heart: how he feared death not at all, but disliked the need for parting with friends like this. The werewolf's heart, too, was full of hopeless, helpless affection he could not express, much of it confused with thoughts of his mate Liudhleeo.

Mercy witnessed them for a while, but demanifested herself before too much time passed. She knew that, whatever they felt now, they would change. She had been a god for long ages now, and she knew that Death was right about mortals: they were filled with one divinity, and then another, and then they changed and changed and changed. She preferred to be absent before they were lost to her entirely.

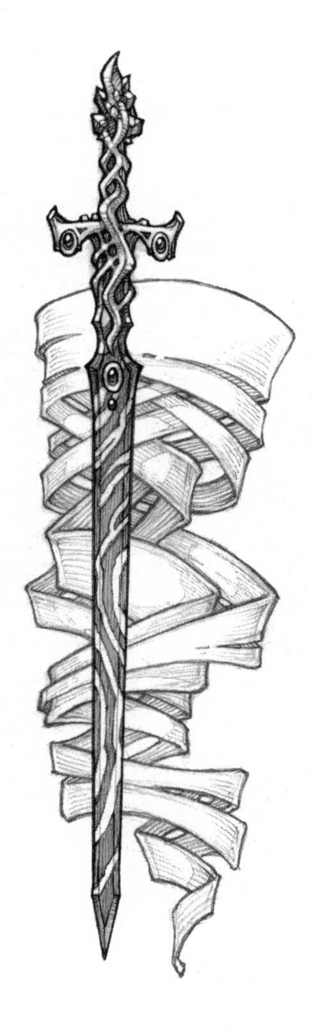

Part Four

The Dire Wolf's Due

The wolf came in, I got my cards,
    we sat down for a game.
I cut my deck to the Queen of Spades
    but the cards were all the same.
In the backwash of Bennario,
    the black and bloody mire,
the dire wolf collects his due
    while the boys sing round the fire.

—Robert Hunter, "Dire Wolf"

Chapter Twenty-five

Friends and Foes

It was a blisteringly hot morning in early spring. The First Wolf of the outliers and their gnyrrand were looking at a bucket of muddy water that Hlupnafenglu had just drawn from the swamp.

"How does it work?" Wuinlendhono asked.

"Like this," Hlupnafenglu said, and dumped the contents of the bucket into an open tube with a downward slope. The muddy water poured down the slope, through a glassy mirrored gate at the base of the slope, then up another slope on the other side. Except the water ran on alone; the mud remained at the bottom of the slope in a sludgy pool. There was a second mirrored gate atop the second slope, and another downward sloping tube beyond. Beneath this tube was another bucket. The water ran into the bucket, and when it was done, the red werewolf picked up the bucket and drank from it.

He offered the bucket to Rokhlenu.

Rokhlenu took it, tasted it, drank a mouthful, and said, "It smells a little odd."

"You can run it through more than once to get it cleaner," Hlupnafenglu said eagerly, and then his face fell. "Chieftain," he said, and bowed his head.

The others turned and saw Morlock standing near, with pale Hrutnefdhu beside him. The day was cruelly hot, but the crooked man wore his usual dark cloak over his ghostly left hand. He didn't seem to feel the heat: his pale grayish skin was dry as bone. He looked at the wooden tubes, at the suddenly abashed Hlupnafenglu and said, "So that was your project? A water cleaner?"

"Yes, Chieftain. I didn't want to bother you with it."

"Not bad. But I think you need more than one turn to get the water really clean. A coil of three or four might do."

"Yes, Chieftain."

"Sketch a design or two and we'll discuss them later."

"Yes, Chieftain."

"This will be important to us," Rokhlenu said, in case the red wolf was disheartened. "Especially if this dry weather continues."

Hlupnafenglu bowed his head, but did not call Rokhlenu chieftain.

"Let's step out of this sun," Wuinlendhono said. "Ghost! It's not even noon yet."

They went back into the First Wolf's lair-tower. The red werewolf remained behind to take apart his apparatus.

"Warm weather for spring," Morlock remarked.

"It's like hell," Wuinlendhono said. "Do your people believe in hell? I never did, but now I think I'm going to live through it."

There was a ragged edge to her voice, and Rokhlenu wanted to comfort her somehow, but he didn't know what to say. The weather was odd, very odd, frighteningly odd.

"I don't suppose you have a magic trick that will make food for us, Khretvarrgliu," the First Wolf said wryly. "We've been living on stores for almost a year, and by next fall they'll all be empty, I guess."

"No," said Morlock, "but if I were you, I would set up a colony on the coast of the Bitter Water. Even the swamp will not last forever, if there are no streams to run into it, and the mirror gates will rinse water clean of salt. Plus the drought will not affect sea creatures much."

There was a silence, and Wuinlendhono said with amusement, "Are you proposing that we eat fish?"

"Citizens will be eating worse by winter," Morlock replied. "At least if you are correct about the stores running out."

Wuinlendhono nodded, still not convinced.

"Besides," Morlock continued, "there are red-blooded animals in the sea and around it. Whales, wave-horses, merkine, seabirds."

"Really? I had no idea! What do they taste like?"

"Seabirds are just birds. I can't say about the rest."

"Yurr. Interesting. Of course, it's a few days' run to the coast. They'd have to smoke the meat on the coast to transport it back here."

The males were silent as the First Wolf thought it through. "And if the drought goes on, we can all just move there," she said at last. "Wuruyaaria will be done, anyway." She put a hand on Rokhlenu's arm. "Beloved, I'm going to do something about this. Do you want me with you when you meet the band from the Aruukaiaduun wolves?"

He did, but he stroked her hand and said, "Want, yes. Need, no. Go save our lives, why don't you?"

She gave a long carnivore's grin to them all and hurried away, her gold-toothed guardians scurrying in her wake.

"Morlock," said Rokhlenu to his old friend, "you don't look well."

"I'm dying," the crooked man said matter-of-factly. The pale werewolf looked at him with alarm.

"You look like you're already dead," Rokhlenu said. "Isn't there anything we can do?"

"Not unless you know where to find a unicorn," Morlock replied.

He used the Latin word, not knowing the term in Sunspeech, and when he explained what he meant, Rokhlenu said dubiously, "There are stories about things like that. Children's stories. What's told of them makes them sound like pets. Imaginary pets."

"I don't know anything about your local kinds," Morlock said. "They lived in the mountains where I was raised. I suppose they still live there."

"Then we'll take you there. Or we'll send there for a horn."

Morlock shook his head. "No. I'll be dead soon. The ghost illness will reach my heart and I'll be done." Again, Hrutnefdhu was looking at him with a stricken expression, but Morlock didn't seem to notice. "I'll teach Hlupnafenglu what I can before I die. I'll do what I can for you before I die. It's not what I would have chosen, but it will have to be enough."

"What about Ulugarriu?" broke in Hrutnefdhu. "Maybe—maybe he could do something."

Morlock opened his right hand, closed it. That seemed to be a dismissal of the subject. He turned to Rokhlenu and said, "I tore down the mirror corridor."

"Yes, I saw that."

"The moonstone failed after I healed Lekkativengu. I can't recharge it with moonlight; it's designed differently than my sunstone. In fact, I don't think it was *made* at all; it may be a piece of a moon."

"How did they get it?"

Morlock shrugged. He continued, "When I was breaking up the silvered glass I had an idea."

He drew a short stabbing spear from a sheath under his cloak. The spear head was glass, woven through with threadlike cracks. And in the center was a silvery wedge.

"In the haft, there's a rune-slate bonded in state to the glass spearhead," Morlock explained coolly. "You stab someone with the spear, break the rune-slate, the glass shatters, and the silver point remains in the wound."

Rokhlenu finally understood the feeling of dread gripping him since Morlock had appeared. "Put it away, please," he said, as mildly as possible.

"I think they'll work," said Morlock, "though I haven't tested one yet. I have enough silver and glass from the mirror corridor to make many of these."

"I'm sure they'll work; everything you make works. But we can't use them."

"They're safe enough for the user. The—"

"Politically impossible. You need to take my word for this, Morlock. I cannot use silver weapons against other werewolves. Every citizen in Wuruyaaria would march against us."

Morlock shrugged, nodded, and sheathed the spear. "Well, maybe I can use the stuff for something else. This really bothers you, does it?" he added, tapping the sheath.

"Yes. It really does."

"I'll get rid of it. You'd better stay here," he said to Hrutnefdhu. "Some silver might be lying around the cavern yet."

The pale werewolf nodded and said, "Either Liudhleeo or I will bring you lunch. You'll eat it or find another den."

Morlock smiled, gripped him by the forearm, punched Rokhlenu lightly in farewell, and left.

"Is he drunk?" Rokhlenu asked Hrutnefdhu. "He smelled like that stuff he drinks. The wine."

"He never drinks during the day," the pale werewolf replied. "But he is drunk every night."

"I wish I'd never given him the stuff. I thought he'd like it."

"I can't tell if he does. It seems to be hurting him somehow. But what does it matter, if he's dying anyway?" The pale castrato's voice was shrill with despair.

They entered the great audience chamber of the First Wolf. She wasn't there. In fact, no one was there. They sat down on couches and talked in low voices about one thing and another: the election, and Morlock, and Ulugarriu, and the deadly weather. They reached no conclusions, but that, Rokhlenu thought to himself, isn't what talking was usually for.

Wuinlendhono appeared presently. She dismissed her guards and began to talk about her plans for the seacoast colony. They were getting more people in the outlier settlement because of their successes in the elections—more than they could really feed, as it was turning out. This was a chance to give some of the newcomers a chance to earn some bite, if nothing else.

Hrutnefdhu left them during this conversation. Rokhlenu waved him an offhanded farewell, involved in discussing the new plans and their political impact with his beloved.

Presently he looked up to see that the red werewolf Hlupnafenglu was standing nearby, patiently waiting for them to notice him.

"What is it, Hlupnafenglu?" he asked.

"Do you know who I am?" the red werewolf asked in turn.

"Yurr." Was the big red werewolf going crazy again? "Aren't you Hlupnafenglu?"

"I am now. Do you know who I *was*?"

"Oh. Before the Vargulleion? No. Is it important?"

"I don't know if it is." The red werewolf looked keenly at the First Wolf. "Do you know who I was, High Huntress?"

She seemed reluctant to reply. Finally she said, "Well. I thought you might be the Red Shadow. I saw him a few times in Apetown. From a distance, mind you. But he didn't look like anyone else I've ever seen, except you."

"I was the Red Shadow."

"All right," Rokhlenu said. "Someone has to explain this to me."

Wuinlendhono turned to him and said, "The Red Shadow was an assassin. You wouldn't have heard about him; you were a respectable person before they framed you. But for five or six years, if you wanted someone killed in Apetown or Dogtown, and you didn't care how much it cost you, you hired the Red Shadow. He never failed. A few years ago, he disappeared. Some people said he was killed by one of his targets, and some people said he had retired to live among the wild packs. But apparently he was in the Vargulleion. Eh, 'Hlupnafenglu'?"

"Yes. I don't know how I got there or what they did to me. I don't remember a lot. But I do remember the murders. Many, many murders."

"Oh," said Rokhlenu. Killing in fights was an accepted part of life in the werewolf city, but secret murder was another thing entirely. "Maybe that does make a difference."

The red werewolf bowed his head. "I'm done with all that. Can't I be Khretvarrgliu's apprentice, Hlupnafenglu? Does it matter that I was the Red Shadow?"

"Not to me," said Rokhlenu. "We were in the Vargulleion together, and we fought our way out together. That matters more to me than the crimes of someone I never heard of until just now."

"But this is a Year of Choosing," Wuinlendhono said gently. "It might matter to the citizens of Wuruyaaria."

The red werewolf nodded, not looking at either of them. "If you say, I will go."

Rokhlenu would have liked to turn him down then and there. *No; stay; you're one of us now*. But it wasn't that easy.

"Let's think about it," he said. "I have a meeting to go to now"—ghosts, that sounded like something a politician would say, but he *was* a politician these days—"so let's talk it over later on, perhaps tomorrow. If you can stay, we want you to stay: not as the Red Shadow, but as yourself, as Hlupnafenglu."

"Chieftain, my real name is—"

"Your real name is Hlupnafenglu, unless you choose otherwise. Think on it."

The red werewolf looked at him with his golden eyes, turned, and walked away.

"I handled that badly," he said to his spouse, after Hlupnafenglu had gone.

"No," she said. "Not if you weren't lying to him. If you really want to keep him around. Because now he probably won't leave unless we send him away."

"I wasn't lying."

"Then go meet with the Aruukaiaduun band. Them you can lie to. They'll be disappointed if you don't."

"Them I live to disappoint."

The Aruukaiaduun band were awaiting him in the old barracks of the irredeemables. Lekkativengu, claw-fingered no longer and wearing perhaps the first pair of shoes he had ever owned, was entertaining them with polite conversation. The subject at hand was the last rally fought between the Sardhluun-Neyuwuleiuun Alliance and the Goweiteiuun with their outlier partisans.

The Aruukaiaduun gnyrrand was a smooth-faced, brown-eyed, shiny-toothed emptiness named Norianduiu; Rokhlenu knew a little bit about him from the old days (as he thought of his life before the Vargulleion), and had not expected much trouble with him. He knew the Aruukaiaduun cantors, as well; they were just inferior versions of Norianduiu.

No, the only person who counted in this embassy was the oldest and ugliest member, a werewolf with no official position in the Aruukaiaduun Pack, the old gray-muzzle Rywudhaariu.

He was nearly a semiwolf. He could assume the night shape, but in the day shape his nose and lower jaw were strangely prominent, almost meeting, and the end of his nose had a strange spongy look, almost like a wolf's nose. His arms were somewhat crooked and leglike, too; he always wore clothes with long sleeves to disguise this.

He was too impaired to run for office; no one liked him enough to vote for him without pressure. But his neck was almost hidden by ropes of honor-teeth he had acquired or extorted over the years. He had been running things on Nekkuklendon, with claws into business on every other mesa, for generations. And he controlled the representatives of the Aruukaiaduun to the Innermost Pack of the city, always through some face-without-a-personality like Norianduiu.

It had kept members of the Aruukaiaduun on the Innermost Pack for as long as anyone could remember. Citizens were more than willing to enlist the famous cunning of Rywudhaariu in the service of the city. But no Aruukaiaduun werewolf had ever been First Singer of the Innermost Pack. That was a job for a puppet master, not a puppet.

This was why Rokhlenu had decided to meet the Aruukaiaduun werewolves alone. The risk was that he would look like a gnyrrand with no followers. The message, though, was that there was only one citizen in the Aruukaiaduun embassy worth talking to. He saw the chagrined looks among the Aruukaiaduun cantors as he approached, and decided that the message had been received. They had been hoping at least to meet his notorious mate, the First Wolf of the outliers. Instead, they would be shuffled off to an underling while the grown-ups talked—as usual.

"Lekkativengu, show the gnyrrand and the cantors around town a bit," Rokhlenu said as he approached. "Citizens, I leave you in good hands"—he winked slightly at Lekkativengu, who grinned and proudly flexed his fingers—"and perhaps we'll talk later. But I must consult with your leader now."

The gnyrrand and the cantors looked at Rywudhaariu, who nodded, and they glumly rose from their couches and shuffled after Lekkativengu into the searingly hot spring sunlight.

Rokhlenu sat down on a couch opposite and tried to look his old enemy in the eye. It was difficult, as old Rywudhaariu was somewhat wall-eyed and he enjoyed making interlocutors uncomfortable by turning his face toward them and his eyes away.

"That was rather high-handed," said the old werewolf, not as if he disapproved. His voice was reedy, not good for singing or speaking.

"Not so high-handed as when your clowns sent me to the Vargulleion."

"That was the biggest mistake I ever made. But you wouldn't be led, old sport, and I'm not ready to lie down and be barked at yet."

"That's to be seen. If you had my people killed, you may find it an even greater mistake."

"I had nothing to do with that."

"That's to be seen, too. But I'm here to talk with you, not as a citizen with a private grudge, but as the gnyrrand of my new pack and the consort of my First Wolf. We have a common interest against this new political alliance of the Sardhluun and the Neyuwuleiuun."

"That's to be seen, in the words of your own refrain. You need us; that's clear. And the Alliance does not need us; that's clear. But it may be in our interest to stand apart, as neutrals, rather than join in a losing side."

"We're not the losing side. We're the winning side. Don't take my word for it. Look what's happened every time the Alliance has tangled with us."

"I have been looking, and I am impressed. But your victories have been very costly for Wuruyaaria, you know. Those airships of the Neyuwuleiuun brought in a lot of slaves and meat-animals. This is going to be a hungry year, and the next one hungrier yet. We'll miss them. And citizens will blame you."

"Slaves do the work once done by citizens. The fewer slaves in the city, the better."

"The better for citizens of very little bite. The worse for citizens of very large bite."

"That may even out."

"You need it to be better than even, in your favor, and I'm not sure that's the way it is."

"You can help with that."

"Maybe I can. What's in it, for me and mine?"

"I can make you First Singer of the Innermost Pack."

Rywudhaariu almost spoke, then paused. He was genuinely surprised. "Would you?" he said at last. "If you could. They are separate issues, I suppose."

"I might: if you give me evidence that you were not involved in the murder of my kin. I'll waive my personal grievance against you. You need not be elected to the Innermost Pack to be First Singer; the Innermost normally choose the First Singer from among themselves, but not always. If a union of the Aruukaiaduun, the Goweiteiuun, and the outliers win the election, the first act must be the admission of the outliers to the treaty. Then I and the gnyrrand of the Goweiteiuun will support you for First Singer. If you can persuade your own unruly band to support you, your election is certain."

"Certain only in the wake of many uncertainties. Still: what an offer! Well, I must think on this."

"Not for too long, though."

"Naturally not. This is a lively election year. A pity if it is really the last."

"The last?"

Rywudhaariu was laboriously extricating himself from the comforts of his couch, but when both his feet were on the floor he said, "Hadn't you heard? The world is ending. That's what all this strange weather means. The gods or somebody—"

"Keep it clean, Rywudhaariu."

"This is how the story goes; I'm not saying I believe it. The gods or somebody have decided that the world has gone on long enough, and now they are burning it alive."

Rokhlenu walked silently beside the old politician for a while and then said, "Yurr. The world changes, but never ends. I can't believe it."

"Oh, I don't believe it, either. Still, if the world changes enough, we may not be able to live in it. I'll leave you here, Rokhlenu," he said at the door of the barracks. "I don't want to inflict the heat outside on you, not if we're going to be friends after all. That sunlight is too much for anyone with red blood still running in their veins. Personally, I rather enjoy it, of course, but I seem to be mostly ice water and mush as I get older."

"Well, see that your ice water doesn't boil over," said Rokhlenu, perfectly willing to stay behind in the shade.

Outside, the rest of the Aruukaiaduun band were waiting, looking bedraggled and unhappy in the fierce light. Not even the harsh sunshine could dim Lekkativengu's spirits, though, and he gladly offered to accompany the Aruukaiaduun werewolves to the southern gate.

Rokhlenu waited till they were out of sight and then braved the bitter light to cross over to the First Wolf's lair-tower and talk with his mate. She was waiting for him in the singing room on the second floor, and they discussed the whole meeting.

"I don't see how we can win," he said, "if the Aruukaiaduun join the Alliance. But I sort of hope Rywudhaariu carries out his threat of staying neutral through the election. I'd hate to give him a chance to bite us on the back of our neck."

"On the back of our anything," Wuinlendhono agreed.

Rywudhaariu had another meeting later that afternoon in the deserted Shadow Market. By then he had dismissed the Aruukaiaduun electoral band and was accompanied by a pack of mute mercenary thugs from Dogtown.

The citizen he came to meet stood alone in the empty marketplace. Wurnafenglu might be a gray-muzzle, but he was proud of the fact that he needed no bodyguards to defend his person or his honor-teeth.

"And so?" he said, as soon as the two werewolves were in conversation range.

"He won't go for it," Rywudhaariu replied. "He's not stupid, just inexperienced, and he's getting more experience every day. I tell you what, if I could gather proof that I wasn't involved in his family's murder—"

"Oh, was that the deal breaker?"

"It was, and he knows it. But if it wasn't, I would toss your Alliance over and join their Union."

"What did he offer you?"

"The chance to be First Singer."

"Yurr. Yes, that was shrewd. If you could have jumped at it, you would have, and the fact that you didn't sang him a whole epic."

"Nonsense. I don't jump at anything without looking it over. I wish you were as bright as our enemy is, Wurnafenglu."

"I have other merits," Wurnafenglu said smugly.

"You must list them for me sometime. That would be useful knowledge indeed. In the meantime, I think we must retreat to our secondary line of attack and rattle the young fellow somehow—get him to do something rash.

What do your spies among the outliers tell you? What is their strength and what is their weakness, and how do we use the one to strike at the other? If we can answer those questions, I may be able to offer you the station Rokhlenu offered me."

Chapter Twenty-six

Death of a Citizen

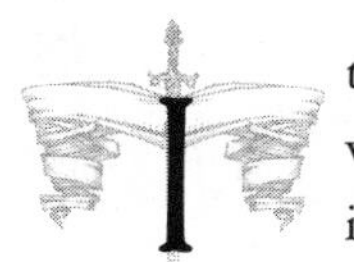

t was already hot the next morning at dawn. Morlock awoke with an empty wine bowl in his hand and a female's screams in his ears.

He dropped the bowl and rolled from his sleeping cloak to his feet. He was not ready for a fight, but tried to look as if he was.

Liudhleeo was on her knees, wailing over Hrutnefdhu's body. His obviously dead body. It still wore the night shape, though the air was filled with sunlight. And the head was missing. Someone had crept into the den while Morlock was drunk, killed his friend, decapitated him, and escaped—not just unharmed, but unchallenged.

He sat down on the other side of the body, her screams and sobs vibrating in his wine-wounded mind. He could not speak to her, could not bring himself to comfort her. He was too ashamed. His friend had been murdered, in his presence, while he lay there drunk. What right did he have to speak to the dead wolf's grieving mate? He was stunned beyond speech, beyond action, by the enormity.

Eventually, Liudhleeo's screams subsided to sobbing, and the enormous glacier of Morlock's shame split through with anger and pain.

There were jars of wine scattered around the den. Morlock got up and threw the nearest one out the window. When he heard it smash on the plank road outside and someone shout in alarm and annoyance, he felt a fierce satisfaction begin to burn within him. He grabbed another jar and tossed it out the window, and another.

Presently feet came drumming up the stairs. He was picking up another wine jar as an astonished Rokhlenu entered through the open door, with Hlupnafenglu following close behind.

"Morlock, what are you—?" Rokhlenu began, but broke off as he saw Hrutnefdhu's decapitated corpse.

"Ghost of all ghosts," Rokhlenu whispered. "What happened here?"

"Our friend was murdered last night," Morlock said, and threw the jar he was holding out the window.

"I was," Liudhleeo said, through her tears, "I was—out. And Morlock was—Morlock was—"

"I was drunk," said Morlock grimly, seizing another jar. "Dead drunk." He tossed the jar out the window.

"Morlock," said Rokhlenu. "Old friend. I think I know how you feel."

"Old friend, I hope you don't. I hope you never do."

"But you could at least toss the jars out the other window. They'd fall in the swamp that way, not into the street."

Morlock considered the question seriously and replied reasonably, "They might not break." He tossed another jar into the street. He continued until there were no more and he was left glancing about in frustration. After a brief internal struggle, he decided not to continue hurling every available thing in the den out the window.

He turned to Liudhleeo, who was bending over Hrutnefdhu's corpse, her eyes wet, though she was no longer sobbing. Hlupnafenglu was standing behind her, staring with a strange, hungry expression at the meaty end of the pale severed neck.

"I'm sorry," he said to her. "You both deserved better from me."

"We both failed him. I should have been here. Oh, I should have been here."

Morlock closed his eyes, imagined waking in the fierce noontime to the prospect of two stinking corpses that had once been his friends, repressed the urge to vomit, and opened his eyes again. "No," he said. "Better that you weren't."

He crouched down across the body from her. She looked at him for the first time.

"I don't know what your burial customs are," he said. "How can I help?"

"That's females' work," Rokhlenu said hastily.

Morlock didn't look at him. "I don't care if it is," he said to Liudhleeo. It was in his mind that she seemed to have few friends, male or female. "How can I help?"

"There is a female—she runs a smoking lair off the market. Name is Ruiulanhro. She has—she has—she can help."

Rokhlenu said, "I know her. I'll send her word."

"Then I will do what I must do," Morlock said.

She bowed her head, breaking their locked gaze.

"Morlock," said Rokhlenu. "Come talk with me a moment."

Morlock stood and walked after his old friend through the door and down the stairs. He felt as if iron spikes were being pounded past his eyes, and every movement threatened to make his gorge rise up through his throat.

Rokhlenu came to a halt underneath a notice near the bottom of the stairs. Morlock had passed it many times, and now, after a fashion, he could even read it. In Sunspeech and Moonspeech it said, *Tenants must bury their own dead. No smoking bloom on the stairways.*

"There is a thing or two I must tell you," Rokhlenu began.

"This is about politics, I guess."

Rokhlenu was silent for a moment, looked past Morlock's shoulder, met Morlock's eye, and said, "Yes, in a way. How did you know?"

"I don't understand it and I don't understand your politics."

"All right. I think this murder was aimed at me—an attempt to make me do something irrational."

"You can leave that to me."

"That's what I'm worried about. The election is in balance just now, Morlock. If the Aruukaiaduun stay neutral, or at least separate from the Alliance, our Union has a fair chance of winning most of the couches on the Innermost Pack."

Morlock looked at him and waited; he could not see why this mattered.

"Most of the City Watchers are members of the Aruukaiaduun,"

Rokhlenu explained, when he saw that an explanation was necessary. "If we go into the city, asking questions, getting in fights, maybe killing someone, it could push the Aruukaiaduun into opposition. That may be the *motive* for this murder."

"Rokhlenu—" Morlock began, and found he could not go on.

"It's dangerous to be too predictable, Morlock," Rokhlenu said. "You're too good a fighter to not know this."

"Rokhlenu, I will have blood for my friend's blood. For our friend's blood."

"Is this what Hrutnefdhu would want?"

"I don't know. It doesn't matter, anyway. I am myself, not him."

Rokhlenu looked away. "I don't want them to get away with it, either. I miss him already."

"Then."

"If—" He glanced up the stairway. There were doors open, citizens gathering on the turns of the stair. He looked back at Morlock. "I have an idea. *You drunken, drooling, farting spongebag of a never-wolf's brach.*"

Morlock was confused, then amused. He thought he saw what Rokhlenu was aiming at. "*Your mother shaved her nose every morning*," he shouted back, red echoes of pain bouncing around his head. "*She could juggle at midnight!*"

"*Don't talk about my mother, you cow-fondling, milk-drinking, ape-toed refugee from a freak show!*"

"*I never fondled your mother—*" Morlock began, and Rokhlenu howled, "*That's* it*!*" and seized him by the shoulders. They struggled for a bit, snarling theatrically for the benefit of the audience.

"Have to take it outside," Rokhlenu muttered. "Need more eyes on this." He released Morlock's shoulders and flew away down the stairs as if he'd been struck.

Even if he weren't hungover Morlock wouldn't have been up to similar acrobatics; the ghost sickness was throwing off the balance of his entire body. But he thundered down the steps as fast as he could, and they broke together through the door leading into the street.

The plank road was littered with broken jars, stained with wine like purple blood. The reek of it nearly did make Morlock furious, and he never remembered afterward the insults he hurled at Rokhlenu in the street. He remembered the awed looks on the citizens standing around, though. The crowd had begun to gather—drawn by screams and hurled wine jars, no doubt—before they took their ostensible quarrel out into the sunlight, and it only thickened as they stood there screaming and shoving each other in the hot morning light.

"Good enough," Rokhlenu muttered eventually. "Have to end it somehow."

Morlock threw back his head and shouted, "Tyrfing!"

The sword, its black-and-white blade glittering like crystal in the day's fierce light, flew from the window of the topmost den and landed in Morlock's outstretched hand.

Rokhlenu spat at his feet. "Go ahead and use it, coward!"

"Get out," Morlock snarled. "Come back with a weapon and we'll finish this."

"I'll come back in my night shape and rip your belly open."

"Dogs bark. Citizens act. This is over."

"It's not over!" shouted Rokhlenu, and stormed away through the crowd.

Morlock turned back to the dark doorway and stepped out of the sun and the gaze of the crowd. There were still citizens goggling on the stairway, but they skittered away like mice when they saw him returning, sword in hand. He mounted the stairs back to the topmost den, his thoughts grim.

If Rokhlenu thought, as he obviously did, that this stagy break between the two friends would help him politically, Morlock was willing to oblige him. But he didn't relish the thought of investigating a political assassination in the largely unknown werewolf city. If Hrutnefdhu could help him—but, of course, it was Hrutnefdhu who had been assassinated. There was Hlupnafenglu, of course. But, if he was not mistaken, Rokhlenu had been trying to warn him about Hlupnafenglu for some reason.

As he approached the still-open door to the den, a thought occurred to him. How had the assassin entered the den? He pulled the door half closed and examined the lock. The glass eye was missing, and the coppery sinews of the lock mechanism had been severed somehow. Not by a blade, he thought: something hot enough to melt copper. Yet it had not set fire to the wooden door. Interesting, and revealing.

Ulugarriu had a hand, or a paw, in this, Morlock decided. At least, he had supplied the means.

Morlock's feelings lightened a little bit. Political assassination was as beyond him as was most politics. But murderous sorcerers were a more familiar matter.

He reentered the den. Liudhleeo was now flanked by two females Morlock didn't recognize, one a semiwolf with a hairless canine face and the other a bitter crone who was staring at Hlupnafenglu with naked hatred. When Morlock entered, she alternated her glare of hatred between the two males.

Morlock got the sheath for Tyrfing, threw it over his shoulders, and sheathed the blade. He tossed a cloak over his ghostly arm and grabbed a bag of money, tying it with his right hand to his belt. Then he stepped over to the red werewolf and said to him quietly, "What did you see in Hrutnefdhu's wound?"

"I don't want to say," the red werewolf admitted. "Maybe I'm wrong. Look yourself."

Morlock did, and then he motioned Hlupnafenglu to join him on the stairwell.

"They can hear us just as well out here," the red werewolf said. "Except that evil old never-wolf, maybe, may her eyes fall out."

Morlock sensed an evasiveness in Hlupnafenglu, a sort of slyness, that was new to him. But not new to Hlupnafenglu, he guessed. Perhaps it had come back to him with his memories.

"The neck was severed below the level of the shoulders," Morlock said. "It would have been easier to sever it higher. But the cutting was done by a practiced hand with a clean sharp blade—a surgeon rather than a butcher. Why?"

"I don't know, Chieftain. But it seemed odd to me."

"How can it be odd? Have you seen many werewolves with their heads cut off?"

"One haunted the prison where we lived, the Vargulleion. I often saw it there."

Morlock was silent a moment under the shadow of the dread memory. Then he said, "You are not answering me. I find that troubling."

"Didn't the gnyrrand tell you about me, Chieftain? I saw him looking at me."

"You will answer my question."

The red werewolf shrugged despairingly and said, "Yes, I have seen many decapitated werewolves. I have cut the heads off many myself. It is the best way to kill a citizen in the night shape. Before I was sent to the Vargulleion I was an assassin. They called me the Red Shadow."

"Oh." Morlock was vaguely aware that werewolves distinguished sharply between assassination and other more open forms of murder. Morlock himself did not, though. "That may be a useful set of skills for us. Rokhlenu thinks this was a politically motivated killing."

The red werewolf was staring at him. "You are not . . . you still wish me to help you? You are still willing to teach me?"

"Yes."

Hlupnafenglu closed his golden eyes, then opened them. "Thank you," he said. "Hrutnefdhu was my friend, too. I would be sorry to miss the hunt."

The stairwell below them was suddenly flooded with females. Looking down, Morlock saw Wuinlendhono at their head.

"All males not dead, get out!" she shouted.

"We were just going, High Huntress," said Hlupnafenglu humbly.

"See that you do," she said briskly, and swept past.

Morlock and Hlupnafenglu edged past the river of female citizens rushing up the stairs. Soon they were standing outside on the stinking wine-stained street in the searing spring sunlight. Some citizens were still standing around, but when they saw Morlock they turned and fled.

"You call it an odd murder, then," Morlock said.

"Yes, Chieftain," said Hlupnafenglu. "It is one thing to sever the head. That makes sense, for a night murder. But why not hurl it out the nearest window? Why carry it dripping away with you?"

"How do you know they did?"

"I smelled it in the stairway."

Morlock nodded slowly. "Then we can trail them—" And then he broke off, staring distractedly at the wine staining the boards. "God Avenger. What have I done?"

The red werewolf punched him gently in his good arm. "Don't gnaw on yourself, Chieftain. We'll walk on the streets nearby a bit, and I'm sure we'll pick up on their scent."

That was what they did, and soon the red werewolf said he had found it.

"Are you sure that's the scent?" Morlock asked, feeling somewhat foolish.

"Fairly sure," Hlupnafenglu replied. "A citizen's blood is a distinctive smell, and Hrutnefdhu's has a tang to it I've never noticed in anyone else's. I'd be surer in my night shape. The wolf's nose is sharper. Hrutnefdhu taught me that when I—when we—when you made me whole. Sometimes I wish you hadn't done that, Chieftain."

"You did seem happier before."

"Maybe happiness is overrated."

Morlock had always hoped so, but said instead, "Should we wait for nightfall? There will be a moon aloft tonight."

"I think the scent might be gone then. Best while it's fresh."

The trail was clear enough. Even Morlock saw a few blood drippings at times. The scent led them to the northern gate, where a few irredeemables were standing guard. Two seemed to be coming on duty, two others going off, and they were standing around talking.

"Khretvarrgliu!" called one of the off-duty guards, and Morlock saw that it was ape-fingered Runhuiulanhu. "What's this rotten froth I hear about you and the gnyrrand fighting?"

Morlock opened his hands and said, "We had words. It's nothing serious."

"Politics?" Runhuiulanhu guessed.

"Sort of."

"I don't know much about politics."

"Neither do I."

"But I know what side I'm on."

"Rokhlenu and I will always be on the same side." Morlock lowered his voice. "But it may not look that way for a while."

"Oh. Oh! I get you! Some kind of strategy?"

"Sort of."

"I know crap-all about strategy either," said Runhuiulanhu, with a certain satisfaction.

"Eh."

"Can I buy you guys breakfast? I just got paid, and my mate bought some sausages. They're guaranteed to contain a certain proportion of real meat. And if they don't, I'll rip the sausage off the walking mouth who sold them to her."

"Thanks, but we're going into town," Morlock said. He didn't like to think of the meat that might be in a sausage made in the werewolf city. "Are you mated?" he asked. "Last time we met you were still . . ."

"Paying for it? I guess so. I thought about what you said that night. Two ape-fingered werewolves ought to be able to get along, shouldn't they?"

Marriage was not among the few topics where Morlock felt he could give useful advice. He hummed and shrugged as noncommittally as possible, and was horrified when Runhuiulanhu said, "Yes, yes, I know what you mean, there."

Hlupnafenglu intervened. "Runhuiulanhu, were you on duty all night?"

"Just since midnight. Why?"

"Did anyone pass by last night carrying a bloody bag or something like that?"

"A bloody bag. What is that, some kind of joke?"

"Can't you smell the blood? I can."

Runhuiulanhu sniffed the air tentatively and he said, "No, I—wait a lope. Wait a lope. Hey, Iuiolliniu," he called to his watch-partner, who was turning away. "Did someone come through here last night with a bloody bag?"

"No one came through all night. Nobody at all. Not that I remember."

"Of course they did. There were those whores walking home from Dogtown; and the guy who kept dropping his lamp and we thought he was trying to burn the plank road, only he was just smoke-drunk; and old Lekkativengu and his bookie friend."

"Oh. Right. But except for them, nobody."

"Yurr." Runhuiulanhu turned back to Hlupnafenglu and Morlock. "Were they going in or out?"

"Out," Morlock said.

"Bloody bag. Bloody bag. You'd think I'd remember that. And yes. Yes, I do remember it. Three of them, right?"

"You tell us."

"Three of them. There was that fuzz-faced goldtooth guard of Her Supreme Wolfiness. Yaniunulu. Which I think she just keeps him around to make fun of him, and why not. And the guy with the bag. He looked kind of familiar to me, but I didn't know his name. All his fingers were the same length. His thumbs, too, I mean."

"Luyukioronu," Morlock said. "They call him Longthumbs."

"Right. You're right! The watchers had us both in lockup before I got sent to the Vargulleion. I guess he got out. Forgery, that's what he was in for."

"Who was the third citizen?"

"That fuzz-face guard. Yaniunulu. That's three."

"That's two."

"Yurr. This shouldn't be so hard. There was Luyukioronu. And fuzz-face, Yaniunulu. And the guy with the bag. That's three."

"I thought Luyukioronu had the bag."

"He did."

"Then that's two."

"All right. Let's see. There was the guy with the bag. And Fuzz-face. And Longthumbs."

"And he had the bag."

"Right." Runhuiulanhu began to look frightened.

"Can you describe him? The third one," Morlock said.

It turned out that he was neither tall nor short, nor of any clear coloration, nor was his scent distinctive, nor was he clearly in the day shape nor the night shape. In fact, Runhuiulanhu could not describe him, or even be sure that it was a male citizen rather than a female citizen. Runhuiulanhu's fear was then more open.

"Don't worry yourself," said Morlock. "I think you've met Ulugarriu."

The ape-fingered werewolf's fear vanished. "Really? You think so? I wish I could remember him!"

"Maybe next time."

They said good-bye, and Morlock and Hlupnafenglu went through the gate out to the plank road.

"The trail is clear," Hlupnafenglu said after a while. "But we'll lose it if it goes into the city."

"Maybe," Morlock said.

"You're full of maybes today, Khretvarrgliu."

"Here's another. The maker who created the moon-clock in Mount Dhaarnaiarnon, and the funicular way, and the other miracles that are credited to Ulugarriu. That maker."

"Yes?"

"Maybe he could make a bag that wouldn't leak."

"Oh, well . . . Well. Yurr. You think he wanted us to come this way? Maybe. Maybe you're right. Then why are we following this trail?"

"The trail is what we have."

The sunlight dimmed as if a heavy curtain had been pulled across the sky. Looking up, Morlock saw this was true: a dense, turbulent, lightning-scarred layer of clouds was spreading over the world, cutting off the light of the sun.

Together Morlock and Hlupnafenglu began to run. If it began to rain, the water would wash away the blood trail. And it was going to rain: the air to the east and south was already blurred with falling water, and the cruelly hot morning air was already retreating before the cool moist air of the storm.

They reached the city's southern gate at the same time as the storm front. But at first it wasn't rain that fell, but hail: great chunks of it, some as large as a child's fist, drumming on the roads and the stone walls and the heads of the travelers, particularly Morlock and Hlupnafenglu. They fled into the open gate and stood there, with the guards and some other passersby taking refuge from the storm.

For a long time, they gazed in unanimous silent wonder at the shallow drifts of melting ice forming in the streets. Eventually, Morlock caught Hlupnafenglu's eye, nodded toward one of the gate watchers, and glanced at his own right thumb. Hlupnafenglu looked baffled, then amused. He nodded.

The big red werewolf sidled up to the gate watcher and said, "Seen Luyukioronu Longthumbs today? I heard he was through here."

The watcher looked sharply at him and said, "You a friend of his?"

There was no mistaking the gate watcher's hostility. Morlock met the red werewolf's eye over the watcher's shoulder and reached out one hand insistently, as if demanding payment.

"He owes me money," Hlupnafenglu said, taking the hint. "The half-rat nipple-biter was running a game off of the outlier market, but he couldn't cover the bets. He said he'd pay me the next time he saw me, only he never sees me anymore."

Hlupnafenglu's newfound facility with lying impressed Morlock, not altogether favorably.

"All right," the watcher said. "I get you. Only it's not my problem, is it?"

Morlock jingled the bag of money tied to his belt.

The gate watcher turned around to look at him. The watcher was a semi-wolf with white fur over a rather vulpine face, but his eyes were human, and they looked searchingly at Morlock. "It's like that? You're with him?"

"Yes."

"All right. Three pads of copper, I tell you where he went. One more, I won't tell him you guys were asking about him."

Morlock reached into the wallet and extracted six copper coins. He dropped them in the watcher's outstretched and rather hairy palm.

"For you and your partner," Morlock said. "We don't care what you tell Longthumbs."

Soon they were out in the hail again, headed for a day-lair run by a night-walker called Iolildhio. Hlupnafenglu knew about it, from his extensive criminal career, but he would not be welcome there. They waited in the shelter of an overhanging wall opposite the dark open door of Iolildhio's joint.

Morlock had decided to watch and wait. Assuming the guard was telling the truth and Luyukioronu, at least, had reached the day-lair and was within, he would not stay there all day. He would satisfy his needs (food, smoke, and sex were what the day-lairs normally provided) and leave. If he was not there, it was possible that Ulugarriu would try to contact them or attack them.

He did not discuss this with Hlupnafenglu, who seemed content to follow his lead. The only thing the red werewolf said while they were waiting was, "I can smell the bloom from here."

Morlock could, too, and he didn't have a werewolf's nose. He nodded.

They waited.

The hail turned to sheets of rain. It filled the already swampy street and ran in through the door of the day-lair. Soon, smoke-choking, half-dressed citizens in varying degrees of wolfhood came stumbling out into the street. The day-lair was flooding. Hlupnafenglu met Morlock's eye and stretched his mouth in a long sinister smile. They would see something soon.

Luyukioronu and Yaniunulu came together out of the dark door, peering up at the sky and holding their hands over their heads in a futile attempt to shield themselves from the savage downpour.

Hlupnafenglu started forward, dashing across the muddy street toward their quarry.

Morlock was taken off guard. He had planned to follow one or the other of the two murderers for a while and see what they were up to, who they contacted. This was especially important in the case of Yaniunulu, who had betrayed his trust: it was important to know who had corrupted him. But he had not discussed this with Hlupnafenglu, who obviously preferred a more direct approach. No longer a red shadow, he was a juggernaut charging through a crowd of citizens bemused by the heavy rain and slipping across shining beds of ice.

Morlock dashed after him.

Luyukioronu dropped his eyes from the sky and saw Hlupnafenglu charging toward him, with Morlock trailing behind. He gaped, screamed, and ran.

Yaniunulu stared bemusedly after him, looked around, saw what Luyukioronu had seen, and ran the opposite way down the street.

Morlock caught up with Hlupnafenglu, pounded on his shoulder to get his attention, shouted, "Get the goldtooth!" and turned, skittering on an ice-lined puddle, to follow Luyukioronu.

The long-thumbed werewolf was already almost out of sight in the torrential rain. Had he plunged into the twisting paths of Dogtown he might easily have left Morlock bewildered, but instead he took a straight route parallel to the city wall, headed for Twinegate.

The rain began to thin out. The clouds were breaking in the east, torn to bits by the winds. Shafts of sunlight illumined the last misty rain. It was already getting warmer again, but Morlock didn't find that unwelcome: he had been battered by the hail, soaked through by the rain. His cloak was heavy with water, but he didn't throw it off: he wanted it to cover the emptiness of his left arm. But the weight was slowing him down; Luyukioronu, though still in sight, was opening up a considerable lead.

Entering the great plaza before Twinegate, Luyukioronu looked over his shoulder to see if he was still being followed. As he did so, his feet hit an icy patch and he rolled in the mud. Morlock drove himself forward; by the time the werewolf had scrambled back to his feet, Morlock was almost on top of him.

He darted into the crowds around the base of the funicular tower. Morlock thought the werewolf was going to circle around it, but instead he charged up one of the stairways, pushing and shoving citizens out of his way.

Morlock followed. He drew his sword as he ran. He disliked shoving people, and he'd found in the past that people were likelier to get out of his way if they saw him approaching with a longsword. So it proved on this occasion, and Morlock again began to gain on Luyukioronu. Eventually, the werewolf heard him approaching and turned, drawing a short sword and a dagger, his dark eyes blazing with panic.

"What do you want from me now?" screamed the werewolf, slashing madly with both blades. "My honor-teeth? You took them before! My money? I spent it all. My female? I spent the money on females; you can hire any of them by the half hour. What do you want? What do you want? *What do you want?*"

Morlock was at a severe disadvantage. Luyukioronu was no master of the sword, but he had two edged weapons and Morlock had to fight one-handed. He had two advantages: he knew how to use his weapon, and it was longer. He retreated a step or two to take advantage of this.

Luyukioronu followed him down, still swinging knife and sword frantically. One of his feet hit an icy patch on the stairs, and he slipped. He reached out his right hand, the hand with the knife, to steady himself on the well of a deep unglazed window set into the wall.

While Luyukioronu was still off balance, Morlock jumped forward and slashed with Tyrfing at the werewolf's right hand. Luyukioronu screamed and, recoiling, dropped the knife and several of his fingers as he retreated back up the stairway.

"Stop!" Morlock said, following him. "Tell me who sent you to kill Hrutnefdhu. If you do, I may let you live."

"I never killed anyone!" Luyukioronu shrieked wildly. "People kill me, they killed me a thousand times, but I never killed. It was a lie what they said about me. An accident. I'm a skilled operator; you should see me."

"I have seen you," Morlock said. "Remember? I gave you twenty copper pads. I sent them by my friend Hrutnefdhu. Remember?"

Luyukioronu seemed to be calming a bit; he considered this question with an inward, remembering gaze. Then he looked up, saw that Morlock had edged closer, and he started away. His back hit the fragile handrail behind him; it gave way beneath his weight.

"No!" shouted Morlock. He did not give a fragmented damn about Luyukioronu's life, but he wanted to know whatever the long-thumbed werewolf could tell him about the murder of Hrutnefdhu. Morlock dropped his sword and let it slither away down the stone stairs, rattling as it went. He leapt forward, reaching out with both hands.

Luyukioronu felt himself beginning to fall, and he reached out with his right hand to grasp at Morlock's left.

But Luyukioronu's mutilated right hand had no fingers, apart from one long thumb, and Morlock's left hand was a patch of mist, the ghostly idea of a hand. Luyukioronu's mutilated hand passed through it; his features convulsed with pain; he fell screaming all the way down the tower until the stones of the plaza ended his fall, his scream, and his life.

"God Avenger!" muttered Morlock (causing Death, who was manifest nearby, to signify hastily against the name of this alien god). He hoped that Hlupnafenglu had caught the treacherous Yaniunulu, or this day was looking bleak indeed.

"Hey!" someone shouted at him. "What are you? Crazy?"

"Maybe," Morlock admitted. He turned to see two armed watchers in city livery coming up the stairs. One had a mace in his hand, the other a drawn sword. The sword was Tyrfing. Morlock remembered he hadn't replenished the talic charge in the sword's crystalline lattice after he had summoned it this morning. If he had, he could have summoned it to himself now.

"Duelling on the anchor stairs is illegal, citizen!" said the watcher in the lead, a citizen with white hair. "Didn't you know that?"

"No."

"Well, it is, and the penalty's a pretty heavy fine. Pretty heavy. You'll find it inconvenient to go to court, and if you can't pay you might even end up in the Vargulleion. You wouldn't like that, would you?"

"No."

"On the other hand, you could just pay us at a bargain rate and save the time, too."

Morlock untied the wallet from his belt and shook it.

"That's the idea," said the watcher approvingly. "Now let's say—*ghost bite me, partner, he's a never-wolf!*" He pointed at Morlock's human shadow falling in the summer-hot sunlight against the gray stone of the anchor tower.

Morlock didn't deny it, since there was no point, but waited to see what the guards would do.

"I've never heard of anything like this!" the white-haired watcher said to his partner. "A never-wolf running around the city killing citizens, a string of honor-teeth around his neck like he's some kind of chieftain."

"Okhurokratu, you are being the stupidest of city watchers I am ever hearing of," his scar-faced partner remarked bitterly. "We've been seeing this guy before, that time when in the Shadow Market you keeping to try rat-wriggling out of the meatcakes."

"I've never been in a meatcake in my life. But I guess I remember what you're talking about: when the young crook tried to pick his pocket."

"He was never him picking his pocket that! The citizen is was saying so!"

"He's not a citizen. He was a never-wolf then and he's a never-wolf now, and if you want meatcakes we can make some out of his liver."

"Stupid, stupid. The citizen is being the one they are calling Khretvarrgliu."

"The—Don't try and slap that turd in my hand. There's no Khretvarrgliu. The Sardhluun made him up to justify that prison break."

Scarface—Morlock remembered the citizen, but not his name—lifted the sword in his hand. "This is being the sword of Khretvarrgliu. My cousin, who is been trying to join with the Sardhluun since forever, he was been always telling me about it. He keeps making it fly through the air to him."

The first guard turned to Morlock. "That true? Can you show me?"

Morlock considered his answer carefully. "If I do, I will have to kill someone with it. There is a curse on the blade." It was a lie, but he owed the City Watchers no truths; they were no blood of his.

"Hm," said white-haired Okhurokratu thoughtfully. "I guess there's been too much fighting on the stairs today as it is. Yoy, partner?"

"Oh, for ghosts' sake," muttered the other watcher, and handed Tyrfing past his partner to Morlock. Morlock gave the bag of money to the surprised and delighted Okhurokratu and received Tyrfing from Scarface, and sheathed it.

"That should cover the fine," said white-hair, weighing the bag in his hand. "I won't say come back again, because I hate the stink of a live never-wolf. But if you come back, remember to bring plenty of this."

"He is being a rat-licker," Scarface said apologetically, "because he can't not be being."

Morlock nodded and walked past them down the long stairway.

It turned out, when he dragged his weary damp carcass back to the outlier settlement, that Hlupnafenglu had failed to catch up with Yaniunulu, and the day became bleak indeed.

The funeral for Hrutnefdhu took place at sunset. They burned the body around sunset (so that it would not end up on some hungry citizen's dinner table in these hard times) and sang songs in Moonspeech to keep the evil ghosts away. Then, when the sun set and they assumed the night shape in the moonlight, they sang songs in Sunspeech to guide Hrutnefdhu's ghost to the place beyond the stars where the good ghosts dwell.

That was how the other werewolves explained it to Morlock afterward, anyway. Then they sat around outside Morlock's cave and reminisced about their dead friend until one by one they went asleep.

Morlock was the last one to drop off. His body was screaming for a drink, and he knew he had a jar or two of wine hidden around the cave. But he sat there in the hot blue moonlight, hating the wine and the thirst for it and the flesh that thirsted, until sleep drew him down into itself.

Another never-wolf was having trouble sleeping that night. His name had been Plackling when he was born, and then they called him Brumerlem when he was weaned, and plain, proud Brum at his man-crowning. Now he was Daytime Twenty-seven, a slave in the anchor-tower of the funicular way, pulling the spoke on the gears during the day that Nighttime Twenty-seven pulled during the night.

Brum, as he still rebelliously thought of himself, lay in the slave barracks not far from the anchor tower and stared at the ceiling and tried not to think about it.

Brum *had* seen him, though—the avenger. He had talked about it with the others on the meal break before the sleep time. Many of them had seen the avenger. They had seen the sword. Some didn't know about the avenger, and others did or thought they did. It was something to talk about, which wasn't nothing. Often they had nothing to talk about and ate their disgusting fodder as solemn and as wordless as cows.

But long after the others had stopped talking, Brum couldn't stop thinking about it. The pain had ended for many of their people on that terrible day and night of the raids. For some it had ended later. But for the people, it was not ended yet. It had not ended for Brum or the others. As long as they were alive, the pain went on. The vengeance was incomplete.

When Brum had been young, he had not believed in the vengeance, not really. But that was before the raids, before the destruction of his people, before he had seen the avenger with his own eyes. Now he was a grown man, nearly fourteen years old, and he knew that the vengeance was real, was needed, and he had seen today that the avenger was still nearby.

Brum silently prayed to his gods in the dark, the Strange Gods. It was the Coranians who had first spread their worship through the north. Brum's people in the old time had persecuted and tortured and robbed and murdered the Coranian prophets. But the Coranians worked certain miracles that impressed the people deeply and led them to believe in the Strange Gods, even as they continued to rob and murder Coranians. When the last Coranian was dead or fled, a shame came upon the people and they began to feel that they had done a great wrong that would be paid for in the fullness of the gods' slow anger. But they also began to believe prophecies of an avenger, who would come in the time of their pain to avenge their destruction.

This meant, as Brum understood the prophecy, that he and his fellow slaves would soon die. And this happy thought kept him awake deep into the watches of the night. It would be over soon. It would all be over soon.

Chapter Twenty-seven

Long Shots

The next day, and for many a day, Morlock went alone into the city to look for Yaniunulu. Hlupnafenglu protested at first, arguing that he should come along, but Morlock pointed out that the outliers needed a maker. Hlupnafenglu, or rather the Red Shadow, was also inconveniently infamous in the more dangerous quarters of Wuruyaaria. Even more important, Morlock needed to be alone. He wanted none of his friends around to watch in pity and amazement as he scratched at nonexistent insects, twitched and shook, and suffered diarrhea or the other panoply of indignities that came when he came off a binge.

He did not bother to swear that he would never put himself in this position again, as he usually did when he quit drinking. He was reasonably sure he would not live long enough to go through this again. The ghost sickness had reached his upper arm by now, and he had a sense that when the deadness that preceded dissolution through his flesh reached his heart, he would die.

The fierce heat of the lengthening days was broken infrequently with savage outbreaks of storm. Whether it was raining or not, Morlock wore a light cloak to cover his ghostly arm.

No one wanted to talk to him at first. Citizens wearing the day shape were not generally welcome in Dogtown, unless they were some kind of semiwolf, and genuine never-wolves (without even a wolf's shadow) were utterly unheard-of. Morlock had to draw his sword any number of times, and fight repeatedly. He took to leaving Tyrfing behind in the cave or Liudhleeo's den. Killing with Tyrfing was always a grim shock, and he dreaded the thought of what it might do to him in his weakened state.

But the nightwalkers of Dogtown grew used to seeing him and smelling him. They respected his ability and, even more, his ruthless willingness to fight. And he always had money to spend, and no one could take it from him or trick it from him; they respected that most of all.

As the days passed and his body slowly recovered, he found out a few things about Yaniunulu. The fuzz-faced semiwolf had money out at loan all over Dogtown—or he used to have it, anyway. For the past month he had been cashing out with all the moneylenders he'd been working with. He was placing the money with bookies, betting on the outcome of the election: betting against the Goweiteiuun-outlier Union.

This struck Morlock as characteristic of a werewolf's sense of revenge: to defeat someone, and profit from it, too. What bothered him was that Yaniunulu had, apparently, put all his money into these bets, so much that it began to change the odds, make them less favorable. (The best odds any bookie would now give was 7-to-1 against the Union; before Yaniunulu had shifted his money, it was only 3-to-1.) He thought it was a sure thing. He had no doubts at all.

That made it all the more imperative that Morlock find him and get him to talk a little about his habits in betting and political assassination. Unfortunately, he seemed to be nowhere at all. He could hardly have gone to ground in Apetown or the mesas of the city: a semiwolf was supposedly an unwelcome visitor at best there. But if he was hiding in Dogtown, he succeeded in eluding Morlock's best attempts to find him.

On the eighteenth day in the sixth month in the year (which Morlock's people called "Marrying" but which the werewolves of Wuruyaaria called, rather unimaginatively, "Sixth-semilunation-of-the-second-moon"), Morlock spent long fruitless hours trying to locate Yaniunulu, and then finally gave up. But before he left town, he went around to every bookie that Yaniunulu had placed bets with, and he made a correspondingly large bet in favor of the Union.

Most of the bookies were unimpressed—they were in the business of lapping up any money that flowed their way—but at least one, a wolf-headed young citizen named Orlioiulu, was quite excited.

"Do you think the Union really have a chance, Khretvarrgliu?" Orlioiulu asked, his pawlike hands trembling slightly as they swept Morlock's coins off his counting board into his cashbox. "I thought you and Rokhlenu were on the outs?"

"Eh," Morlock replied. "He may be sort of a bastard. But that's not always a bad thing in an election." He hoped *bastard* implied what he thought it did in Sunspeech; the word certainly caused Orlioiulu's eyes to gape wide.

When he returned to the outlier settlement through the south gate in midafternoon, he was glad to see Lekkativengu conferring with the guards. Most of the old irredeemable crew had guessed that the quarrel between Morlock and Rokhlenu was a political fiction, but Lekkativengu knew it for a fact and had often served as a go-between for the two friends.

The no-longer-claw-fingered citizen tried to look sternly at Morlock, but ended up grinning broadly. Morlock couldn't help smiling a little in response. But his voice was harsh as he held the wooden betting tickets out to the werewolf and said, "Hey, citizen. Give these to your chief. Tell him I expect them to pay off."

Lekkativengu took the tickets, gaped, nodded, grinned again, and capered off.

Morlock waved at the gate guards, who did not appear equally glad to see him, and trudged back to the east-side den that he now shared with Liudhleeo alone.

The outlier settlement had changed a good deal since he had first seen it. There was a respectable wooden wall running all the way around it, for one thing—much of the wood dephlogistonated, so that it could not catch fire under any circumstances. There was even a gate with guards and a watchtower on the eastern margin, just in case enemies braved the silver-infected hills and tried a sally that way. Morlock's cave was not within the palings: he had several surprises planned for his Sardhluun acquaintances, if they ever came to visit him. Also, it helped maintain the fiction that he was at odds with Rokhlenu and Wuinlendhono.

Liudhleeo was sleeping when he entered, curled up in her day shape in a pool of bitterly hot sunlight. He tried to avoid waking her, but she leapt up with a gasp when he eased himself down on the floor across the room from her.

"Who is it?" she shouted.

"Me," Morlock said. "Sorry to wake you."

Unselfconsciously, she rolled across the floor and looked in his face. "Are you all right?" she asked. "Are you hungry? Are you thirsty?"

Morlock only ate and drank at intervals because he knew he must; he was never hungry or thirsty anymore. He considered this a bad sign, but did not want to discuss it with Liudhleeo, who had a habit of worrying too much.

"No to all that," he said. "You should take care of yourself, not me."

"Yurr. Don't be a bore like everyone else. 'Take it easy, Liudhleeo. Don't worry about it, Liudhleeo. We'll take care of it, Liudhleeo.' Hrutnefdhu, may he sing beyond the stars, is dead, but I feel like I'm the one wrapped up in linen for a funeral."

"Stop barking at me."

"Oh, that's more like the Khretvarrgliu I know and unrequitedly love."

"Stop that, too. Or I'll be polite to you again."

"Anything but that." She stood and looked down at him, smiling a long predatory smile. Her face went blank; she turned her head sideways and said, "Someone is on the stairs. Rokhlenu, I think."

It was Rokhlenu, his hands full of wooden betting tickets. "Every now and then," he said without preliminary remark as he entered, "I start to believe that you will stop doing weird things. And then something like this happens." He waved the tickets in his hands.

"I'd have written you a note," Morlock said, "but I still can't write Sunspeech very well. And I can't write Moonspeech at all."

"Well, well. Illiteracy in a citizen of your eminence is a shame, but no crime. I take it you wanted to talk to me about something and that you don't actually intend me to make good these bets."

"You can keep them. They are bets on the Union's final victory in the elections, at odds of seven to one."

"Seven to one against our victory?"

"Yes."

"That seems a little high."

"Yes."

Rokhlenu sat and listened while Morlock told him what he had found about Yaniunulu's finances.

"He must know something," Rokhlenu reflected. "Or thinks he knows something. He thinks that there is no chance we'll win."

"Yes. I don't know what it is."

"I think I do. I expect that the Aruukaiaduun will side with the Sardhluun-Neyuwuleiuun Alliance. Bastards."

"Hm." Morlock reflected and asked, "If I called you a bastard, would it be an insult?"

Rokhlenu was amused. "Naturally. Why? Wait: have you been calling me a *bastard* around Dogtown?"

Morlock repeated his conversation with the bookie and added, "What I meant was that you were tough and relentless, even though I was angry at you. Insults like that can carry this meaning in other languages."

Rokhlenu shook his head, and looked sourly at Liudhleeo, who was holding her hands over her face and shaking with silent laughter. "I suppose it can," he conceded grudgingly. "It's pretty poisonous language, though."

"Sorry."

"No, no. You were right. Just the thing to keep up the illusion that we're against each other. But I have to admit this odds thing bothers me a little."

"Beyond Yaniunulu, you mean?"

"Yes. It's the bookies who are setting the odds, and other people will know about it, even if they never place a bet. It makes us look like losers, and that's always bad. No one likes a loser."

"Eh."

"Long shots, then, if you don't like *losers*."

"It doesn't matter to me; I was just going to say something."

"I'm sorry; I'm not used to that sort of wild behavior from you. What were you going to say?"

"We could send citizens into town to place bets with bookies. Lots of bets."

"Yes, but we couldn't do it on credit; we'd have to use money—but I was forgetting. You can make the stuff."

"So can Hlupnafenglu. I taught him how to make gold and copper, anyway. I take it weights of the metals will pass as currency; I wouldn't want to counterfeit coin."

"No, of course not. That would be wrong. They might send you to the Vargulleion."

Morlock smiled wryly and opened his hand.

"Yurr," Rokhlenu said, after some silent thought. "I like this. I like this betting idea a lot. It's a new way to get the ears of the citizenry. If the odds start sliding our way, everyone will start talking about it. Let's get started on it tomorrow."

Morlock looked at him, looked out at the sunlight, and looked back at Rokhlenu.

"I know there's daylight left," Rokhlenu said, "and that many a bookie does business after dark. But there's a rally tonight on the Goweiteiuun's home mesa, up on Iuiunioklendon. I need to get some sleep now, and—given what you've told me—send a message or two to the Goweiteiuun gnyrrand and his band of happy warriors."

"I forgot," Morlock admitted.

"Well, I guess if we ever saw each other these days I might have mentioned it." He looked dubiously at Morlock for a moment, and Morlock thought he was going to say something about his health or appearance. But what he actually said was, "This farce about us being enemies may have run its course. I'll talk it over with the First Wolf; her instincts on these things are better than mine. But you had certainly better not join us tonight."

Morlock hadn't planned to, but he felt a pang when Rokhlenu said this. He thought it might be more a reflection of his illness than electoral politics . . . and, probably, it was justified under both headings.

"What about me?" said Liudhleeo, briskly, looking from one old friend to the other.

"The rally will be all-wolf. It will be a two-eyed night," Rokhlenu said, meaning that two moons would be aloft, "and all our fighters will be in their night shapes. So I don't think we'll need your services as healer, tonight, Liudhleeo; I hope not."

She nodded, and said, "I hope not, too. Send for me if you need me."

Rokhlenu said he would and, after some more talk about this and that, he left.

It was a solemn, if not a silent, crowd assembling in the amphitheater on Iuiunioklendon that evening just before sunset. Most of those present were native to the mesa, and most of them belonged to the Goweiteiuun Pack. The election didn't seem to be going well for them; their reckless union with the lawless outliers had brought other packs into alliance against them—and everyone had at least heard a rumor that the Aruukaiaduun Pack would join the Alliance.

There were claques of citizens favoring the Sardhluun and the Neyuwuleiuun. They made noise occasionally, barking their slogans about unity in solitary strength. But no one was quite sure what they meant, and they didn't catch on with the crowd at large. And the barkers didn't sound very happy or confident: this was a make-or-break rally for the Alliance, and both packs had lost a great deal in this election already. Even if they ultimately won, the cost might prove too high to be borne.

Plus, almost everyone was hungry to some extent. Food was scarce and expensive, and growing more expensive daily. The weather was so bad that people expected the rest of the year and next year to be even worse. And if it got much worse, many citizens would simply starve to death. Concerns like these tended to blunt the edge of slogans that were not about food.

One enterprising merchant from Apetown made a great deal of money in a short time by offering for sale a completely novel form of food: fish sausages. Each sausage was guaranteed to contain a certain proportion of real fish, caught on the shores of the Bitter Water and rushed for sale in the great city of Wuruyaaria before it could spoil by magical means the seller was unfortunately unable to disclose, interesting though they were. His audience was skeptical, but in this grim year they could not afford to be scornful. The merchant sold all his fish sausages at a remarkable profit. If he had thought to provide himself with a couple of guards, he might even have taken the money away with him. Still, he lived, and both he and his customers and those watching had learned something interesting and useful: werewolves would eat fish, if sufficiently hungry, and would pay well for the privilege.

The sun set, and presently the major moon, Chariot, peered out in somber brilliance through the bloody stain the sun had left on the eastern sky. Every citizen who could do so assumed the night shape. Then, as one, they turned to the west to look at the minor moon, Trumpeter—smallest of the three moons, but standing fiercely bright in the western sky.

It was time for the rally. The Goweiteiuun gnyrrand, Aaluindhonu, was the first candidate to appear, followed by his bold cantors and their brave band of volunteers. So Aaluindhonu described them in his opening song, but it would probably not have occurred to anyone else to do so. One of the cantors was actually trailing his tail on the ground, like a puppy who had been shouted at.

But Aaluindhonu sang well and fervently. There were rumors about him, and the crowd whispered them to each other as he sang. They whispered that he once had semiwolf kin in Dogtown, and the Sardhluun had killed them. Others said, no: the semiwolves were held hostage by the infamous First Wolf of the outliers, and others told other stories. But everyone had felt doubts about the gnyrrand's dedication to victory earlier in the Year of Choosing, and no one doubted it now.

In his song he hit the Neyuwuleiuun very hard, pointing out that the airships had never before been used against werewolves, and that if they could be used against the outliers then why not against the citizens of Dogtown? Of Apetown? Of Iuiunioklendon? Not only had the Neyuwuleiuun Pack committed a crime, they had failed: their vaunted airships had been struck from the sky by the daring and skill of the outliers. Bad enough to elect criminals to lead them—but *failed* criminals?

Which brought him to the Sardhluun. For years they had taken money and resources from the city to house prisoners in the Vargulleion and the Khuwuleion. Some they had killed, for meat or mere cruelty. Some they had sold like cattle to the wild packs. When a brave remnant had broken free from their sluggish hold and brought the truth to Wuruyaaria, the Sardhluun dogs had been powerless to stop it, just as they were powerless to answer that dreaded question. Where were the prisoners of the Khuwuleion? Where were the prisoners of the Khuwuleion? *Where were the prisoners of the Khuwuleion?*

The refrain infected the crowd, most of whom were anti-Sardhluun anyway. As they sang, the outliers raced into the amphitheater, green-and-gold streamers tied to the cords of honor-teeth around their necks. Their appearance raised the first genuine cheer of the night. When that subsided, the great gray werewolf who led them, the dragon-killer Rokhlenu, began to sing.

He sang that the outliers and their Goweiteiuun partners had founded a colony on the shores of the Bitter Water. He said that even if the harvest of the land failed and all the cattle died, the harvest of the sea would go on forever, fresh with life in the cool blue water. This, in essence, was the contrast between the Sardhluun-Neyuwuleiuun Alliance and the Goweiteiuun-outlier Union. The Alliance were dishonest jailors and failed sky-pirates. The Union dared to think in new ways to save the lives of citizens in these troubled times. Did citizens want the vicious past of the Alliance or the shining future of the Union? The choice was theirs.

His song was brief, convincing, eloquent, and had several direct references to food. The audience howled their approval at the two-eyed star-spangled sky.

Suddenly there were new bands charging into the fighting ground of the amphitheater. The gnyrrands of the Sardhluun and the Neyuwuleiuun, grimly silent, running side by side with their bands of cantors and a stunningly large crowd of volunteers in their wake. The Alliance werewolves ran silent circles around the werewolves of the Union, and the crowd fell silent too. The Alliance was waiting for something, and the crowd waited also.

It happened. Five standard-bearers appeared at the amphitheater gates. But instead of flags, on the standards were the heads of citizens. Most were rotting, almost skeletal. But one was freshly killed: his blood was still dripping, his eyes still shining with tears in the moonlight.

Between the standard-bearers came the Aruukaiaduun band and their volunteers, teeth bared, snarling, ready to fight and kill. They charged straight at the Union werewolves, and as they did so the Alliance werewolves broke their circle formation and charged inward.

Few in the amphitheater recognized the heads on the standards, but Rokhlenu thought that he knew them. They were the heads of his father and brothers. The shock of seeing them was great, so great that he didn't even feel it as grief. He had long mourned them as dead. It maddened him a little to think that his youngest brother, one of the two who had disappeared around the time the others were murdered, had been alive until moments ago. It was his head that was still dripping on its pole. They had killed him just now to torment Rokhlenu, make him lose control.

He would not give them that.

He snarled a directive at his reeve, Yaarirruuiu, and at Aaluindhonu. They'd suspected they would be outnumbered, although not this badly, and had planned a retreat. He sang they should execute that plan now—but added they should kill the standard-bearers if they could.

The Union wolves struck as a body against the Aruukaiaduun band rushing down on them and sent the newcomers into confusion. Soon the Aruukaiaduun were entangled in the advancing lines of the Alliance werewolves.

The Union werewolves made their escape in the confusion, killing several of the standard-bearers as they went.

Rokhlenu sang one last line to the audience as he stood in the amphitheater gate, the last to leave as his enemies bore down on him. He sang that this was the meat and drink the Alliance would serve Wuruyaaria: their own flesh and blood.

Then he turned and vanished into the night.

Now, at last, the Alliance gnyrrands sang their songs. They welcomed the Aruukaiaduun werewolves to their band, and the Aruukaiaduun gnyrrand acknowledged his pack's worth and the new Alliance's glory. They talked a good deal about sternness, lonely strength, the need for order, and they boasted time and time over of their victory.

The crowd, apart from the Alliance claques, was mostly silent. It was true the Alliance had won the rally, but they had won in the ugliest possible way. It was not against the rules to overwhelm your opponents with the number of your volunteers, as the Alliance had done, because very little was against the rules in the Year of Choosing. But it was a very low-status way to earn a victory. Many remembered and repeated Rokhlenu's last words. And everyone noted that the Alliance werewolves said nothing at all about food or famine.

Morlock spent part of the afternoon teaching Hlupnafenglu a new set of multidimensional polytopes, and the red werewolf reciprocated by teaching Morlock how to read. Written Sunspeech he could understand, after a bit of effort, but he was deeply ignorant of the ideograms used in Moonspeech. He did not think he would live long enough to make much of this knowledge, but he had to have something to do at night besides drink, and he thought reading might be worth a try.

The last part of the afternoon they spent playing cards. Hlupnafenglu was unlike most werewolves in his disinterest in gambling, but he loved the deck of paper images and often used them in the mantic spells Morlock had taught him.

Before sunset, the red werewolf returned to the old refectory of the irredeemables to eat. It was thought the Sardhluun might try some sort of night attack after the rally, however it went—and, anyway, Hlupnafenglu wanted to wait for the rally results with his fellow irredeemables.

Morlock returned to the den he shared with Liudhleeo and spent some time reading a scroll that Hlupnafenglu had given him, written in Sunspeech ideograms. The exercise of recognizing ideograms was fairly interesting, the story less so. It was some minor epic about two immature werewolves in the night shape and their human slave, Spilloiu. It was possible that the lines had some sort of poetic force that Morlock was not sophisticated enough to recognize. They seemed mostly to be exhortations that one child shouted at the other to look at Spilloiu as he ran or did not run. Morlock finished the scroll and, irritated by the inefficient format, sliced the pages apart with a razor and sewed the pages together to a cloth binding to make a passable codex book. He was wondering what to use for a cover when Liudhleeo came home, her hands full of covered dishes.

"I brought dinner," she said.

"Not supper?" he said. He had just learned the ideogram for that word. (*See Spilloiu! See Spilloiu fetch supper!*)

"Don't be more ridiculous than you can help. Supper is a meal eaten by sophisticated citizens after a night howling about the town. Dinner is eaten by working-class citizens around sundown."

"Dinner, then."

"That's what I said."

She set the dishes down on the floor next to him and gracefully sat down across from him. "You'll never guess what it is."

"Not meat, I hope."

"Not for you." She uncovered one dish, plucked out a steaming fragment, and popped it in his mouth before he could protest.

"Hm." He chewed the oily, leathery stuff for a moment. "Smoked fish of some kind."

"Yes!" She was absurdly delighted. "The First Wolf gave it to me. It's from the new colony on the Bitter Water. I had my friend Ruiulanhro cook it up. She runs a hot-pot as well as a smoking lair and a poison shop, you know."

Morlock hadn't known. In fact, he wasn't sure what a hot-pot was: some sort of restaurant or refectory, it seemed. "It's good," he said.

"Do you really like it?"

He did. He was never hungry or thirsty, but his illness seemed to be intensifying all his sensations. He didn't feel the need to eat, but the act of eating was intensely pleasing.

"I have red meat, of a sort, for myself," Liudhleeo added. "You may partake if you like. It's guaranteed not to come from a never-wolf. In fact, it looks to be some kind of bird."

A seagull, Morlock guessed, looking in the dish. This had not been smoked, and was somewhat gamy by his never-wolvish standards. Also, it had not really been cooked so much as warmed, and the innards did not seem to have been removed at all. "No thanks," he said. "I'll stick to the fish."

"Knew you would. Coward."

Morlock shrugged, picked up a piece of fish, and ate it.

"Have you been practicing your ideograms? Oh my ghost, what have you done to Hlupnafenglu's little reader?"

"Made it into a proper book." He lacked the terminology for codex books since, apparently, he had just introduced them to Wuruyaaria.

She licked her fingers fastidiously and flipped through the primer. "I suppose it's easier to handle," she said.

"The pages won't crumble as it gets older," he pointed out.

"Nice stitching. You sew better with one hand than most people do with two."

He nodded to acknowledge the compliment. She gave him an amused glance and held the gaze too long for Morlock's comfort, so he glared at her a little. She dropped her eyes then, but not her smile.

They ate and talked desultorily until about sunset, and then they walked down through the hot humid air of evening to the marketplace to wait for election news with the other outliers. Liudhleeo walked on his left side and casually put her arms around him when the crowd threatened to push them apart. A little too casually: as he looked sideways at her profile, he thought she was enjoying the experience of being Khretvarrgliu's escort. Not improbably, that was why she had resisted the change to the night shape.

There was a carnival atmosphere in the market: torches and lamps lit the place almost as brightly as day. The citizens swarmed in the night shape, the day shape, and every gradation of semiwolf in-between. The air was dense with smoke from cooking fish and other seafood—a pleasant smell, in a town that had come very near to famine. Another noticeable smell was bloodbloom, one of the few crops hardy enough to thrive in the nightmarish weather of the past couple years, and more in demand than ever.

One female citizen was wandering the crowd, selling bowls of bloom to all and sundry. She was a semiwolf who wore the day shape except for bristling doglike fur that covered her from head to toe, and hence she had dispensed with the apish vulgarity of clothing.

Liudhleeo saw her, and was no longer interested in having people see her. She turned her head against Morlock's shoulder and seemed to shrink into herself.

But the smoke-selling semiwolf saw her and cried out, "Liudhleeo! How are you, you slinky bastard's brach?"

"Putting the bite on things, Ruiulanhro," Liudhleeo replied politely, but said nothing more to promote conversation.

Ruiulanhro, however, needed no encouragement. She looked Morlock up and down and said, "So you must be the never-wolf she's trying to regrow her hymen for?"

"Eh," Morlock said. "Thousands have."

"When I—What was that? What was that? Never mind. I don't really want to know if you're joking or not. I guess there's more to you than meets the eye, anyway. Have a bowl of bloom."

"No, thanks."

"On me!" she protested.

"I don't smoke."

"Oh, I don't think you two are going to get along. Have a bowl on me, gravy," she said to Liudhleeo. "For old times' sake. We miss you round the old den. We'll still be there when this one is off hunting fresher hymens."

"Thanks, Ruiulanhro," Liudhleeo said. "But not bloodbloom. Spiceweed, if you've got it."

"Some. I was expecting more children to be here." She blew a spark onto one of the bowls of herb on her tray and then offered it to Liudhleeo. She took it, saluted Ruiulanhro with it, and inhaled deeply of the smoke. Some of it reached Morlock; it smelled of cinnamon and cloves.

"Farewell, my meatpies," the vendor said. "I was young once." She moved on through the crowd, hawking her smoky wares.

After a moment of silence, Liudhleeo said reflectively, "So this is what it is like to long for death. I've often wondered."

"Don't gnaw yourself."

She looked at him gratefully. She offered him the fuming bowl and said, "It doesn't make you drunk, exactly. It's mostly for scent and flavor."

"I'm getting plenty," he said.

Her eyes widened in alarm. He gripped her shoulder briefly to tell her nothing was wrong. She smiled waveringly. Inhaling smoke deeply, she nestled into his side.

The news came soon, and it was worse than anyone expected. There was much resentment at the reports of how many volunteers the Alliance had brought to do their fighting, and the reports of severed heads as standards raised howls of rage from every quarter of the crowd. Morlock had seen werewolves do worse, even to other werewolves, but apparently the fact that this happened in the city, in an election rally, was genuinely shocking to the citizenry. About politics he knew very little, but he wondered if the Alliance might have gone too far.

Around midnight, Rokhlenu and his cantors made an appearance in the market square. The outliers gave them a loud welcome, howling and shouting. There was a great deal of singing and speaking going on, most of which Morlock didn't understand; werewolves could follow many songs at once, with a skill he had not yet learned to match. But he did see, or thought he saw, that Rokhlenu was ill-at-ease, never standing in one place for long, his eyes scanning the crowd of citizens.

This would be the first rally the outliers could be said to have lost, at least as far as Morlock knew, and perhaps that was all that was bothering his old friend. But Morlock added some things together: the number of severed heads the Aruukaiaduun had displayed, the number of Rokhlenu's brothers (plus his father), the fact that at least one of the heads was a fresh kill, according to reports, and that two of Rokhlenu's brothers had been reported missing when the others were killed.

No wonder Rokhlenu was distressed: the Aruukaiaduun had been boasting openly that they had killed his family, and he had been compelled to flee from the rally. Morlock knew his old cellmate fairly well, and guessed that shame and grief would be eating away at him now.

Rokhlenu stopped scanning the crowd; he was now looking directly at Morlock.

Morlock met his eye, across the surging tide of citizens. He pointed deliberately at Rokhlenu, then at himself. He pointed at himself, then Rokhlenu. What he meant was, *You and me against them*. Although he didn't think his friend knew it, he added the Dwarvish signal *blood-for-blood*: his hand clenched twice in front of his chest.

Rokhlenu grinned a long wolvish grin. He threw back his head and laughed. Either he had understood what Morlock had signalled, or understood something else that put his mind at ease.

"You don't say much," Liudhleeo said wryly at his side, "but you sure seem to make it count."

"Eh."

"Except when you say that."

Rokhlenu's laugh had surprised most of the audience, and they fell quiet, watching him. Into the semi-silence he sang a clear, concise song. It was true they had been defeated, and the taste of defeat was bitter. But one rally was not the election, and they would force that bitterness down their enemies' throats until they learned to love it. They would pay blood for blood. He thanked the citizens for coming and suggested, in brief, that they go home and begin working for the defeat of the criminal Alliance.

The crowd roared. The word *criminal* struck at the heart of their anger. Were they dogs or cattle, for the rope-twisting Aruukaiaduun to kill for their entertainment? They were citizens of Wuruyaaria, and there would be a reckoning. So they said to each other. Rokhlenu and his cantors were gone from the rostra, and the meeting was breaking up.

Morlock and Liudhleeo were at the edge of the market and found it easy to slip away on a side street. They were soon away from any crowd, but Liudhleeo kept her arm around him and he did not push her away. They walked home in silence and climbed the dark narrow stairs to the den.

She didn't say anything, so neither did he. He planned a long day tomorrow, making copper and gold so that they could flood the bookies with bets on a Union victory. The night was hot, as the nights always were these days, so he stripped to his shirt and lay in the shadows against the wall under an open window.

He had almost fallen asleep when he felt her press up against his back.

He turned to face her, holding himself up from the floor by his right hand.

Her red eyes were black in the blue moonlight. She whispered to him, "I don't need you to say anything. I don't need you to feel anything for me. I don't even want that. I know you don't care. I don't care that you don't care. But please. Please. Please."

He did care, but he didn't tell her that. He felt death in him and near him all the time, and she was alive, was life. Her lean naked body was strangely beautiful. Her mouth was hot and wet and smelled of cloves. She pressed it against his as she frantically tore the buttons from his shirt and they at last met, skin to conscious skin.

He worked for two straight days making copper and gold. He invested a third day in helping his old apprentice to teach his new apprentice the making of copper and gold. He thought of his new apprentice as the apprentice of his old apprentice, Hlupnafenglu, but no one else seemed to. His new apprentice was the clumsy thief who had tried to pick his pocket in the Shadow Market, a young citizen who was named Lakkasulakku.

Now that he had two apprentices, he never taught the same thing to both. His idea was that they could pool the skills he taught them after his death. They both looked disturbed when he told them this, but he could not understand why: he could feel the dead area preceding dissolution creeping up his neck and through his chest. His shoulder was beginning to fade. They could cherish illusions if it suited them; he didn't have the time.

In the evening and the night, there was Liudhleeo. He learned more about her in a few days than he had in the previous six months. She was intent on sharing everything with him: the details of her day, healing the semiwolves and never-wolves of the city; her brutal childhood in a fosterden on Iuiunioklendon; how she had escaped to live in the necropolis of Wuruyaaria, the long eastern slope of the mountain that bristled with the tombs of the city's eminent dead; how she had met Wuinlendhono there and how they had come together to the outlier pack; how Wuinlendhono had risen and risen while Liudhleeo fell further and further until . . . well . . .

She poured her words into him as if they were coins and he was a strongbox to protect them. Sometimes he wanted to tell her to stop, to save her secrets for someone who would be alive to share them with. But, of course, it was the imminence of his death that made him safe to talk to. He was like one of the eminent dead she knew so well from the necropolis, a grave and mostly silent counsellor.

Her physical hunger for him was as intense: a dark longing in which pleasure had very little place. He understood the horror and repulsion that drew her to him, and he pitied her for them. But he never said this to her, because he felt it would drive her away. And he wanted her at least as much as she wanted him.

She was alive. She was life. And he was dying.

He had not forgotten his debt to avenge Hrutnefdhu, her mate whom he could follow but never replace. He went several times into Dogtown to place long-shot bets for the outliers, and the bookies grew to know and trust him well. He became quite adept at reading the notes on betting slips, a mish-mash of Sunspeech and Moonspeech. And he believed that some of the bookies, at least, would pass the word to him if they saw Yaniunulu again. No one seemed to esteem him much: an odd-smelling mutt with a habit of sneering at people; more bark than he had bite.

One day he was in the cave, teaching Lakkasulakku how to fold molten glass, when Hlupnafenglu came in, a small strip of wood in his big red hands.

"A runner from the city brought this, Khretvarrgliu," he said. "It's from that bookie in Dogtown, Orlioiulu."

Morlock looked at it. It was scraped on the same sort of wax-covered wood that they used for betting tickets. The ideograms told him that Yaniunulu ("the dog-faced betrayer") had been seen, and that Morlock ("Khretvarrgliu") should come see Orlioiulu ("friendly purveyor of chance and mystery") soonest.

Morlock's reading had progressed fairly well, but it was as a maker that the note interested him.

"Elegantly carved ideograms, wouldn't you say?" he asked, showing the note to the werewolves.

"Yes, Khretvarrgliu."

"Sure," said Lakkasulakku. "What's it say?"

"A lie," Morlock said. "Have you ever seen Orlioiulu?"

Hlupnafenglu nodded, and then gave a slow smile. "He has paws for hands. He could not have drawn these figures."

"Not with these angles of incision," Morlock said, who had examined the note very closely indeed.

A shadow fell across Hlupnafenglu's face. Looking up, they saw that Liudhleeo had entered the cave.

It turned out she, too, had received a note. Written by the same hand, but not signed Orlioiulu, it said that if she wanted news of her mate's murder, she should consult her new mate.

"This looks very much like a trap," said the red werewolf with great satisfaction. "Let me go, Khretvarrgliu. I missed him once; let me bring him home this time."

"No," Morlock said. "I'll go. From you they would merely hide. Also, you may be recognized—not as yourself, but as who you were."

"Morlock," Liudhleeo said evenly, "I am frightened."

"I'll be careful."

"For myself, you selfish pig. They meant this note to divide me from you. I'm worried they may be coming for me."

"Hm. Not impossibly. Another reason for you to stay, Hlupnafenglu. You can defend her with the resources of the cave. I'll leave Tyrfing, also. Kill with it only if you must, but in that case kill without mercy."

Hlupnafenglu, who had been the Red Shadow, bowed his golden head. "Khretvarrgliu, I will. I will spend my life for hers, if need be."

"You can't do this," whispered Liudhleeo. "You cannot do this. You stupid ape-faced—you've only got one hand!"

"I'll have three," Morlock said. "Lakkasulakku will come with me."

"Right, Chief!"

Now Liudhleeo was weeping silently as Morlock armed himself and his apprentice from the gear in the cave. He turned to her at last. "I'll see you tonight," he said.

"Tonight you'll be dead. I'll never see you again."

"If not tonight, then soon. Good-bye, Liudhleeo," he said, and kissed her shocked weeping face. He turned away and walked down the hill in the bitterly bright sunshine. Lakkasulakku followed him, whistling noisily as he rattled down the wooden steps.

Orlioiulu's betting booth was closed, much to the annoyance of some semiwolvish patrons who wanted to lay bets on the weather. A prominent citizen was claiming the sunlight would soon be hot enough to boil water at noon, and the locals wanted to get some action going on it. Orlioiulu would give odds on anything, but he wasn't here to give odds on anything and his loyal customers were upset.

"Poor old Orlioiulu," Morlock remarked to young Lakkasulakku.

"Think he's dead?"

"Yes. Our correspondent will have killed him."

"Bastard."

"Yes. They will show us some bait, soon. I'll follow it. You wait a hundred breaths or so and follow me from a distance. Get me?"

"I get you, Chief."

Before long, they saw their bait: fuzz-faced Yaniunulu lurking at the mouth of an alleyway, craning his neck to peer toward Orlioiulu's betting booth. He was even wearing the gold tooth he had earned as a member of Wuinlendhono's guard, just so that no one could miss who he was.

"Pretty raw," whispered Lakkasulakku. "He must be desperate."

Morlock was also. He nodded, turned away, and sauntered openly toward the alleyway.

Yaniunulu affected not to see him until he had crossed half the distance to the alley. Then the fuzz-faced semiwolf started, and turned back to run up the alley.

Morlock loped after him, not too swiftly. He was fairly sure Yaniunulu wasn't really trying to escape him, and he wanted to have a look at whatever trap he was headed into before it closed on him.

By the time Morlock reached the alley, Yaniunulu was at an open doorway, looking over his shoulder. When his eyes met Morlock's, he fled through the doorway.

"Too obvious," said Morlock aloud, and drew one of the stabbing spears sheathed over his shoulder. He followed Yaniunulu through the open door out of the cruel sunlight.

He waited for his eyes to accustom themselves to the shadows before he moved.

What he saw, presently, was a dim corridor with Yaniunulu standing (somewhat twitchily) at the far end. The corridor floor had a dark seam down the middle, and it looked like the edges did not fully meet the walls on either side.

"Eh," Morlock said. The trap was so obvious he had to be concerned it was simply the mask for another more subtle one. But before him was one of the citizens involved in his friend's murder. If he could not get him to talk, he would not let him get away.

He threw the spear in his hand.

He was ten paces away from Yaniunulu, and he was ill and feeling weak. But he was still Morlock Beast Slayer: the spear passed through the werewolf and pinned him to the wall behind. Yaniunulu screamed and struggled to free himself.

Morlock crouched down and pounded on the corridor floor with his fist. The two sides of the floor folded apart as he had expected. They were set on axles, it seemed, about a handsbreadth away from the walls; the space between the wall base and the floor had been left to allow the floorboards to swing freely when the trap was sprung. Below was a filthy stretch of water that looked like a sewer—and smelled like one, too.

Morlock tested the strength of the axle holding one of the swinging floorboards; it seemed strong enough to hold his weight. Balancing with his right hand against the wall, he stepped onto the upright edge of the floorboard and walked across to where Yaniunulu was still vainly struggling against the spear that pinned him to the wall.

The wound was grave, straight through the middle of the werewolf's body. But it hardly bled at all.

"What are you, citizen?" Morlock asked. Yaniunulu's dark eyes, void of expression, met his, but there was no other answer.

"Not what you appear, at any rate," Morlock observed. He drew his other spear and, striking vertically, slashed Yaniunulu from the base of his neck to his belly.

The werewolf's loose brown garment fell away, and great folds of his furred skin parted like curtains. Through the gaps Morlock saw several small creatures, hardly larger than his fists. They had pink-and-brown mottled skins, void of hair, and long gray tails. Their faces were strangely human, but for the long ratlike snouts. He had wounded one of the rat-things, and evidently killed another, but the rest chittered angrily. One issued a high screeching sound like a command, and the ratlike beasts began to abandon the Yaniunulu simulacrum they had been operating.

They held long glittering razors liked swords in their hands, and they moved toward him menacingly.

He decapitated one with his spear when it approached him incautiously and kicked another into the slime of the open trap. He made a great sweeping feint with the spear, and the rough line of ratlike beasts broke. They fled, a dozen or so, across the edge of the floor trap and away into the harsh sunlight at the corridor mouth.

Morlock examined the now-motionless simulacrum of Yaniunulu. It was a fascinating piece of work. The skin and fur and bone seemed to be real and alive, but it was all just a shell, with levers and pulleys to be operated by the tiny crew of rats. It was marked nowhere MADE BY ULUGARRIU, but it hardly needed to be.

The corridor was a dead end that gave no clear entrance into the rest of the building. Morlock turned and followed the rats across the trap and into the cruel sunlight outside.

The rats had long since fled, but he saw a familiar figure lying on the ground at the head of the alley: Lakkasulakku. Several citizens were bending over him, not obviously with kind intent. Morlock ran over, brandishing the spear still in his hand, and they retreated.

Lakkasulakku was bleeding copiously from wounds in his foot and thigh. A swelling bulged on his forehead; he had been struck there. Morlock thought bitterly of the razorlike blades of the ratlike beasts. Had he followed them straight out, they might not have had the opportunity to do this.

He sewed up the greater wounds with thread and needle he had with him in a stray pocket and bound up the wounds with strips torn from his clothing. Then he tossed the young citizen over his shoulder and loped off down the street.

Lakkasulakku's face was pale, and oily with sweat; his breathing was irregular; he had been unconscious since Morlock had found him. But Morlock thought he could be saved by a healer as skillful as Liudhleeo. He made his way back to the outliers as swiftly as he could.

The sunlight was growing gray for Morlock by the time he reached the southern gate. He was glad to see one of the old irredeemables on duty at the gate, although he could not remember the werewolf's name. He was about to ask that the guard help him haul Lakkasulakku to Liudhleeo's when the guard said to him, "The gnyrrand wants to see you, Khretvarrgliu."

"Later," Morlock said. "I have to get this young citizen to a healer."

"She—" the irredeemable began, then paused. "There was a thing that happened at your cave. That's what I heard."

The day got grayer still for Morlock, though the sun was as fierce as ever. "Can you take care of my friend?"

The irredeemable bowed his grizzled head. "An honor, Khretvarrgliu. The gnyrrand and—and—and the others are at the First Wolf's lair."

Morlock, relieved of the burden of Lakkasulakku, ran as fast as his weary legs would carry him to the First Wolf's tower. The goldtooth on duty at the entrance saw him coming and simply stepped aside.

The bodies were laid out on biers in the main audience hall on the ground floor. Hlupnafenglu was staring at the ceiling with what Morlock would have called an expression of mild interest, were it not for the raw red hole in his unmoving chest. The other body was headless and already wrapped in linen, but Morlock recognized it as Liudhleeo's from its outline.

Wuinlendhono was bent over Liudhleeo's body, sobbing. She had one of the dead linen-wrapped hands gripped in both of hers. Rokhlenu stood beside her, his hands on her shoulders, his face clenched with grief and worry.

Wuinlendhono looked up with red eyes as Morlock approached. She dropped the dead hand, shook off Rokhlenu, and stood between Morlock and the corpse as if to protect it from him.

"If she," she said. "If this. If you. If. If this. If this was because of you. If *this* happened because of *you*. I'll kill you myself. You sheep-stinking, ape-faced, never-wolf, *plepnup* bastard. I will kill you."

Morlock stepped around her. The neck was severed in the same way as Hrutnefdhu's had been. Hlupnafenglu's neck was untouched. Of course, it was possible that the killer had planned to remove Hlupnafenglu's head in the same way, but had been interrupted. He would ask about how the bodies had been discovered, if he had a chance, and if he could get someone to talk to him instead of screaming at him. But, even if that were the case, the killer (or killers) must have killed them both and then proceeded to decapitate Liudhleeo's corpse first. This had been done for a reason.

The linen wrappings were falling loose from the hand Wuinlendhono had been weeping over. Morlock looked at the hand, then picked it up and further unwrapped the linen to get a better look at it.

"Leave her alone," Wuinlendhono shrieked, and began to pummel him. "*Leave her alone!*"

He turned and held the dead hand up in front of her face. "Do you recognize this hand?"

The unexpected question shocked her into stillness. Presently she said, "I recognize it. I first saw it ten years ago. I was fleeing from the Goweiteiuun after killing my husband. I ran into the necropolis. I stole food from the funeral gifts; that was how I stayed alive. Once I saw a hand reaching for the same piece of rotten meat that I wanted, and I bit it. See the scar? See the scar there, on her hand? That was where I bit it. We fought, Liudhleeo and I, and she—we fought. She didn't kill me, though I guess maybe she could have; I was near starving, weaker than a chicken. She was running away, too. She said we should go to the outliers. I. She. I went with her. Came here with her. I don't know what I would have done. Without her. And now. Now I'll have to."

"This is not Liudhleeo's hand."

"Liar. That won't save you."

"She was smoking spiceweed every day for the last month—bowl after bowl of the stuff. It stained her hands and her fingers. Do you see any stains here? Use your dog's nose. Do you smell the spiceweed?"

Wuinlendhono's dark eyes widened with anger and wonder. Then she closed them tight, and her face wore a remembering look. "I saw her only twice the last month. That was your fault: this stupid game you and Rokhlenu are playing. But she was smoking. She was smoking spiceweed both times. It does stain your fingers, and your teeth. That's why I never." She opened her eyes. "What is it you are saying?"

"Liudhleeo may be dead," Morlock said. "But this is not her body."

Wuinlendhono took a step back, straight into Rokhlenu's arms. He wrapped them about her, and she let herself rest upon them, closing her eyes, her face growing calm.

"How can that be?" she asked at last, not opening her eyes.

Morlock had an idea or two about this. He had been thinking of that strange flesh-machine the ratlike beasts had been using, the simulacrum of Yaniunulu. Perhaps this corpse was something like that. Perhaps there was some other explanation. But there was no reason to say all that when one word would do as well.

"Ulugarriu," he said.

Wuinlendhono screamed. Her body arched with the force of it. She screamed until all the air had left her lungs and the scream sank to a croaking, gurgling snarl.

Rokhlenu held her patiently through all of this.

She lay in his arms for a time, neither speaking nor moving.

Then she opened her eyes and stood. She looked at Morlock and said, "You will find the truth of this. You will go and find the truth of this. We will hold a funeral over these things as if they were our friends. Is that Hlupnafenglu's body, do you think?"

Morlock nodded. "Probably."

"Well, we will pretend this thing is her body and burn it with Hlupnafenglu's. It's a kind of blasphemy, but we've all done worse, I guess. And you will find the truth of this."

Morlock said nothing. Nothing needed to be said.

She turned to Rokhlenu and said, "Beloved. Thank you. I needed you, and I will need you, but now I need to be alone. Please don't follow me away." She walked off and disappeared into a stairway.

Rokhlenu waited until she was gone, and then turned to Morlock with something like relief in his face. "What is Ulugarriu after, do you suppose?"

Morlock shrugged.

"He seems to have been interested in the cave. He ransacked it before he left."

Morlock nodded, almost pleased. This confirmed that the killer had not failed to behead Hlupnafenglu for lack of time.

"It looks like Hlupnafenglu left her, came back to find her dead, and then stabbed himself with a glass dagger. That's how we found him."

"That's how it was meant to look."

"I'm afraid he took your sword," Rokhlenu added. "Unless you hid it somewhere."

"No," said Morlock. "I left Tyrfing with Hlupnafenglu. And it is gone?"

"Yes."

Morlock laughed. It was the best news he had heard on this evil strange day.

Rokhlenu was looking at him with open amazement.

"I'll explain," Morlock said.

But first he turned to his dead friend. The red werewolf's body had been washed, but not yet bound with linen. Morlock took some lying ready nearby the bier and wrapped up the red cold hands in the cloth. Then he put his hand on Hlupnafenglu's eyes and whispered a prayer that Those Who Watch would welcome this apprentice through the gate in the west.

"Good-bye, my friend," he said at last. "I hope you have all the breakfast you need or want, wherever you are now."

Then he turned away and walked from the audience hall with Rokhlenu beside him. Someone else would have to stand the vigil over the corpses: there was much to do.

The next morning found Morlock walking through Twinegate in full daylight with a lit lamp.

"Sun's up," said one of the watchers. "Don't know if you noticed."

"I'm looking for a citizen," Morlock said.

"Good luck. There might be one or two in the city somewhere, if you're not choosy."

"I'm choosy," said Morlock, and walked on into the sunlight with his lamp.

Morlock's plan was a simple one. The killer (Ulugarriu or his agent) had taken Tyrfing. That might even have been the motive for the attack on the cave, a possibility that gnawed at Morlock a little: if he had taken Tyrfing with him to the city earlier, Hlupnafenglu might be alive now. But never mind that: the killer had taken Tyrfing, and nothing else it seemed, because Ulugarriu had wanted it. So the sword was with the killer, or Ulugarriu (if there was a difference) now.

And Morlock could find Tyrfing. He had implanted a talic impulse in the crystalline lattice of the sword, so that he might summon it to him at need. That meant he was still in talic stranj with the blade. If he had been in full possession of his Sight, he would simply have summoned a light trance and walked until he reached the blade and the killer. But the ghost sickness, or whatever was causing it, had weakened his talent so that even going into a light vision kept him from taking volitional action in the world of matter.

Still, the matter was easy enough. Morlock lit a lamp, went into a trance, and went into talic stranj with the flame. When he descended to normal awareness, the flame was still linked to his magical blade: the flame burned brighter in its direction.

The lamp had led him here. It would lead him to Tyrfing. And then he and Ulugarriu would have a long-overdue conversation.

The bright edge of the flame guided him through Twinegate Plaza into Apetown. He came at last to a sort of shop, but the sign outside the shop was blank and there was no name or symbol on the door.

He kicked the door open and entered.

The shop within was dim: all the windows were shuttered. The brightest lights in the room entered with Morlock: the fierce sunlight of the spring morning and the lamp he held in his hand.

By their light he saw in the room's shadows an old citizen in the day shape sitting in front of a shop counter. Behind him, on the counter, glittered Tyrfing.

"Are you Ulugarriu?" he asked the old citizen.

The old citizen's lower jaw swung open like a gate. Through the grayish lips peered a mottled pink-and-brown face, almost human but for the long ratlike snout.

It screeched. Morlock heard someone behind him and reached out his hand to summon Tyrfing, but a blow fell on the back of his head and he lost consciousness before he could speak.

Chapter Twenty-eight

The Stone Tree

Morlock awoke to the weary certainty that he was imprisoned again. The dank stone floor was familiar; the stench of unwashed bodies and the crash of iron doors was familiar. There was no cord of honor-teeth around his neck. For a moment, before he opened his eyes, he was afraid that the desperate New Year's escape and all that followed had been a delusion of his madness and he was still in the Vargulleion.

But as soon as he looked around him, he knew the fear was groundless. This was not the Vargulleion. The cell had no window; the walls seemed to be baked brick; and the cell doors had proper locks on them. Nothing he couldn't handle with the slightest excuse for a lockpick and a little time, though. They had taken his cloak, and all the useful and useless items he had tucked away in its pockets. But he had a long stiff wire or two sewn into the seams of his breeches; they might do the trick, if he could get a few moments unobserved.

There was only one guard outside his cell door, a solemn-faced semiwolf with a long face and hairy ears, wearing the dark regalia of the City Watchers.

"Why don't you shave those ears?" Morlock asked him, adding other insults that occurred to him, or that he remembered werewolves using to each other over the months he had been in or near Wuruyaaria.

But the watcher didn't even seem to be aware he was being insulted. He just looked at Morlock solemnly and with a little awe.

Presently a tall citizen with grizzled hair and a great torc of honor-teeth on his chest appeared, strolling up the corridor.

"I'll sit the watch for a while," he said.

The watcher stood slowly. "I think he was trying to get me to fight, Chieftain."

"You were too smart for that, I hope."

"Me, fight Khretvarrgliu?" The watcher seemed genuinely appalled. "Never."

"That's right," the grizzled citizen said agreeably.

The watcher wandered off, and the werewolf with the torc said to Morlock, "But we've already had our fight, haven't we, me and you? We've fought, and I've won."

"Your name is Wurnafenglu," Morlock said.

"It is," the werewolf said, quite pleased. "You were not in a condition to converse when last we saw each other. I'm glad things have changed."

"We have not fought. You are wise to keep this door between us. I'll kill you if I get the chance."

"But I won't give you the chance!" Wurnafenglu said triumphantly. "No, indeed. That's why I win, Khretvarrgliu. I'll keep you on the other side of this door as long as it suits me."

"That's what you thought before."

"I'll keep you on the other side of this door as long as it suits me," Wurnafenglu repeated, raising his voice. "On a day soon to come, I will have you chained and dragged forth. I will take you to the highest mesa of the city, and I will execute you there between the Stone Tree and the Well of Shadows, as the climax of our final rally against those mongrels who now call themselves the Union."

"Why wait?"

"A good rally takes preparation. Plus, our astronomers say there will be an eclipse of the sun on that day. That will impress the rabble."

"Your fellow citizens, you mean to say?"

"That's what I did say. The important people are already with us."

Wurnafenglu spent some time talking about his plan of independent strength through partial unity. Morlock didn't listen, but spent the time thinking about things he had seen and people he had known.

Presently he saw a decapitated man holding his severed head like a lamp. The man was standing next to Wurnafenglu, as he had stood beside him so many times in the Vargulleion. Wurnafenglu had never seen him then and didn't see him now. But Morlock did. He wondered if his madness was returning—if, perhaps, the ghost sickness was driving him insane.

"No," said the severed head in Wardspeech, one of the languages Morlock had grown up speaking. "I felt an impulse to manifest to you. I am War."

Morlock mulled this over for a bit, and said in the same language, "You are one of the Strange Gods?"

"I am."

Wurnafenglu asked him what the ghost he was babbling about, but Morlock had no trouble ignoring him. "Do you know Death?" he asked.

"She is one of our company. I don't count her as a friend, but we often work together, of course."

"Why have you chosen to show yourself to me?"

War dismissed the question with a wave of his free hand. "I do what I choose, and I don't explain myself even to myself. I should thank you, though. This has been the most entertaining Year of Choosing that I remember."

"I have nothing to do with that."

"Never lie to a god. What's the point? I was manifest when you and your friends escaped the Vargulleion. I was manifest when you fought the Sardhluun on the ground and the Neyuwuleiuun in the sky. I watched the battles your friend has been fighting."

"They call them rallies, I think."

"Never bandy words with a god. He may take offense."

Morlock shrugged and opened his right hand.

"You are indifferent, I see. But in a way, we are old friends. And I often visited you in the Vargulleion."

Morlock nodded. "Do you know Death?" he asked.

"No one really knows her; she is the strangest of the Strange Gods."

"I think I met her, once."

"'Met' is improper usage. She may have allowed you to perceive her manifestation. Yes, I visualize that. I don't understand it, though. Perhaps you can ask her about it when you see her."

"You visualize my imminent death?"

"Not visualize, no. All things are in flux, and visualizations of the future are near valueless. Still, if I were a gambling god, I would not bet on your living to the next moonset."

Morlock turned his face away and sensed without seeing War demanifest himself. When he looked back at the corridor, both War and Wurnafenglu were gone and the semiwolf watcher had returned and was staring at him, the long doglike jaw somewhat askew.

Morlock wondered why he was so impressed. Clearly he had heard stories of Khretvarrgliu. But it was not impossible he somehow felt without understanding the manifestation of the Strange God. He had few honor-teeth: one of those Wurnafenglu called the rabble.

"I am not angry at you," he said to the guard in Sunspeech. "I am rarely angry. But when I am angry, I will blot out the sun. Do you understand me? I will blot out the sun."

The watcher gaped at him, but did not respond. Morlock decided he would try again with the next shift.

Days passed. Eventually the day for his execution came. The corridor filled with watchers, most of whom stared at him in open terror: he had spent each shift working on their minds. His heart fell, though, when two watchers actually entered the cell. They weren't jailhouse guards. In fact, they were the pair he had met before, patrolling the Shadow Market and again on the stairs of the funicular tower: white-haired Okhurokratu and his scar-faced partner—Snellingu, Morlock remembered. Okhurokratu had chains in his hand; Snellingu a drawn sword.

"Be coming along, Khretvarrgliu," said Snellingu.

Morlock rose to his feet, prepared to fight if there was a chance.

But there was no chance. Other guards with clubs entered, and they struck Morlock about the head and shoulders until he lost consciousness.

When he awoke, he was being carried up the long stairs of the funicular tower by the white-haired werewolf and the scar-faced one.

"Are you being awake?" grunted Snellingu. "Why don't you get walking, then?"

"Eh," said Morlock. "Why not?"

He thought there might be more chance for escape while on his own feet, although it turned out he was wrong about that. His right hand was chained to his leg; his legs were chained to each other: there was barely enough slack for him to climb a step at a time. His left hand was free, of course, but there was little it could do. His cloak had been taken, and his ghostly arm was bare to the shoulder, looking strangely insubstantial in the fierce morning sun. They were already halfway up the long tower stairway: there was no chance of his getting away—unless he took the quick route, over the rail. He thought about it coldly, then decided against it. He wasn't the resigned type. He would put them to the trouble of killing him, if there was no other way he could inconvenience them.

He turned his eyes back up the stairwell and met the gaze of the white-haired guard who was leading the way upward. "That's right!" Okhurokratu said, in a relieved tone. "No point getting us into trouble."

"Don't be trying to be talking him into it," called Snellingu from below.

Morlock said nothing. He thought he heard someone saying, *Kree-laow! Kree-laow!* He looked into an unglazed window as they passed it on the stairwell but could see nothing within: the light difference was like a black curtain.

As they climbed, Morlock kept his eyes on the funicular ways. He would have liked to see the gears within the tower, but he thought he understood how the ropeways worked. There was one upward way and one downward way that were in constant motion. At regular intervals, crews atop the towers attached the rope-woven cars to the upward way and detached them from the downward way.

They finally reached the top. Morlock looked with interest at the crews hitching and unhitching the basketlike cars. When a car came down the way, the crew fixed it to the tower with an anchor like a great hook. The passengers got out and trudged away via the down staircase on the far side of the tower. Then the crew unhooked the car from the ropes and carried it over to the near side of the tower. They anchored it, hooked it to the upward rope, but did not fasten the hitch, so that the funicular ropes ran through the hooks without carrying the car away. They motioned the waiting passengers to embark. The waiting passengers were Morlock and his two guards: the way had apparently been cleared before them.

The crews were looking very unhappy in the fierce light and humid air, but they didn't appear to be slaves.

The guards sat down at some distance from him: white-haired Okhurokratu at the left-hand window, opposite to Morlock, scar-faced Snellingu with his back against the wicker-screened window in the front of the car. They had probably been warned against coming within reach of his ghostly hand. This was wise, as Morlock would certainly use it against them if he could. It had occurred to him that if he could distract one of them with it long enough to get a spear, he might kill them both, in which case matters would be very different indeed. He could not hope for real escape, but he did plan on causing harm to those who would kill him.

Morlock covertly tested the wicker screen on his right by pressing his elbow against it. It didn't give much. Probably it would be difficult to kick one of the guards out without being speared by the other. If he was going to try anything on the funicular, it would be best if he freed his hand first. He thought about the difficult task of teasing forth the wire from the seam while the guards were watching him, and wondered if he could get them to distract each other.

The crew cast off the anchor of the car and simultaneously did something to the hitches, fixing them to the cable leading upward. The car jerked into motion and carried them out over the city.

Morlock asked the watchers, "Are they all free citizens on the roof crews?"

"Yes," Okhurokratu said. "They tried slaves a few times, but it never worked. Not lively enough when it counts. It used to be free workers on every spoke down to the ground, and things worked better then."

Snellingu made a rude whistling sound with his wounded lips.

"My old gray-muzzle used to work the gears," Okhurokratu said. "Since they went to using slaves, he hasn't had an honest day's work and I've got to support him. A free citizen, supporting his gray-muzzled dad and half his brothers. Can you feature that?"

"The funiculars are working the same way they have been always doing, and you are just being angry about your sloppy-lazy family, which is boring to me."

"Ah. You don't know what it's like."

"I am knowing; you are all the time telling me. I am not caring."

"Ah. You—"

"So, Khretvarrgliu," said Snellingu. "You are being impressed by our funicular ways? Is it not being impressive? Don't be listening to my partner; he cannot be being happy unless he is being unhappy."

This turned the conversation back to Morlock, which was awkward, as he had the tip of the wire between his thumb and index finger. "Could be improved," he said. "It's a long walk up."

Both the watchers laughed. "Of course it's a long walk," Okhurokratu said. "What would you do about that? The funicular has to be high so it can clear the mesas."

"The same sort of gears that power the funicular could work ropes running up and down the tower. Put platforms on the ropes; people can ride up." He was hindered by the lack of a technical vocabulary in Sunspeech—and, anyway, he really only wanted to distract them.

The watchers fell silent, distracted by the image in their minds of elevators rising and falling. "Too much work for the tower-slaves," Okhurokratu said eventually. "They're only flesh and blood."

"Get other crews. The gears could be worked from the ground, or from the top of the tower. Adding another level there might be the best thing."

The two watchers looked at each other. Morlock deftly palmed the wire now freed from the seam.

"They would never be going for it," said scar-face doubtfully. "The big-teeth."

Morlock shrugged. He looked at a hand crank on the ceiling of the car.

Nodding toward it, he said, "That's for—" He paused. He didn't know the Sunspeech word for *emergency*, though he had been in many and caused more than a few. "If the ropes stop," he concluded finally.

"Yes," grumbled Okhurokratu. "Happened to me, once—on the up way, which is the worst. Had to crank for half the afternoon just to get to the next tower. That never happened when they used free workers."

Snellingu rolled his eyes. "How would you be knowing? You have been saying you were only a pup when they were had starting to use slaves."

"My gray-muzzle told me."

Both watchers turned their gaze directly at Morlock, now—not especially interested in him, but efficiently minding him. There was nothing he could do while they were watching him, so he looked out the window.

They were riding high above the city. Morlock felt strangely inspired, almost the way he had felt when he was flying. The city had a kind of beauty, seen from here: it was full of trees, bristling with lair-towers. There were running streams, silvery in the bitter sunlight, and open pools that glared back at him. He saw the citizens going about their business in their day shapes in the cruel summery light. None of them looked up to see him pass on toward his death. They would go on doing the same thing tomorrow when he was dead. In that moment, they almost mattered more to him than he did to himself, even though they looked smaller than . . . than those ratlike things with the human faces.

"Were you two there when I was arrested?" he asked the guards.

They looked uncomfortable. "We were only doing our jobs," Okhurokratu said defensively.

"Yes," agreed Snellingu.

Morlock wondered why they said that—why they thought it would make a difference to him. But since they clearly had been there, he asked the question he really wanted an answer to. "Did you see that thing inside the old citizen—the thing running him like a puppet?"

"Were-rats," White-hair said, and scowled. "I hate those guys."

"Why are you hating them?"

"They smell bad, and I can't understand what they say, and they make me feel creepy. And that meat-puppet they had really bothered me."

"The old citizen," Morlock prompted him, when it seemed like he would say no more.

"Citizen my third testicle. That thing—didn't it bother *you?*" he asked his partner explosively. "Now I have nightmares that half the people I run into are just meat-puppets run by were-rats. It would explain a lot of what's wrong with this town. But you're not bothered; I can tell by the smug expression on your face."

"Not me. I would be knowing."

"How?"

"They are smelling bad. You are saying so."

"Where do the were-rats come from?" Morlock asked. "Do they have a borough, like Dogtown or Apetown?"

"The were-rats are living on Mount Dhaarnaiarnon. Everyone is knowing that."

"I'm not from around here."

"I am almost forgetting. Even though you are smelling like a never-wolf."

By now they had reached Runaiaklendon Tower. Morlock was hoping for a moment or two of distraction as they disembarked and reembarked on the funicular car—but they didn't disembark at all; the guards kept their seat and the tower crew hustled the car and its passengers from the Twine-Runaiaklendon line to the Runaiaklendon-Nekkuklendon line.

By now Morlock's cupped right hand was resting lightly on the manacle binding his thigh. If he could open that lock, it would effectively free his hand . . . and give him a weapon, as the leg manacle swung on the end of a short chain might do a lot of damage in the right hand (that is, Morlock's).

Unfortunately, it was no good. The wire rasped audibly against the metal of the manacle. Morlock could hear it, and he knew the two werewolf watchers heard something, too: their ears seemed to twitch. He moved his hand away from the manacle in a way he hoped did not look furtive. He would have to wait until there was more noise and less alertness.

The noise came at every changeover, but unfortunately the guards' alertness increased then also. When they were riding up the final line, from Iuiunioklendon to Wuruklendon, Morlock had to admit to himself that he would not be able to free himself before he arrived at his place of execution.

The funicular anchor on Wuruklendon was the lowest of all—not even a tower, really, just a raised platform. The door of the car was opened from the outside, and white-haired Okhurokratu, all friendliness dropped, stood and gestured with his spear at the door.

Morlock stood and walked out the door into the late-morning sun.

On the platform the crew was standing well clear of him, fearful looks on their faces. Around the anchor-station on the ground was a small army of campaign volunteers, divided into companies of the Sardhluun (black-and-green tunics), the Neyuwuleiuun (red-and-green tunics) and the Aruuka-iaduun (resplendent in blue and gold). They were armed, also, and their weapons were in their hands.

Wurnafenglu stood at the head of the Sardhluun volunteers. "Come down, Khretvarrgliu, come down!" he cried. "We have an errand at the Stone Tree!"

The Sardhluun werewolves cheered him enthusiastically, the others of the Alliance less so.

"That's our next First Wolf, partner," Okhurokratu remarked quietly to Snellingu behind Morlock. "And I hate that guy."

"I am not liking this," the scar-faced partner replied. "I am being glad the Sardhluun dogs will be doing the actual kill."

"What's to like? It's a job, partner. Citizens don't have to like their jobs; they just have to do them."

Morlock walked down the wooden steps, trying to conceal the wire in his hands without seeming to conceal anything.

This station was different from the others. Most of the gears were underground, but one set was exposed to the outer air, just below the platform. He gazed hungrily at it, and couldn't help speculating on how their efficiency might be increased.

The slaves working the wheels on the upper level looked up from their work and saw him as he descended. He recognized none of them, but they seemed to recognize him; some seemed to be muttering *kree-laow*. He nodded at them and turned away toward his enemies.

The line of weapons bristled as the volunteers lifted them threateningly against him. He looked at them, rattled his chain, and smiled. Some of the ones nearby turned their eyes away and seemed embarrassed. But no one lowered a weapon.

The volunteers surrounded Morlock like an honor guard, the nearest ones a spear's-length distance from him on every side. He walked among them and tried to see past them.

Wuruklendon was strangely like a wilderness. If anyone had ever lived there, it was so long ago as to leave no traces. There was underbrush and small trees—and rising over all a great gray branching structure that stood against the misty blue sky: the Stone Tree. It did look like a leafless tree, but Morlock guessed it had been built, rather than grown. The ends of the branches seemed to trace out three-dimensional representations of higher-space polytopes. He would have been interested to know if the branches changed position over time, but he doubted that anyone within hearing distance would answer his question.

Not far from the trunklike base of the Stone Tree was a dark hole in the ground, bordered by a crumbling stone wall. The Well of Shadows, no doubt.

Beyond the well, the ground fell steeply away and the eastern slope was littered with the shapes of tombs, mausoleums, and monuments all the way down to the hilly plain at the base of Wuruyaaria's mountain. This was the necropolis of the city, where wealthy and wellborn citizens honored their dead.

Between the well and the tree was a wooden platform with three levels.

The volunteers parted, and Morlock was prodded with spears to step forward and climb the scaffold to the highest platform, where there were leg manacles on chains that were nailed to the wood.

Once there he turned and looked out at the crowd gathering for the rally, and the execution.

A volunteer in the green-and-black tunic of the Sardhluun had followed Morlock up the stairs. With a grim look on his face, he knelt down and fastened the manacles to Morlock's ankles. Then he stood and looked Morlock in the eye.

"So much for you, Khretvarrgliu," he said. "My brother died in the Vargulleion on New Year's Night."

"I hope I killed him," Morlock said.

The Sardhluun volunteer's long face worked, as if he were trying to spit, but could not quite manage it.

"If your mouth is dry," Morlock said, "perhaps Wurnafenglu can moisten it for you."

It was a version of an insult he had heard Lakkasulakku shout at Hlupnafenglu on one high-spirited afternoon recently. He had no clear idea what it meant. But the Sardhluun volunteer obviously did. He staggered backward; one foot missed a stair, and he tumbled down the long wooden scaffold to the bottom.

A small, ugly victory on the way to an even uglier defeat. Wurnafenglu looked at the fallen Sardhluun volunteer, who was carried away unmoving, looked up at Morlock, and smiled, exposing all of his white sharp teeth. He pointed at the sky and turned away, still smiling. Morlock spent some time wondering what he had meant. *Enjoy your last noon. Your time is short. The eclipse is coming*. Something like that, perhaps.

The three gnyrrands of the Alliance had gathered on the third platform, along with their reeves and cantors. Citizens without colors or weapons were gathering to watch the rally, but they were still outnumbered by the sea of armed and uniformed volunteers. The Alliance had found so much success with their last rally that they were taking no chances at all with this one. If the outliers and the Goweiteiuun showed up, the gnyrrands and cantors would be killed, with as many of their volunteers as seemed necessary. The election would end today. So ran the rumor of the crowd as it reached Morlock, standing alone on the high scaffold. His hand rested naturally on the manacle binding his thigh.

Wurnafenglu was forcefully asserting his right to speak for the entire Alliance before the execution. The other two gnyrrands of the Alliance seemed unhappy about this, but the one in Aruukaiaduun colors was a nonentity, not even addressed with respect by his own cantors, and the Neyuwuleiuun gnyrrand lacked Wurnafenglu's fierce hunger for the crowd. Also, they were constrained by the time, if they were really trying to orchestrate Morlock's execution with an eclipse—and time was certainly an issue: one of the reeves had mounted a sundial on the corner of the platform, and was constantly consulting it.

Presently, Wurnafenglu mounted to the second platform and began to speak. His speech was about the grief and the glory of being a solitary citizen of Wuruyaaria. From solitude came strength and courage; from unity, weakness and fear. But when the strong united with the strong bravely to oppose the cowering weak, were they not creating a kind of disunity that led to greater strength? But if some would weave the city into a disharmonious unity, weakening its strength, then the city must defend itself by cutting that part of itself out, like a gangrenous limb. So Wurnafenglu reasoned with his audience, taking both speaking parts.

The reeve watching the sundial made a significant gesture.

Two other reeves opened a long box: in it lay a long spear, painted black and green. Beside it glittered Tyrfing, unsheathed and unbound in any way that Morlock could see.

Someone in the crowd shouted that the sun was disappearing. Everyone looked up, including Morlock. Cries of wonder and fear swept the crowd, and Morlock was not immune from the same feelings. He wished, at some time in his long life, he had spent some time understanding the mysteries of eclipses, the subtle gestures of the stars, all the open secrets the sky unveiled every night.

Wurnafenglu shouted in a commanding voice, "And so the sun itself demands the death of the never-wolf who poisoned the city!" This drew the eyes of most, if not all, of the crowd back to him. One of the reeves, the one wearing Neyuwuleiuun colors, handed Wurnafenglu the spear dark with Sardhluun black and green.

Morlock pulled the unlocked manacle free from his leg. He reached out his still-manacled hand and called loudly, "*Tyrfing!*"

In the faded light of the vanishing sun, the monochrome blade flew glittering through the air to Morlock's outstretched hand.

Wurnafenglu gaped for a moment, then realized what had happened. He charged up the stairway to the execution scaffold.

Morlock shattered the shackles on his right ankle and then Wurnafenglu was upon him. Morlock swiftly brought Tyrfing up to parry Wurnafenglu's spear.

Tyrfing's edge sheared away a strip of black-and-green pigment from the spear's shaft. Underneath, the spear gleamed like glass.

"Your own work," Wurnafenglu whispered. "Think of that when I stab you through the heart with it."

Morlock didn't answer. With their weapons bound together, Wurnafenglu was clawing at his face. Morlock reached out with his ghostly hand and inserted empty fingers into Wurnafenglu's right eye socket.

The gnyrrand screamed and the day went dark. The disc of the sun had completely disappeared, and the three moons stood forth in the suddenly dark sky like unequal glaring eyes.

Werewolves rippled and howled in the cascade of sudden moonlight, assuming the cloak of their animal forms.

Wurnafenglu did not have the discipline to resist the night shape. His wolf's shadow rose over him and recast him in its image.

In the moment of transition, Morlock's ghostly hand tore a deep furrow through Wurnafenglu's being, doing fearful damage to both his shadows.

Wurnafenglu fell heavily on the stairs. His head was half wolf, half man; his legs were crooked and lupine; he lifted clawed but human hands at the uncaring sky.

In horror at himself, at what he had become, Wurnafenglu lay aghast in the brief night.

Morlock shattered the manacle on his left ankle. He stepped forward and struck down with Tyrfing as if it were an executioner's sword.

Wurnafenglu's monstrous head fell from his bristling severed neck.

To inflict death with Tyrfing was always nightmarish, but Wurnafenglu's death in the terror of his distortion was a kind of damnation. It nearly carried Morlock's spirit with it into the darkness, and Morlock fought for long moments to keep his life in his ailing body.

In this trancelike state he seemed to see the Strange Gods gathering in the sudden night by the Well of Shadows. They got on their hands and knees and drank from it like dogs.

Then the moment passed and he was wholly himself again, Wurnafenglu's death dismissed, the Strange Gods no longer visible.

He unbent himself and looked out at the crowd.

The Alliance had planned his execution to coincide with the eclipse, so that the terror and ecstasy of transition would be yoked in the minds of the citizens with the Alliance's victory. The result had been somewhat different.

Morlock held his bloody sword toward the sky and shouted, "Citizens of Wuruyaaria! I await your next champion."

The gnyrrands, reeves, and cantors still on the scaffold scampered or rolled down the stairs to the ground, hampered by their clothing in their night shapes.

Dim misty bars of sunlight fell from the sky, breaking the darkness. The eclipse was ending. Another cascade of transitions spread through the crowd, howls becoming screams as their human shadows fell on them and forced them to resume their day shapes.

The monuments of the necropolis also seemed to be changing shape, moving up the long slope. Morlock stared at them, bemused, until he understood what he was seeing. It wasn't the monuments. It was an army of werewolves who had been hiding among them, waiting for this moment of confusion to strike their enemies.

They came in every shape: men and women trailed by wolvish shadows, wolves paired with crouching human shadows, and every grade of semiwolf in-between. But they had clearly resisted both transitions, hiding from the sky among the mausoleums, and they came with clear minds, bared teeth, and drawn blades. They wore the red and blue of the Goweiteiuun and the green and gold of the outliers, and they fell on their enemies of the Alliance.

Rokhlenu, wearing the day shape, ran in the vanguard. Beside him, bearing a green-and-gold banner in one hand and a glass sword in the other, was Wuinlendhono.

Morlock charged down the stairs of the scaffold, kicking and stabbing at stray werewolves as he went. Shouted chants were rising on the edge of the crowd toward the funicular station—perhaps a rally of the Alliance. He could do the most good (or the most harm, depending on how one looked at it) if he joined with the outliers.

The green-and-gold wave was sweeping toward him also, Rokhlenu and Wuinlendhono at its crest. They met, laughing, by the Well of Shadows.

"You are in good time, my friends," Morlock said.

Rokhlenu stared at him with haunted blue eyes. "We couldn't attack before," he began to explain. "The—"

"I meant what I said," Morlock said firmly. "No banter."

"Ghost no," gasped Wuinlendhono. "No banter. I *hate* banter."

They turned and led the Union werewolves in a charge straight through the chaotic clusters of the Alliance volunteers. Many died; many fled; the spectators to the rally had long since run off to a safe distance.

Long before they reached the funicular, they heard chanting. It was in neither Moonspeech nor Sunspeech nor any language that they spoke, but Morlock at least recognized it: "*Kree-laow! Kree-laow! Kree-laow!*" The slaves of the funicular station had risen in rebellion. They were attacking the spectators and Alliance werewolves from behind with their chains as weapons. Many of the slaves had already died, their bodies scattered about the plain of Wuruklendon, but others were still streaming out of their subterranean tower, eager to take up the fight.

"Rokhlenu!" shouted Morlock, when he saw this through the dust and blood of the election rally. "I need to take the funicular slaves out of here. Will that hurt your Union?"

"Take them," Rokhlenu said instantly. "Get as many as you can clear. We'll meet you back in Outlier Town."

"We may meet there," said Morlock. He was thinking about Mount Dhaarnaiarnon, and were-rats, and Ulugarriu.

"Oh?" said Rokhlenu, obviously surprised, but there was no time to talk the matter over. "In any case, good luck to you, my friend."

"And to you, and all of yours," said Morlock, and they parted there in the midst of battle, much as they had met.

Morlock ran straight at the ragged line of slaves and shouted in Sunspeech, "Do you understand me? Do you know me?"

"*Kree-laow!*" they shouted, saluting him with their bloody chains. "*Kree-laow!*"

"*Do you understand me?*"

"We understand you, Khretvarrgliu," said one in Sunspeech. "This is the hour of vengeance and atonement. Where do you wish us to die?"

"This is the hour of escape. We will make our way down the face of the city and free as many of our people as we can. If we die, we die, but if we escape we may live—for a little while," he added, thinking of his own illness.

"That may not be, Khretvarrgliu, for armed werewolves guard the downward ways."

"Let me through!"

They parted and Morlock dashed to the edge of Wuruklendon.

A band of dark-coated City Watchers stood blocking the stairways down to Iuiunioklendon.

"Citizens," said Morlock, "give way or die. I will not tell you twice."

Some of the watchers did in fact flee down the stairs at his approach. But others stayed, led by a white-haired werewolf and one with a scarred face.

Morlock beat the spear blade of the scar-faced guard aside and passed Tyrfing through his heart. The death-shock was grievous, causing Morlock's knees to buckle, and the white-haired guard cried out with rage and made as if to stab him. But then the guard went down before a tide of chain-swinging slaves; his cries of anger changed to fear and then fell silent forever.

Morlock straightened himself and looked about. The guards who had not fled were dead or dying.

"We go down and out," he said, as clearly as he could. "Mesa by mesa, tower by tower. We rescue our people as we go. If we get separated, fight your way out and flee south; all will head that way who can."

"But what of atonement, Khretvarrgliu?" said one.

Morlock had no idea what they were talking about, but he didn't want to admit it, lest he lose authority in their eyes. "Dying is easy," he said. "It is over in a moment. Atone by living. Live as well as you can, for all who have died. It is all you can do."

This seemed to satisfy them. They armed themselves from the fallen guards and began to move down the winding stone stairways, the first stones of an avalanche that would sweep the city clear of slaves.

Morlock went with them. But first he paused to cover the hands of two dead guards: one with white hair, the other with a scarred face. If it was important to atone, and if death was an atonement, they had atoned.

Chapter Twenty-nine

Election Results

Rokhlenu watched Morlock go, then turned back to the rally, where the fighting had broken up into a chaos of separate combats, clouds of dust dimming the colors and scents of the factions.

"We'll never find the Alliance leaders in this mess," Rokhlenu remarked to Wuinlendhono.

"You want my advice?"

"Yes."

"Don't bother with the leaders. Better that they survive today, hated and toothless. Who'll vote for them now?"

"Right. I'd rather kill the volunteers, anyway."

His wife looked at him in some surprise.

"I want them to know," Rokhlenu said grimly, "that if they march to an election as if it were a war, a war is exactly what they'll get. The Aruukaiaduun would never have put my family's heads on poles if they hadn't known a private army was marching with them. It won't be so easy for them to recruit one, next time."

"Yurr. Well, if nothing else, it thins out the voters committed to the other side."

In fact, there was not much more fighting and no more killing. The

Alliance leaders had quietly absconded down the necropolis slope once the Union charge had passed by, and when the Alliance werewolves realized this they began fleeing themselves, or tearing off their colors and surrendering themselves.

They let the Alliance citizens keep their weapons and collect their dead. They sent the Union dead and wounded back to the outlier settlement by the necropolis road: Rokhlenu didn't want to make a display of their losses, which were not nothing.

But he did want to make a display of their victory. Both packs of Union werewolves raised their banners high and ran together in good order down the winding stairs to Iuiunioklendon market square.

There the Goweiteiuun citizens parted company: most of them had dens on Iuiunioklendon. "And it would be a long walk back up, thanks to your friend," said Aaluindhonu, the Goweiteiuun gnyrrand, as they parted company. He gestured up at the motionless funicular and laughed.

"We should call for an election soonest," Wuinlendhono said. "I think we have the bite for it."

"Tomorrow after sunset, I suggest," Aaluindhonu replied, looking at both Rokhlenu and Wuinlendhono to see if they approved. When they nodded, he said, "I'll send a message to the First Singer when I get back to my den. He'll have plenty of time to send heralds to sing the news tonight, and shout it tomorrow."

They said good-bye, and the outliers continued onward and downward.

Rokhlenu and Wuinlendhono didn't talk much as they walked; they were both tired, and the head of a crowd was no place for a conversation of consequence. But once he asked her, as they passed the abandoned funicular tower on Iuiunioklendon, "Do you think I was wrong to tell Morlock to take the slaves out?"

"No," said Wuinlendhono. "For one thing, he'd have done it anyway. But I think the political harm will go to the Aruukaiaduun. They played a rough game and lost. Everyone knows it. They will have to hire workmen to open the funicular ways again, but no one will thank them for it; everyone knows they would rather have slaves."

But it was clear, long before they reached Twinegate, that at least one of the ways would not be reopening soon. The anchor-gate in Twinegate Plaza was bright with flames and dark with smoke in the afternoon shadows. Someone had set the wooden mechanisms inside the tower on fire.

They stood on the verge of Runaiaklendon mesa and watched the tower burn for a while.

"Morlock has written 'I was here' on the face of the city in letters of fire," Rokhlenu said. "People will be reading it there for a long time."

"No doubt," said Wuinlendhono. "That tower isn't going to stand much longer. Let's go home through the Dogtown Gate. We don't want to be punctuated by falling periods."

Hours later, Rokhlenu and Wuinlendhono were alone at last, settling down for a brief nap before sunset, when she asked, "You don't think you'll see him again, do you?"

"I wouldn't bet either way," said Rokhlenu. "Not on him. But I don't think he expects it. He's old; he's sick. If he can get the never-wolves to safety, it may be the last thing he can do. His future is closed in, and he's out of tomorrows. I'd loan him some of ours, if I could."

"Over my day-barking body you would," Wuinlendhono replied, and bit him somewhere he'd notice.

Morlock was not, in fact, shepherding the never-wolves to safety. He had sent them away south to fend for themselves, and he was, at sunset, rounding the edge of the city's necropolis and headed for the slopes of Mount Dhaarnaiarnon.

He had felt bad about parting company with the ex-slaves, but most of them had not seemed to expect his help. They were natives of the northern plains and knew the region better than he did. Also, some of them kept referring to atonement and some sin by their ancestors in the distant past, and he found it hard to stay patient with this. He had done things since noon that he felt some guilt for; if the never-wolves weren't committing their own misdeeds by now, it was long past time that they start.

As for him, he had to untie the knot of mystery surrounding the murder of his friends and find vengeance for them. He did not honestly think that he would succeed, but if he were even to try, he would have to confront Ulugarriu. Morlock was wondering if he might be a were-rat, or perhaps a colony of were-rats, passing the name *Ulugarriu* down generation after generation to create the legend of an immortal maker. But if he was not a were-rat, or among the were-rats, the were-rats certainly knew him and were working with him.

Morlock walked around the marsh south of the outlier settlement and came at his cave through the silver-tainted hills to the east.

He was surprised and pleased to see a sallow-faced Lakkasulakku hard at work over the forge, folding and refolding glass for weapons.

"Good evening, apprentice," he said, when the young citizen leaped up at his approach.

"Khretvarrgliu!" shouted Lakkasulakku. "They said they were going to execute you!"

"They tried. They won't again, I think."

"Then the Union won the rally?"

"I think so, though I left before it was done. I am here only to collect a few things and leave again."

"I hope—I hope you don't mind. . . . They needed weapons for the rally, and I thought—"

"I don't mind. Everything in the cave is yours as much as mine, save Tyrfing alone, because of the burden that goes with it."

"Chieftain," Lakkasulakku said, bowing his head.

Morlock pounded him on the shoulder. Together they gathered a cloak, some cold-lights and provisions, and a few other things Morlock thought might be handy. Before the sun disappeared behind the shoulder of the hill, he was off again, waving farewell to Lakkasulakku, who stood disconsolate before the mouth of the cave. Morlock never expected to see him again and, as a matter of fact, he never did.

Sunset found him on the lower slopes of the volcano. He was tempted to drive onward, but he knew too much about mountains to try ascending one in the dark. Also, he was deathly tired. He wrapped himself in the cloak, although the air was still hot, and lay down. He was awake for a long time, looking at a strange fiery light burning on the undersides on the incoming clouds. It was odd, as if the city were on fire and the clouds were reflecting it. But the city was not on fire.

The next morning, he ate some bread and drank some water, because he knew he must, and began the long climb to the mountain's summit. It took him most of the day, and throughout it he kept alert for the sound and sight—even the smell—of the were-rats.

Evening's red light found him lurking under the lip of the crater, above the great moon-clock in the mountain's face. He kept hearing fugitive sounds he thought were were-rats' voices. But whatever way he turned, he seemed to get no closer to them, and they often roamed farther away.

He wondered if they might have nests inside the crater. The idea took him up to the edge of the crater.

The sun disappeared beyond the eastern rim of the world. Two moons stood out abruptly in the night sky: Chariot was burning darkly on the red rim of the western horizon: it would set soon, and summer would begin. Trumpeter stood somber above: in a few days, it would set, too, and the night skies would be dark until Horseman returned. Morlock watched, his quest for were-rats forgotten, as Chariot slid down beyond the eastern edge of the world and its light was lost.

"*Khul gradara!*" Morlock said, when Chariot was gone. "Good-bye, moon."

He turned back to the vast echoing pit of the volcano crater. He thought he heard some sort of sound coming from it. He kept his eyes fixed on the darkness in the crater, hoping he might see something as his eyes grew used to the dark.

Something pushed him, hard, on the back of both legs and he tumbled helplessly into the crater. He heard were-rats chitter in triumph behind him, but he still could not see them. He slid down the surface of the crater and, before he could recover, fell into the open pit at the bottom.

He was falling straight into the mountain. Shadows spun around him as he fell.

At about the time Morlock was briefly encountering the were-rats, Rokhlenu was acclaimed First Singer of Wuruyaaria.

Heralds had been crying the election up and down the mesas of the city all night and day, and by sunset the surviving candidates and all citizens interested in voting were gathered on the great plain west of the city. The crowd was gathering around a dais built near the Bitter Road. On the dais were five couches, and in front of the couches stood five citizens, their necks a-bristle with honor-teeth: the incumbents of the Innermost Pack.

Rokhlenu and Aaluindhonu, with their reeves and cantors and supporters, stood on the south side of the road. The gnyrrands for the Alliance and their fellow candidates and supporters stood on the north side of the road. The candidates wore no colors or scents, but their supporters carried the pack banners high. As citizens arrived at the assembly, they joined one side or the other. They also had the option of standing aloof, but tonight few were availing themselves of this.

In fact, few stood by the Alliance candidates. Long before the sun set, it was clear that the election was a landslide for the Union. An election in Wuruyaaria could be a drawn-out business, with voters changing sides through the night as bite, or the perception of bite (which was the same thing, really, in the hour of choice), shifted from one pack to another. It could be complicated by the fact that one citizen's bite, and consequently his vote, might be greater than another's.

But tonight there was no question: the citizens were almost uniformly rejecting the Alliance. To be brutal, criminal, and reckless was one thing. To fail was another, and Wuruyaaria's citizens had no mercy on it. The only citizens standing with the Alliance were the candidates' closest relatives, ones who could not vote with the opposition (or stay away) without shaming their blood.

The sun set.

All citizens turned eastward. The moonlit tide of transformations swept over them, and they cried out in voices human and lupine, bidding Chariot farewell and summer welcome.

When the major moon had set, when the citizens had recovered from their transformations, Aaluindhonu gave Rokhlenu a wolvish grin and trotted over to the dais, where the retiring singers of the Innermost Pack were leaping down from the dais.

He congratulated the retiring First Singer, an old acquaintance of his from the Neyuwuleiuun named Skuiulaalu.

Skuiulaalu thanked him loudly, then more privately wished him good luck: he would not have chosen to take the high couch at this strange and dreadful time. Citizens said the world was ending, and Skuiulaalu half believed them.

Aaluindhonu laughed, skipped past the old singers, and leapt up to the dais. He prepared to mount the high couch of the First Singer.

There was a storm of protests from the crowd. It broke forth without warning, and it was intense, furious. It raged on both sides of the road. Neither the Alliance nor the Union voters would accept Aaluindhonu as First Singer. The Alliance disliked him, and neither side respected him.

Instead, the voters chanted or howled the name of Rokhlenu.

This was not as the gnyrrands had arranged it between themselves and their fellow candidates. But the electorate was a fickle master, not under anyone's control. Strictly speaking, they had no say in the matter, but it was a foolish politician or a brave one who defied the unanimous wish of his constituents.

Rokhlenu met Aaluindhonu's angry eye and tilted his head sideways: an inquiry. Aaluindhonu hesitated, then lowered his gaze: a submission.

Rokhlenu leapt forward, bounded up to the dais, jumped atop the high couch, and stood there, looking out at the crowd.

The electors howled their approval. Even the Alliance voters seemed caught up in the moment. It was a triumph to make songs of, a tale that would be told for a thousand years. Half a year ago, Rokhlenu had been a prisoner in the Vargulleion. Tonight he was the First Singer of Wuruyaaria.

Least moved, of everyone there, was probably Rokhlenu himself. It would have meant more if his father and brothers had been there. Ghost, it would have meant more if Morlock had been there. His beloved was there, proudly waving a green-and-gold banner, and that meant a great deal. It meant more than the rest of the crowd rolled together in a carpet. Meeting her, mating her: that was his true triumph in this half year, the triumph of his life. That was what he would make songs of, when he had time.

When the crowd's shouting began to subside, Rokhlenu summoned the candidates they had agreed on to the Innermost Pack: two from the Goweiteiuun cantors and his own reeve, Yaarirruuiu. The Goweiteiuun were to have a majority of singers on the Innermost Pack, in return for their welcoming the outliers into the treaty. That seemed to be a settled question when the voters saluted him as First Singer, but he was determined to keep his deal with Aaluindhonu.

Rokhlenu's first song as First Singer was brief. He promised two things, though. First, there would be a new source of food in the outliers' colony on the Bitter Water; they could not control the weather, but they would not sit idle while it killed them. That was the behavior of a dumb beast, not a werewolf. Second, there would be justice for every citizen. He repeated that: justice for every citizen, no matter what his bite.

"Where are the prisoners of the Khuwuleion?" shouted someone—a semiwolf still wearing the day shape. Others took up the cry, in Moonspeech and Sunspeech.

Rokhlenu silenced them with a commanding howl. The question, he sang, had been asked, and asked again. It would never be forgotten. Soon it would be answered. There would be justice for every citizen.

Then he dismissed them to their celebrations. The first night of summer had come; the Choosing had ended.

Wuinlendhono and her mate spent the night going to other citizens' celebrations. They finally got back to her lair-tower just before dawn.

While they were grooming each other before lying down, she met his eye and whispered a question: Was he unhappy? They had succeeded, against very long odds. He was due a little triumph. Was anything wrong?

Rokhlenu had been singing the role of a magnanimous victor all night, and it was a relief to tell what he really felt. But he sang, in the end, he was glad: no one could take the outliers away from her now, not after what she had achieved—

—what they had achieved, she snapped.

—what she had achieved. And they would be together now, forever. That was the greatest victory of all.

She told him to prove it, and their minds turned to other matters.

The next morning he had not slept much, but his mind was clear as ice (which he wondered if he would ever see again: it was another murky glaring day). He and Yaarirruuiu woke early so that they could climb the long stone stairs up to Iuiunioklendon, where the first meeting of the Innermost Pack traditionally took place. Aaluindhonu had commandeered the audience hall of the Goweiteiuun's Inner Pack for the occasion.

The first issue they tackled was the admission of the outliers under the name of the Ekhaiasuteiuun ("the border-runners"), as chosen by a majority of the outlier citizens. A copy of the treaty was sent down to the outlier settlement for the First Wolf to sign.

As the other singers began to rise from their couches, Rokhlenu said, "And now for the main business. I want the Aruukaiaduun gnyrrand and the Werowance of the Sardhluun arrested."

This quelled anyone's interest in leaving. Three of the singers were standing with their mouths open, but no song or speech came from them.

Aaluindhonu smiled wisely, as if he had been expecting something like this from the hotheaded young First Singer and said, "Understandable, but quite impossible."

"Essential," Rokhlenu disagreed.

"What charges will you prefer?"

There was a smiling ambiguity in Aaluindhonu's question that Rokhlenu disliked intensely. He said bluntly, "The Werowance, as the representative of the Sardhluun Pack, is guilty of theft from the city. They took money every month for the feeding and housing of prisoners they had sold as slaves or butchered for meat. That's a crime against the city, against every citizen."

"Subject to a certain interpretation—"

"That is nonsense, my friend, and you know it. The disbursements were marked in the city accounts 'For the maintenance of prisoners.' The dead do not require maintenance."

"Yurr. I see what you mean. You have actually read the city accounts?"

"Skuiulaalu sent them to my residence last night, of course. I read the relevant parts as I walked up here this morning. Yaarirruuiu has them, at least a portion of them."

"You have hit the ground running, I see. It bites me to admit this, but I think our fellow citizens made the right choice. But what is it you have against the gnyrrand of the Aruukaiaduun? What is his name again?"

It turned out no one there could remember his name. But Yaarirruuiu had some notes from the campaign with him, tucked into the city account books (he had held them while Rokhlenu read them), and after consulting them he could tell his fellow singers that the gnyrrand of the Aruukaiaduun was named Norianduiu.

"All right," Aaluindhonu continued smilingly, "what have you got against poor Norianduiu?"

"Murder. The Aruukaiaduun under his leadership secretly murdered my family. Their display of the severed heads as campaign banners at that damned rally was an open admission. My youngest brother had been dead less than an hour. You saw the head, Aaluindhonu: what do you think?"

The old politician's smile was finally gone. "Yes," he said finally. "Yes, you've got something there. But won't it look like you're using your position for private vengeance?"

"No. Because if I were, I'd go after Rywudhaariu. Everyone knows that he pulls the strings in the Aruukaiaduun Pack. But Norianduiu was legally responsible for the campaign, so he will be charged. I'm putting this to a vote. I want unanimous support. If I don't get it, I'm going to resign my office and kill those rat-bastards with my own teeth and claws. Because if the secret murder of citizens is not a crime, if theft from the city is not a crime, if treating female citizens like meat for export is not a crime, then nothing is a crime because there is no law. And if there is no law, there is no city. Say your say; do it now."

They all agreed to the arrests. But Aaluindhonu added hesitantly (no longer smiling, thank ghost), "But, Rokhlenu, a suggestion."

"Yes?"

"You should not direct the arrests or prosecution yourself. Let me do it. I can get justice without appearing vindictive. It will be better all around that way."

Rokhlenu had never found himself able to trust Aaluindhonu; they had been thrown together by circumstance rather than choice. But he did trust

Yaarirruuiu, and he saw his former reeve approved the plan, so he nodded. "Good. I'll leave it to you, then."

"There's something else we could do to diminish the appearance of a grudge," one of the other Goweiteiuun singers said—a citizen named Naaleiyaleiu. He was unremarkable, except for his overuse of the pungently piney pack-scent of the Goweiteiuun. "The Neyuwuleiuun are fending off some attack on their northern colony—the place that served as a hunting ground and a station for their airships. If you take some fighters and defend the Neyuwuleiuun, it will show this is not about the election."

Yaarirruuiu was nodding at this, but asked, "What kind of attack? We don't want to lose our First Singer on his first day on the job."

They all smiled at that. Some laughed.

"Werebears, I'll bet," the other Goweiteiuun singer said. (Dhuskudheiu was his name.) "There have been lots of them roaming around the fringes of the city."

The smiles faded. Werebears were nothing to laugh about.

"I'll go and reconnoiter," Rokhlenu said thoughtfully. "If it looks too risky, we'll get out and come back with a stronger force."

They all agreed, and on that note the Innermost Pack ended its first meeting. Rokhlenu and Yaarirruuiu left, hauling the city account books, deep in conversation. Dhuskudheiu departed on some mission of his own—possibly lunch. Aaluindhonu started to go, paused by Naaleiyaleiu's couch a moment as if he would speak, twitched his nose, then hurried on.

Naaleiyaleiu was left alone in the chamber, chittering to himself. Eventually, his jaw swung open like a gate, exposing the long-nosed pink were-rat within. Naaleiyaleiu's hand reached into a pocket and grabbed a jar of scented oil. Naaleiyaleiu's hand doused the were-rat in Naaleiyaleiu's head generously with the scent, and then did the same for the were-rats controlling the other parts of the body.

Naaleiyaleiu had a more difficult job than most of the meat-puppets scattered through the city. But it was nearly over, thank Ulugarriu: so, at least, Naaleiyaleiu's crew chittered hopefully to each other.

Rokhlenu left later that afternoon. He picked a crew of nine irredeemables to go with him, and Yaarirruuiu was not among them, much to the latter's annoyance.

"Look," Rokhlenu said, when he had heard his fellow singer's fifteenth reason why he should come along. "I need you around town to keep an eye or two on that slippery Aaluindhonu." And that convinced him.

But he did take Lekkativengu and eight other survivors from the fifth and fourth floors of the Vargulleion. And, on reflection, he stopped by Morlock's cave before he left and had Morlock's remaining apprentice, a reedy little citizen with a big nose, get him two of those nightmarish glass spears with a silver core in the head.

He disliked even the feeling of being around them, and when he rejoined his fighters he knew that they felt the same way; their faces fell and they started to twitch. So he explained to them about the spears. His thinking was: werebears don't like wounds from silver any better than werewolves do. His fighters agreed, but they still weren't enthusiastic.

To placate his fighters, Rokhlenu stopped by Ruiulanhro's poison shop and picked up some spearheads imbued with wolfbane. That cheered them up a little: citizens didn't get to use poison weapons very often, but in their former lives as criminals many irredeemables had been fond of them.

It was well after dark before they got anywhere near the Neyuwuleiuun's northern colony, and that was intentional on Rokhlenu's part. He wanted half his crew to wear the night shape, the better to sense danger, half of them to retain the day shape, so that they could use weapons. But as it turned out, only Rokhlenu himself and ape-fingered Runhuiulanhu had practiced the discipline of resisting the call of the night shape. Rokhlenu wasn't happy about it, but it was his own fault: he had picked the crew. He and Runhuiulanhu divided the weapons between them, abandoning what they could not carry.

They ran onward, past the western shoulder of Mount Dhaarnaiarnon. The great moon-clock in its face seemed almost to be watching them, but Rokhlenu dismissed the idea impatiently as it occurred to him.

It looked almost as if the plains north of Dhaarnaiarnon's foothills were on fire. There was a sullen brooding redness there that shifted and shifted—not quickly enough for fire, not steady enough.

Rokhlenu almost turned back, then. There was something odd about this. The air around them was furnace hot. No one would have reported this as an attack of werebears. It was beginning to look like a trap. Certainly he wanted to go back and have a long conversation with his fellow member of the Innermost Pack, the scent-addicted Naaleiyaleiu.

In the end he decided to go onward. This, whatever it was, might have something to do with the freakish weather bedeviling the city. It might be a cause of the weather; it might be an effect. But this near to the city, it certainly represented a danger. He was now the First Singer of Wuruyaaria. He led his fighters on.

Rather than head straight onto the plain where the red shifting mystery lay, he climbed the last foothill to the north to reconnoiter. His fighters followed him up.

From the ridge at the top of the hill he looked down on the plain and the monstrous thing it contained.

It was like a bug, he decided—a helgrammite or many-legger, grown to incredible length. It sprawled from east to west without any obvious ending. It was coal black in color, but around the edges of its carapace it glowed with sullen red light.

Perhaps it was more like a plant than an insect. It seemed to be sinking roots deep into the ground, all along its length that he could see. And it had more than one branch.

"Chieftain," said Runhuiulanhu urgently, gesturing behind them. "Look!"

Rokhlenu looked and disliked what he saw. Two branches of the thing, whatever it was, were closing around the hill they stood on.

"Who's fastest?" he snapped. "Lekkativengu and who else?"

"Taakhyteiu," said Runhuiulanhu, and there was general agreement.

"Lekkativengu. Taakhyteiu. As soon as I'm done talking, you get out of here. Get back and tell Wuinlendhono and Yaarirruuiu what you saw here—and *no one else*. Go."

The two werewolves fled down the southern slope toward the closing gap.

"You three: go with Runhuiulanhu. You three: come with me. Runhuiulanhu: each of us will take one branch. If it's a beast, we can fight it. If we can't kill it, we can at least keep it from killing our messengers. If we survive, so much the better. Get me?"

"Got you, Chief." Runhuiulanhu and his crew ran down to attack the branch curling around the hill from the west. Rokhlenu and his crew took the eastern branch.

Two of Rokhlenu's werewolves jumped straight at the nearest point of the eastern branch with reckless courage, one at a rootlike leg, the other at a lateral plate. They didn't seem to slow its progress at all, but they hung on for a moment or two, screaming. Then Trumpeter's dim moonlight could not heal them anymore and they burst into flame and died.

"God bite this damned thing!" Rokhlenu swore. He could hardly bear to close with it, the heat was so fierce; the boiling glass in Morlock's cave was nothing compared to it. He seized a poison-tipped spear and darted in close, slashing at one of the rootlike legs. A blue glowing mist emerged: what the beast used for blood, he supposed. Immediately rootlike tendrils reached out toward the blue glowing scar: to heal it, he guessed. He darted back in to widen the wound. The spear shattered in his hands, scattering red shards of molten metal. He jumped back, burned and cut by the hot metal, poisoned by its venom. He could feel it spreading in his veins from the wound.

He glanced over to see his last remaining comrade had been pierced through the eye by a metal fragment. He was as dead as if he had been stabbed with silver.

Silver. Rokhlenu remembered the dreadful weapon he carried. He drew it from the shoulder sling and stabbed the beast with it in the side, stabbing fiercely but without hope. He hated the thing, and he hated silver, and he wanted to use one hate to hurt the other.

And it did. The silver-cored glass spear shattered from the heat of the beast, but his slashing desperate cut opened up a long blue wound in the beast's side.

Nor was that all. Again, rootlike tendrils reached toward the wound. But so did several legs. They sank deep into the beast's own side. It was not trying to heal itself. Somehow, it was feeding on itself—struggling to consume the blue glowing fog that lay within itself. And he had slowed its progress, as it turned on itself.

Turned on itself. That was it. He could not defeat the thing, but it could and would defeat itself, if it could be wounded deeply enough.

He wondered if the messengers had gotten away. He looked up to see Lekkativengu standing alone and indecisive in the red-tinged moonlight—but beyond the closing ring of the beast's branches.

"Get out!" he screamed. "Get back! Runhuiulanhu, use the silver spear! Then get away!"

He did not see Runhuiulanhu, and wasn't even sure he was still alive. But Rokhlenu realized that he himself was already dead. If he could give his fighters a chance to get away, he owed them that.

He raised his hands toward dim uncaring Trumpeter and summoned the night shape upon himself.

When he arose as a wolf, shaking off his harness and tunic, time had passed. The narrow blue wound he had opened in the beast was nearly blocked by the beast's own hungry tentacles.

Rokhlenu leapt at the furnace-hot blast of the beast . . . and found the blue fog seeping from the beast was strangely cool. He planted his teeth on one of the ragged edges of the wound and pulled with all his strength. If he could kill it, or lure it into killing itself, his death might not be for nothing. It might save his beloved from dying the same way.

That was his last thought. There were no others. In a way, there never had been, none that mattered.

Chapter Thirty

Makers Meet

Morlock fell into the pit, and shadows spun around him as he fell. He thought at first they were birds, but when one passed without pain through his ghostly hand he realized they were impulse clouds.

Conditions were hostile in the extreme, and he had, perhaps, moments before his fall killed him. But he forced his mind into the discipline of vision. The world of matter fell away, and he was surrounded by clouds of intention and desire, bereft of any will to wield them.

Morlock wielded them. He wrapped the impulse clouds around him like a cloak, slowing his fall.

Time and the perception of time are altered in the experience of visionary rapture. Morlock had no idea how long he fell. He simply became aware, at some point, that he had struck the ground with some force. Not enough to kill him, he guessed, since his awareness was still anchored by his body.

With his Sight in its current decrepit state, it was even harder for him to dismiss a vision than to summon one. Slowly, deliberately, he rewove the ragged threads of his conscious awareness. As he became more and more aware of physical pain, he knew he was getting closer to escape from the vision that had saved his life.

He finally opened his eyes. The world was coal black, edged with burning red. Even without being in rapture, he could feel the swarms of impulse clouds surrounding him. If they had been water, he would have been drowning in them.

He sat up slowly. His body ached a bit, but all the parts that were still there still worked. Tyrfing was still strapped to his shoulder. If someone had tried to kill him, they had failed. He took his time about getting to his feet: there was no hurry, since no one seemed to be trying to kill him at the moment.

The light was dim and bloodred, coming from a distant source that (Morlock thought) was toward the east. Morlock had spent much of his life underground, and he thought he knew what the light was from. He reached into a pocket of his cloak and drew out a cold-light, tapping one end gently on the pommel of his sword to activate it. By its cold moonlike rays, Morlock picked his way through the field of boulders he found himself among, trending westward—at any rate, away from the fiery light.

He spent a long time stumbling about in the great chamber he found himself in at the base of the volcano. He did not find any vents or air currents that suggested to him a way out. He did form the tentative conclusion that the floor of the cavern, despite its unfinished appearance, was artificial, perhaps the roof to a cavern still further below. And he definitely discovered that it was littered with corpses. Some were relatively fresh; some skeletal; some mummified; several had turned to stone.

This was all very bad, Morlock thought. If he was going to a dangerous confrontation, he preferred to have a line of retreat ready. Still, there was at least one other possibility open.

Light footfalls approached him, over and among the boulders and littered corpses. He felt an incongruous lightness of spirit hearing these sounds: it had been centuries since he had heard their like. But they did indicate the presence of danger, so he hid the cold-light under his cloak.

The footfalls fell silent. Then Morlock heard them again: moving away this time, hesitantly at first, then with more confidence and speed. Morlock didn't try to keep up, knowing that was impossible, but did struggle to keep within earshot.

Presently they came closer to the source of the red light, and Morlock caught glimpses of his quarry against it. It was a tall beast, with shoulders about as high as Morlock's, with goatlike legs and body. It was most dangerous, of course, because of the long tapered horn that sprouted from its forehead.

The source of the fiery light was a river of molten stone. They were fairly close to it now, enough so that Morlock felt uncomfortably warm.

The unicorn began to wander aimlessly up and down the banks of the burning river. Morlock peered out from behind a boulder. There was a bridge, glittering white in its own light, that passed over the river. The unicorn was pacing up and down in front of the bridge, guarding it. The beast was bloodred, but for its black wisping beard and black-slotted eyes, but apart from that it resembled the Swift People Morlock had known (mostly from a distance) in the mountains of his youth.

It was Ulugarriu's doorkeeper, Morlock guessed, to keep out any unwanted visitor who made his way down here.

The unicorn stepped lightly over to the bank of the river and lowered its head to drink from the molten stone.

Morlock thought this a good time to try the bridge. He left his boulder behind and stealthily made his way toward the bridgehead.

Not stealthily enough, though. The unicorn lifted its head and swung about on guard. Fire dripped from its black beard; the black slots in its red-on-red eyes fixed on Morlock; its red spiraling horn was aimed directly at his chest.

It did not charge. When Morlock moved to one side, it moved to keep its horn pointed at Morlock. When he took a step forward, it took a step forward. When he stepped back, it did nothing.

Morlock was puzzled. Before, when he was so far distant from the bridge that he couldn't see it, the unicorn had seen him or sensed him and moved to attack. Now that he was actually near the bridge the unicorn guarded, its behavior was merely defensive. It would not let him pass, but it did not attack.

Then he realized: it was the cold-light, of course. He pulled it out from under his cloak—and was nearly stabbed through the heart by the unicorn, bearing down on him, glaring with silent rage. Morlock swiftly hid the light again. The unicorn stopped in its tracks. Its equine nostrils trembled with frustration or fury. It backed away slowly, staring at Morlock, waiting to see what he would do.

Morlock waited until it had backed up to the bridgehead and stopped. He stared off idly into space for a time. Then he spun about, snatched the cold-light from his cloak, and threw it as far as he could away from the river.

The red unicorn charged past him, furiously intent on the inimical light.

Morlock ran like a thief to the bridgehead, then up on the arching white bridge. The cool glowing light protected him from the killing heat of the river, as he had hoped.

Beyond the red river were dark grassy fields scattered with pale flowers like asphodels. Morlock moved cautiously here; the light was dim, and there were shapes moving about.

When he was well into the dark fields, he approached one of the people wandering there. It was a citizen wearing the day shape; his face was oddly familiar, but Morlock was not sure in that dim light if he knew him.

The citizen did not seem to see him at all. He turned and walked off, his indifferent face dimly lit by the distant bridge and river.

Morlock walked on. The shadowy figures paid attention neither to him nor to each other. At times they bent down on their hands and knees and grazed like cattle on the faintly glowing asphodels. Morlock detoured around one of these. Glancing down as he passed, he recognized the pale mottled face. It was Hrutnefdhu.

"Old friend," Morlock whispered. "You are alive. You are alive after all."

But he could not believe it as he said it. Hrutnefdhu's empty eyes looked at nothing in particular as he chewed his cud of flowers.

Morlock turned away. But now he had a reason to look at every passing shadowy face.

He found her by the banks of a narrow stream, near the end of the asphodel fields. Her cupped hands were full of water, and she was lapping delicately at it with her tongue.

He knelt on one knee and touched her russet hair with his right hand. "Liudhleeo," he whispered. The name meant *She-who-remembers-best* in the werewolf languages. He asked her desperately, "Liudhleeo. Liudhleeo. Don't you remember me? Don't you remember the city, the world above—the sun, the moons, the stars?"

Liudhleeo continued to drink as if he were not there. When the water was gone, she opened her hands and stood. She walked away, her lips wet and motionless, without ever having looked at him.

He stayed kneeling there beside the stream for a long time, his head bowed. Finally he said to himself, "If this is life, it seems worse than death."

He stood and stepped forward into the stream. About midway across, he began to feel that he should really go back—that he must, in fact, go back. The water was up to his knees by then. He ignored the impulse and strode forward; the odd feeling faded, disappeared entirely as he stepped out of the water on the other side.

He squelched over the shoulder of the hill that faced him on the other side.

Beyond the hill was a sort of house. The walls were like slabs of brownish ivory bone; there were no doors, exactly, but there were gaps in between the bones. The roof was a kind of canopy of glowing moss.

He walked up to the house and hesitated before it. A voice called out to him from one of the gaps, "Well, you made it this far, damn you. You might as well come in."

The voice was oddly pitched, not exactly a male's or a female's.

Morlock stepped through the gap and found himself in the familiar confines of a maker's workshop. The making was different than any art he normally practiced, but he could not mistake the lighting, the long tables, the racks of tools, the posture of the citizen who was bending over some sort of bowl, incising its broad rim with Sunspeech ideograms.

"Give me a moment, old friend," called Ulugarriu. "The image in this bowl of dreams simply won't come clear, and it will be rather important to our conversation. That is, if you don't intend to simply strike me dead."

Morlock walked closer. He eyed the long lean build of the maker, as much as could be seen in the folds of the long silk gown. He examined the russet hair, the pale mottled features, the dark eyes. Ulugarriu was conscious of his inspection and seemed to enjoy it. The werewolf maker finished the task at hand, gave a satisfied look into the bowl of dreams, and turned to face Morlock.

"I can't tell," Morlock admitted at last. "Which one are you? Are you Hrutnefdhu, or Liudhleeo?"

"I'm both, of course, and others besides."

"God Avenger."

"Please don't talk in that filthy way. I know you don't mean any offense, but still. Foul language upsets me a little."

Morlock shook his head, dismissing the issue. "Both is neither," he said.

"I don't see why. I was really there, you know—all the time."

"Through your meat-puppets. Is that what those things on the field are?"

"In a manner of speaking. The real meat-puppets, as you call them so gracelessly, are the things I make for the were-rats."

"Good of you."

"Were-rats are people, too, and they are often helpful for my purposes, which is more than I can say for some. But the bodies on the asphodel fields I grew from seeds of my own flesh. I let them wander the asphodel fields when I'm not using them, because it's better for them; meat-puppets I keep in vats sealed with gel until they're needed. They're not me. But the simulacra really are me, extensions of myself, and I can direct my intentions through them. And that is how I usually operate: the way we spoke on the airships. It's been ages since my body here has felt the light of the moon or the sun."

"Meat-puppets."

"Shh. You don't really understand yet, Morlock. I was afraid to appear before you through a mere simulacrum—I was afraid your Sight would sense my absence and the game would be over. I don't have much in the way of Sight myself, and I don't fully understand it. In extreme cases, I can have my skull and heart transferred to a simulacrum, and that is how you knew me, as both Liudhleeo and Hrutnefdhu. That was the reason for Liudhleeo's late-night excursions and Hrutnefdhu's habit of early rising—so that I would not have to operate one simulacrum by remote while inhabiting the other. I was afraid your Sight would catch me at it. But if one or both were sleeping, you would not expect them to be fully present."

Morlock closed his eyes, remembering. How often had he seen his two friends together, and awake? Not often, if ever. "God Sustainer. How blind I was."

"Please: I asked you already about the language. And it's not your fault about not seeing. One of my best magics is a kind of indirection, and I deploy it constantly when I'm, you know, up there. It has been very useful in my conflict with, well, certain enemies I shall tell you of."

"You mean the Strange Gods, I suppose."

Ulugarriu's dark eyes glared at him. "God. God damn it. Do you already know every God-bitten thing I was going to tell you? If I'm not a God's brach-bastard of a bastard's brach! God! God! God!"

Morlock disliked to see Ulugarriu upset, probably because he was reminded so much of his two lost friends. He reached out and put his hand on the hysterical werewolf's shoulder.

This calmed Ulugarriu down. "I'm sorry. I'm so sorry. I just had a series of surprises planned, leading to a conversational coup of some importance, and you've screwed my plans already. Well, what else is new? May I ask how you know about the Strange Gods? Have you seen them?"

"At least two. I saw Death in the Bitter Water early last year, and War in the jail in Wuruyaaria on the day of my execution."

"Oh yes. You killed Wurnafenglu, didn't you? Wish I'd seen that with my own eyes. I hated that evil son-of-a-brach-and-her-bastard."

"Who didn't?"

"He didn't, but he was about it. War and Death, you say? Not Wisdom?"

"Just War and Death. Why?"

"I'm working on a theory about Wisdom, that's all. He ceased appearing in my visualizations some time ago. I think Death may have killed him, which would be very interesting indeed. Do you know anything about their plans for the city?"

"They both said something, but I didn't pay any attention."

"Now that was a mistake, my friend. War is a liar, it's true, and proud of it, which is worse, but on the rare occasions Death speaks it's wise to listen. Even her lies can be revealing, because she's so bad at it."

"I didn't pay any attention because I don't care. If Wuruyaaria is wiped off the map it's nothing to me."

"But . . . but . . . your friends live there!"

Morlock met the other maker's eyes. "Not so many as before. And the others can live somewhere else, if need be."

"I knew I should have killed you. I should have outright killed you when

I had the chance. You don't care about anyone but yourself. Oh, *shut up, Ulugarriu, shut up*."

The werewolf maker looked away from Morlock for a time. Eventually Ulugarriu said in a subdued voice, "I know that's not true. I should know. On that night, on New Year's Night, I really thought I was going to die in that stupid corridor. After all my long life, and all the things I'd done, and all the things I still might do, to die that stupid way, because I couldn't nerve myself to run away in front of you and poor Rokhlenu. And you saved me. And I . . . I . . . I loved you for that. For other things, too. But to you. To you it was like nothing. It was just a thing that you did, like eating or breathing or cutting your fingernails. On the rare occasions you bother to groom yourself, you ragged bastard."

Morlock found that the enemy he had come to kill was embracing him and sobbing. Ulugarriu's head was pressed against his head as if listening to his heart. Liudhleeo had sometimes done the same. He stood there and waited for the other maker to calm down.

"You really don't know what's going on, do you?" Ulugarriu asked. "Or is it that you don't care? Why don't you ask? Why don't you ask? Don't you care? I know you don't care."

"Ask what?"

"Whether I am male or female."

"Then. Are you male or female?"

"Neither." Ulugarriu looked up into his face and hissed the words. "That's what you'd say. Because *both* is *neither*."

"Eh."

Ulugarriu leapt back and laughed bitterly. "Oh, I was wondering where we'd hear that one! Concise, but meaningless, the inarticulate maker's all-purpose reply! Stock up now, folks, supplies are limited! Brilliant! Brilliant!"

He looked at Ulugarriu and shrugged.

"Oh, god. Oh, ghost. Never mind. Yes, my old friend, I was born with both male and female genitalia. But don't worry. My parents followed the traditional practice of giving me before puberty to the ghost-sniffer, who applied the traditional remedy of castrating me with a silver knife and searing the wound with poison. This will normally kill the child, solving the problem for everyone, don't you see, but I was always an inconsiderate brach and I lived. I was afterward some use to the ghost-sniffer, as acolyte and as sexual object, but only when he was too smoke-drunk not to find me disgusting."

Ulugarriu was silent for a time and then said, "I killed them all, of course, in time. My parents, the ghost-sniffer, the females who held me down while he cut me, everyone who watched and laughed and gave helpful advice. They are all dead, and the only reason I regret it is because I can't kill them again and again."

Morlock nodded grimly.

"Oh," said Ulugarriu, "you don't really mean that. What you want to say is—"

"I say what I want to say," Morlock interrupted. "What I do not say, I don't want anyone to say for me, particularly when they will blame me for it. You say you are my friends, Hrutnefdhu and Liudhleeo. Would they oblige me in this?"

"Liudhleeo would oblige you in any way at all," said Ulugarriu, "as you know. I am sorry, though. This is how I live, you see: through many masks and under many names. I have not spoken to someone openly, as myself, in oh so long. Except for the Strange Gods, and only then when I couldn't avoid it."

Ulugarriu put a long pale hand over a red mouth and laughed silently. "But it's so funny. You still don't know whether to kiss me or kill me, whether to call me he or she. There's no word for what I am, because all of you pretend I don't exist, that people like me don't exist."

"I would refer to you as 'they,' if I were talking to someone else about you."

"What? Why?"

"That's what we do in the Wardlands when someone has more than one sex."

Ulugarriu looked at him through narrowed eyes. "Yurr. They. They. I think I like that." Ulugarriu pressed their hands on their temples. "There are so many people in here. And, oh honey, they cause me a lot of trouble sometimes. Excuse me."

Ulugarriu fled up the long room and out a side doorway, leaving Morlock alone in the workshop. When they did not soon return, Morlock found a stool and sat down on it. Soon he was laying his head down on a nearby table, and very soon he was asleep.

He woke on a couch that smelled intensely of cloves and faintly of more intimate scents. He had no clear memory of how he had gotten there, or of the recent past. "Liudhleeo," he said sleepily.

"I am here," Ulugarriu said.

Memory stabbed through him. He sat up, propping himself on his good arm.

Ulugarriu was sitting next to him on the couch (clearly, their own couch). They held a wooden bowl out to him. "I don't suppose you've eaten much, lately."

"I'm never hungry," Morlock admitted. "I eat because I know it's time."

"And down here you never know what time it is. That's one reason I like it. It's also one reason I hate it." Morlock sat straight up, and they handed him the bowl.

"I thought about killing you while you slept," Ulugarriu said. "It would solve a lot of problems."

"I'll be dead soon anyway. That should solve those problems."

"And you don't care."

"Everyone has to die sometime."

"I don't. I mean, apparently, I don't."

Morlock ate the porridge and waited for them to go on.

"I think I'm about six thousand years old," Ulugarriu said. "I'm not sure, because every so often I go to sleep. And I sleep for a long time, and when I get up I'm a little younger than when I lay down. I age very slowly, so it seems to average out."

Morlock nodded. "Then the city is your child."

Ulugarriu winced. "Yes. Yes, I suppose so. I was never able to have children, thank you so much for reminding me. And, oh I don't know. After everyone I had ever known had died, I got sort of bored and I started trying different things. It was interesting. When I wasn't working on the crafts of lifemaking, I sort of did things with the city as a hobby. And the two pursuits merged, until the city became my greatest act of making."

"You didn't make the mechanisms—the moon-clock, and the funicular, and so on."

"No—nor the excellent sewer system. Different citizens came up with these ideas over the years, and I filed them away and eventually arranged for them to be implemented."

"What happened to the citizens who came up with the ideas?"

"They would be dead by now anyway, Khretvarrgliu. I couldn't have people just randomly setting up lyceums of machine making and other ugly crafts. The city is mine, my long life's work. Do you understand?"

"Yes. But I don't agree. A city belongs to those who live there. And they belong to themselves."

"Do it for them, then. Not for me, but for them."

"Do what?"

"Help me fight the Strange Gods. Oh, they're not invulnerable; don't let them fool you. They hate Wuruyaaria because they need the Well of Shadows, and the city feeds on it."

"Feeds on it? How?"

"Why do you think there are so many werewolves around here? They've been imbued with, what is it you call them, impulse clouds from the Well of Shadows. The Stone Tree was created to gather them and concentrate them in the Well. But since the growth of the city, well, there has been less to go around."

"And the gods need them."

"The Strange Gods do. They were once men and women, like you and your people. Long ago, they found a way to ascend to godhood, identifying their selves with abstract elements of human nature. Each one sacrificed himself—or herself—on the Apotheosis Wheel to a specific deity. And they became that deity. They have the powers that go with their spheres: Love or Cruelty or War or Death. But they need to be refreshed by shadows—by impulse clouds, as you say—to sustain the identification. Without that, their powers fade. They may even die. Wouldn't that be wonderful?"

Morlock was dying himself, and did not feel any measure of the other's enthusiasm. He shrugged and handed them the bowl. "Thanks for the porridge."

"And now you'll be going?" Ulugarriu scowled at him. "You came here to kill me because I killed your friends. That robbed you of your purpose. I can give you another purpose. Will you hear me out?"

"I've been hearing you. I am done with purposes. I am nearly done with everything, I think."

"Listen. Just listen. If you're dying, what's your hurry? You might as well die here with me. I doubt anyone in the world loves you as well as I do, and I'll feel that way even if I have to put the knife in you myself."

"Eh."

"Please, please don't say that. I never know what you mean by it. Never mind. Come and look at something with me."

Ulugarriu stood, and he followed them out of the dimly lit sleeping chamber back into the bright workroom.

At one end of the room was a kind of bottle, about the size of a woman or a man. Both ends were twisted together. To Morlock's practiced eye the bottle looked as if it was made with glass interwoven with sunlight. He sensed a talic pressure also, even without summoning the rapture of vision.

Inside the bottle was a figure, misty and indefinite in form. Sometimes it looked like a woman, sometimes like a sword, sometimes like nothing Morlock could recognize.

"You see," Ulugarriu said proudly. "I captured one. The one they call Justice. The power of justice is anywhere that people behave justly—which is why this is one of the weaker gods, I guess. But the Strange God named Justice has to manifest herself in a particular locus of space-time. They can be trapped by a crafty hunter with the right materials."

"What is this made of?"

"Light. Glass. And heretical opinions: the Strange Gods are entities of the human domain, so human action can influence them."

Morlock looked at Justice writhing, trapped behind glass.

He reached for his sword, but it was not on his back, of course. No matter: he could feel its nearness. He called out, "Tyrfing!" and held up his right hand. The sword flew glittering to his hand.

"Are you going to kill her?" Ulugarriu cried, surprised and delighted. "Khretvarrgliu, my stalwart. I knew you—Do it. Kill her. I've learned as much as I can from her. Then we can fight the rest of them together. Eh? Oh, say 'Eh' to me for once in your life."

Morlock, ignoring them, summoned the lowest level of vision. In the talic world, uniting spirit with matter, he was a pillar of black-and-white flames, and Tyrfing his focus of power showed the same talic pattern. Ulugarriu, in contrast, was a cloud of chaotic lights. Justice in her prison became more vivid and terrible, displaying the colors of a dying god. Her chains were the exact color of a thousand screaming voices.

Morlock swung the blade; it shattered the chains and the prison of glass and light.

Justice rose towering over them. One of her hands was gray, lacking talic force. Tyrfing had passed through it, and it seemed to have affected her somehow for the worse.

Morlock expressed regret: he had not meant to harm her.

Without answering, she moved to exact justice from her jailor.

Morlock stepped between the alien god and his enemy. He raised his sword, willing to do damage if Ulugarriu was harmed.

Justice, baffled, ceased to manifest herself. When Morlock was sure of this, he lowered his sword and dismissed his vision.

"—ghost-bitten god-licking brach-up of a bastard!" Ulugarriu was shrieking.

Morlock leaned on his sword like a staff. The effort had cost him much, too much. He felt his tunic settling from his left shoulder down to his side. His shoulder had become too insubstantial to hold the fabric up. And the area around his heart was numb, set for dissolution. In another day he would be dead, or a living ghost.

He snarled wordlessly at Ulugarriu, who seemed taken aback.

"At times I forget you're not a werewolf," they said. "But that's because you're so much like a werewolf."

He turned to leave.

"Wait!" Ulugarriu said. "Look at the visualization I've been simmering in my bowl of dreams. This will matter to you. I promise you it will."

They led him down the long workroom to the broad-rimmed bowl of dreams, in its own wooden stand near the door where Morlock had first entered.

"Look!"

Morlock looked. He saw the insectlike instrument of the Strange Gods, sprawling across the northern plain. It was black lined with red fire. The land beyond it was brown and dead.

"What does it do?" Morlock asked.

"Ah! You are interested! I call it the Ice-Binder. It seems to eat cold."

"Eh."

"Oh, ghost. Not that again."

"Cold is merely the absence of heat."

"That's what I used to think, and I still think it. But apparently, heat can also be treated as the absence of cold."

"Hm."

"How I shall miss your lively conversation when you're gone!"

Morlock knew that two contradictory scholia might sometimes be used to explain and account for the same phenomena, and he even knew some math to describe such situations, but he was not interested in augmenting Ulugarriu's already considerable powers, so he said nothing.

"So this thing will gradually make this area unlivable, is that it?"

"Yes, except for the gradually part. I've been holding it off for years—using various dodges. It acts like it's alive, but it doesn't really seem to be. It certainly doesn't think. So I've used phantom cold waves and other tricks to slow its progress. But now it's about to sweep over the city."

"How are we seeing this? This is not a vision."

"You don't tell, but you ask, ask, ask. All right; I don't mind. The Strange Gods don't have anything like your Sight, either, but they do have what they call visualization. They gather information throughout their sphere and use it to create understanding of things as they are, or were, or will be. Their minds are not limited by physical constraints; they can use the whole world to think in, or remember. I can't, but I found that I can gather information through mantic spells to create images of things-as-they-may-be."

"May be? Sounds uncertain."

"That's what you get when you look at anything, youngster: something that *may be* there."

Morlock tapped the rim of the bowl of dreams, sending ripples through the visualization. "This, itself, is interesting. But I still don't care what happens to Wuruyaaria."

"No? Look there! A band of warriors, led by the new First Singer, has come north to investigate the Ice-Binder. They're trapped on the hill there. They're fighting so that some of them can get out."

Morlock didn't even glance at the image. "They will die, or live. It makes no difference to me."

"No?" Ulugarriu's russet eyebrows lifted in wonder. "Well, I made a promise to you earlier. I'm not withdrawing it—*what was that?*"

"You tell me."

"They made some sort of hole in the Ice-Binder. Not enough to do any lasting harm, and now they're dead, as you say, but it's more than I've been able to do. If we could find out what they used—"

"I am dying, Ulugarriu. Even if I wanted to help you, I would be of no help to you."

"Yes, but you need not die. I could—we could. That would be the first matter of business, you see. I would take your word you would help me. Then I, of course, could help you."

"You can cure the ghost sickness."

"Well. In a word. Yes."

"Because you caused it."

"Well, I. May have. Unintentionally."

"What were your intentions?"

"To make you more pliable, of course. That was the whole purpose in getting you into the Vargulleion. That fathead Wurnafenglu said he could break anybody. But you wouldn't be broken. You wouldn't cooperate in any way. I admired you for that, still do, but it was inconvenient. The Strange Gods had sent you north on some mission that was disrupting all visualizations—even they were complaining about it, if you can believe it, self-centered brachs. I thought if I could get you working for me, you know, things might be fine after all."

"You planted that spike in my head. And it was *meant* to do this. To do *this* to me." He waved his ghostly hand in Ulugarriu's alarmed face.

"No! Really, I mean that. The spike was just a precautionary measure. I had no idea it would be in that long, or that it would make you suffer so. I was glad to take it out, so glad. But I couldn't have you—have you. Sort of running around with your full Sight, seeing through things and me and things. I just couldn't. So after I took the spike out I. Well, I did something else, didn't I? I let you have some of your Sight, and you weren't insane anymore, though you will never be what I would consider wholly sane either. The ghost. The ghost illness. Well, that wasn't meant to happen. I think I know why it's happening, and I can stop it. If you'll promise to help me."

"Would Hlupnafenglu have gone the same way?"

"No. He had another problem. He couldn't stand his memories of being the Red Shadow. When I met him in Apetown he was going to kill himself. I experimented on him with the electrum spike. It did make him pliable and freed him from the burden of memories."

"And made him an idiot."

"A cheerful idiot is not to be despised, not by creatures like us, my friend. It was you who gave him his memories back. Without those, he might have been happy."

"Did you kill him?"

"He killed himself."

"That was how you made it look. You killed him."

"I'll swear to you on binding oaths, I did not kill him. As Liudhleeo, I persuaded him to leave me alone for a time, and then I planted the headless Liudhleeo-simulacrum, stole Tyrfing, and fled. He must have killed himself after he found the body. He bore a heavy burden of guilt, you know."

"No," Morlock said bitterly. "No, I didn't know."

He turned away.

Ulugarriu sighed. "Wait," they said to his back. "Ambrosius, listen. The way down to the underworld is easy. The dark door lies open night and day. But to retrace your steps and escape again to the upper air—for that you'll work. For that you'll suffer."

"Drop dead."

"You're nearer that than I am, old friend."

Morlock did not answer. His cloak and other gear were on the stool where he had first sat down to rest. He donned them, sheathed his sword, and walked out of Ulugarriu's house.

He passed swiftly through the asphodel fields, lest Ulugarriu try to talk to him through any of those masks, and was nearly running by the time he reached the shining bridge over the river of fire.

On the far side, the red unicorn had resumed its place at the bridgehead. Now it was pawing at something on the ground. Morlock could hardly see it in the glare from the bridge's light, but as he came closer he thought it was the dark splintered remains of the cold-light he had thrown away earlier.

He felt through the pockets in his cloak and shirt to see how many cold-lights he had left. The unicorn looked up and saw him on the bridge. It casually moved aside to let him pass: apparently it only guarded against people trying to enter—if, in fact, that was what it had been doing before. Perhaps it had only wanted to destroy the hated light, and now it had.

Morlock sidled past the uninterested unicorn. He had a thought on how to get that horn.

Morlock found an upright stone a little under his height. He draped his cloak over the stone. Standing behind the stone and resting his head atop it, he inched his arm under the cloak and pulled a cold-light from one of its pockets. Holding it behind the cloak, he tapped it lightly against the stone to activate it.

At the sound, faint even to Morlock, the red unicorn became completely alert. It stared straight at Morlock with its slotted red eyes.

Morlock shifted his stance a little and pushed the light out from beyond the cloak.

The unicorn lowered its horn and charged, in a single silken motion. Through each odd writhing gallop, neither like a horse nor a goat, the long spiraling horn was aimed straight at the same point; it never wavered.

The impact of the unicorn shook the stone. The horn was buried deep in the rock, about where Morlock's heart would be, if the stone had been his torso.

And it was stuck. The unicorn planted its delicate cloven hooves and pushed against the rocky ground, but it could get very little purchase.

Morlock pocketed the cold-light as the unicorn watched him with frenzied gaping red eyes. He drew Tyrfing from the baldric over his decaying shoulder.

"I'm sorry, Swift One," Morlock said. "Need drives me." He struck at the base of the horn and cut it cleanly through, about a thumb's width above the brow.

The docked unicorn leapt back and stared bemusedly at Morlock. It looked at the stump of its horn sticking out of the stone and stepped back farther.

"I hope it will grow back," said Morlock, not supposing the unicorn understood him, or would care if it could. Resting Tyrfing against the stone's side, he drew the cold-light and tossed it as far and as fast as he could.

The unhorned unicorn followed the arc of the light with delighted angry eyes and immediately ran after it. Morlock had actually thrown it harder than he intended: the cold-light landed in the river of molten stone. The unicorn dove in after it and disappeared from sight. Presently it appeared again, spraying fire from its nose and mouth. When Morlock turned away, it was still diving about like a porpoise in the fiery river.

Morlock picked up Tyrfing and began to hew away at the top of the stone. If he could have used two hands, he would have. But eventually he had split the top of the stone and was holding the red horn of the unicorn in his hand. He tucked it away in his cloak and walked away from the river of fire.

He came to the place where he felt the impulse clouds swirling through the air like leaves in autumn. He lay down among the stones and the corpses and, holding tightly to Tyrfing as his focus, summoned the rapture of vision.

It did not come easily, but he was in no hurry this time. He focused and unfocused. He thought and he dreamed. He unwove his consciousness and in its place spun a vision as deep as his wounded powers could permit.

When he was deep in rapture, he began to draw impulse clouds to him. They flocked to him like birds to scattered grain, eager to be directed by a living will. When he was densely cocooned with the shadowy clouds, he directed them to lift him upward.

As he rose through the cone of the dead volcano, he saw much with his inward eye that had been hidden before. He saw a network of underground channels like dark rivers, leeching impulse clouds from the Well of Shadows. He saw the unlife of the fiery beast to the north and the thousand winters it carried in its cold veins. He saw the colonies of were-rats up and down the slopes of Mount Dhaarnaiarnon. More were dead than alive: the cruel weather had been deadly for them, too.

The impulse clouds lifted him above the lip of the crater. It was night, and they began to disappear in the open air; they could not carry him much farther. He unbound them from his will and let them dissipate in the faint misty starlight.

He knew, rather than felt, that his body slid down the side of the volcano for a while until it came up against a tumble of stones. Carefully, as deliberately as he could, he rewove his conscious connection with his dying flesh. It took a long time, and he didn't have much time, but he was strangely unconcerned.

He had come looking for knowledge and for vengeance. He was leaving with knowledge and guilt—and a unicorn's horn. That added up to something very like hope.

Chapter Thirty-one

Plans and Devices

Morlock made his way back to his cave past the necropolis covering the eastern face of the city. No moon was aloft, but there were faint lights moving among the tombs, no doubt from citizens who had taken refuge in the graveyard, or were robbing the graves for meat. The slopes of the city were outlined in fire. Morlock wondered if the city was on fire. But he was not especially concerned: his friends would be safe enough in the outlier settlement. As he climbed the ridge above the silver-waste fields, he saw that at least two mesas of the city were stained with fire—Iuiunioklendon and Nekkuklendon. The outlier settlement, in contrast, was unusually dark and quiet—there were usually some citizens abroad during the night, but tonight it seemed almost funereal. Perhaps they were helping fight fires in the city.

He was deeply weary when he reached his cave, but he set immediately to his task. He could not afford to rest; he might wake up dead, or unable to work. The fragmentary page he had purchased from Iacomes described a mirror made from a unicorn's horn, but not how to use it. He was fairly sure he could make the mirror, anyway.

He broke up the unicorn horn with Tyrfing and ground the shards to powder with a diamond mortar and pestle. The powder had a gritty sandlike quality, and he hoped to melt it like sand to make glass for the mirror. He eventually succeeded in doing so, though it took his entire choir of young flames working for hours in a reflective furnace. He poured the bloodred molten glass into a shallow mold, cooled it, polished it, and cut it into an octagon, to match the form sketched on his fragment.

He had intended to treat the back with quicksilver or some other reflective agent. But the glass, though thin, was opaque. Its redly opalescent surface was not especially reflective, even when polished.

He picked it up with his right hand and looked intently at the faint image of himself he saw on the surface. It seemed faint and ghostly.

On impulse, he tried to pick up the mirror with his left hand. The drifting mist that were the fingers of his left hand, unable to move anything more substantial than a leaf, closed on the red glass and easily hefted it in the palm of his left hand.

Fairly easily. It felt heavy—heavier than it should—heavier than a dead body. But he could hold it.

And the image of himself on the red surface suddenly became much clearer. It was indeed ghostly, a drifting mist in Morlock's image. But the gray eyes were luminously clear, even through the red glass, and his mirror-left hand and arm looked hale, unharmed.

The mirror-Morlock met his eye and said, "So it's come to this. *I* have to save *you*."

It occurred to Morlock that his reflection was drunk. His heart sank. He would have spoken, but he found he could not.

After brooding a while, the mirror-Morlock said resentfully, "You'd never do it, you know. If our positions were reversed. You hate me. You'd rather die than be yoked to me forever. Well, I hate you more. But I'm not an idealist, like you are. The only way I can go on living is if you do. So buy me a drink, sometime; we'll call it even."

The mirror-Morlock reached through the mirror with his misty right-reversed hand and past Morlock's eye, pushing the misty fingers deep into his skull. Morlock would have backed away or protected himself somehow, but he could not move: his free will seemed to have been wholly seized by the mirror-Morlock.

The mist-fingers moving through his brain were searing agony. But eventually he felt them close on something, an alien presence, like a splinter of glass or metal lodged in his mind. The fingers drew it forth. This, too, was agony, but also a relief, like a weapon being drawn from a wound. At last, healing could begin.

He briefly saw the dark splinter in the mirror-Morlock's misty hand before he passed out.

When he awoke, it was still night. Or perhaps, it was night again. His head was pounding like a drum; his throat was as an old shoe buried in the desert; he was hungry enough to eat a live stoat and too weak to chase one even if it were right in front of him.

But he didn't care about any of that. Because the wound in his spirit was gone; his arm and hand were whole again, and even without summoning the rapture of vision, he knew his Sight had been healed as well.

The red mirror lay shattered in his hand. He thought about what the mirror-Morlock had said. He wondered if this flaw, this division of himself into drunk and sober Morlocks, had been the entering point for Ulugarriu's hostile magic. It was worth considering.

He found some flatbread and a bottle of water in a breadlocker and ate and drank, exulting in the freedom to use his left hand. When his thirst was finally satiated, he grabbed the fragments of the red mirror and started to juggle them. When that no longer amused him, he threw glass daggers, left-handed only, at marks on the cave wall. He spent an hour or two writing in the palindromic script of ancient Ontil, which requires the left hand and the right hand to write simultaneously. In short, he engaged in a bacchanalia of sinister chirality.

He was still exulting in his regained hand and the hope for life that had returned with it when he looked up and saw that the sun had risen. He felt briefly ashamed that he had been wasting time so childishly.

"No, to hell with that," he said aloud, changing his mind. If self-hatred was the secret door by which this illness had entered him, he was going to lock that door—mortar it shut, if possible. "Look," he said, addressing his despised drunken self. "I'm not going to buy you a drink. But there must be something else I can do to amuse you. Let me know."

There was no response, but Morlock didn't really expect one; he was aware he was talking to himself, that there had never been more than one Morlock.

He packed a knapsack with flatbread, cheese, and bottles of water; he took a few glass knives and a glass sword from the weapon rack. He noticed someone had taken two of the silver-core glass spears. He wondered what they had been used for: Rokhlenu had been so set against them. Perhaps someone else had been less squeamish.

Everything else in the cave he left for Lakkasulakku. The young citizen was not much of a maker yet, but he was intelligent and quick-fingered and he knew some useful skills. Morlock thought he would do well.

Morlock had decided to leave Wuruyaaria. It was no place for him, if gods were clashing with immortal werewolves there and both had plans for him. It was no place for his friends, either: he was going to recommend to Rokhlenu and Wuinlendhono that they flee to the shores of the Bitter Water and wait for the Strange Gods' vendetta against the city to play out. That would be their choice; he had made his, and it was a great weight off his crooked shoulders.

He ran down the wooden steps to the wicker boat and poled himself across to the eastern gate of the outlier settlement. The gate was unguarded, which struck him as odd at first, but then he realized that the election must have passed and with it the time for open warfare between the packs.

He had not gone far into the settlement before he realized that something was wrong, though. There were no sounds of city life at all in the hot still air: not a single voice, or any footfall beyond his own. The settlement had been abandoned.

It was the same through the market and all the way to the First Wolf's lair-tower. Not only was the tower empty, it had been cleared of its contents. There was no destruction; it had not been looted. The tenant had decided to vacate.

As he was looking about the second floor, he did notice some citizens around the old headquarters of the irredeemables. He descended to the street and went over to investigate.

That, too, was almost empty. But Wuinlendhono was there, wearing dark clothes that must have been uncomfortable in the hot heavy air. There were a half dozen irredeemables present also; Wuinlendhono seemed to be giving them some sort of instructions when Morlock entered, and she, seeing him, broke off.

She was looking oddly at him. They all were, except Lekkativengu, who had turned his eyes away, his face dark with shame.

"Khretvarrgliu," Wuinlendhono said, "have you come for the funeral? It is over, I'm afraid."

Morlock assessed the mourning quality of her face and clothes, the sullen anger in Yaarirruuiu's face, the shame in Lekkativengu's. He knew then that his friend Rokhlenu was dead.

"I didn't know," he said. "I've been—" *to the underworld and back; baiting unicorns; talking to myself* "—away."

The anger in Yaarirruuiu's face faded. "Your hand is better, Khretvarrgliu."

"Yes."

"I'm so glad," said Wuinlendhono's voice. Her face said, *What do I care?* And Morlock completely understood this.

"How did he die?" he asked. Wuinlendhono winced, and he added hastily, "I'm sorry. I will ask someone else."

"Lekkativengu can tell you," Wuinlendhono said, in tones that were almost too even. "He was there."

Now it was Lekkativengu's turn to wince. But under the First Wolf's cold dark eye and with a minimum of prompting, he told the story of Rokhlenu's last fight and death.

Morlock listened with bowed head. He was thinking of those images he had briefly seen in Ulugarriu's bowl of dreams before turning his face away. The images of Rokhlenu fighting desperately, the images of his friend dying alone. He wished, now, that he had taken the time to look at them. But that was done, and he wrapped Lekkativengu's words around what he had seen, and he thought he had learned something important.

Lekkativengu had finished speaking, and an embarrassed silence reigned. Morlock looked up to see that the citizens were all eyeing him, waiting for him to speak.

"I'm glad you, at least, returned, my friend," he said to Lekkativengu.

He could tell the werewolves thought this was in very poor taste. Even Lekkativengu seemed to be offended.

"Should have died with his chieftain," Yaarirruuiu muttered.

"His chieftain didn't think so," Morlock replied. "And neither do I. It was a tale worth hearing."

They all bowed their heads as if he had said some sacred word. "Yes," said Wuinlendhono eventually. "And it will be a song worth singing, in time."

She shook her head and lifted it. She calmly wiped away the tears that were leaking from her eyes and said, "Khretvarrgliu, we are leaving for our colony on the Bitter Water. We would welcome you, if you wish to join us. In my stalwart's name, for my stalwart's sake, you will always be welcome in any dwelling of mine."

"No, thank you," Morlock said, thinking that the coils of the gods were difficult to escape. "I am glad you are going, and taking the outliers with you. I will go and see if I can kill the beast that killed Rokhlenu. Blood for blood."

"Blood for blood!" the werewolves cried.

"Let us help you, Khretvarrgliu," Yaarirruuiu said eagerly. "We'll fight alongside you to avenge our chief."

"The First Wolf needs you," Morlock pointed out. "Besides, my weapon will be made of silver, like Rokhlenu's. Only a never-wolf could wield it."

"Of course! Of course!" cried a new voice from the doorway. "They had to have some way to slay the beast themselves. But they didn't want us to be able to do the same. Brilliant, really. I wonder who thought of it: most of those gods don't strike me as being terribly bright."

"Is it—oh ghost," whispered Wuinlendhono. "Is it you, Liudhleeo? Have you—have you come back?"

"Not exactly, sweetling," said the newcomer gently. "You knew me as Liudhleeo, and as Hrutnefdhu, and as others still whose names may someday occur to you. But my true name is Ulugarriu."

The werewolves bowed their head in reverence and fear at the great name.

Morlock, of course, did not. He looked coldly on the werewolf maker and said to them, "You visualized this moment."

"It appeared faintly in my bowl of dreams," Ulugarriu acknowledged. "But I could not be certain of it. Events I myself may take part in do not visualize clearly for me. And by then I had already decided to come help you, if it came to this."

"Then you don't know if we will slay the Ice-Binder or not?"

"No—not 'know' exactly. In fact, if I were a bookie, I wouldn't give good odds on us. But it's a fight I wouldn't miss, my friend."

The citizens left before noon. Ulugarriu and Wuinlendhono spent some time talking urgently together in the arch of Southgate, while Morlock and the others stood apart. In the end, Ulugarriu tried to put their hand on Wuinlendhono's face and she recoiled, her face a mask of fury. Ulugarriu looked mildly on her, bid her farewell, and walked away without looking back.

Wuinlendhono stared after Ulugarriu in frustrated rage. Her eyes caught Morlock's, and her expression changed as if she had been stabbed. He had reminded her of her dead husband, he guessed. She raised her left hand in farewell; he did the same. The irredeemables, shouting their good-byes to him, surrounded her in a guard formation and they ran off together in long loping strides down the plank road to the marsh's edge.

Morlock left Ulugarriu to their own devices in the empty town. He returned to his cave to forge the weapon that had come into his mind when he had heard Lekkativengu's story. For it, he would need silver, a great deal of silver. Collecting it from the silver-wastes would probably be quicker than transmuting it out of swamp mud, so he spent much of the first day doing that.

A crow flew into the cave that night after dark. After remarking that it was as hot as a bonfire outside and as hot as fifty bonfires in the cave, she asked if he was coming home for supper anytime soon. His den-mate wanted to know.

Morlock said he was surprised that there were any crows left around Wuruyaaria and suggested that she and anyone she cared about should get out.

The crow absentmindedly agreed and wondered if he had any of that bread stuff around?

Morlock gave her some crumbled flatbread and then observed that he had used the rest to stoke his smelting furnace. This was a lie, strictly speaking, but he didn't want crows hanging around Wuruyaaria hoping for more handouts from Morlock. Whether they defeated the Ice-Binder or not, the region was likely to be unhealthy for some time.

He set the molten silver to cycle through a fifth-dimensional pattern of mirrorglass pipes and went down the hill, across the marshy water, through the empty gate, and up the lair-tower to the den he had shared with Liudhleeo and Hrutnefdhu—or, as it turned out, Ulugarriu.

Ulugarriu had set a low table on the floor; there were several covered dishes on it and bowls of clean water. There were two couches set on opposite sides of the room, and Ulugarriu was spreading a sheet on one as Morlock entered. They watched him as he took in the scene, and then they said stiffly, "We needn't both sleep here if you dislike it. The den below this is vacant. In fact, nearly every building in town is vacant. But . . . anyway, I promise not to touch you. I'm well aware that you find me disgusting."

"No," Morlock said, "but we should sleep in separate couches at least. I haven't decided whether I'm going to kill you yet."

"Haven't you, my stalwart?" Ulugarriu turned to finish their work on the couch, then turned to face him again. "That seems unusually indecisive."

"I don't believe your story about Hlupnafenglu's death, but it may be true. If it isn't—"

"It is true!"

"If it is true, you, at least, can't swear to it. According to you, Hlupnafenglu committed suicide in your absence."

"Oh. I guess you're right."

Confident assertions beyond the evidence were one symptom of lying; Morlock had noticed others in Ulugarriu's account, but did not choose to say so.

"Aren't you being incautious in telling me of this, Morlock?" Ulugarriu continued. "I might kill you to protect myself."

"No. You need me to do your fighting for you."

"Oh! That's true, I suppose. When I caught you in my intention, you also caught me. Life is odd sometimes, isn't it?"

"Yes. What's for supper?"

"Nothing remarkable. Some dried fish, cheese, peas, a bit of smoked seal (I think). I didn't bother to heat it up, because . . ."

"It's hot enough already, yes. Thanks for gathering it."

"It was no trouble, dear." They sat and began to eat without ceremony.

"Your appetite certainly has returned," Ulugarriu remarked approvingly.

Morlock nodded. "Not dying agrees with me."

"Well, I agree with it. Can I ask you a personal question?"

Morlock shrugged.

"Taking that as a yes—aren't you reluctant to share a meal with someone you may later have to kill?"

"Not if I've warned them. Then there's no deceit."

"So you were being polite. In your rather brutal way. How strange you are."

Morlock shrugged again.

"Tell me what you did today or I'll say something disturbingly personal."

"I collected silver ore discarded in the waste hills and smelted it. I left it cycling through a five-space web of mirrorglass tubes."

"I didn't get that last part—but never mind. Once you have the metal, isn't that enough? Can't you make your weapon?"

"No, I don't want to use regular silver. As metals go, it's too soft to make a good weapon. Also it melts too easily."

"You're going to change it somehow?"

"Yes. You know that quicksilver is a form of the metal even softer and more malleable than regular silver."

"Of course. Though some people say it's a different metal entirely."

Morlock waved aside this superstition without bothering to discuss it. "There is a form of silver opposite to quicksilver: harder, more brittle, with a much higher melting point."

"I see. Sort of a deadsilver."

"Yes. Once I extract its phlogiston, it should be suitable for the weapon I have in mind."

"What is that, exactly?"

Morlock sketched it on the surface of the table with the point of a knife.

"I see," said Ulugarriu at last. "How can I help? I can't work the silver with you, obviously."

"We'll need a lot of cable for this plan to work—strong and lightweight."

"Yes—yes I can provide that. But it will burn, I'm afraid."

"We'll dephlogistonate it."

"Of course. I'm looking forward to learning that technique from you; it will be so useful."

In fact, Morlock believed that Ulugarriu already knew how to remove phlogiston from matter. He wasn't sure why they were lying to him about this—mere habit, perhaps. But it was a useful reminder that Ulugarriu could not really be trusted.

The meal was done, and Morlock said, "You brought the food, so I'll clear up."

"Oh, ghost," said Ulugarriu, and tossed an empty dish out the window. "Let the swamp have it. We'll be here a few days, but I can always scavenge clean dishes when we need them."

They threw the dishes out the window, laughing a little, and turned in on their separate couches.

The next day, Morlock left the silver to unquicken in its five-web and built a ballista out of lumber from abandoned buildings in the outlier settlement and rope that he borrowed from Ulugarriu's cable-making project, which they had set up in the empty marketplace. Ulugarriu had rapidly built a rope-winding machine out of wood, and by the time they were done, citizens were already bringing in fiber to feed into it.

"Are they extensions of yourself?" Morlock asked Ulugarriu, when several of these blank-eyed citizens dropped off loads of hemp fiber and left.

"No," Ulugarriu said uneasily. "Just citizens who owe me favors. Well, most of them are were-rats running meat-puppets, all right?"

"It's all right with me," Morlock said. He took his rope and left.

Death and Justice, manifest as sisters (which they once had been), were walking arm in arm under the Stone Tree. Justice had swords for hands and Death had reaping knives, but apart from that they made a charming pair, for those who were there to see them.

"And so the werewolf city is dying at last?" Justice signified.

"The instrument threatens it more every day. There were riots and murders through the election season, and then more rioting after the new First Wolf was treacherously sent to his death. Yes, I think it is dying, if not yet dead."

Justice shook her monochrome head. "I saw so little of this. My visualizations were disrupted by my manifestation's captivity."

"Not just yours," Death replied. "Everyone's visualizations have been uncertain, lately. But all that is soon to end."

"Yes. It will be relief to have the plan fulfilled."

"It will be a relief. A great relief."

"Why are the others not manifest, yet? Were we not to meet at this space-time locus?"

"They are here, Justice, but you cannot see them." Death unfolded a piece of space-time and said, "Look."

The Strange Gods were all present. Even Wisdom was there, or at least the shell of Wisdom. Justice knew from his manifestation that he was dead, had long been dead.

Each of the gods, except Death, was bound in a web of otherness that Justice saw, but did not understand.

"What is this, Death?" she asked.

"This is the plan," said Death. "I have labored over it for thousands of years. Each of you is trapped (yes, you, too, Justice) in a talic web of my weaving. Each thread of the web is woven to a cluster of human lives. And if you move to break that thread, the lives will be affected in a way inimical to your nature. See poor War there, I caught him first, while he was enjoying the riots after Rokhlenu's death. If he tries to free himself in time, the Anhikh Kômos will make peace with the Ontilian Empire. If he tries to free himself in space, the Mupuvlokhu tribes in northern Qajqapca will lay down their arms and unite. If he tries to take effective action without freeing himself, other things inimical to his nature will happen."

"Why? Why are you doing this?"

"So that I can kill you. If gods take action inimical to their nature, their manifestation becomes more loosely associated with their nature. If that separation becomes permanent, death will occur."

"I know that. I know that. I am asking you why."

"So that death will occur. I act according to my nature, and my nature is Death. You are mortal, and my task has been to reap your lives. You have been cunning. You have used power and magic and skill and patience. You have evaded me for long ages, but you could not escape me. I am Death."

"You weren't always Death. We were sisters once."

"We were once, but we are not now. All your symbols, all your dreams and hopes, all that you were and were not and wished to be, all this is nothing to me. Stop your signifying, Justice. I am Death, and I always have the last word."

Chapter Thirty-two

Last Words

On the second night of the ninth month, the month Morlock called Tohrt, he took the nexus holding his choir of flames and carried it to the bone-dry grassy slope to the east. He set the nexus down and broke it open.

"Run free," he said. "Live and die as flames do, my friends. You need not leave the nexus, but I may not return to feed you anymore."

They were young, as flame-choirs go, and eager to escape and explore the world outside. Long branches of flame were already spreading across the dead dry hillside as he walked away. He did not look back; he'd said harder goodbyes than this, lately.

Horseman was a bright white eye in the western sky. Ulugarriu was impatiently waiting in their wingset by the door of his cave. It was time to go avenge Rokhlenu or die as well as he had.

The ballista Morlock had built was a relatively light weapon, if a powerful one, to start with. After Morlock had leached forth its phlogiston and covered it with weight-defying scales harvested from the unfinished wingsets, it was approximately as heavy as a happy thought.

For Ulugarriu, the thought was a rather grim one at the moment, though: resting on the firing slot were two hooked and flanged spears made from deadsilver.

"I can come back for these," Morlock said, noting the look of dread that Ulugarriu was giving the spears.

"No," said Ulugarriu. "We'd best do this all at once."

The werewolf maker took a long look at the rising moon, took a long breath, and knotted the lift ropes to the harness of their wingset. Morlock had been doing the same, and he met their eye. "Ready?" he asked, and they nodded.

The two makers gripped their wings and launched from the earth. The ballista came after them, dragged by the ropes.

They had practiced this a number of times, but it was different now—because of the silver spears, weighing down the ballista—and because this wasn't practice.

They flew straight up at first, into the hot blue night. When they were well above the level of the city and Mount Dhaarnaiarnon, Morlock called out, "Now!" and they levelled off, heading north.

Ulugarriu could already see the thing. At least there was a smoky red line of fire there that became clearer and clearer as they approached.

There were citizens abroad on the mesas of Wuruyaaria, but not as many as you would expect on a moonlit night. Ulugarriu wished they were down there, wearing the night shape, singing and causing trouble.

They felt an awkward tug on the load-bearing ropes. It almost pulled them off course. Looking around for the answer, Ulugarriu saw that Morlock was veering to the right, toward the high mesa of Wuruklendon.

"What are you doing?" Ulugarriu screamed.

He called back something about something and the Stone Tree.

"Don't care!" they screamed back. "North!"

He got the *eh* expression on his face: they just bet he was muttering it to himself. But he bent his course northward until there was a little slack on the load-ropes.

The dark shoulder of the volcano was below them now, with the moon-clock and its one luminous eye rivaling the rising moon to their left.

Then the beast was below them, a red-black border burning from west to east.

It was a stupid sluggish burning worm that was poisoning Ulugarriu's world, and they hated it. They wished they knew how it worked.

The turbulent wind carried them up, upward, up—an intense updraft caused by the heat of the Ice-Binder. The air was pretty hot, but not hot enough to ignite the phlogiston-imbued metal scales—that was Ulugarriu's deepest dread about this business.

Then they were past the updraft and trending downward.

"There!" Morlock shouted.

Ulugarriu saw it: a small hill just north of the Ice-Binder. It was dark and lifeless as everything the Ice-Binder left in its wake.

They turned, in fairly good order, and glided down to perch on the hilltop; the ballista dropped down on the hillside below them.

They unhitched their load ropes and fetched the ballista. They set it up on the slope, about two hundred paces from the undulating red-black side of the Ice-Binder.

Morlock bound one of the lightweight coils of rope to one end of one of the deadsilver spears. He pushed the spear (harpoon, really) into the firing slot from the front, and then dropped the coil on the ground where it could run free.

"What if you miss?" Ulugarriu said stupidly. "We should have brought more than two shots."

Any other male Ulugarriu had ever known would have said, *I never miss*, or something equally fatuous. Morlock simply tapped the rope bound to the end of the spear. Of course: they could simply drag the spear back and try again.

It was only then that Ulugarriu realized how terrified they were of this. They definitely weren't thinking clearly.

Morlock cranked up the ballista, took several sightings, adjusted the height and position of the ballista, and said, "Watch out."

Ulugarriu was already well away, so Morlock released the firing bolt; the ballista kicked like an angry donkey and the deadsilver spear was gone, trailing the rope after it into the night. After a moment, though, the rope stopped. Ulugarriu looked up and saw a faint blue light around the side of the Ice-Binder. Soon this was obscured by dark tendrils rising from the Ice-Binder itself.

"Clean hit," Morlock said. "I think the hook is in place."

"It works," Ulugarriu said wonderingly. "It feeds on itself."

"It doesn't feed," Morlock disagreed.

With deliberate speed, he performed the same set of actions for the second deadsilver spear, firing a little further east this time, so that the ropes wouldn't get tangled.

"West or east?" Morlock asked.

"West," Ulugarriu said, with dry lips. They went and bound the rope from the first harpoon to the harness of their wingset.

Morlock was doing the same with the rope for the other spear.

"Morlock," said Ulugarriu, "what if this doesn't work?"

"Then we'll think of something else."

"What if it *does* work?"

"Then get away as fast as you can."

Ulugarriu knew what he meant. This thing had millennia of perpetual winter locked in its guts, all the cold of the world's far north. They were hoping it would be released more or less at once. If so, this would be no place to linger.

"Then," Morlock said, and took to the air.

Ulugarriu had a speech planned, witty yet tender, designed to make Morlock less inclined to kill them, should the occasion ever arise. They gaped after the winged back of the disappearing never-wolf. "Gaaaah!" they shouted, and took to the air flying westward.

Due west and fairly low, at first. They didn't want to pull the harpoon loose, but drag it through the side of the Ice-Binder, doing as much damage as possible.

Soon the cord on their harness jerked, holding them back as they strained with their wings to fly forward.

That was good. It meant that the hook had set.

Now came the hard part. Ulugarriu pumped, with their arms and legs, as hard as they could. At first, it seemed as if they were trying to fly through stone. Then something gave a little; then something more. Soon they were plowing forward slowly—not as if the air were stone, but perhaps a thick unpleasant sludge. Which it sort of smelled like.

They looked back over their left wing and saw a gratifyingly long scar of blue light opening in the Ice-Binder's side. It wriggled at the edges, as the Ice-Binder's legs turned to feed on itself.

Ulugarriu was repelled, but also pleased, and they turned with a fierce grin to drive themselves a little farther west, to drag that hook through the Ice-Binder's side a little longer.

It was a lot longer. Ulugarriu lost track of time, but a good deal of it had surely passed when they felt a shadow pass between them and the moon.

Ulugarriu looked up curiously, and saw something high in the sky, like a tower. A falling tower. And on top of the tower was a kind of mouth ringed with dark flashing teeth.

It was the Ice-Binder—the end of the Ice Binder. Ulugarriu's first thought was that it was coming to attack whatever was hurting it, that is, Ulugarriu themself. They thought furiously, then regretfully loosed the rope tied to the wingset's harness. They had done as much harm to the Ice-Binder as they could; now it was time to save themself.

Except it was already too late, it seemed. As Ulugarriu flew free from the rope, the many-toothed worm head swerved to follow. Ulugarriu twisted in the air, veering left, and the worm head followed again.

Ulugarriu hoped fiercely that they had at least killed the thing that was about to kill them when a winged silhouette impinged on the sky between them and the falling worm. Morlock. That crazy brach's bastard.

"What are you doing?" Ulugarriu shrieked. "You were going to kill me anyway!"

Morlock arced high, drawing the attention of whatever the worm used for eyes. It followed him, bending upward again.

Morlock vaulted straight in the air, spun in the sky, and began to fall.

He had released both his wing grips, Ulugarriu saw. He was holding that sword of his, Tyrfing, in both hands. He fell past the questing worm mouth and scored a shining blue wound down the side of the worm. The worm mouth turned its teeth on its own wound and began to tear at it. Morlock fell past, dropping his sword, clutching at his wing grips.

But the close passage with the blazing hot surface of the Ice-Binder had kindled the phlogiston-imbued scales on his wings. Morlock was burning, and burning he fell to the ground and lay there.

Ulugarriu stooped like a hawk, driving themself to the point where Morlock had crashed to earth. They pulled up at the last minute and stalled in the air, dropping down beside the fallen maker.

The fall had actually extinguished most of the fires on Morlock's wings. He had rolled in the dusty ground. Morlock was starting to move.

"Be still!" Ulugarriu shrieked, and heaped dust on his wings until the flames were dead.

"You hurt anything?" said Ulugarriu. "Idiot. You were supposed to be pulling the hook in the other direction."

"Rope broke."

"My ropes don't break! You must have done something wrong! You're always doing everything wrong! You should have let it kill me, you idiot, don't you see? Now you'll have to kill me or I'll have to kill you."

"Ulugarriu," said Morlock, "it's snowing."

"It—" It was snowing. Ulugarriu stared mutely at the white flakes falling like a benediction around them in the moonlight. Towering over their heads, stretching eastward past Dhaarnaiarnon, the Ice-Binder was busy ripping itself to shreds, releasing deep winter into the humid air of midsummer. "It's snowing!"

"Yes."

"We have to get out of here!"

"Yes."

Ulugarriu found they wanted to rage some more at Morlock about something, anything, but now was not the time, obviously. "Where away? The volcano? It's still our best bet, I think."

"Yes."

"Will your wings carry you? You lost a lot of scales."

Morlock stretched his wings testingly. He nodded. "Yes."

"Say something else!" Ulugarriu shrieked in his face. "Say something else! Say anything else! Say *eh*, or something!"

Morlock shouted, "Tyrfing!" The deadly blade flew from the ground by the self-eating Ice-Binder into Morlock's outstretched right hand. He sheathed the blade over his crooked shoulders and then gestured politely at the sky.

After you, Ulugarriu interpreted the gesture. They leapt into the air and flew westward, giving the Ice-Binder a wide berth, then taking a long steep turn eastward, running alongside the dying monster through the sudden moonlit snowstorm.

Ulugarriu marvelled at the ferocity of the thing's self-attack, as pitiless toward itself as if it were alien to its own being. Morlock was right, they realized. This thing was not really alive. It was a mechanism, not an organism. But it was a mechanism designed to look like an organism—a parody of life, made by something that hated life. Ulugarriu wondered who had made it. It seemed beyond the scope of the Strange Gods.

When they were over the dark shoulder of Dhaarnaiarnon, Ulugarriu looked back to see how far Morlock was behind. They assumed he would be flying more slowly, because of the lost scales.

Morlock was not behind them at all.

Ulugarriu felt the bite of panic and shook it off. They circled slowly in the air, scanning the snow-scattered sky.

They caught sight of a winged man flying slightly to the south, toward Wuruklendon atop Wuruyaaria.

Morlock. He had been hollering something about the Stone Tree earlier. But didn't he realize they had to get somewhere safe?

Ulugarriu hesitated, then followed. It was barely possible he knew what he was doing.

Morlock wearily relaxed his arms and let himself fall the last few feet to the ground of Wuruklendon.

The scaffold of his execution had been dismantled. No one else was present. To all appearances, he stood alone in the moonlit snowstorm under the Stone Tree.

But he could feel something happening. He knew something was happening. He remembered his brief vision of the Strange Gods drinking from the Well of Shadows. And he remembered this feeling from the time he had died in the Bitter Water.

"Death!" he shouted. "I feel your presence! Show yourself! I have something to say to you."

Death manifested herself not far from him, in the form of a spider with a woman's face.

"If you wish," the woman's face said. "It is a foolish wish, but I owe you this at least for the service you have done me."

"I reject your service. I will not serve you. I will not serve."

"You have already served me. I give you the gift of everything you have, which I will take back whenever it suits me. Go now. I'm working." She disappeared. But Morlock felt that she was still present somehow.

Morlock drew Tyrfing and summoned the rapture of vision.

The scene transformed itself as he entered the talic realm. All around the Well of Shadows he saw the Strange Gods in their various manifestations, bound with strange dark webs of talic force. The webs all ran to and through Death, still spiderlike, her manifestation perched on a branch of the Stone Tree.

Death was hard at work. If Morlock had his way, she would work still harder yet.

Morlock slashed with Tyrfing at the talic webs running from the Strange Gods. Without looking, he knew several of them were free. Death signified a statement that nearly struck him dead; he was saved only because he didn't fully understand the symbolism. But he kept on slashing, and soon the other Strange Gods were signifying back at Death, and the time-space locus was full of clashing symbols.

The Strange Gods all were unbound now; even hollow Wisdom was free to fall to the earth and stare with empty eyes at the snowthick sky.

The Strange Gods assumed their most terrifying aspects. They rose to gigantic heights. They turned all their power together against Death.

And it was nothing to her. Morlock saw that immediately. What were all the powers of human life to Death, that surrounds and defines all life? Nothing.

But he saw something else. There was Death, a Strange God among others, and there was death, the uncaring essence that ends all entity. They were different, somehow, though joined.

Morlock kicked off from the ground. Sustained by the wounded levity of his wings, he rose to the branch where Death was perched. In the instant that they occupied adjoining loci time-space, the living maker and the manifestation of Death, he struck at the spidery presence with his cursed sword, severing the woman's head from the spider's body.

The manifestation of Death became disorganized and ceased to represent an individual identity.

Even in long ages, Death cannot die. Death continued to stand at the end of every road, the darkness framing the light of everything that lived until it lived no longer.

But the Death who had been one of the Strange Gods, who had once been a woman, who had walked arm in arm with her sister Justice on the western edge of the world and talked of the way things were and the way things should be, that Death was gone.

In this limited sense, Death was dead.

The death of the greatest of the Strange Gods shook the world. The surviving Strange Gods, dismayed, fled into widely separate loci of space-time.

Morlock, struck from his vision, from awareness, and nearly from the world, fell from the Stone Tree and lay motionless on the snow-covered ground of Wuruklendon.

He was not, however, alone.

Ulugarriu followed Morlock to the high mesa. They heard him shout his insane challenge to the Strange God of Death. They saw, with perfectly reasonable terror, the manifestation of Death. After the manifestation disappeared, they were bemused to see Morlock draw his sword, luminous black-and-white in the storm's shadows, leap up on his fire-scarred wings, and strike at the empty air above the branch of the Stone Tree.

The death of Death shocked Ulugarriu—but Ulugarriu walked freer from death's shadow than some, and they soon recovered.

When they raised their head and looked at the sky, Ulugarriu saw a storm, blue with continuous lightning, striding high above Mount Dhaarna-iarnon, a wave of blue light brighter than the moon in the one-eyed sky, a wave as tall as the world, deadlier than the god Morlock had just killed.

The Ice-Binder had destroyed itself; the millennia of winters were loosed on the world, and the storm was heading this way. It was already too late to reach the crater of the volcano.

Only one bolt hole remained, and Ulugarriu used it.

They ran over to where Morlock lay under the Stone Tree and dragged his unconscious form to the Well of Shadows. They tried to pry his sword loose from his fingers, but the unconscious maker clutched tight to the grip and would not let go.

"Be that way then!" Ulugarriu shouted at him, and pushed him into the Well. They jumped in afterward.

The fall was long, so long. But Ulugarriu hoped the wings would keep them, both of them, from being crushed by the fall.

The storm fell howling across the mountain, shaking it like a blue earthquake. Ulugarriu dreaded the thought of a direct lightning strike down the well, but none came. Eventually they struck the ground in a tangle of wings and bodies; the storm front passed. There was silence and darkness for a long time.

Ulugarriu seemed to awaken. Between Morlock and Ulugarriu, who lay at the stony base of the Well of Shadows, stood a young woman with no mouth, holding a faintly glowing lotus flower in her hand. Ulugarriu knew she was the manifestation of the Strange God called Mercy.

"All right," Ulugarriu said grumpily. "I suppose you gods always win in the end. Just be quick about it."

Mercy signified her dissent from this in symbols that were too intense to be clear to Ulugarriu's baffled mind.

"Talk to me, can't you?" they shouted. "Or go away! You make my head hurt with your signifying."

A red-lipped mouth formed in the lotus flower. Mercy spoke through it in Moonspeech.

"I am not interested in killing you, poor Ulugarriu," Mercy's flower said.

"I opposed the plan of the other Strange Gods, and worked to overcome it in the end. It was in my nature to do so, and it would be against my nature to slay you now. Besides, you saved my agent Morlock, and I'm grateful to you for that. Blood for blood, as he would say, poor man."

Mercy reached down and caressed Morlock's scarred sleeping face with her flower.

Ulugarriu watched this with interest, thinking furiously all the while. "I thought it was Death who appeared to Morlock in the Bitter Water. That's what he told me, anyway."

"She did, and she thought she was acting for herself when she saved him from drowning. But it was I who prompted her to act against her own nature, separating her manifestation from the phenomenon that sustained it. It took time for that seed to blossom, but now it has, and she is finally at peace."

Ulugarriu lowered their head and thought about this for a long time. Finally they said quietly, "Are you telling me that *that* was what this whole thing was about? Everything that happened was so that you could bring death to Death?"

"I was sorry for her suffering, which was more terrible than you or I can imagine, and I wanted it to end. That was my purpose, and it was very simple. Other entities had other purposes (you among them, Ulugarriu), and so the pattern of events became very complex."

Ulugarriu raised their head and saw in the light of Mercy's lotus that Morlock was gone.

"What have you done with my stalwart?" they blurted.

"Hardly yours, poor Ulugarriu. I hid your presence from him, and he has gone his way through the dark roads under the earth. Don't be afraid for him; he has lived much of his life underground, poor man."

"We didn't have a chance to say good-bye."

"I can't see very deeply into his mind, Ulugarriu. It is almost as strange to me as yours is. But I do know that he might have felt obliged to kill you for what you did to his friend, and I felt obliged to prevent that."

"I did not kill Hlupnafenglu!"

"I know. I was referring to Rokhlenu."

"Oh." Ulugarriu thought it over and decided it was fruitless to make a denial. "Everything would have been fine if Aaluindhonu or someone like that had been elected to lead the Innermost Pack. I couldn't have Rokhlenu as First Singer, don't you see? The city's social pattern is a delicate thing, and too-rapid change will create chaos. Don't you see?"

"No," said Mercy, making a protective sign against the name of the alien god Chaos, "but it's not necessary that I do. Do you think Morlock would see?"

"I guess not. Thanks."

"He would have been sorry if he found out afterward you were pregnant."

Ulugarriu was silent for a time, and then said feebly, "I'm not pregnant."

"Your simulacrum Liudhleeo is. Or is my visualization in error?"

"No," Ulugarriu admitted finally. "You're right. It is pregnant. I haven't been sure what to do about that. What does your visualization say?"

"I see no unclarities. The child will lie in Liudhleeo's womb for two years. He will be born with a full set of teeth and a full head of hair. Not even you will consider him handsome, but he will have very long, strong, clever hands. You will call him Fenrir Ambrosius."

"I bet I'll think he's handsome."

The red mouth on Mercy's flower smiled gently. "What will you bet, poor Ulugarriu?"

Morlock walked many long twisting ways under the ground, seeking a way out of the warm ghost-thick darkness and into the cold light of life.

He finally followed a breath of bitter air to a shallow snow-filled flaw in the earth. Cutting his way through with Tyrfing, he emerged in a trench filled with snow, and the gray light of a daytime blizzard.

The dirt of the trench smelled and tasted like silver ore to him. If he was not very much mistaken, he had emerged close to his cave on the verge of the outlier settlement.

He thought of taking refuge there from the cold, but shook the thought off. He had shed that skin.

The framework of his wings had broken in his several falls; as wings, they were unusable. But the scales that still remained on them kept him light on his feet, and he could wrap the wings around him like a coat, until he found (or made) better.

Not far off, he was interested to see a steaming pit in the snow, about three hands wide. He slogged closer and peered over the edge.

At the bottom of the pit was the flame nexus. Three shivering flames, the last of his choir, were quarrelling over the last bit of wet smoky fuel.

"Friends," he said, "I'm headed south. Care to come with me?"

They accepted his offer with dignified, if sparky, restraint. He reached down and lifted the nexus out of the pit.

He fed them scales off his broken wings, and they assured him that metallic phlogiston was the best thing ever, even better than coal, unless he actually had any coal. Since he didn't, they gladly continued to consume the burning metal. This, in turn, warmed Morlock.

Sheltering the three flames under his wings from the midsummer blizzard, the crooked man took the long road south.

This, Iacomes, is the extent of my visualization. May I return now, to rest among my stones?

Appendix A

Calendar and Astronomy

1. Astronomical Remarks

The sky of Laent has three moons: Chariot, Horseman, and Trumpeter (in descending order of size).

The year has 375 days. The months are marked by the rising or setting of the second moon, Horseman. So that (in the year before *The Wolf Age* begins) Horseman sets on the first day of Bayring, the penultimate month. It rises again on the first of Borderer, the last month. It sets very early in the morning on the first day of Cymbals, the first month of the new year. All three moons set simultaneously on this occasion. (The number of months are uneven—fifteen—so that Horseman rises or sets on the first morning of the year in alternating years.)

The period of Chariot (the largest moon, whose rising and setting marks the seasons) is 187.5 days. (So a season is 93.75 days.)

The period of Horseman is 50 days.

The period of Trumpeter is 15 days. A half cycle of Trumpeter is a "call." Calls are either "bright" or "dark" depending on whether Trumpeter is aloft or not. (Usage: "He doesn't expect to be back until next bright call.")

The seasons are not irregular, as on Earth. But the moons' motion is not uniform through the sky: motion is faster near the horizons, slowest at zenith. Astronomical objects are brighter in the west, dimmer in the east.

The three moons and the sun rise in the west and set in the east. The stars have a different motion entirely, rotating NWSE around a celestial pole. The pole points at a different constellation among a group of seven (the polar constellations) each year. (Hence, a different group of nonpolar constellations is visible near the horizons each year.) This seven-year cycle (the Ring) is the basis for dating, with individual years within it named for their particular polar constellations.

The polar constellations are the Reaper, the Ship, the Hunter, the Door, the Kneeling Man, the River, and the Wolf.

There is an intrapolar constellation, the Hands, within the space inscribed by the motion of the pole.

Solar eclipses are rare but not unheard-of. They do not involve the three known moons. Some speculate that there is a fourth nonluminous moon whose course runs north–south through the sky. Others insist that the sun has a nonluminous hemisphere that appears as the sun rotates at irregular intervals.

2. The Years of the Wolf Age

The calendar below was first developed in the Wardlands, and then spread to the unguarded lands by exiles. In the Wardlands, years are dated from the founding of New Moorhope, the center of learning. The action of *The Wolf Age* begins in the 465th Ring, Moorhope year 3247, the Year of the Reaper. But in the Ontilian Empire, the years are dated from the death of Uthar the Great, a system that came into widespread use north and south of the Kirach Kund. According to that scheme, the action begins in 335 A.U.

335 A.U.
3247 M.Y., Year of the Reaper in the 465th Ring

1. Cymbals.

New Year. Winter begins.
1st: Chariot, Horseman, and Trumpeter all set.
8th and 23rd: Trumpeter rises.

2. Jaric.

1st: Horseman rises. 13th: Trumpeter rises.

3. Brenting.

1st: Horseman sets. 3rd and 18th: Trumpeter rises.

4. Drums.

1st: Horseman rises. 8th and 23rd: Trumpeter rises.
Midnight of 94th day of the year (19 Drums):
Chariot rises. Spring begins.

5. Rain.

1st: Horseman sets. 13th: Trumpeter rises.

6. Marrying.

1st: Horseman rises. 3rd and 18th: Trumpeter rises.

7. Ambrose.

1st: Horseman sets. 8th and 23rd: Trumpeter rises.

8. Harps.

1st: Horseman rises. 13th: Trumpeter rises.
Evening of the 188th day of year (19 Harps):
Chariot sets.
Midyear—summer begins.

9. Tohrt.

1st: Horseman sets. 3rd and 18th: Trumpeter rises.

10. Remembering.

1st: Horseman rises. 8th and 23rd: Trumpeter rises.

11. Victory.

1st: Horseman sets. 13th: Trumpeter rises.

12. Harvesting.

1st: Horseman rises. 3rd and 18th: Trumpeter rises.
6th: Chariot rises, noon of 281st day of year. Fall begins.

13. Mother and Maiden.

1st: Horseman sets. 8th and 23rd: Trumpeter rises.

14. Bayring.

1st: Horseman rises. 13th: Trumpeter rises.

15. Borderer.

1st: Horseman sets. 3rd and 18th: Trumpeter rises.

336 A.U.
3248 M.Y., Year of the Ship in the 465th Ring

1. Cymbals.

New Year. Winter begins.
1st: Chariot and Trumpeter set. Horseman rises.
8th and 23rd: Trumpeter rises.

2. Jaric.

1st: Horseman sets. 13th: Trumpeter rises.

3. Brenting.

1st: Horseman rises. 3rd and 18th: Trumpeter rises.

4. Drums.

1st: Horseman sets. 8th and 23rd: Trumpeter rises.
Midnight of 94th day of the year (19 Drums):
Chariot rises. Spring begins.

5. Rain.

1st: Horseman rises. 13th: Trumpeter rises.

6. Marrying.

1st: Horseman sets. 3rd and 18th: Trumpeter rises.

7. Ambrose.

1st: Horseman rises. 8th and 23rd: Trumpeter rises.

8. Harps.

1st: Horseman sets.13th: Trumpeter rises.
Evening of the 188th day of year (19 Harps):
Chariot sets.
Midyear—summer begins.

9. Tohrt.

1st: Horseman rises. 3rd and 18th: Trumpeter rises.

10. Remembering.

1st: Horseman sets. 8th and 23rd: Trumpeter rises.

11. Victory.

1st: Horseman rises. 13th: Trumpeter rises.

12. Harvesting.

1st: Horseman sets. 3rd and 18th: Trumpeter rises.
6th: Chariot rises, noon of 281st day of year. Fall begins.

13. Mother and Maiden.

1st: Horseman rises. 8th and 23rd: Trumpeter rises.

14. Bayring.

1st: Horseman sets. 13th: Trumpeter rises.

15. Borderer.

1st: Horseman rises. 3rd and 18th: Trumpeter rises.

Appendix B

Names and Terms

NOTE: This glossary doesn't include terms that are used only once and glossed in adjoining text. The descriptions include some data that might be considered spoilers.

Aaluindhonu ("Born in bright call"): the Goweiteiuun gnyrrand.

Aruukaiaduun ("Rope makers"): One of the original three treaty packs; they predominate on Nekkuklendon; their colors are blue and gold.

Dhaarnaiarnon: volcano north of Wuruyaaria.

Dhuskudheiu: Goweiteiuun cantor, later singer on the Innermost Pack.

Ekhaiasuteiuun ("the border-runners"): name of the outliers on admission to the treaty; electoral colors are green and gold.

gnyrrand ("growler"): leader of a pack's electoral band in a Year of Choosing.

Goweiteiuun ("Ghost-hunters"): the original treaty pack (so they claim); they predominate on Iuiunioklendon; electoral colors are blue and red.

harven coruthen ("chosen-not-given"): a Dwarvish term for voluntary associations as strong as blood kinship.

Hlupnafenglu ("Steals-your-food"): insane never-wolf; irredeemable; later: Morlock's apprentice.

Hrutnefdhu ("Skinmaker"): a castrato who served as trustee in the Vargulleion.

Hurs krakna (untranslatable): a Dwarvish expression of surprise or dismay.

Hwinsyngundu: cantor in the Sardhluun electoral band.

Iacomes: non-werewolf who created the Vargulleion.

Iolildhio: pimp in Dogtown.

Iuiolliniu: easily bewildered outlier guard.

Iuiunioklendon: second-highest mesa of Wuruyaaria; the Goweiteiuun predominate.

Khretnurrliu ("Man Slayer"): bestial semiwolf killed by Morlock in the Vargulleion.

Khretvarrgliu ("Beast Slayer"): the name given Morlock by the irredeemables for killing Khretnurrliu.

Khuwuleion ("the Stone Lair"): prison for female citizens kept by the Sardhluun.

Lakkasulakku: inept thief, later Morlock's apprentice.

Lekkativengu ("Clawfinger"): irredeemable semiwolf; chosen as backup by Olleiulu.

Liudhleeo ("Remembers-best"): healer of the outlier pack; mate of Hrutnefdhu; friend to Wuinlendhono.

Liuunurriu: semiwolf book vendor in the Shadow Market.

Luyukioronu Longthumbs: inept artist and murderer; capable forger.

Naaleiyaleiu: Goweiteiuun cantor, later singer on the Innermost Pack.

Neiuluniu: bookie who cheats Lakkasulakku.

Nekkuklendon: third mesa of Wuruyaaria; the Aruukaiaduun predominate.

never-wolf: (1) a human being (i.e., a non-werewolf); (2) a slur for werewolves who never assume the night shape.

Neyuwuleiuun ("Lair-weavers"): One of the original three treaty packs; they predominate on Runaiaklendon; electoral colors are red and green.

nightwalker: a werewolf unable to assume the day shape.

Norianduiu: Aruukaiaduun gnyrrand.

Okhurokratu: white-haired city watcher.

Olleiulu ("One-eye"): Rokhlenu's right-hand semiwolf among the irredeemables.

Orlioiulu: dog-faced bookie in Dogtown.

plepnup (plural: *plepnupov*): a castrated werewolf.

Rogerius: a bronze head in the workshop of Iacomes.

Rokhlenu ("Dragonkiller"): born Slenkjariu in the Aruukaiaduun Pack.

Ruiulanhro: runs a smoking den among the outliers.

Rululawianu: yellow semiwolf who escapes on New Year's Night.

Runaiaklendon: fourth and lowest mesa of Wuruyaaria; the Neyuwuleiuun predominate.

Runhuiulanhu: ape-fingered irredeemable.

ruthen coharven ("given-not-chosen"): a Dwarvish term for blood relatives.

Rywudhaariu: the gray eminence of the Aruukaiaduun, who framed Rokhlenu.

Sardhluun ("Bear-killers"): the fourth treaty pack; electoral colors are black and green.

Skuiulaalu: First Singer when the novel begins.

Slenginhuiuo ("Fur-like-silk"): Wuinlendhono's mother.

Slenkjariu ("Fur-like-wires"): Rokhlenu's name before he killed the dragon.

Snekknafenglu: thug-for-hire.

Snellingu: scar-faced City Watcher.

Spilloiu ("Spot"): pet human in an easy reader.

Taakhyteiu: a fast werewolf, irredeemable.

Ullywuino: prostitute in Dogtown.

Ulugarriu ("Ghosts-in-the-eyes"): legendary immortal maker of Wuruyaaria.

Uyaarwuionien ("third half-lunation of the second moon"): Brenting, the third month

Vargulleion ("the Beasts' Lair"): prison for male citizens; kept by the Sardhluun.

vifna: a term in Moonspeech meaning roughly "gall; nerve; an impressive disregard for norms."

werowance: presides over internal pack affairs.

Wuinlendhono ("Born-in-dark-call"): first wolf of the outlier pack (later the Ekhaiasuteiuun or "border-runners").

Wurnafenglu ("Moon-stealer"): prison-commander; gnyrrand of the Sardhluun electoral band.

Wuruklendon: first and highest mesa of Wuruyaaria, where the Well of Shadows and the Stone Tree are located.

Yaarirruuiu: irredeemable; later Rokhlenu's campaign reeve; still later a singer on the Innermost Pack.

About the Author

James Enge lives with his children in northwest Ohio, where he teaches classics at a medium-sized public university. His short fiction has appeared in *Swords and Dark Magic* (Eos, 2010), in the magazine *Black Gate*, and elsewhere. His previous novels are *Blood of Ambrose* (Pyr, 2009), which was listed on Locus Magazine's Recommended Reading for 2009, and *This Crooked Way* (Pyr, 2009).